Praise for Rosanne Bittner's Mystic Dreamers series

Mystic Visions

"Rosanne Bittner retains her title as a premier Indian romance writer. . . . Poignant and startling." —*Romantic Times*

"Bittner's descriptions of Lakota life are impeccably researched, with impressive scenes of visions and ceremonies . . . bringing a variety of intriguing Native American characters to life." —*Publishers Weekly*

"Beautifully written and structured. . . . [*Mystic Dreamers*] is the West of blood, tears, and transcendent dreams."
—Loren D. Estleman, award-winning author of *White Desert* and *The Master Executioner*

Mystic Dreamers

"Rosanne Bittner's stories are powerful because she creates memorable characters who enlighten readers as they rekindle the magical spark that belonged to the first people to love this land." —*Romantic Times*

"Filled with suspense and high emotion, quests and visions, this compelling love story is sure to please Bittner's fans and to win over new converts." —*Booklist*

D0707255

Also by Rosanne Bittner

Mystic Dreamers
Mystic Visions

MYSTIC WARRIORS

Rosanne Bittner

TOR®

A TOM DOHERTY ASSOCIATES BOOK
NEW YORK

This is a work of fiction. All the characters and events portrayed in this book are either products of the author's imagination or are used fictitiously.

MYSTIC WARRIORS

Copyright © 2001 by Rosanne Bittner

Map by Mark Stein Studios

A Tor Book
Published by Tom Doherty Associates, LLC
175 Fifth Avenue
New York, NY 10010

www.tor.com

Tor® is a registered trademark of Tom Doherty Associates, LLC.

ISBN: 0-812-56543-6
Library of Congress Catalog Card Number: 200108960

First edition: May 2001
First mass market edition: February 2002

Printed in the United States of America

0 9 8 7 6 5 4 3 2 1

Many thanks to my patient husband, Larry;
and to even more patient editor, Andrew Zack;
and to my agent, Denise Marcil.

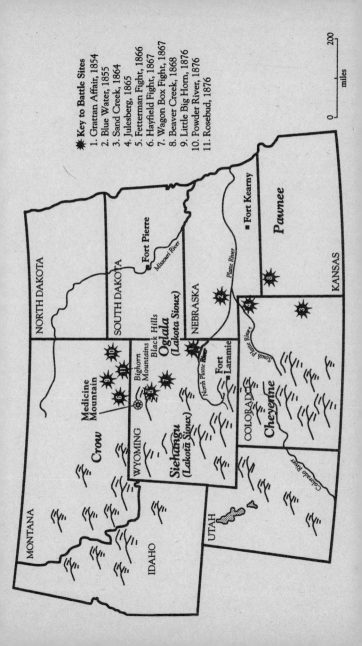

Key to Battle Sites
1. Grattan Affair, 1854
2. Blue Water, 1855
3. Sand Creek, 1864
4. Julesberg, 1865
5. Fetterman Fight, 1866
6. Hayfield Fight, 1867
7. Wagon Box Fight, 1867
8. Beaver Creek, 1868
9. Little Big Horn, 1876
10. Powder River, 1876
11. Rosebud, 1876

0   200
miles

PREFACE

In all three of my *Mystic Dreamers* books, I refer to the Feathered One. This Being is my interpretation of a representative of the Phoenix, a mythical Being, half man, half eagle, who some Native Americans believe will rise from the flames of fire as a symbol of the return of their ancestors, after the white man has destroyed himself. Native Americans believe they will then reclaim land that has always rightfully belonged to them.

There are many theories about the "Rise of the Phoenix." I do not claim that mine is the right one.

The main characters in this story are fictitious; however, every event involving the Lakota and battles with soldiers is true, including attacks by soldiers on peaceful camps, and also the hanging of two Oglala chiefs and a Cheyenne chief at Fort Laramie, their bodies left to rot rather than being buried. I do mention real historical Indian leaders in this book such as Crazy Horse and Sitting Bull; as well as actual army leaders, such as George Custer. The events surrounding them are true.

To avoid confusion, it should be noted that among Indian tribes there were often several "chiefs," not just one; and no man had to follow any directive from these respected leaders if he didn't want to. Thus, treaties were often signed by a few leaders, but seldom by all. Those who did not sign took it for granted they did not have to abide by those treaties.

In this story I mention "old" Crazy Horse. The Crazy Horse of historical fame was the son of a man named Crazy Horse. The younger Crazy Horse was called Curly in his youth. His father gave him his own name as a sign of great honor, after the young man proved his worth as a warrior.

The Medicine Wheel mentioned in all three of my *Mystic Dreamers* books does exist, on top of Medicine Mountain in northern Wyoming. Events that transpire there in this book are fictitious.

It should be noted that the Native Americans in this story would, of course, speak in their own tongue. However, their dialogue is presented here in English.

A good deal of the facts in this story came from information found in the following books:

Frazer, Robert W. *Forts of the West: Military Forts and Presidios and Posts Commonly Called Forts West of the Mississippi River to 1898.* Norman, OK: University of Oklahoma Press. 1965.

Greene, Jerome A. *Lakota and Cheyenne: Indian Views of the Great Sioux War, 1876–1877.* Norman, OK: University of Oklahoma Press. 1994.

Hook, Jason. *American Indian Warrior Chiefs: Tecumseh, Crazy Horse, Chief Joseph, Geronimo.* New York: Firebird Books, Sterling Publishing Co. 1989.

And from various articles in *True West*, *Old West*, and *Nebraska History* magazines.

He is a warrior, even today, more than a century after his death. One needs only to watch the heavens to see him riding there in the clouds, his muscular body decorated with beaded arm bands, red war stripes painted down his cheeks, black surrounding his eyes, coup feathers tied into his straight, black hair, a bone hair-pipe breastplate worn over his chest. He sits on a horse like no other, and beside him rides his first-born, Brave Horse . . . and on the other side his wife, a holy woman of the Oglala, Buffalo Dreamer.

Do you see them there? They live to this day in that place where all Oglala have gone before, waiting for the day when the earth again belongs to them. Can that day be far away?

They will come down from the skies, those mystic warriors, and claim what always belonged to them.

PART ONE
Broken Promises

What treaty that the whites have kept has the red man broken? Not one. What treaty that the white man ever made with us have they kept? Not one. When I was a boy the Sioux owned the world; the sun rose and set on their land; they sent ten thousand men to battle. Where are the warriors today? Who slew them? Where are our lands? Who owns them? What white man can say I ever stole his land or a penny of his money? . . . Who has ever seen me beat my wives or abuse my children? What law have I broken? Is it wrong for me to love my own? Is it wicked for me because my skin is red? Or because I am a Sioux; because I was born where my father lived; because I would die for my people and my country?

—SITTING BULL, OGLALA

AUGUST 1855

Time of the Hot Moon

CHAPTER ONE

"TAKE A LOOK!" Cooper Baird handed his spyglass to his friend, Clement Dees. "First one I've ever seen. I've heard of white buffalo, but in all the years I've trapped and hunted out here, I've never seen one."

Clement steadied the spyglass while Cooper remained crouched beside him. "It's a white buffalo skin all right," Clement answered. He kept his voice to a low whisper. "From what I can tell, there's nobody down there but one brave and his squaw." He handed back the spyglass. "Shouldn't be too hard a job for four men."

Cooper swatted at a fly on his cheek. "You never can tell with the Sioux. There's likely plenty more nearby. Don't forget what happened to them soldiers under that Lieutenant Grattan. The Sioux are feelin' their oats, right boastful and ready for more killin', most likely; kind of like a wolf. Once it gets the scent of blood, it's ready for more."

"In this case it's one man and his squaw, not a whole war party," Clement argued.

Both men slithered down the rise that hid them from the Indian camp below. Cooper shoved his spyglass into a loop on his belt. "As long as we keep things quiet and don't end up with a war party on us. I seen the remains of Grattan and his men. It weren't a pretty sight, let me tell you. Most of the bodies could hardly be recognized, all chopped up and riddled with arrows." He brushed off his already-soiled buckskins. "Still in all, we can get good money for somethin' like that white robe, it bein' so rare and all. I say we try for it."

Clement shrugged. "You're the one who was just gripin' about the mood the Sioux are in. It's a big risk."

Cooper headed toward the gully where he and his hunting party were camped. He whistled softly to signal two more men waiting in the brush. Clement was right. This was not a good time to be out here hunting buffalo, but the animal's hide was garnering a damn good price back in St. Louis. Hunting the great beasts was becoming the new sport, a damned exciting one for men who liked the challenge, and Cooper liked nothing better than trying something he'd never done before, including the idea of stealing a white buffalo robe from the Sioux.

He ducked into the thick brush surrounding his camp, followed by Clement. Bob Powers and Jim Liskey waited there for them, both men holding pieces of jerky in their hands, their most practical nourishment in times when making a fire meant danger. No white man in these parts wanted to be spotted by the enemy. Sidearms, knives, and rifles were kept handy.

Liskey nodded to both arriving men before biting off a piece of the hard, dry meat. "See any buffalo?" He wiped at his nose with the sleeve of his stained buckskin shirt.

Cooper winced at the sight of Liskey's left eye, which was really nothing but a sewn-up hole. A large white scar ran from above the eye down across the man's cheek and lips. A drunken Sioux brave had done that to him. No one hated Indians more than Jim Liskey. "Saw somethin' even better than buffalo. There's a white buffalo robe spread out on a tepee the other side of the hill."

Liskey's eyebrows shot up in surprise. "White?"

"White. Never seen anything like it, and it's already cleaned and stretched. All we need to do is go down there and take it from an Indian camp."

"That easy, huh?" Powers replied, snorting in laughter. "No, thanks."

"There's only one tepee, a man and woman camped alone."

"And probably a couple thousand more nearby," Liskey grumbled. "You know how wily the Sioux are. Least ways, I know. If you want your hide roasted over an open fire, go get the damned robe by yourself."

"I've got an idea for gettin' it with no trouble," Cooper answered.

"The robe is laid out over tepee skins, maybe to air out," Clement added. "Looks like some squaw is down there lookin' for turnips or somethin'. There's a brave with her, sittin' off smokin' his pipe. Looks to us like they're alone, probably feelin' right cocky after the Grattan thing; but that don't matter much, long as it's just the one Indian."

Liskey shrugged. "If it's true they're alone, why don't you just pick off the man with your buffalo gun and go get the robe? You could bring along the squaw for all of us to share."

"Sounds tempting," Cooper answered. "But you were right that there could be a couple thousand more someplace nearby. Them bastards can pop up out of the tall grass like prairie dogs. Don't forget that any Sioux in these parts are likely ripe for another fight. I don't aim to go shootin' off my gun to let them know we're here."

Powers chuckled. "That damn fool Grattan deserved what he got, goin' up against half the Sioux nation with a lousy thirty inexperienced soldiers. And what for? Just because one Sioux warrior shot an old, lame cow that belonged to a damned Mormon. The cow wasn't worth a shit to begin with."

"I don't give a damn about how many soldiers died or what the reason was," Cooper grumbled. "All I know is I want that white robe. You other three willing to help me get it?"

The other three glanced at one another warily.

"I don't know," Powers answered skeptically.

"What's your plan?" Clement asked.

"I figure on sneakin' down there and doin' it quietly, after dark," Cooper said. "If one or two of you can create some kind of distraction, I can make off with the robe. We could have our horses someplace nearby and ride off, hard and fast, right toward Fort Kearny. We're only a day's ride from there. Fact is, the soldiers would probably be right glad to know there's some Sioux so close by. Last I heard, they was gettin' ready for a new campaign against the murderin' bastards under a General Harney, I think. We can furnish them some information when we get there."

Liskey rubbed at his shriveled eye socket. "I hope they kill every last one of the bastards."

Cooper snorted, gathering phlegm at the back of his throat, then coughing it up and spitting it out. "We ain't gonna' kill these. Not if we can help it. That's my orders."

"Why not?" Clement asked. "Seems to me the easiest way to get the robe."

Cooper scratched at the several-day-old stubble on his face. "And that's the best way to bring the whole lot of them after us. All I want is the robe, and with nobody hurt and no horses stole, they won't be so likely to come after us. They might not even know why we were there till later. That will give us time to get away." He grinned. "And as far as I know, we'll be the first to arrive in St. Louis with an albino robe."

"They're sacred, you know." Powers said.

"Sacred?" Clement removed a floppy, leather hat.

"The white buffalo. The Sioux consider them sacred. You can bet that robe means a hell of a lot to whoever owns it. And if you steal it, you might regret it."

Cooper chuckled. "How's that?"

Powers shrugged. "Who knows? You might have all kinds of bad luck once you steal it. The Sioux religion is pretty powerful stuff. You mess with somethin' sacred to them, and you could have a heap of trouble on your hands."

Cooper shared in the snickers of Liskey and Clement, shaking his head. "It's *their* religion, not mine," Cooper said derisively. "I don't have *any* religion, and I ain't superstitious. I ain't worried about some damn object a bunch of wild Indians think has magical powers. The only magical powers that robe has is the magic to put money in our pockets."

"Whoever is in charge at Fort Kearny won't take kindly to us stirrin' up the Sioux again," Clement reminded him.

"They don't need to know nothin' about it. We'll hide the

white robe and just ride in like a huntin' party done with its job. Besides, the Sioux are riled up over other things. They'll stir up enough trouble all on their own." He took a piece of jerked meat from his pants pocket and bit down on one end of it, yanking off a piece. "You three gonna help me?"

They all grinned and nodded, and Cooper thought how nice it was going to be getting back to St. Louis. He wouldn't mind being the center of attention over that fine white robe. He bit off another piece of meat, feeling very satisfied.

CHAPTER TWO

BUFFALO DREAMER LAY next to Rising Eagle, listening to the distant cries of coyotes. A west wind rustled the leaves of the nearby cottonwood trees. Her husband sighed and rolled to his side, resting his head on his hand as he faced her.

"There is much change in the air," he said softly.

Buffalo Dreamer stared up at the twinkle of a few stars she could see through the smoke hole of the tepee. The view was clear tonight, for she'd made no fire. "A new season will come soon," she answered.

"It is not just the seasons of which I speak," Rising Eagle answered. "Our children are mostly grown. Brave Horse is a man now, a warrior of twenty-one summers; and one day soon we will give our adopted daughter away in marriage. Little Turtle is growing fast and already doing well in the warrior games, anxious to become a man. Songbird is already learning much from Running Elk Woman. She is still young, but eager to be grown."

"Running Elk Woman has been a good replacement for my mother. Your aunt has become like a grandmother to our daughter." Buffalo Dreamer swallowed against a sudden urge to cry. "I still miss my mother so."

Rising Eagle sighed deeply. "I often think about all the loved ones we lost to the white man's spotted disease, all the friends who have left us over the years, so many due to the white men and their soldiers. When we were young life was good, free and happy. Now all these changes because of the *wasicus*. No matter what we do, they keep coming. All the soldiers we killed not long ago will be replaced by twice as many . . . and they will come again."

"And we will continue defeating them until they give up," Buffalo Dreamer assured him. She reached up in the darkness and touched his face. "Don't forget that in my dream of long ago, our people surrounded and killed many more soldiers than those who were killed last summer. That means we have more victories ahead of us, and as long as we possess the robe of the white buffalo, we have much power."

Rising Eagle moved on top of her, resting on his elbows. "It will all have to happen soon. My hair is showing gray at the edges. Soon I will be considered an elder, and I will not have so much power and strength riding against the enemy."

Buffalo Dreamer laughed lightly in spite of her misty eyes. She could not see him well in the darkness of only a sliver of a moon; but she knew her husband was also smiling. "You will always have power," she answered, running her hands over his still-muscled arms. "You are a holy man, a man of vision, one who has seen and heard the words of the Feathered One. As far as your physical strength . . ." She moved her hands up and over his shoulders. "You have not changed, my husband, and you still do not have the big belly of an elder."

Rising Eagle leaned down and licked at her lips. "You are the one who has not changed. We have been together for twenty-three summers, and still your hair shows no gray. You have borne many children." He ran a hand over a naked breast, down over her waist, and around under her hips. "But your body is still that of a young woman . . . and I still burn for you."

The warm night required no clothing. Buffalo Dreamer could feel her husband's hardness pressing against her groin. "Then I should put out the fire," she said seductively, moving her own hands down along his back, to his bare hips, around to touch that part of him that still made her ache to feel him inside her. She opened herself to him, groaning when he entered her, taking delight in these two days they had chosen to spend alone while others watched over their two youngest children. There were times when a man and woman had to do these things, knowing hard times may lie ahead, knowing their own bodies were aging, and that moments like this could become more rare.

For the next several minutes they reveled in lovemaking, taking and giving, sharing each other's ecstasy, loving in the most intimate, most intense way a man and woman could love.

Buffalo Dreamer's pride in Rising Eagle had not waned over the years. She was herself a holy woman, the only one among their People who'd seen and touched the white buffalo. Her dreams often evoked visions of the future.

Rising Eagle was a man of even greater vision, a man with healing powers, and the only warrior in generations who'd seen and heard the Feathered One, the great Being who spoke for *Wakan-Tanka*. He was a man held in high esteem by the entire Lakota Nation, and he'd chosen her because of a vision. A stranger when first he came for her, she'd learned to love him deeply.

She felt his life spill into her. She would never stop wishing that life could take hold again, but she knew it was not to be. Instinctively, she'd known that after the birth of her youngest child, Songbird, she would never have another. Now it was grandchildren she must look forward to, but she still enjoyed the pleasures of lovemaking.

Rising Eagle could have his pick of any young maidens he chose, yet he had kept his long-ago promise that he would never take another wife. He was a man who honored his word, unlike the white man. He seemed to honor nothing he promised, and it was a white man's disease that had stolen away two of their children, her own mother, and many friends and loved ones . . . the white man's disease that had left small, white, pitted scars on Rising Eagle's handsome face.

He rolled away. "Tomorrow we will return to the main camp. We need to hunt more buffalo before the weather changes. Those who go to Laramie for promised supplies bring back only rotten meat and blankets eaten by moths. It is just as I told the others when I refused to sign any treaties. We cannot depend on the white man to keep one promise he has ever made. We can only rely on the hunt for survival. We will move into Crow and Shoshoni country if that is the only way to find more buffalo. We will drive them out, as we have done in the past, in spite of the white man's orders to make no more war against other tribes."

"Apparently the soldiers learned a good lesson last summer when we killed all those who attacked Conquering Bear and the Brule. They have not disturbed us since."

"Perhaps not. But we must remember we cannot ever trust them. We must always be on guard."

Just then one of the four horses tethered outside whinnied. Then another.

Rising Eagle and Buffalo Dreamer both quickly sat up. Rising Eagle grabbed his hatchet and a knife, and Buffalo Dreamer reached for her tunic, slipping it over her head as her husband, still naked, ducked outside to determine what had disturbed the horses. Buffalo Dreamer thought she heard something behind the tepee. She quickly grabbed her own knife and darted outside. "Who is there?" she shouted in her own tongue.

She heard a man cry out then, over near the horses. She ran in that direction, yelling Rising Eagle's name.

"I am here!" he called to her.

She hurried toward the sound of his voice, several yards past where the horses were tethered. When her eyes adjusted to the darkness, she could see Rising Eagle standing over a man writhing on the ground. The culprit wore buckskins, and his hair was dark and tangled. She did not need to see him well to tell that he was a white man. She could tell by his smell, a sweet, sweaty, dirty smell she'd already learned most white men carried. It made her nose curl.

"He was trying to steal a horse," Rising Eagle told her. He looked around. "I think there were more. I heard them running away."

"What were white men doing out here with so many of our people close by? Don't they know we'll kill any white man we see?"

"They're probably buffalo hunters," Rising Eagle sneered. "The kind who kill the sacred beast just for its hide, leaving the rest to rot!" He looked down at the man he'd just caught and stabbed. He kicked him onto his back, and the man groaned. "Good. He is still alive. We will take him to the bigger camp and let the women and elders decide what to do with him!"

Buffalo Dreamer could feel the eagerness in his voice. They would make this man suffer for the way he and his kind were destroying the buffalo. The Lakota would make an example of this white man for others who dared to come into their hunting grounds. He would not die quickly or easily.

"We should bring the horses closer," she said.

"Hush!"

Buffalo Dreamer quieted as her husband listened with keen ears. Then she, too, heard the sound of horses riding off.

"They are going," Rising Eagle said quietly. "They have left their wounded friend behind. I'm not surprised." He looked down once more at the man at his feet. "We can leave the horses where they are. I do not think they will be back."

"Are you hurt, Rising Eagle?"

"No." He kicked at the wounded man once more. "We will leave this one here until morning. Let him suffer." He put a hand to her waist and walked with her back to their tepee.

"I thought I heard one of them near the tepee," Buffalo Dreamer told him as they walked. "But then I heard someone cry out. I was afraid it was you, so I—" She drew in her breath, grasping Rising Eagle's arm. "The robe!" She left him then, her heart pounding as she ran. She reached the tepee, feeling around where she'd left the robe spread over the tepee skins to air in the sun all that day. It was not there.

"No! No!" she whimpered. She felt around more, getting down on her hands and knees and feeling around on the ground, hoping it had simply slipped down. Tears welled in her eyes as she searched, feeling around in the grass, her stomach tightening into a painful knot. "It's gone! Rising Eagle, the robe is gone!" she cried out.

She felt his presence then, felt his own horror.

"I have lost it!" Buffalo Dreamer wept. "I was careless, and I lost it! I did not think anything could happen with us out here alone." She sucked in her breath in a great sob as she felt Rising Eagle grasp her arms and pull her up.

"But we were *not* alone," he said, obvious rage in the words. "Again the white man has come to try to destroy us! Again they show no honor for what is pure and *sacred*!"

"This is a bad, bad omen, Rising Eagle," Buffalo Dreamer wept. "It will be a curse on our people, and it is my fault!"

He gripped her arms tighter and gave her a light shake. "It is *not* your fault! It's just another sign of how evil the white man is. *They* are the ones who will suffer! As soon as it is light, I will follow the tracks of whoever stole the robe. I will find him and I will *kill* him!"

Buffalo Dreamer shook her head. "You will not find him. I know it in my heart." She hung her head. "I have lost the white buffalo robe . . . after all these years. You were right, my husband. There *is* change in the air . . . a terrible change . . . worse than we thought possible."

Rising Eagle pulled her tight against him. "The change will not affect just us, Buffalo Dreamer. It will also affect the *wasicus*!"

CHAPTER THREE

"BRAVE HORSE."

His name was spoken softly, timidly, by a female, bringing Brave Horse to alertness. He looked up from where he sat alone under a cottonwood tree near the creek, and his heartbeat rushed when he saw Yellow Bonnet emerge from nearby bushes. For years, almost since the day his father captured her from a white man's wagon train, he saw Yellow Bonnet as a golden vision, all pink and white and yellow, so different from Indian girls. He'd watched her grow into a woman, a true daughter to Rising Eagle, one who was now ready to be courted. His father would, of course, not allow her to go to anyone but the most honored of warriors. But Brave Horse could not be such a suitor, because Rising Eagle considered him Yellow Bonnet's brother.

He stood up, setting aside his prayer pipe. "What is it, Yellow Bonnet?"

She stepped a little closer, her willowy body making the fringes of her tunic dance fetchingly. She wore her blonde hair in two queues over the front of her shoulders, as was customary for a female who had passed from childhood into womanhood. "I wish to speak with you." She looked around cautiously. "I know I am not to be alone with any young man, but you are my brother. If someone sees us, we are just brother and sister talking."

"Of course." Brave Horse caught the question in her eyes . . . the doubt. "What is it you wish to speak to me about?"

A crimson blush moved into her cheeks. "About . . . what I just said . . . you being my brother." She closed her eyes and breathed deeply as though for courage, then boldly faced him. "You really are *not* my brother. We are not even of the same people, even though my heart belongs to the Lakota."

Brave Horse frowned, confused. "I don't understand." He was sure he detected tears in her eyes as she quickly looked away.

"I have seen how you look at me sometimes," she said, "and I know you have . . . special feelings for me, as I have for you. I watch with great pride when you win a horse race, or when you win at spearing games. You are tall and skilled . . . and most handsome, Brave Horse. At your first Sun Dance sacrifice, my heart swelled with love, as well as with agony for your pain."

Brave Horse felt warm all over, watching her brush at tears, obviously having great difficulty with her words.

"It is a different kind of love than a sister for her brother," she went on. "And if I were not certain in my heart . . . that you have the same feelings toward me, I would not be standing here now, risking my own pride and honor by telling you this. I only thought . . . you should know. If I am wrong, then you should tell me so and I will discuss these feelings with our mother. Buffalo Dreamer will know what to do. She might tell Rising Eagle that I should wed someone else as soon as possible, so that I can learn to accept another man into my heart and . . . forget the forbidden feelings I have for you."

Brave Horse could not believe what she was saying, nor could he prevent the rush of love that swept through him. Hesitantly, he stepped closer to her, close enough to touch her. She remained turned away, her arms crossed almost defensively.

"Look at me," he told her. "Never hang your head as though ashamed, Yellow Bonnet."

She wiped away more tears, then faced him.

"Love should never bring shame," he said gently. "My mother and father raised you to be among the most honorable of young women. You have celebrated all the same ceremonies as the Lakota girls. You have learned to build tepees, to make clothing, skin and tan hides, to make pemmican. You know how to build a travois, how to make war shields, how to do quill work and bead work. You are brave and you are . . . beautiful . . . more beautiful than any young Lakota woman in our tribe. You have never shown fear, not even the first day my father brought you to us when you were much younger. Your own mother chose her freedom over yours, and she never came back for you. I always felt sorry for you because of that. My own mother would die before she stopped searching for me. She even rode into battle against the Pawnee once to help find me after they stole me as a baby. And now . . . to tell me how you feel, knowing my father would consider this forbidden . . . that only shows me how brave you truly are." He took a deep breath. "And I am brave enough to tell you in return that I have loved you . . . almost since I first became aware of you as a woman, and myself as a man."

More tears spilled down her cheeks. "Then I was right," she said, quickly wiping at her nose with the back of her hand for lack of anything else.

Brave Horse nodded. His heart went out to her, and he reached out, pulling her into his arms. She moved her arms around his waist to embrace him, and the feel of her full breasts under her soft tunic brought a tingle to his bare chest.

"I am so happy to know for certain that you feel this way," she said. "So happy to finally admit my feelings for you."

Brave Horse kissed her light hair, darkened somewhat by the buffalo fat she used to keep it shiny and lustrous. He could not resist leaning down to rub her cheek, trembling at the feel of her against him, so close, so soft. Her mouth came close to his, her lips full and pink. He licked them, feeling a painful need in his loins that caused him to suddenly let go of her and step back. "I do not wish to offend you, or to ruin your honor."

Yellow Bonnet again reddened, smiling nervously as she, too, stepped back.

"Knowing how we feel, you should go now," Brave Horse added.

She nodded, twisting her fingers together as she looked at him longingly through tear-filled eyes. "What will you do?"

"I will speak with Rising Eagle and Buffalo Dreamer."

"They will be angry, especially Rising Eagle."

"I know how to reason with my father. He will be angry at first, but he will take time to think about it. When he understands that it is possible he will lose his son by having him banished from our tribe, he will see that the right thing to do is to let us be together."

"Banished? Why would *you* be banished?"

Brave Horse grinned. "For doing the dishonorable thing and running off with you without Rising Eagle's permission."

Her eyes widened. "You would *do* that?"

He studied her lovingly, drinking in her shape, her beautiful blue eyes. "Yes. Now that I know how you truly feel, it will be impossible not to want you for myself. If my father made you marry another, I would steal you from him, bringing even more shame on myself and risking death at the hands of your husband."

She put a hand to her chest. "Brave Horse!" she said in wonder. "You are the son of Rising Eagle! I could not *let* you do such a thing. I would not go! Your reputation and honor are much more valuable than our feelings for each other."

He slowly shook his head. "I am not so sure. But first we will see if we can be together the proper way. If not, I will pray about this, seek a vision. Perhaps then I will know what I must do. I only know that not to have you as my own would be a pain worse than death."

Yellow Bonnet's lips quivered as she replied. "I feel the same." She started to cry again. "And knowing you understand . . . and that you share these feelings . . . makes my heart ache from happiness!"

"Rider coming!" someone shouted from the nearby camp. "It is Buffalo Dreamer! She is alone!"

Immediately Brave Horse's conversation with Yellow Bonnet was interrupted. "Go quickly!" he told her. "Come back to camp from another direction!" He darted away, heading toward camp, his emotions running high with a mixture of happiness over

learning about Yellow Bonnet's feelings, and excitement over the
kind of news his mother might be bringing. Was it good, or bad?
Why had she come back alone? When he reached camp he saw her
talking excitedly to others, her horse looking lathered. Whatever
her news, it was very important.

He ran up to where his mother stood, and as others parted, he
saw a man tied by the ankles to the back of Buffalo Dreamer's
horse, his clothes torn and mostly ripped off from being dragged,
his skin a mass of blood.

"White men have stolen the white buffalo robe!" his mother
cried upon seeing her son.

Brave Horse's joy over learning of Yellow Bonnet's love quickly
turned to feelings of alarm. Nothing held more importance to his
father's clan, and to his mother's strength and esteem than the
white robe. Losing it could have disastrous affects on the Lakota!

CHAPTER FOUR

BRAVE HORSE AND his best friend, Curly, watched with great satisfaction as men hanged the bleeding white captive by his ankles from a tree limb, leaving his head only a few inches from the top of the fire built to slowly roast his brains. The man had already been beaten with fists and sticks by several women, who had then peeled away a good deal of his skin while the man screamed and begged for mercy, only proving how weak and cowardly white men were.

Now the captive hung limp, occasionally groaning as his fingers, which hung directly in the flames, caught fire, then his hair. Death would soon claim him, and justly so. Brave Horse wished all *wasicus* who came into this land would die.

"Just punishment!" Curly sneered.

"Aye," Brave Horse replied. "And I hope his death will help heal my mother's heart. This has been hard on her."

"Do you think Rising Eagle will find those who took the robe?" Curly slowly walked around the tortured captive, wrinkling his nose at the smell of burned hair and roasting flesh.

"He will try his best," Brave Horse answered. "The loss of the robe has destroyed my mother's spirit, and it will mean bad times for us. When the white buffalo came to my mother and offered itself many years ago, it spoke to her and told her that as long as she possessed the robe, only good things would come to the Lakota.

She and my father cut into its heart while it was still warm and they ate of it. Later more white men came into our hunting grounds, but in spite of that we have continued to do well. We even killed all those soldiers last summer. It was a great victory, our sign to the white man that he cannot come here and take our land and break treaty promises without suffering for it. Now white men have stolen the robe, as though to bring themselves the power it gives."

"What if Rising Eagle cannot recapture the robe?"

Brave Horse looked at his good friend, a very unusual young warrior of only fourteen summers, three years younger than he. Curly got his name from the waves in his unnaturally light-colored hair. He was quite handsome, in spite of looking different from most Lakota, and soon he intended to seek his first vision, a beginning of his journey to manhood.

Curly's father, Crazy Horse, claimed his son's unusual physical attributes meant he was gifted, that the Great Spirit had special plans for him. Already the young man was nearly as adept at the hunt, at the use of bow and arrow, tomahawk, and spear, as any accomplished warrior. He expected to complete his own vision quest soon, hoping to learn what it was the Great Spirit expected of him.

Brave Horse didn't know what to think of it all. He only knew in his heart that great things would come of Curly, and he intended to be a part of them. Whatever Curly ended up doing, Brave Horse wanted to be at his friend's side. Often they talked about dreams and visions, and they always rode side by side in attacks on enemy tribes.

"If my father cannot recapture the robe, then we must all be prepared for the worst," Brave Horse continued. "We must be strong and watchful. As long as white men possess the white robe, we must never trust any of them." He folded his arms, arrogantly studying the prisoner who hung roasting and bloody over the open fire. "The elders will hold a council meeting to discuss all of this. We should go and listen."

"What will your mother do?"

Brave Horse's heart felt heavy, knowing Buffalo Dreamer felt a deep sorrow over this, as though she had lost a loved one. "She will pray. Already she has cut off her hair in mourning, and she has gone into the hills alone. She will let blood and pray for an answer, pray for the return of the robe."

Curly sighed. "I hate the white men. They have been nothing but trouble ever since I can remember."

Brave Horse nodded, as thunder rumbled in the distance.

"A storm is coming," Curly commented.

"Indeed," Brave Horse answered.

Rising Eagle halted his horse when Fort Kearny came into view. Rain poured down in torrents, but he hardly noticed. The sight of hundreds of new recruits at the fort took precedence over all other concerns.

More soldiers! Why were they here? Was the white men's leader ordering new attacks on the Lakota because of all the soldiers he and others had killed the past summer? They had all *deserved* to die. The soldiers had killed the Brule chief, Conquering Bear, over the butchering of one sick cow that was of no use to the white men anyway.

Thunder cracked and rumbled as he watched the movement below. His heartbeat quickened at the sight of all those soldiers, and he felt sick at knowing he had failed in finding and retrieving the white robe.

As he'd tracked those who'd fled, he'd found one man lying on the ground with his head cracked open. From what he could tell, the man had ridden into a tree branch in the dark. Several hours later he'd found yet another man lying on the ground with his britches down, a snake bite on his hip. He'd apparently been relieving himself when a rattler took offense. Rising Eagle took solace only in the fact that the thieves were quickly learning that stealing the white robe would only bring them bad luck. He'd sent the man he'd originally captured back to camp with Buffalo Dreamer. By now he, too, was dead.

Three dead. From the tracks he'd continued to follow, there had been one left, and it was most likely that one who had the robe, since he still had not found it. If only he did not have to wait until dawn to follow them, he might have caught up with them in time to recapture the sacred buffalo robe.

The last man's tracks had led toward Fort Kearny, but the recent downpour had washed the tracks completely away. Still, he strongly suspected the man was headed here, where he would be safe. Not far back he'd found a dead horse, one of its legs crooked and broken, a bullet hole between its eyes. More bad luck for those who dared take the white robe! Apparently this last man had finished his flight on foot in the drenching rain.

Mud ran in rivulets all around him. He knew he dared not go down to the fort, well aware that right now any Lakota man a soldier saw in his rifle sight was fair game. If he went into the fort after the robe, he would be shot down without question. And now that the robe was lost to his people, they would need his leadership . . . and Buffalo Dreamer would need his support.

He turned away, disheartened. It was possible the sacred white buffalo robe was lost to them forever.

CHAPTER FIVE

"WHAT THE HELL?" Sergeant Paul Miliken stared down at the man who'd staggered into the gates of Fort Kearny and then collapsed. He clung to a soggy buffalo robe he'd dragged along. Several men gathered to stare at the curious new arrival.

"Who is he?" one soldier asked.

"How in hell do I know?" Miliken answered, irritated by the rain that soaked his shirt. "Close the damn gates!" he barked at one of the men. "And get a blanket and a stretcher!" He knelt down beside the collapsed civilian and leaned close. "Hey, mister, what's your name? How did you get here? Where's your horse?"

The man lay flat on his back, staring vacantly. Miliken shook him lightly. "Mister! Who are you? What's happened to you?"

"The . . . robe," the man muttered.

Miliken lifted the buffalo robe, and in spite of its muddy condition, he could see it was from an albino buffalo, something very rare. He held up one end of it so the civilian could see it. "This what you're talking about? What do you want to tell me, mister?"

The man's eyes widened. "Get it away from me!" he practically screamed. "Get it . . . the hell away from me! It's . . . cursed!"

"Cursed?" Miliken studied the sodden robe a moment, then pulled it away. Its weight made it impossible to toss it far. "What's your name?" he asked the stranger again. "How did you get here?"

The man managed to raise his head slightly, and Miliken ordered one of the men to give him his trench coat. He held the coat over his own head and over the civilian as the man spoke.

"Name's . . . Cooper," he said. "Cooper Baird. That robe . . . I took it from an . . . Oglala man. It's . . . bad medicine. Lost . . . three other men coming here."

"Lost? Where are they?"

"Sioux captured one. Jim Liskey. Bob Powers . . . he got his head cracked open . . . hit a tree branch. My friend Clement Dees . . . got bit by a rattler. My horse broke his leg . . . couple miles back. I had to . . . shoot him." The man winced as though in great pain. "And my chest feels like a horse . . . is sittin' on it. You gotta help me . . . please! And get rid of that robe. It's an albino . . . sacred to the Sioux. I tell you . . . it's cursed! It's . . ." He winced again, then gasped and collapsed.

Miliken leaned close to feel at Cooper's neck for a pulse, then threw back the trench coat. "The man's dead!" he exclaimed. He stood up, thinking how Cooper Baird's arrival had at least broken up the boredom of the day. There would be plenty to talk about tonight over the usual game of cards.

The man who had gone for a blanket and stretcher returned then, bringing the fort doctor with him.

"Forget it," Miliken told the doctor. "He's dead."

The doctor frowned. "The soldier who came for me said this man arrived on foot, dragging an albino buffalo robe with him."

Miliken nodded. "I had a chance to question him a little. He claims he and three other men stole the robe off the Sioux. One of them was captured, and another one was killed when he rode into a tree limb. The third man was snakebit and died." He looked down at Cooper. "Now this one is dead, too. And most likely the one the Sioux captured is also dead by now, probably tortured to death. This guy called himself Cooper Baird. He claimed the deaths of the others were because of the robe—said it had some kind of special powers because it belonged to the Sioux, said it was cursed."

"Damn," someone muttered.

In spite of the rain, they all stared at the robe in quiet astonishment.

"Attention!"

All stiffened respectfully when the fort commander came stomping up to them after yelling the order. "What's going on here, Sergeant?" the scowling commander asked.

Miliken saluted. "Lieutenant Spear, sir, this man came staggering into the fort on foot. Claims him and three friends stole that white buffalo robe from the Sioux. Now all four of them are dead. He said it was because of the robe—says it's cursed."

"*Cursed?*" Lieutenant Richard Spear looked down at the robe. "Hogwash!" he grumbled. He leaned down and picked up one end of the robe, holding it away from himself because of its muddy condition. Rain ran off the hood of his coat and down over his shoulders as he looked around at the other soldiers present. "If you men are this afraid of a damned buffalo skin once owned by the Sioux, how in blazes are you going to face the Indians themselves when we go after them for what they did to Lieutenant Grattan and his men?" He held the robe out to the sergeant. "*Take* it!" he ordered.

"Sir?"

"You heard me! Take hold of the damn thing! Carry it over to the blacksmith's and have him hang it up somewhere so it can dry out!"

The sergeant hesitantly took the robe.

"It's just an old buffalo robe! And since it is a white one, I'll keep the damned thing myself for a souvenir. Ought to stir up a good conversation when I go home some day. In the meantime, you and your men had better shape up. It won't be long before you'll be facing Lakota warriors. If you let this damned robe spook you, you'll all be worthless to me! Some of you men bury this man's body. See if he has anything on him that might tell us where he's from so we can notify relatives."

Miliken nodded. "Yes, sir."

The lieutenant glanced at the rest of the men once more with a look of disdain before marching back to his quarters. The doctor turned away, and Miliken ordered four men to burial detail.

Reluctantly, he gathered up the robe, heavy from the rain. He walked toward the blacksmith's, telling himself that Cooper Baird's bad luck was simply of his own doing. It was no surprise that one of the men was captured when they stole the robe. A man couldn't expect to steal from the Sioux without suffering for it. The other two men simply died by freak accidents. Considering the weight of the wet robe, it was no wonder Cooper Baird died. He'd probably had a heart attack from walking so far carrying the damn thing. Trouble was, why didn't the man just let go of the robe in the first place? Did it have some kind of magical spell over him?

Thunder cracked again, and he looked out at the surrounding hills. Lightning lit up the deep gray sky, and his chest tightened at what appeared to be a man sitting on a horse in the distance.

Indian? Damned if the bloody Sioux didn't give him the shivers. He stared at the spot a moment longer. Lightning flashed again, and the figure was gone. He quickened his steps, hurrying faster to the blacksmith's. He grunted then when he hoisted the robe over a wooden fence.

"Take this thing inside!" he shouted to a sergeant who stood just inside the smithy's shed. "Lieutenant Spear wants it hung up to dry." He did not remain for the sergeant's questions. He simply left, glad to get away from the white robe. "Spear can have the damn thing," he muttered.

SEPTEMBER 1855

Moon of the Drying Heat

CHAPTER SIX

"WE WILL GO to Medicine Mountain and pray." Rising Eagle hoped the words would give strength to Buffalo Dreamer, who sat nearly silent, her head hanging, her hair a mass of uneven shocks from being fitfully whacked off with her skinning knife. Above all others, Rising Eagle knew the extent of his wife's agony and sorrow over losing the white robe. It had represented hope, life, successful hunts, bounty, and peace for the Lakota. It was literally a weapon against the intrusion of the white man, for possession of the white robe protected the Lakota from all outside forces. Now it was gone. More than that, it was in the hands of *wasicus*.

Buffalo Dreamer's arms bore fresh scabs where she had cut herself in sacrifice to *Wakan-Tanka* as she prayed for protection for the Lakota and for the return of the robe. Almost overnight his beautiful wife's hair had begun to show streaks of gray. It sickened Rising Eagle that he had not been able to bring the robe back to her. He, too, had prayed vehemently, fasting often, cleansing himself in the sweat lodge, seeking an answer to this dilemma. When she finally met his gaze, pain shot through him at the sight of the dark circles under her big, brown eyes. Still, he at least saw a ray of light in those eyes.

"Can we go soon?"

He got up from where he'd been sitting and praying before the central fire. He came around to where she sat and knelt in front of her. "First we must go on one more hunt. You know that we still do not have enough meat and robes stored up for winter."

She nodded, her eyes tearing as she reached out and touched his face. "And now the hunts will be less successful since the robe was stolen."

He took hold of her hand and kissed her palm. "You do not know that for certain. You must think about this as a test, Buffalo Dreamer."

She frowned. "A test?"

He kept hold of her hand. "I have prayed and fasted over this, just as you have. I remembered all the things I was told by the Feathered One about the hardships that would come when the white man came. I remembered our son's vision of an iron horse that would bring many more white people here. We have not yet seen this iron horse. Nor have we seen your vision of many Sioux and Cheyenne surrounding hundreds of soldiers and killing all of them. That means all of these things are yet to be. It also means we must be very strong now, stronger than ever before. We must be united, brave, and true to our beliefs. Losing the white buffalo robe awakens us to this. It shows us we must always be ready for the white man's trickery."

She slowly nodded. "I have always trusted your visions and your power, Rising Eagle."

"Then trust me when I tell you that you've lost none of *your* power. You have been truly blessed by the buffalo spirit. The robe has been stolen, but only the Lakota have eaten of the heart of the white buffalo. And only you have seen her and have spoken with her. If the white man thinks he will destroy our power and our hope by taking the robe, he'll find out he is wrong. And to help us find the strength and guidance we need, we'll go to Medicine Mountain, where we have always found the answers to our troubles."

She leaned forward and pressed her cheek to his. "I was thinking I would like to go there. It's as though we have been together so long that we read each other's thoughts."

Rising Eagle lay her back and stretched out beside her. "We'll move our camp to Blue Water Creek. From there the men will look for buffalo. If *Wakan-Tanka* chooses to be good to us, we will find enough meat to get us through the winter. We know we can't count on receiving everything the white man promised in his last treaty with us. What meat that does come will be full of worms. The other things they bring are useless. Pots and pans and beads and worn blankets will not fill our children's bellies."

He held her close, listening to the distant cry of a coyote. The body of the man he'd captured the night the robe was stolen had been dragged off to a gully. Perhaps those coyotes were still feasting on what was left of his bones.

OCTOBER 1855

Moon of Yellow Leaves

CHAPTER SEVEN

FLORENCE KINGSLEY SMOOTHED the skirt of her dress before answering the front door. Through the lace curtain at the oval window she could see her visitor, Herbert Helmsley. The newspaper reporter had asked for an interview, and after a good deal of prompting by some of the ladies in her Bible study, she'd finally agreed.

She still found it rather silly that the people of Springfield, Illinois were so consumed with curiosity over the fact that she was a full-blood Lakota woman. Some of her husband's parishioners still stared at her longer than necessary, probably trying to picture her in a tunic standing beside a tepee, her long, black hair braided and wrapped in beaded rawhide.

There were times when she longed to live that way again, but she'd spent too many years now as a white woman. She doubted she could ever go back to her old way of life. Now she wore her long braids wrapped and pinned neatly around her head, and her clothes were a far cry from a simple deerskin tunic.

She took a deep breath before opening the door. She hated being the center of attention, and she hoped her green cotton day dress was appropriate for the visit.

She greeted Helmsley with a smile. "Mr. Helmsley, please come in."

The short, wiry Helmsley, grinning almost nervously, thanked her and stepped inside, carrying with him a tablet and pencil. He removed his felt hat, and Florence took it from him and hung it on a hook in the hallway of the small, neat parsonage she shared with her husband, Preacher Abel Kingsley. She showed Helmsley into the parlor, offering him a seat in a rather worn, but clean settee. Most of what she and Abel used, including the house in which they lived, belonged to the Methodist Church next door; Abel refused offers of new furniture, feeling it was not fair to spend church offerings on himself. Other than true necessities, he felt everything should go toward the church's needs, and to helping the poor.

"Would you like some coffee?" she asked Helmsley.

"Oh, no, thank you," he replied. He positioned a tablet on his knee and took a pencil from a pocket inside his jacket. "Now, then, shall we begin?"

Florence sat down in a rocker across from him, placing her hands in her lap. "I'm a little nervous about this, Mr. Helmsley."

He laughed lightly, rolling the pencil between his thumb and forefinger. "Oh, believe me, Mrs. Kingsley, I am more nervous than you are. Your husband's congregation would just like to put a little piece about you in the *Herald*, welcoming you and explaining a little more about how you came to be here. I don't mean to put you on the spot, ma'am, but a full-blooded Sioux woman can't help but make people in these parts curious, what with all that's going on out West, Indian attacks and such. I see that besides yours and Reverend Kingsley's son, William, you also brought with you an older son, uh, Robert, I believe his name is?"

"Yes. Robert is my son by . . . by my first husband." *I was never really married to the man. It was after I was banished from the Oglala tribe for making trouble for a holy woman. I lived at Fort Pierre with a trapper. He was a drunk, and he was cruel. I became an alcoholic.* She certainly was not about to tell this man all of that. Abel Kingsley, a missionary out to "save" the Lakota, had saved her, from alcoholism and prostitution. They fell in love, and now she was Abel's wife, an educated, respectable woman, thanks to Abel.

"My first husband died." *He was killed by an Oglala man, Rising Eagle, a man I once loved. He killed Robert's father because he was cruel to me. I still and will always love Rising Eagle for that.* "After that," she continued aloud, "I could see that life would not be easy at a white man's fort, especially for my baby son, who looked so Indian. I therefore gave him to the Oglala to raise, where he would be loved and more accepted. They called him Spirit Walker."

She watched Helmsley begin to scribble notes, noticing his fingers looked slim and bony for a man. He was young and eager, a man who'd questioned her and Abel about the "Wild" West.

"When Spirit Walker was eighteen years old, he found me at Fort Laramie during the Big Smoke there in 1851," she continued. "He decided that because he was half white, he wanted to learn more about that part of himself; and so he came to live with me and Abel. We discovered him to be extremely intelligent. He learned reading and writing and math very quickly. He's turned out to have above normal intelligence. All his teachers have been amazed. Now he is taking exams for entrance into college. He wants to be a doctor. Robert loves to help sick people, and when he lived among the Oglala, he worked with their medicine man."

"Medicine man?" Young Helmsley looked up from his writing. "Isn't that just a bunch of chanting and shaking of rattles? Does your son expect to be a doctor by knowing how to sing over sick people?"

Florence caught the derision in his voice. "No. He fully understands the white man's way of healing; but I assure you, Mr. Helmsley, that there is much to be said for the healing powers of a Lakota medicine man. Robert knows this, and he just might end up using some of those healing methods along with the white man's modern solutions. You should not underestimate the power of Lakota medicine."

He looked down and made more notes. "No, ma'am. No offense." He cleared his throat. "So, Robert is twenty-two now?"

"Yes. My husband fully adopted him as his own, and we gave him his white name."

"And what was your name before you married Abel Kingsley?"

Florence still felt a tinge of nostalgia at the memory of her life growing up among the Oglala. "It was Fall Leaf Woman."

"And why did you leave the, uh, the Oglala, is it?"

"Yes." She thought a moment, not wanting to reveal certain things that were none of this man's business. "Well, I guess I left because I was just young and curious. We sometimes traded at Fort Pierre, and being unfamiliar with white man's ways, life there fascinated me. On one visit, I decided to stay there, as many other Lakota often camped in the area, so I was not alone. I grew to like the handy things the white men used for cooking, the different foods they had, like sugar and flour and spices. I guess I stayed too long, because after a while I realized I could not go back to my old life. Then my husband came to the area to preach, and I began learning about Christianity. The next thing I knew, I was becoming more white than Lakota, and Mr. Kingsley and I fell in love. We married, and for a while I helped him preach to and teach the Lakota. That is how we ended up at Fort Laramie for the great treaty signing there; and that is how I finally found my first-born son again."

"I see." Helmsley wrote on for several seconds before continuing. He studied his notes a moment before leaning back to study her a moment. "Can you tell me a little more about life as a Lakota?"

Florence breathed deeply before answering. "I can tell you that my people are not nearly as wild and vicious as people here make them out to be. They have families, and they love their siblings and parents and children just as the white man loves his. They do many of the same things whites do, except that they don't conduct their day by the clock. They don't have fancy homes and buggies. I assure you, though, that the tepee is quite clean and quite comfortable. If you like, you could do a series article on Lakota life. I could explain to you how we build a tepee, how we kill and clean the buffalo, and what all the parts are used for. Contrary to the white man, Mr. Helmsley, the Lakota waste nothing. Everything they use comes from the earth, and is returned to the earth. And most of what they need to survive comes from one thing—the buffalo. The only other thing they need are wild herbs for healing, and dead trees for wood; although they don't even always need that, since buffalo chips can be burned for cooking and for warmth."

"Buffalo chips?"

Florence smiled at his ignorance. "Yes. It's really just dried buffalo dung, Mr. Helmsley. They make a wonderful fire that is nearly smokeless, but of course a wood fire is better for smoking meat." She watched Helmsley turn red at her reply.

"I see." He shook his head. "I also see that you are right about needing a series of articles. I am sure there are many things you could tell me about Indian life. For now we'll just talk about how you came to be here in Springfield, the wife of the preacher of the local Methodist Church. Did Abel Kingsley preach out West for a long time?"

"Several years. I can't even remember exactly how long. We came back here so that Robert and our own son, William, could get a better education; and because Robert's sister is ailing and he felt he should be with her."

Helmsley nodded. "And how do you like it here, ma'am?"

Florence thought a moment before answering. "It's very nice. The congregation has been kind and accepting. Abel is well liked, and so whoever he loves is loved and accepted by his parishioners."

"What do you think about some of the fighting going on out west, Mrs. Kingsley? Do you know any of the Indian leaders who are stirring up trouble, like Rising Eagle? And some new man who's been getting attention lately, Red Cloud?"

Florence felt her heart flutter. "Well, sir, I have never met Red Cloud . . . but I do know Rising Eagle." *Oh, yes, I know him well. I loved him once, when I was very young, before he became a holy man and married the woman he was told to marry through a vision. It broke my heart. I told lies about his wife, to make her look bad, and for that I was banished from the tribe.* "Rising Eagle is the one who raised Robert."

"He *did*? My goodness! I shall have to also talk to Robert and find out what the man is like! This is splendid!"

"I can tell you that Rising Eagle is a holy man among the Oglala, revered by them. He has great spiritual powers." *Should she tell him that Robert was born with deformed fingers and toes; and that after Rising Eagle took him as a small baby to Medicine Mountain, where he prayed over Robert and was struck by lightning, Robert was healed? No. People like Herbert Helmsley and* those in her husband's congregation did not believe such stories. They would think her a crazy woman.

But it was true.

"This is amazing!" the man muttered as he scribbled. "We have so much to talk about, Mrs. Kingsley!" He met her gaze then. "And I must say, you are so distinguished and refined, and you seem so well educated. You certainly are not the picture of the typical sav— I mean, well—"

"Savage?" Florence finished for him.

"I'm sorry. I—I didn't mean to insult you."

Florence smiled sadly. "You do not insult me, Mr. Helmsley; but you do insult the Lakota as a whole. They are not savages. They are men and women who love each other and their families. They are a very spiritual people, who live close to Mother Earth and respect her. They pray constantly. Their very lives are a constant prayer. They shed blood in sacrifice to *Wakan-Tanka* to show him they are willing to suffer to have their prayers answered. They grieve over the loss of a loved one, and they do not lie, Mr. Helmsley. The reason for the present uneasiness is due to the fact that our government has lied to *them*, many times over. They continue to break treaty promises, confusing and angering the Lakota. To them a man's word is his word. They do not tolerate lying."

Helmsley kept writing. "Well, you just can't stop progress, or land-hungry settlers now, can you? It's just a fact the Lakota will have to face. I'm sure something can be worked out."

Florence said nothing, beginning to feel irritation at this man's ignorance. "What else would you like to know, Mr. Helmsley?"

"Well, I saw your husband over at the church, and he said he'd be along any minute. I'd just like to talk to both of you about how you met, how long you've been married, what life was like out west preaching to the Indians, you know, that sort of thing. And how old is your youngest son, Mrs. Kingsley?"

Again Florence felt her heart skip a beat. "William is nine years old." *And he is not my son.* No one knew except Abel. Robert did not know. William certainly did not know that she was not his mother, or that Rising Eagle was his true father. William's mother had been a white captive of Rising Eagle, who had "claimed" her, as the Lakota way of shaming her white husband and convincing white men to leave Lakota hunting grounds or suffer the consequences. Rising Eagle gave her over to soldiers after that, never knowing that she was carrying his child, a baby she did not want. Florence herself helped deliver that baby at Fort Laramie, and his white mother told her she could keep the boy. She'd missed raising Robert, and so she loved that baby with all her heart, especially because he was Rising Eagle's son.

Only she and Abel knew that. Now that William was older, she was afraid to tell him the truth, for fear he would no longer love her as his real mother. The child seemed to be having a terrible conflict over his identity, and children at school often teased him because he looked so Indian. They called him "wild" and a "savage." Her one regret over moving to Springfield with Abel was that William was having such a hard time being accepted. But Abel wanted to come home for a while to be with his ailing sister; and he'd done so much for her over the years. He deserved to be here if that was what he wanted. Surely William would adjust in time.

"He certainly looks all Indian," Helmsley commented.

"Yes, he does." *He looks just like his father, a great warrior, a holy man.* Could William ever understand how honored he should feel, being the son of Rising Eagle? He'd never known that way of life. He would surely hate her if she told him the truth, and he would be devastated and teased even worse if people knew his father was what people around here considered a "savage." "He is very smart, Mr. Helmsley, and quite handsome, don't you think?"

The reporter smiled and nodded. "Yes, ma'am. I see you keep his hair cut short the way it ought to be."

Ought to be? An Indian man took pride in his long hair. It gave him strength. "Keeping his hair long is important to a Lakota man, Mr. Helmsley. I keep William's short because he lives among white boys and wants to look as much like them as he can."

Helmsley sighed. "Well, ma'am, I guess there is a whole lot I don't understand about the Sioux culture. I sure want to learn, though. I do hope you're serious about allowing me to question you for future articles."

"Certainly. I don't mind." Florence wondered if this man could ever truly understand the Lakota way. It was something that lived in the heart, not something you could just learn, like in a textbook. Even a white man or woman could have a Lakota heart, but it took a great deal of prayer and understanding, and it was almost impossible without first living among her people.

She heard the door open and close then. That would be Abel. She always felt more relaxed in these situations when Abel was around. Her husband entered the parlor, walking over to shake Helmsley's hand. She thought Abel looked more tired than usual, and he was showing a good deal of gray about the temples. Her husband kept himself immaculate, but always dressed simply. A long time ago she'd learned to do seamstress work to earn money when she was alone, and now she made most of Abel's as well as William's and Robert's clothes.

Abel ran his hands through his thick hair and took a seat near her, then turned to her with a smile and a wink, telling her with his dark, snappy eyes that she didn't have to worry. He was here to smooth over the rough spots. Abel knew full well things like an interview by a white reporter made her nervous. Abel was her hero, her protector. He was the kindest, most patient and forgiving man she'd ever known. He took her from the steps of a saloon, when she was an alcoholic and a prostitute, and he transformed her, educated her, married her. She loved him. Yet in spite of his goodness, she would never love him as she'd loved Rising Eagle, nor did he *make* love the way Rising Eagle made love, wild and free and passionate. That was one of the differences between white men and Lakota men. Still, she had learned to love the white man's way, because Abel had been her salvation.

She rose and walked to a window while Abel and Herbert Helmsley talked. She could see William walking home from school, his head hanging, a pout on his face. Poor little William was not happy. She wondered if he ever would be.

LATE SEPTEMBER
1855

Moon When the Deer Paw the Earth

CHAPTER EIGHT

BRAVE HORSE RODE past Yellow Bonnet at a gentle lope, enjoying the look of love in her eyes. He tried to tell her with his own gaze that he was ready to do something about that love. Every bone in his body ached to hold her again, longed to do much more than that. The commotion and his mother's terrible grief over losing the white buffalo robe had put a halt to his intended talk with her and his father about Yellow Bonnet. Out of respect for Buffalo Dreamer, he had waited; but now she seemed in slightly better spirits, and his father was always in a better mood when heading into another hunt. Perhaps this was a good time to approach the subject of the love he held in his heart.

The entire tribe was headed for Blue Water Creek, and recently they had been joined by a band of southern Brule. That made his chances of winning his mother's approval even better, since she originally came from the Brule nation of Lakota. She was with her own people again, her heart warmed at seeing how happy her father was. Old Looking Horse was growing weaker, but being around old friends seemed to give him more energy. He even intended to join the younger men in this hunt.

Brave Horse suspected his grandfather might be thinking this could be his last hunt. He did not want to miss it. Often he talked of one day joining his wife, Tall Woman, in a better place beyond the stars. Buffalo Dreamer's mother had died of the white man's spotted disease several years earlier, the same awful disease that had killed Brave Horse's young brother and sister. Part of the reason Rising Eagle stole Yellow Bonnet from the wagon train was to bring another daughter to Buffalo Dreamer.

Brave Horse charged past Rising Eagle, letting out a yip of joy, then turned his horse and trotted back to his father, who grinned.

"You are very happy today."

Brave Horse nodded. "I am." It suddenly struck him how odd it would be to ask permission of his own father to court someone. He always thought he would be going to some other warrior for such a favor. His father's attitude that Yellow Bonnet was his sister made this very awkward. He glanced at his mother, riding a gray spotted Appaloosa directly behind her husband. Most women walked behind the warriors, leading more horses and travois that carried their belongings and sometimes small children. But Buffalo Dreamer was a very honored woman, and she often rode with her equally-honored husband, who belonged to the Brave Hearts. Red flannel tied at the end of his lance was the sign of that particular society.

"I wish to talk to both of you," Brave Horse said, looking from Buffalo Dreamer to Rising Eagle. He slowed his own sturdy red-coated gelding and rode at a gentle walk between his mother and father then.

"What is it you wish to tell us?" Rising Eagle asked.

Brave Horse took a deep breath for courage. "Something has happened . . . to my mind and heart. I am old enough and accomplished enough now to marry." He stared straight ahead, allowing the initial thought to sink in.

"I suppose twenty-one summers is old enough," Rising Eagle answered.

They rode on silently for several long seconds before Buffalo Dreamer spoke. "Is she an honorable Lakota woman?"

"Yes." Brave Horse felt his heart pounding harder.

"Will she cost many horses and meat? Robes?"

"I do not know. I have not yet asked her father permission to court her."

"I don't recall you playing your flute outside any young woman's tepee," Buffalo Dreamer told him. "Does she even know about your interest in her?"

Brave Horse decided it was best not to tell them he'd spoken alone with Yellow Bonnet. "I'm not sure. She will know soon, though, when I begin courting her. I'm hoping she won't take too long setting out a bowl of food for me so that I know she's interested. Then I can speak with her father about her price."

"She would be a fool not to want the son of Rising Eagle," Buffalo Dreamer told him. "And her father would be equally foolish in not allowing a courtship."

That is how I am hoping he will feel.

"Why do you come to us about this?" Rising Eagle asked. "You should just begin courting her."

"It is as mother said. I'm the son of Rising Eagle. I feel I need your approval of the girl I . . . love." Now he could feel his father's eyes on him.

"Love? You are this sure?"

Brave Horse swallowed. "I am."

Buffalo Dreamer laughed lightly. "This is exciting! Who is she?"

Brave Horse felt light-headed. "That's the hardest part. She's . . ." He took another deep breath. "She's Yellow Bonnet."

The dead silence that followed made Brave Horse feel like cringing. Rising Eagle slowed his horse, taking hold of the bridle to Brave Horse's own mount and coming to a full halt. Buffalo Dreamer did the same, and Brave Horse wondered if he should just bolt and run.

"*Yellow Bonnet?*" Rising Eagle said, the name coming out in practically a growl.

Brave Horse squared his shoulders and faced his father. "Yes, Father. I have loved her for a long time, in more ways than just as a brother. She's not of my blood. I have a right to love her."

"You are *right*!" Rising Eagle barked. "She is *not* of your blood! You should marry a *Lakota* woman!"

Brave Horse raised his chin. "And how many times have you said yourself that Yellow Bonnet *is* Lakota at heart? Is there no better way to be Lakota? The body is only a vessel for the spirit, and her spirit is Lakota, even though her skin and hair are light. Yet she carries none of your blood, nor the blood of any Lakota man or woman. She is free to be courted by me if I so choose."

He noticed Rising Eagle stiffen, and hated sounding defiant of his father. But his love for Yellow Bonnet gave him the courage he needed; and his father knew the words he spoke were true and defied argument.

Rising Eagle looked away as others in the migrating camp passed them by, including Yellow Bonnet. Brave Horse glanced at her, but she looked away and kept going as though not noticing. He knew her own heart was probably pounding furiously, her mind racing with curiosity.

"Our son is right, my husband," Buffalo Dreamer spoke up.

Rising Eagle cast her a scolding look before meeting Brave Horse's gaze again. "Not only do I disapprove, but even if I approved, it would be impossible for me to ask of my own son what I would have asked of another suitor."

"Ask what you wish. I will go out and get as many horses as you want, suffer whatever torture you want, bring as many gifts as you want. I would not want you to ask any less of me than you would another."

With a scowl on his face, Rising Eagle looked away again. "You have given me much to think and pray about. I cannot give you an answer now."

"I understand, Father."

"I adopted Yellow Bonnet as my own. To me she is your sister. It would be incestuous to wed her."

"You know that in reality it would *not*. And you also know that Yellow Bonnet deserves to be happy and to make her own choice when it comes to a husband. You should ask her what *she* thinks of all of this. If she does not want me in return, there is nothing left to talk about. I will simply have to live without her at my side. Can't you at least ask her if she would allow me to court her?"

Rising Eagle sighed deeply. He glanced at Buffalo Dreamer again.

"You must at least consider it," she told him.

Rising Eagle sat frowning a moment longer, still holding the bridle to Brave Horse's mount. "Do you feel pain from the want of her?"

Brave Horse grinned a little, realizing his father apparently understood such pain. "Yes," he answered boldly.

Buffalo Dreamer laughed lightly. "Our son is smitten, Rising Eagle. To deny his request is to risk losing him by running off with Yellow Bonnet."

Brave Horse felt deep embarrassment, but he could not help smiling at the disgruntled look on Rising Eagle's face and at the way Buffalo Dreamer had of needling him sometimes.

Rising Eagle remained sober. "This will take much thought," he said. His eyes narrowed as he drilled a look into Brave Horse. "No son of Rising Eagle would shame his father in such a way," he said, the words sounding more like an order than a comment.

Brave Horse did not answer.

"You will accompany us on the hunt," Rising Eagle continued. "It is best for now that you are nowhere near Yellow Bonnet. After the hunt I will give you my decision."

Brave Horse nodded. "That is all I ask of you."

Their gazes held a moment longer before Rising Eagle turned his horse and rode off to catch up with the other leading warriors who headed the procession. Brave Horse turned to his mother. "Do you think he'll allow it?"

Buffalo Dreamer studied him lovingly. "I will speak to him in the privacy of the tepee."

Brave Horse grinned then. His mother seemed to have great powers of persuasion "in the privacy of the tepee." He wondered if someday Yellow Bonnet would have such power over him in their own tepee.

CHAPTER NINE

BUFFALO DREAMER HUNG a piece of buffalo meat over a strip of rawhide to dry, then noticed movement on the north edge of camp. Suddenly and unexpectedly, several men on horses appeared in formation, and a rush of alarm swept through Buffalo Dreamer like a knife.

"Soldiers!" she exclaimed to her sister-in-law, Many Robes Woman. Rising Eagle's sister ceased scraping membrane from a buffalo hide and looked up, then quickly rose, dropping her bone hide-scraper.

"Why do you think they are here?"

"We'll soon know," Buffalo Dreamer answered. "Look there! The Brule chief, Little Thunder, is riding out to greet them." Her chest tightened when she turned to see even more soldiers gathering to the south. "I don't like this. They are all around us, and our men are away on the hunt!" She shoved her knife into her belt. "I think we should begin striking the lodges and gathering the children."

"But we have all this meat to dry and hides to cure," Many Robes Woman protested. "Maybe they will go away."

Buffalo Dreamer called for her youngest daughter, six-year-old Songbird, to leave her playing and come closer. "I'll go and find

Little Turtle," Many Robes Woman told her, hurrying away to find Buffalo Dreamer's son.

"Help me gather some food and blankets," Buffalo Dreamer ordered her daughter. "Where is Yellow Bonnet?"

"I don't know, Mother. Have the soldiers come for us?"

Buffalo Dreamer sensed the fear in her little girl's voice. "I have no idea. Most of our men are gone on the hunt, so we must be wary."

She and Songbird hurriedly filled parfleches with meat, and in moments Little Turtle and Many Robes Woman arrived with horses, helping tie on some supplies. Many Robes Woman's son, Fox Running, accompanied them.

"I'm glad I stayed behind this time," he said, ducking inside his mother's tepee and coming out with a quiver of arrows slung over his shoulder and his bow in his hand. "I wish I had a white man's rifle."

"One day all our men will own them," Buffalo Dreamer told him as she threw a blanket over one of Rising Eagle's sturdy Appaloosa mares. "Until then we can only make do with what we have."

"I heard the chief, Little Thunder, arguing with the soldiers," Fox Running told them. "They want us all to move south of the Platte River, or we will be considered hostiles and can be shot or arrested. They say we are here against the last treaty. Little Thunder told them we cannot move until our men come back and until we are through drying our meat and cleaning and curing the hides. The soldier leader, who calls himself General William Harney, said we must leave it all behind and go. He has five stars on his shoulders, a high chief among the white man's army."

Buffalo Dreamer fumed. "We can't survive the winter if we leave everything behind! That's ridiculous! Why is it so important we leave before we finish preparing the meat? And why can't they wait until our men return?" She lifted Songbird onto the back of the Appaloosa and ordered her son to get up on another horse.

Fox Running gave the reins of his own horse to his mother. "If something happens, ride hard to the south."

"But there are soldiers all around us, my son!" Many Robes Woman argued.

"I and the few men here in camp will aim our guns and arrows at those to the south to open an escape route. We—"

His words were cut off by a shuddering boom, followed by a whistling sound in the air.

"The big guns!" Buffalo Dreamer exclaimed. Before she got the words out an explosion at the center of the village blew a tepee to shreds and sent shrapnel flying in every direction.

Women and children began screaming and running. Buffalo Dreamer leaped up behind Songbird, kicking the horse into a hard run and yelling at Little Turtle to follow. The soldiers' howitzer fired again, and seconds later another tepee exploded close to Buffalo Dreamer as she passed it. She felt a sharp sting to her left leg, and her horse stumbled. She managed to rein the well-trained mount to steadiness and kept riding, one arm wrapped around Songbird.

"Where is Yellow Bonnet?" she screamed to Little Turtle.

"I don't know!" the boy answered.

Buffalo Dreamer galloped her mount toward a ravine, where she ordered Little Turtle to stay low and protect his little sister. She lowered Songbird, then daringly rode back into the melee of screaming women and children, shouting soldiers, gunfire, and exploding shells. Several tepees were on fire. Women, old men, and children lay dead and wounded.

Why? Her people had not raised a hand to the soldiers. They had no reason to do this! Bullets whizzed past her as she ducked down and maneuvered her horse around bodies, darting in every direction in her search for Yellow Bonnet. To her horror she witnessed a soldier ride down on a fleeing little boy and slash him through the spine with his saber. Some of the women lay with their dresses thrown over their heads, their stomachs slashed open. One was pregnant, the baby torn out of her! With one quick glance toward where the big guns sat in the distance, she saw a man with white hair shouting orders.

Soldiers swarmed through camp now. She had no choice but to

head back toward the ravine again, where she'd left Songbird and Little Turtle. Many more women and children had fled to the same ravine, but already soldiers were there, too, deliberately slaying even more women and children! The air became a din of screams, gunfire, and thundering horses. It was impossible for Buffalo Dreamer to continue her search for Yellow Bonnet. She had to save herself and the two children she'd left here. She screamed their names, finally finding them huddled behind Little Turtle's horse, which lay dead.

"Climb up! Climb up!" she yelled, reaching down for Songbird and yanking the child up in front of her. Little Turtle managed to jerk himself up behind her. Buffalo Dreamer charged away, not sure what had happened to Many Robes Woman, her good friend of so many years. If only their warriors were here instead of off hunting. Rising Eagle and the others would have chased away these soldiers, perhaps even killed all of them for attacking a peaceful camp of innocent women, children, and old men.

She glanced back once more to see nearly the entire village on fire. They would lose all their meat and robes! There had been no time to save anything but themselves, and bodies of those who were not even able to do that were strewn everywhere.

She kept riding, not even knowing where to go, until finally she reached the northern bank of the Platte River, where the trees were relatively thick. She stopped there, climbing down and telling the children to hide in the brush along the riverbank. She smacked the horse and chased it away, afraid if soldiers saw it they would look for its rider. She huddled into open tree roots then, hoping to remain undetected until they could be sure the soldiers were gone.

It was only then that she again felt the sting in her leg, and she looked down to see a gaping wound from shrapnel. Blood ran from it, mixing into the river water.

So, now we know what murderers and cowards the Blue Coats are, and the cost of losing the white buffalo robe.

CHAPTER TEN

CAUTIOUSLY, BUFFALO DREAMER moved from her refuge along the riverbank, listening intently for any sound. She heard only the wind. No birds sang. She heard no voices, no whinnying of horses, no soldiers' shouts, no gunfire.

"Follow me, children," she said, grimacing with pain as she began walking back toward the campsite. She looked down to see the gaping wound on her left calf had stopped bleeding, but because water had been washing over it for so long, the open area looked like fresh meat, rather than being scabbed.

She put her arms around her children, who helped her walk. She realized it would soon be dusk, and she prayed, hoped, she would find someone, anyone still alive.

After a long, painful walk, they mounted the last low rise before camp. When it came into view, Buffalo Dreamer gasped, then cried out with terrible mourning at what she saw. Songbird also began crying, and Little Turtle ran off, saying he was going to try to find Yellow Bonnet. From where they stood, Buffalo Dreamer could see dead bodies scattered everywhere: men, women, and children who had been chased down and deliberately slaughtered.

"He is a *butcher*!" Buffalo Dreamer moaned, referring to the white-bearded General Harney. No enemy tribe would kill this way. Not even the Pawnee would kill so relentlessly.

With tears streaming down her face, she walked among the dead, recognizing many she'd called friend for years. She spotted Many Robes Woman, who lay sprawled on her back, her dress thrown over her chest and a deep gash opening her belly and privates. Since the first day Buffalo Dreamer came to Rising Eagle's family as a young bride, his sister had been her good friend . . . so many years together . . . so many memories. Few were as friendly and happy as Many Robes Woman. Buffalo Dreamer turned away and vomited from overwhelming agony and sorrow.

Finally she found the strength to kneel closer and move Many Robes Woman's dress back down to cover her.

"Mother!" Little Turtle shouted then from several feet away. "It is our sister! Yellow Bonnet!"

Buffalo Dreamer grasped her stomach. She managed to rise and limp to where her son stood over the white woman who had come to them as a young captive and was adopted into their family. She'd loved Yellow Bonnet as her own, and now the lovely young woman lay with a deep slash over her face and throat.

Buffalo Dreamer wondered how she was going to bear so much sorrow. She sat alone amid what seemed nearly a hundred dead bodies, and already buzzards circled overhead. She threw back her head and began the trilling chant of sorrow. Yellow Bonnet's death would surely fill Brave Horse with a deep hatred for the white soldiers who had murdered this young woman he'd loved and wanted to marry. Her death, and the death of Rising Eagle's sister, would fill Rising Eagle's heart with an even deeper hatred for the *wasicus*.

When the hunters returned to see this devastation and slaughter, there would be no way to measure their need for vengeance. What she saw here was almost more than a person could take, and Buffalo Dreamer felt as though her own heart was being ripped in half.

For nearly an hour she sat wailing her death song, young Songbird crying beside her, while a stunned Little Turtle continued wandering among the dead bodies, returning at different times to tell her of more familiar friends and relatives he'd found dead. One was old Runs With The Deer, Rising Eagle's uncle, the very man who had come to her father's camp so many years ago to announce that Rising Eagle had chosen her through a vision to be his wife. He was a dear, dear man, a respected elder, one who had always held great importance among the Lakota. Dead, too, was Running Elk Woman, the wife of Bold Fox, another of Rising Eagle's uncles. She, too, had been a dear friend, and like a grandmother to Yellow Bonnet and Songbird.

"Mother, Moon Painter is also dead!" Little Turtle told her, referring to the old medicine man in whom the Lakota put great trust. Little Turtle looked away, then walked off, his shoulders shaking as he sobbed silently.

"I hate them!" the boy said brokenly, clenching his fists. "I *hate* the white man soldiers! I will ride with father and with my brother, Brave Horse. We will kill *all* of them, just like in your dream!" He ran off, screaming more words of bitter hatred, mixed with pitiful sobs and wailing.

Through tear-filled eyes, Buffalo Dreamer watched her son, her heart aching for him. Beyond where he walked she noticed someone coming toward them, an old Indian man. At last! It was good to see someone else had survived. She rose and stumbled in his direction, realizing as she drew closer that it was Many Horses, another of Rising Eagle's aged uncles. She hurried closer and grasped the old man's hands. "Where were you?" she asked.

The old man's eyes showed tears as he shook his head slowly. "Once I was quite a warrior. Now I feel only shame that I could not stop this and protect all of you," he answered. "I ran and hid like the others."

"It was the only thing left to do," Buffalo Dreamer reassured him.

Many Horses nodded, then closed his eyes. "They killed Looking Horse," he said brokenly.

Buffalo Dreamer felt yet another arrow pierce her heart. Her treasured father, an elder of the Brule tribe, was dead. She let go of Many Horses's hands and turned away.

"They took many of the surviving women," Many Horses continued. "I do not know where they took them, but they marched them away on foot. Some were wounded. What do you think they will do with the women, Buffalo Dreamer?"

She barely knew how she should feel. So much loss, so many to grieve over, so many to bury. She scrambled to think straight. "They will hold them for ransom," she answered.

"But what ransom could we pay? We have nothing the white man wants."

Buffalo Dreamer scanned the surrounding landscape. "Yes, we *do* have something they want. We are standing on it. The only way we will get our mothers and sisters and daughters back is to agree to leave this place and never come back." She met Many Horses's gaze. "As of this day I, too, am a warrior, Many Horses. When Rising Eagle and my sons ride against the Blue Coats, so will I."

Many Horses put a hand on her shoulder. "Always you give us hope, Buffalo Dreamer. No matter what has happened, your presence gives us hope."

Buffalo Dreamer felt the great weight of responsibility. Though her own heart felt shattered, her grief overbearing, she had to stay strong for the Lakota. She was Buffalo Dreamer, their holy woman.

CHAPTER ELEVEN

RISING EAGLE KEPT his painted Appaloosa at a dead run, charging ahead of the other hunters, his heart pounding with dread at what he might find when he reached camp. The wounded scout who had managed to find and warn them had brought the terrible news of the soldiers' attack on their peaceful camp, a story of death and horror. A number of women had been marched off to Fort Laramie, to be held there until he and the other Lakota leaders would agree to another treaty.

What kind of men hid behind women? What kind of men attacked wives and mothers and sisters to get what they wanted? If they had attacked while he and the other more apt warriors were present, they would never have succeeded in such a slaughter!

His most agonizing dread was Buffalo Dreamer, his daughters, Yellow Bonnet and Songbird, and his youngest son, Little Turtle. He had lost enough when a son and daughter died years ago from the white man's spotted disease.

Before he died from his wounds, the scout had said that nearly all the dwellings and supplies had been burned or otherwise destroyed, other supplies stolen, horses stolen, women marched away as prisoners! If getting their women back took too much time, winter would be upon them before they could again hunt in order to store up enough supplies to survive. The white man had so far not kept any of his promises to provide enough food and blankets to sustain them, which meant many would die this winter . . . all because of this cowardly soldier attack on innocent women, women who were doing nothing more than preparing meat to keep themselves and their children alive through the cold season.

Many white men would *die* for this! Their *women* would also die! Their horses would be stolen! Their children would be taken captive! There must be a retaliation for this insult! They had attacked and killed soldiers before. They would do it again—and again and again—until the white men learned the Lakota would not put up with their despicable behavior! Many whites might have to die before they understood this was Lakota land, and it would *stay* Lakota land!

Beside him and only slightly behind him Brave Horse also rode hard. Rising Eagle knew his first-born son must surely be dreading what might have happened to Yellow Bonnet. Rising Eagle had decided that if Brave Horse truly loved her enough to risk his own father's anger for it, then perhaps there was nothing left but to allow his son to marry Yellow Bonnet. He'd planned to tell him so, but now . . .

They reached a small rise that led down to the village near Blue Water Creek. The sight was enough to make even a seasoned warrior like Rising Eagle gasp in horror. He drew his horse to a halt, sod spraying in all directions as the sturdy steed planted his hooves into the soft earth. Brave Horse kept riding, surging past him, shouting Yellow Bonnet's name. A few other warriors followed, but most stopped alongside Rising Eagle, murmuring their astonishment and horror.

"Buffalo Dreamer," Rising Eagle whispered. Was she down there? All he saw were dead bodies sprawled everywhere. Even from here he could tell some of the women's dresses had been thrown over their heads, as though to deliberately insult them further, even in death. Buzzards circled overhead, and the stench of death met his nostrils. It would take days to erect scaffolds to bury all the bodies. This place would become a Lakota burial ground, never to be used for camp again. And if any white man stepped foot here, the Great Spirit would see that he died a terrible death!

He closed his eyes when he heard Brave Horse cry Yellow Bonnet's name again, this time with a ring of terrible anguish. That could only mean he'd found Yellow Bonnet dead. Rising Eagle could see his son standing beside a body. He raised his arms, and Rising Eagle knew Brave Horse would cut himself in mourning. Already he was singing a death chant.

He saw a woman and two children helping someone erect a scaffold. From here it looked like Buffalo Dreamer. *Please let it be her*, he prayed silently. He headed toward the camp of death, others following. Brave Horse's good friend, Curly, rode past them, also singing a death chant. This was indeed the worst loss the Lakota had ever suffered to the Blue Coats.

He rode closer, forcing back tears when he realized it was Buffalo Dreamer helping with the scaffold. How he wished there was a tepee where they could go to be alone so that he could hold her. He could not show such emotion in front of the other elders. He dismounted before his horse even came to a full halt, hurrying to where Buffalo Dreamer stood. He felt as though someone were ripping out his heart at the sight of her. She'd cut her hair even shorter in mourning for their daughter, and surely for other friends and relatives who'd been killed here. Fresh scabs showed where she'd cut her arms to let blood in grief, adding to the many other scars on her arms from mourning, nearly all caused by the white men. He noticed an ugly wound then on her left calf.

"Buffalo Dreamer! You are hurt!" He could not resist showing his mixture of great relief at finding her alive, and devastation over the death that surrounded them. He gently touched her cheek.

She met his gaze, her eyes showing her awful grief. "I will live, and Little Turtle and Songbird are alive," she said. "We managed to get away and hide. But Yellow Bonnet . . ." She looked away. "I could not find her in time. And your sister . . ." She closed her eyes. "Many Robes Woman is dead." She shuddered. "Also my father . . . and your beloved uncle, Runs With The Deer. Also Running Elk Woman, and old Moon Painter. Your uncle, Bold Fox, still lives. He has been helping with the scaffolds, but there are too many dead for us to build scaffolds quickly enough."

Rising Eagle saw old Bold Fox not far away, hacking at a young tree with his hatchet. The old man looked bent and broken, and Rising Eagle knew the agony he must be suffering at losing Running Elk Woman, his wife of so many years. He could not help the tear that slipped out of one eye and made its way down his cheek. "Many white men must *die* for this!" he groaned.

"It is because the white robe was stolen," Buffalo Dreamer answered. "We have lost its protection. We must try to get to Medicine Mountain, Rising Eagle." She met his eyes then. "The power and strength we draw from the top of the mountain is all that will help us now, my husband."

Rising Eagle nodded, glancing over to where Brave Horse knelt on his knees beside Yellow Bonnet's fly-covered body. "We will bury these bodies as best we can. Some will have to be buried the white man's way, though I do not favor putting their bodies into the earth, away from the sun. Still, Mother Earth will hold them close. We will cover their graves with many rocks to keep away the wolves. Some of us must go to Fort Laramie to free the rest of the women."

How much was one man, or even one Nation, expected to bear? Why did the white man fear sharing this land with the Lakota? There was plenty of room for all, yet the *wasicus* insisted it be only theirs.

The air became filled with others singing their death chants. The elders would have to gather for prayers and purification. They would have to seek advice from *Wakan-Tanka* about this. And they would have to go to Fort Laramie and face the very soldiers who had done this, swallowing their pride long enough to get their women back.

"The soldiers will probably want us to sign yet another treaty," Buffalo Dreamer told him.

Rising Eagle clenched his fists, rage filling him to painful proportions. "I will sign no treaty! Some of the others may sign, but their signatures will mean *nothing*! It will only be done so that our women will be returned. If the white man wants to believe another treaty means peace, he will discover his error!" He touched her shoulder. "Let the others go to Laramie and do what they must do. You and I will go to Medicine Mountain, as we had planned, even though winter will be upon us by the time we return. We will have to take warm robes and sturdy horses." He looked around the camp. "There is nothing left here. We will have to go north along the flat river to where the rest of the Brule are camped to get supplies." He glanced at his still-weeping and mournfully singing oldest son, then looked down at Buffalo Dreamer. "It will take many winters for Brave Horse to no longer feel the pain of this. I will have him return to *Paha-Sapa* with the rest of the Lakota, where he will himself need to fast and pray for an answer to what we must do now. You and I will go to Medicine Mountain alone." He ran his fingers into her hair and grasped it tightly. "We will not let this defeat us, Buffalo Dreamer."

She looked across the destroyed camp, alive with flies and the cries of mourning. "No enemy tribe has ever done this to us. This new enemy is unlike anything we have ever known."

Rising Eagle drew her close, fighting his own need to weep openly.

"We will go to Medicine Mountain," he told Buffalo Dreamer. "And no white man will stop us!"

EARLY OCTOBER
1855

Moon of Falling Leaves

CHAPTER TWELVE

BUFFALO DREAMER HUDDLED under a bearskin robe, singing her plea to *Wakan-Tanka*, willing to sit here on top of the world and even risk freezing to death, if that was what it would take to bring an answer to her prayer.

> Wakan-Tanka, *hear me.*
> I am nothing in your eyes,
> Yet I beg you for strength.
> Show me the way to be strong.
> Save my people.
> Show me the way to be strong.
> I am nothing in your eyes,
> But you love your people.
> Show me the way to be strong.
> Wakan-Tanka, *hear me.*

Though the wind howled fiercely on Medicine Mountain, Rising Eagle wore no shirt as he danced and sang around the sacred circle of stones. He'd painted stripes down his cheeks and across his chest in his prayer color of white. His songs comforted Buffalo Dreamer.

Here was where they always came to find answers. Here was

where they always found strength, where the Feathered One himself once appeared to Rising Eagle.

Already winter was whispering its way into the valleys below, making it a dangerous time to be in this high place. They'd risked being trapped by a sudden snowstorm on their way here. The risk was much higher at this elevation, but it was worth the danger to come here to pray.

Weather was not the only danger. Whites lived and traveled too many places in this land now, and they were too eager to raise their long guns on the Lakota for no reason at all. A Lakota man and woman traveling alone became fair game to the *wasicus*. In spite of the danger, she and Rising Eagle had pressed on for days on end to get here, keeping to places where they would least likely be seen. How frustrating to have to hide in this land where once all the Lakota rode free, over hills and valleys and mountains, grasslands and waterways, all of it belonging only to them.

Buffalo Dreamer clung to the belief that such freedom would be theirs again someday; perhaps not in her lifetime, but someday, far in a future she would never see except from above. The Feathered One once predicted to Rising Eagle that the white man would one day destroy himself. Only the true Human Beings, the Lakota, would survive.

She was so hungry and cold that she began to lose track of her thoughts, and of Rising Eagle's dancing and singing. Vaguely she thought about the fact that he wore only his winter moccasins and leggings, the stinging wind whipping his bare chest and arms as he danced. She knew it mattered little to Rising Eagle. Such suffering was a form of prayer and sacrifice to *Wakan-Tanka*. He sang:

> See me here, Wakan-Tanka.
> Do you see me here?
> I pray to you.
> I sing to you in the cold wind.
> I ignore my warmth for you.
> I ask for strength, Wakan-Tanka.
> I ask for victory over the wasicus.
> I ask that they give our women back.

Bring me answers, Wakan-Tanka.
Do you see me here?

Alone they sang and prayed. Rising Eagle, too, had fasted for several days before they managed to guide their horses to the top of this mountain, from which it was possible they would never descend. Here they could starve to death, freeze to death, but if their prayers meant that the Lakota would be strong over the white man, victorious against the *wasicus*, their sacrifice would be well worth the effort, even unto death.

She leaned over and tented her robe around the sacred fire, allowing its smoke to engulf her, cleanse her. She stared at the glowing coals, sensing that they whispered to her.

Fire, fire . . . from out of the fire will come the Feathered One, rising as a Phoenix, man and eagle, breathing new fire and new life into your people. The fire of hope will burn eternally . . .

The fire of hope. Yes, it was hope to which they must cling, waiting for the day when the Feathered One would rise from the fire to bring back all ancestors and bring a return to freedom and plenty. A sudden peace filled her, and after breathing once again of the sacred smoke, she wrapped the warmed robe around herself and lay down beside the fire.

Rising Eagle danced until he was hardly aware of the snow, the wind, the cold. There was only this place, this sacred, sacred place, where he always found strength, and where he'd even found a miracle. Here his first-born son was conceived, and here his adopted son Spirit Walker's once-deformed fingers and toes had been healed. No place on earth was more sacred, or more important to him, than Medicine Mountain. Here he always found new strength and new hope. On this mountain he felt he could live forever; and here, when his days were ended, he would come to meet the Feathered One, who would carry him to that wonderful place in the heavens where all his loved ones had gone before.

Surely *Wakan-Tanka* would hear him at this place on top of the world. Surely the Great Spirit would see the sacrifice he was making, so cold now that numbness took away the pain. He continued singing.

> *Do you see me here?*
> *I pray to you in the cold wind.*
> *I ask for strength,* Wakan-Tanka.
> *Do you see me here?*

It was then he heard the voice in the wind. *Do not fear.*

He stopped dancing and spread out his arms, listening, listening . . .

Hope is eternal. Listen to the voices of your ancestors. They sing in joy, knowing one day there will be no more death.

Tears sprang to Rising Eagle's eyes, from the joy of realizing *Wakan-Tanka* still heard his prayers, knowing he had not lost his spiritual closeness with the Great Beyond. The wind howled around him, swirling stinging snow against his bare chest, back, face, and arms. "Strength," he said, feeling weak but refusing to fall. "Give me strength."

You are stronger than you know, and hope is never lost. It lies in the heart. Remember, even if the white man seems to win, he will lose. The rivers are of your blood, the birds are your voices, the earth your flesh. The Earth will always belong to the Lakota.

The wind suddenly died, and the sun broke through the thick, dark snow clouds. It stopped snowing, and the sun shone on Rising Eagle with an unusual warmth.

Rising Eagle smiled. Yes, *Wakan-Tanka* had heard his prayers! He was even blessing his freezing body with a wonderful warmth. Hope . . . he had hope, and he felt a new strength flow through his veins.

He lowered his arms and turned to gaze at Buffalo Dreamer, who still lay curled into her bearskin robe. He walked near her, kneeling to add wood to the dwindling fire, wood they had carried here in bundles on horseback. Flames flickered higher, and the fresh wood crackled and popped as it heated.

Rising Eagle moved under the robe beside Buffalo Dreamer. At last he could warm himself better as the sun again disappeared behind a billowing cloud. He pulled Buffalo Dreamer closer.

"Hope is never lost," he whispered in her ear. "It lies in the heart."

Weakly she replied. "The fire of hope burns eternal."

Rising Eagle's heart soared with new hope in spite of the loss of the white robe. Her words told him that once again this holy woman had experienced a dream connected to his own.

DECEMBER 1855

Winter Moon

CHAPTER THIRTEEN

LIEUTENANT RICHARD SPEAR threw off the white buffalo robe, cursing. "Damned spooky piece of fur!" He got up, kicking it farther away. "Goddamn weather!" He shivered as he yanked open the door of a pot-bellied stove and threw in a few more pieces of wood, an almost futile attempt at fighting a driving wind that forced the bitterly cold air from outside through cracks around the windows of his quarters.

"How in hell did I end up in such country!" He closed the stove door and opened the draft. The wood burst into flames, and he decided to let it burn hard for a few minutes, grumbling about the poor supply of wood out here in prairie land.

"I'll never understand why the U.S. government is so goddamn bent on opening up this country, or why anyone in their right mind would consider settling out here," he muttered. He raised the wick on his lamp to see better, then took the army blankets from his cot and wrapped himself in them. He stayed close to the stove for warmth, studying the white buffalo robe still lying where he'd kicked it in anger. He'd been so cold he'd decided to take it down from where it hung tacked to the wall over his desk, using it for extra warmth. Its insulating benefits helped him readily understand why the robes were so important to the Indians in the deepest throes of winter. He'd never experienced anything warmer, and he

wanted dearly to cover himself with it again; but the damn thing
had such an affect on him mentally and emotionally that he wasn't
able to sleep. Every time he shut his eyes he heard singing and
chanting, jingling bells and rhythmic drumming. It was so real that
he'd jumped up four different times over to open the door and listen. He heard nothing outside, and he knew damn well the Sioux
seldom bothered making war in winter. They had enough to do just
to keep warm and keep their families fed. Still, every time he lay
back down and covered himself with the robe, the singing and
drumming returned.

He had no idea what time it was now, but he knew he'd lost
several hours of sleep. The only reason he could figure for the
singing and drumming he heard was that it had something to do
with that damn robe. He felt like a fool thinking that, but there was
no other explanation.

He closed his eyes and waited. All he heard was the crackling
of the burning wood, but no chanting and drumming. "I'll be
damned," he said softly, amazed.

He sat up again, reaching over to close down the stove draft so
the wood would settle into hot coals. He stared again at the robe.
Could that damn buffalo hunter, Cooper Baird, have been right,
saying the robe was cursed? Look what taking it had done to Baird
and his men.

Angrily, he flopped back down onto the cot. Was he losing his
mind? He felt like an idiot. He sure as hell couldn't admit his problem and questions to any of the men. He would have to come up
with an excuse for getting rid of the robe. He was so shaken by his
experience that now he didn't want it around at all, not even on
the wall over his desk.

He lay back down again, shivering as he pulled his blankets
around his face to warm his nose. Damned if he wasn't afraid of
that buffalo robe. He sure couldn't admit *that* to anyone! Maybe for
now he would hang it in the mess hall. That would give him time
to think about it, and time for the men to have a better look at it.
Maybe someone would speak up, pay him something just to have it
for himself. It would make quite a prize for a soldier to take home
with him one day and show off to his family. Someone would

probably claim he took it off a dead Indian he'd killed in some brave battle, or perhaps that he'd gone on a dangerous buffalo hunt and shot the white buffalo himself. The thing was food for all kinds of stories.

Again he tried sleeping, but it still didn't work. This time trying to figure what to do with the robe kept him awake.

"*Sonofabitch!*" he fumed, kicking away his blankets again and getting up to storm to the door. He opened it a crack and shouted.

"Miliken!"

Sergeant Miliken, on guard duty nearby, replied loudly. "Sir!"

"Get over here!" Spear shut the door, hearing Miliken's clumping footsteps as the man walked along the boardwalk in front of the officer's quarters. "Sir!" he shouted again from outside the door.

Spear opened the door and let the shivering sergeant come inside. The ear flaps to Miliken's winter hat were pulled down, and Spear couldn't help feeling a little sorry for him, having night duty in such weather; but an army man had to do what he had to do. "I'm sure you'd like whatever excuse you can find to get in out of the wind," he told the man.

"No, sir, I don't mind at all."

"Well, I have a little job for you. I want you to pick up that damn white buffalo robe over there and take it to the mess hall."

"Sir?"

"You heard me."

"*Now,* sir?"

"Are you hard of hearing, Sergeant?"

"No, sir."

"Then do what I told you."

"Yes, sir."

Miliken moved past him then, walking over to pick up the robe. He slung it over his shoulder, and although Miliken was over six feet tall, each end of the large robe hung down to his feet, front and back, part of it dragging the floor. "Anything else, sir?"

Spear ran a hand through his graying hair, thinking to himself that he was getting much too old for a soldier's life. He'd be retiring next year, and he could hardly wait. "Nothing else," he answered. "Thank you, Sergeant."

"Yes, sir."

Miliken left, and Spear closed the door, glad that in spite of the bitter cold they had been spared heavy snow. Snow from a storm several days ago had dissipated, leaving frozen ground behind. He did not doubt, however, that they would experience dangerously deep snows before winter ebbed. The only good thing about that was that it kept the Sioux in their tepees and out of trouble. However, such snows also made it difficult for the soldiers to hunt, and for supplies to get through. He hoped this would not be another winter of near starvation. He could only hope the damn buffalo robe would not bring bad luck to the entire fort.

He returned to his bunk, breathing a sigh of relief that the robe was gone from his possession. "Good riddance," he muttered, glad Miliken had not asked for an explanation. He was not about to give one. He was in command here, and he didn't have to give a reason for anything he did.

He lay back down and rolled into his blankets again. The room felt a little warmer. He breathed a deep sigh. Now he could sleep.

AUGUST 1856

Moon of Dry Heat

CHAPTER FOURTEEN

BRAVE HORSE WATCHED Curly grab up a handful of gopher dust and toss it over his horse and his own body. His chest was painted with white dots, representing hail spots.

"Why do you cover yourself with dust?" Brave Horse asked his good friend.

"One day I will tell you," Curly answered. "It is part of my vision. I have told no one yet what I saw."

"You know my vision," Brave Horse told him, keeping his voice low. Both were in a gully below a rise, the other side of which lay an Arapaho camp. "I should know yours."

Curly grinned as he deftly leaped onto the back of his painted war pony. "You will know soon enough. For now let's go take some Arapaho scalps and steal some horses!" He signaled to other young men who rode with them, all ready and eager to make a name for themselves by counting coup on the Arapaho. Such things were important to gaining respect from the elders; even more important, this was good practice for fighting white soldiers, which Brave Horse had no doubt would be their greatest challenge one day.

His heart burned with eagerness to take a *white* man's scalp! The blue-coated soldiers would forever pay for what they had done at Blue Water Creek! The picture of how he had found Yellow

Bonnet would never leave him, nor would the hatred in his heart for the *wasicus*.

He and Curly and many of their young friends had planned this hunt, a hunt for enemy Arapaho, not for buffalo. There would be time enough to prove themselves in a buffalo hunt. To count coup on an enemy and steal their horses would win them much more praise and favor. The only thing more fulfilling would be to fight white soldiers.

Curly let out a fierce war cry, and Brave Horse screamed even louder, as both young men tore out in the lead, charging their painted horses up the rise, the hooves of their cohorts' horses thundering behind them. Brave Horse paid no attention to arrows that began singing past him, although he realized the Arapho must have somehow already spotted them, for they were dug in behind rocks at the top of the hill, a barrier against their reaching the Arapaho camp on the other side.

Curly began riding back and forth in front of the defenders, screaming his war cries and daring their arrows to touch him. Brave Horse did the same, yipping and shouting, picking up on Curly's brave venture. Their diversion helped the others get closer to let loose their own arrows.

Finally Curly and Brave Horse retreated, along with the others, resting their horses behind boulders and shrubbery at the bottom of the hill, laughing at the excitement of the battle.

"Not one arrow touched me!" Curly said, fire in his dark eyes.

"Nor me," Brave Horse answered. "Maybe they will think we have magic about us and will be afraid and give up."

"Let's charge them again!" Curly again rode away, and the others followed. Brave Horse saw in the very young Curly a true leader in the making. He respected the fact that the young man had been a part of his father's vision, although the true link would not be known until Curly revealed his own vision. He'd gone on his own vision quest the year before, but said nothing about it when he returned. If it was close to Rising Eagle's, they would then know that Curly was destined for great things. Brave Horse felt no jealousy for him. The Great Spirit had reasons for choosing whomever he wanted to bless with special gifts of holiness or good medicine or leadership. His own blessing was simply being the son of Rising Eagle. He carried the man's blood, and that alone made him special. The first-born son of such a man was expected to follow in that man's footsteps, gradually rising to the same prominence. Brave Horse was determined to do just that, no matter what the sacrifice.

For nearly two hours the constant charges continued, until several Arapaho and Oglala lay dead or wounded. The remaining Arapaho men finally left their barricade of rocks and headed over the rise to run to their hunting camp.

"Let's go!" Curly shouted to Brave Horse. His heart pounding with excitement, Brave Horse and the rest of the Oglala followed Curly over the rise, charging into the camp, screaming death songs they hoped would plant fear in the hearts of the defending Arapaho.

Brave Horse charged past fleeing women and children. He had no interest in killing females and young ones. Such things were cruel and took no bravery. Instead he headed straight toward an Arapaho warrior whose bow was raised. The man loosed his arrow, but Brave Horse knew the timing of such things. He fell to the side of his war pony, feeling a brush of air as the arrow sang past him. He moved to an upright position then, charging the enemy warrior and swinging his hatchet. He landed it into the side of the man's head, splitting it open. He whirled his horse as the Arapaho warrior fell, then quickly dismounted and grabbed a fistful of the man's long, black hair. Using the same hatchet, he whacked off the hair, along with the scalp to which it was attached. He held up the scalp and let out a scream of victory.

In the distance he saw Curly taking another man's scalp. Other Oglala warriors charged about the camp, killing and pillaging. Brave Horse shoved the scalp into the waist of his breechcloth and rode down yet another warrior who came at him with a lance. The man raised his arm, ready to sink the lance into Brave Horse's war pony, or perhaps into Brave Horse's leg. But Brave Horse let out a scream and suddenly veered left, then immediately reined his horse right, appreciating the animal's agility and obedience. He and

Rising Eagle had been training this gray Appaloosa gelding for months, and it paid off.

The sharp whirl to the right knocked the warrior off balance, sending him sprawling onto his belly. Brave Horse jumped off his horse again, and he was onto the warrior's back before the man could rise. He grabbed the man's hair and yanked backward, using his hatchet to slash the man's throat, then taking a second scalp.

He screamed even louder at his prize. Rising Eagle would be proud of his success here! These Arapaho would think twice about ever entering Oglala hunting grounds again!

He pushed the second scalp into the waist of his breechcloth and remounted. He shoved his hatchet into a corded loop attached to his lightweight saddle made of deerskin stuffed with grass. Then he reached behind himself and retrieved his bow and an arrow from the quiver that hung behind his back. He positioned the arrow, letting go of it and watching it land in the back of a fleeing warrior. Then he rode about the camp, grabbing the ropes to several Arapaho horses. He then rode farther out to gather other horses that had scattered.

He jumped down and used rawhide cords he'd brought with him to form a noose around one horse, then brought the cord back and tied yet another noose around a second horse. Other Oglala men were snagging more Arapaho horses. Brave Horse tied his cord to a third horse, one that already had a rope tied to it. He attached his cord to it, then brought that rope back and tied it to the next horse, and then another, until he had five horses strung together.

His heart sang with joy at the vision of riding back to camp with two Arapaho scalps and five horses! He was indeed a true warrior now! The rest of the Oglala men were looting the Arapaho tepees, taking food, robes, anything they could carry, as well as more horses. The camp was alive with yips and shouts of victory. Brave Horse's only regret was that it was not white soldiers he'd killed.

"Curly took an arrow!" a young Oglala man shouted to him as he rode past.

Brave Horse felt alarm. He spotted Curly's mount in the distance, and he headed toward him. As he drew closer he could see an arrow sticking out of Curly's left thigh. Curly was obviously in pain, but he made no sound. "Curly!" he shouted when he reached him. "Is it bad?" Curly looked angry and confused.

"I do not understand," he confessed, pain in his voice. "Arrows are not supposed to harm me."

"How do you know this?"

"Because of my vision."

"Then you must tell your father or mine about your vision, so that you fully understand it."

Curly nodded. "I will, but not yet. I am embarrassed, because an enemy arrow struck me."

"There is surely some explanation."

Curly grinned in spite of his agony. "I took three scalps!"

Brave Horse laughed. "And I took two! And look! Five horses!"

Curly laughed with him. "You did well, my friend."

"And I will tell your father about how you rode back and forth right in front of the enemy with no fear. He will be proud of you no matter what, Curly. You are a true leader!"

The young man closed his eyes and swallowed. "Pull out the arrow and I will tie it off," he told Brave Horse.

Gritting his teeth, Brave Horse took hold of the arrow, knowing how badly it would hurt to yank it out, pulling a good deal of flesh with it, no doubt.

"Quickly!" Curly said, stiffening.

Brave Horse yanked with all his power. The arrow popped out, and Curly only grunted. Then he took a piece of rawhide tied to the side of his horse and tied it around his thigh to slow the bleeding. "We should go now. I will need the prayers and healing powers of Walks With Wolves."

"Yes," Brave Horse answered. "Will you be all right, Curly?"

His friend nodded. "It is worth the wound. Besides, it hit no bones. It will be very sore, but there is no real damage, except to my pride."

"You should not fret about it, Curly. There could be a good reason. One day when you share your vision with others, perhaps then you will understand."

Curly nodded, looking around to see most of the other Oglala men had taken what they wanted and were heading away from the camp. "Let's go home," he said to Brave Horse.

Brave Horse knew he meant the Black Hills, *Paha-Sapa*, which would forever be home to the Oglala and all the Lakota. That was one place that would never be taken from them, and now they were both trained and ready to fight to keep them, no matter what the cost.

JUNE 1857

Moon of Making Fat

CHAPTER FIFTEEN

BRAVE HORSE BREATHED deeply, allowing the steam from the sacred stones to cleanse him from within. He shared the sweat lodge with his father; as well as with Curly and his father, Crazy Horse, a Lakota medicine man, Walks With Wolves, and his granduncle, Bold Fox. Old Bold Fox had aged dramatically since losing his wife at Blue Water Creek, but ever since Rising Eagle and Buffalo Dreamer returned from Medicine Mountain two summers past, Bold Fox seemed to get a little stronger and more vital each day, taking much hope in the strength the first two had found after praying at the sacred mountain.

Brave Horse himself felt a new happiness after his and Curly's raid on the Arapaho last summer. The capture of many horses and two Arapaho scalps had greatly enhanced his place among the Oglala as one of their most promising young warriors, along with Curly. Both spent a good deal of time in prayer and sacrifice, looking for answers to the sorrow of Blue Water Creek, looking for new strength and power, enough to one day ride against the white soldiers in victory.

Crow Chasing Woman came inside the sweat lodge then to pour more water over the hot rocks. She was the wife of the clan's previous medicine man, Moon Painter, who died at Blue Water Creek. Now Crow Chasing Woman, who was very wise in proper healing prayers and the use of special herbs, often helped Walks With Wolves, who had discovered his healing powers when he prayed fervently over a grandchild who had fallen from a horse last winter and was trampled. Several of his bones were broken, but the boy recovered remarkably well under Walks With Wolves's strong healing powers.

Crow Chasing Woman left, closing the entrance flaps again so that the moist heat inside became close to unbearable, yet no man complained. It was important to be completely cleansed and filled with the spirit of *Wakan-Tanka* before joining other leaders who had come here to the sacred Black Hills for an important conference. Thousands had gathered to discuss what should be done about the *wasicus* from here on. After seeing the atrocities of which they were capable, especially at Blue Water Creek, it was obvious the white man could never be trusted, nor could a man logically reason with *wasicus*.

Shihenna leaders had also joined them here, and outside the sweat lodge could be heard rhythmic drumming and singing. Warriors danced and women trilled their approval of plans to stop any further white advances. Here in the sweat lodge, which both Curly and Brave Horse felt honored to share with their elders, all sat quietly praying, allowing any weaknesses or impure thoughts to be shed through intense perspiration. It was always best to purify one's self and suffer a little before joining in dances and prayers for victory, and before making grave decisions.

"I think that now would be a good time to share with you what I saw in my vision quest three summers past," Curly spoke up, surprising all of them. "I have never told my father, or even my best friend, Brave Horse."

All were silent for a moment, until old Crazy Horse spoke. "I have never asked you, my son, because I knew you would find the right time. Yes, this would be a good time. The holy man, Rising Eagle, is with us, and our medicine man, Walks With Wolves. We would be honored to know of your vision, and to help interpret it for you."

Curly glanced at Brave Horse, sharing a look that told Brave Horse how important it was to him that his good friend also hear about his vision. He turned then to his father. Telling stories of battle and bravery, or of vision quests, was a favorite mode of entertainment for Lakota men, and Brave Horse could feel Curly's pride and excitement at sharing his experience.

"I lay for three days on gravel," the young man began. "I kept stones between my toes to help keep me awake, but all that time I saw and heard nothing. I had no dreams. I had already gone without food for several days, and without water those three days." He faced Rising Eagle. "I became discouraged and rose to go to my horse, but then the earth seemed to be moving beneath my feet. I became dizzy and fell under the shade of the tree where my horse was tied."

He turned to his father again. "When I looked up at my horse I saw a light-haired man on its back. My horse began to float above the ground. The man who rode him wore blue leggings. He wore no face paint and a hawk's tail was tied into his loose hair. There was a small brown stone tied behind his ear, and beads in his scalp lock. He did not move his lips when he spoke to me, but rather seemed to speak through his eyes. He told me to never wear a war bonnet or to tie up my horse's tail before going into battle. I am to throw dust over my horse before fighting the enemy, and I should never take anything for myself."

He paused, and the others waited quietly for him to continue. Brave Horse pondered the story, wondering at its meaning. He'd experienced his own vision five summers past, one that told of a black, smoking iron horse that would come into Lakota land and bring many whites with it. They had yet to see such a horse, but he did not doubt his vision. All visions held truth and meaning.

"Then the man on my horse rode into the sky against other warriors," Curly finally continued, staring at the hot stones. "Their arrows disappeared before reaching him. A storm came, and the man then only wore a breechcloth and moccasins against the cold. The hail turned into white spots on his chest and lightning cut a flash mark across his face. A red-backed hawk flew above him. What was strange was that the man's own people seemed to be trying to hold him back, grabbing him by the arms." He turned to his father again. "That is when you woke me and scolded me for going out alone for my vision quest instead of taking you and a medicine man along. But I did have a vision, Father, and now I need to know what it all meant."

Crazy Horse turned to Rising Eagle. "You told me once that you dreamed of a young warrior named Crazy Horse, and that you believed that young man was my own son."

Rising Eagle nodded. "Not only that, but my vision was of a young man who rode through the sky with hail spots on his chest, a bolt of lightning painted on his cheek, and a brown stone tied behind his ear."

Walks With Wolves gasped and began chanting a song to *Wakan-Tanka*, praising him for the wondrous connection between Rising Eagle's dream and Curly's vision, for surely it meant great things lay ahead for young Curly, to be seen in a vision by such an esteemed holy man as Rising Eagle.

Crazy Horse sighed, studying his son for a moment before answering. "I believe, because of Rising Eagle's dream, that the man on the horse was yourself. This means you must wear the small stone behind your ear and a hawk's tail in your hair, which you should leave loose when riding into battle. You should paint a lightning bolt on your face, and hail spots on your chest, wearing only a breechcloth and moccasins when going into battle. The hawk is your guiding spirit, and with its guidance and the protection of the thunder spirit, enemy bullets and arrows will never harm you. Those who ride with you will also be safe. However, because the vision told you to take nothing from battle, you were wounded in your fight with the Arapaho last summer. That is why an arrow pierced your leg. From now on, Curly, you must remember to never take anything with you when you leave a battle, not even an enemy scalp. Simply fight bravely to save what is yours and to protect the women and children. You are destined to be a great leader, my son, so you must obey the vision spirits."

Curly glanced again at Brave Horse, and the two young men grinned in eager excitement. "Yes, Father," Curly answered.

"Do not think your powers will make your life easy, my son," Crazy Horse continued. "Things are never easy for one of such power and importance. Rising Eagle can tell you so. You must be diligent in abiding by the proper behavior of an honored warrior, and you will often be tested. I fear the vision of our people holding you back could mean that one day your great leadership will bring jealousy among the Oglala, perhaps arguments over the right thing to do. The white man is clever, and perhaps will find a way to divide our people."

"Never!" Curly answered.

"We must trust our visions and act accordingly," Rising Eagle warned the young man. "Perhaps other Oglala leaders will try to hold you back or turn against you. Either way, you must do what you know in your heart is right to do."

"We will speak of your vision to Black Elk, whose opinion we will also seek. He, too, is an esteemed holy man among us. I am sure Rising Eagle agrees that Black Elk should also hear your story."

Rising Eagle nodded, and all fell silent again as they sat sweating out their impurities for several more minutes before Rising Eagle spoke again. "Rest in the knowledge, Curly, that you are destined to become a great leader among us. I am proud that my son calls you friend. Now it is time to leave and let others take their turn in the sweat lodge before our meeting tomorrow with all the elders."

Walks With Wolves nodded. "I think that our sons should be there, Rising Eagle."

Brave Horse wanted to jump up with pride at the offer.

"I agree," Rising Eagle replied.

"And our holy woman, Buffalo Dreamer, should also attend as one of the circle," Walks With Wolves added. "Your prayers and those of your wife are important to our decisions, Rising Eagle."

Rising Eagle nodded. "Buffalo Dreamer will be honored." He raised his prayer pipe then, which he'd kept lit. He offered it to the four directions and smoked it, then passed it to the others who did the same. Once all had drawn on the pipe, Rising Eagle announced it was time to leave the sweat lodge.

They wrapped blankets around their naked bodies and exited the sweat lodge, the warm air outside actually feeling cold at first when it hit Brave Horse's face. Curly joined him as they left the area, then suddenly stepped sideways, nudging Brave Horse. "We will enjoy many victories together, won't we, my friend?"

Brave Horse grinned. "I look forward to it, especially when we get a chance to ride against the Blue Coats who killed Yellow Bonnet."

"We will continue practicing on enemy tribes!"

Curly hurried off then to his own tepee, laughing as he ran. Brave Horse chuckled, shaking his head. He realized this was the happiest he'd felt since Yellow Bonnet's death. He glanced around at the hundreds of tepees set up in the Black Hills camp, Oglala, Hunkpapa, Minneconjou, Sans Arcs, Blackfeet and the Two Kettles tribes. Yes, they were still strong! Yes, there were many victories ahead! The white man would one day greatly regret his atrocities against the Lakota!

CHAPTER SIXTEEN

THUNDER RUMBLED IN distant black clouds, as though to accent the power of *Wakan-Tanka* and thus the power of the Lakota leaders who sat around the large central fire, blessed by the Lakota medicine man, Walks With Wolves. Never had the words of hope spoken to Buffalo Dreamer held more significance than now. Thousands of Lakota had come to the sacred Black Hills, along with their friends, the Shihenna. If the white soldiers thought there was power in numbers, then here lay the strength of the Lakota: brave men, highly skilled in battle, better fighters than any Blue Coat soldier.

She realized that two winters had gone by since the awful slaughter of loved ones at Blue Water Creek. Some of their leaders had signed yet another treaty after that, but only as a way to free their loved ones. Spotted Tail, Red Leaf, and Long Chin had surrendered themselves and were imprisoned. Because of that, Spotted Tail's clan had chosen not to come to this council, afraid of more trouble. Buffalo Dreamer feared that was a sign of coming division among the Lakota, as predicted in young Curly's vision. That made it all the more important for the rest of them to remain strong and united.

The scene today renewed the hope in Buffalo Dreamer's heart that she and Rising Eagle had realized on Medicine Mountain. She stood behind Rising Eagle at this council meeting. Her husband was now a revered elder at the age of forty-nine winters. She felt proud of how virile a man he still was, and of the fact that Rising Eagle was *naca*, a supremely important leader.

The circle of elders passed a prayer pipe before beginning council. It rested now on Rising Eagle's lap as he opened the talks.

"I believe that we all agree that this place, our beloved Black Hills, must never be given to the *wasicus*," he told the others. "More than once my dreams have warned me of this. The Feathered One Himself commanded me to never allow anyone to take *Paha-Sapa* from us."

The others nodded their heads. Rising Eagle wore a splendid bonnet of eagle feathers, gifted to him by old Bold Fox. His aging uncle wanted to be sure his most treasured possession went to the right person before he should die, and he had told Rising Eagle he was the most worthy of it. Bold Fox sat now at this council, bent over, his eyes closed, his braided hair an almost-brilliant white. His arm muscles hung limp, and his belly pooched out over the waistline of his leggings. Bold Fox was the last remaining blood uncle to Rising Eagle. Buffalo Dreamer knew that she and Rising Eagle would actually rejoice when he passed on, for he would go to a place where he would be young and strong again, and where he could again be with his beloved Running Elk Woman. Not long ago, Many Horses had walked the road to heaven, another beloved uncle gone to be with his wife, taken away many years ago by the white man's spotted fever.

"The white man is hungry for our land," Walks With Wolves offered. "I have no doubt he will even try to take *Paha-Sapa*. Our greatest challenge one day will be to protect this sacred place."

"We will always keep the Black Hills," Owl Crier, a Kit Fox leader, declared. "We will *die* before giving up this most sacred place!"

Again, all nodded, and behind the elders several younger warriors, including Brave Horse and Curly, raised their fists and shouted excited war cries.

"We will *never* surrender!" Brave Horse shouted. "Death to the *wasicus*!"

Cheers went up from his cohorts, young men from many different clans, all ready to fight, all ready to show their prowess and be able to brag about counting coup on Blue Coats. Since Yellow

Bonnet's death, Brave Horse had changed, all his youthful joy gone, except when he became excited about making war. Otherwise Buffalo Dreamer's son seldom smiled or laughed. The only one who seemed to be able to bring a smile to his face was his good friend, Curly, and sometimes his younger brother, now renamed Thunder. Brave Horse's hatred of the *wasicus* could not be matched. At twenty-three summers Brave Horse had twice suffered the Sun Dance ritual, deliberately pulling at the skewers in his breasts, yet emitting no cries of pain. Already he'd garnered a good deal of respect, and he hoped to soon be appointed Shirt Wearer, beginning a climb to his father's prominence.

Curly, too, though three years younger, already held high respect among the Oglala. Because Rising Eagle himself had seen Curly in a vision long before he knew him, there was no doubt he, too, was destined for glory.

Another man quickly realizing respect from the elders, Red Cloud, now rose. Red Cloud was adept at trading with whites, but he was also wily and clever, not really trusting them. He stretched out his arm then to indicate to everyone present the importance of what he had to say.

"We must remain united," he declared. "The white man has strength in numbers, and so must we. I, too, will fight to the death to keep the Black Hills, but I will fight for more than that. Anyone who wishes to follow me will help me keep not only the Black Hills out of the hands of the white man, but also Medicine Mountain, all the mountains of the big-horned sheep, and all the fertile valley along the Powder River, where we have always hunted."

There followed more cheers and war whoops. Buffalo Dreamer breathed deeply of the hope and courage she found here today. Red Cloud sat down, and yet another fast-rising young warrior, *Tatanka Yotanka*, Sitting Bull, stood up. About the same age as Brave Horse, he and Brave Horse and Curly often rode and hunted together, or went on horse-stealing expeditions together.

"We are many, and we are strong," Sitting Bull told them. "If our elders say we must fight to keep the Black Hills, and if our esteemed leader, Red Cloud, says we must even fight for the Powder River, we are ready to do so!" The young warriors cheered even louder.

The council meeting lasted several more minutes, several of the elders voicing their support of a stand against the white man, as well as offering sage advice to the younger warriors not to allow their eagerness to get in the way of making wise choices in battle, and especially to remain true to their visions. Then Rising Eagle stood, indicating that all the other elders should also rise.

"It is agreed, then, that we will remain united in our fight against the *wasicus*," he said. "We have discussed much here today, and we know that our strength lies in numbers. This we must always remember, because of my wife's vision of long ago." He raised his own fist. "One day, my brothers and fathers, we will ride in many thousands, surrounding many Blue Coats, and we will kill *all* of them!"

More cheers.

"The white man will remember this battle forever! And forever he will speak our names with fear and awe!" Red Cloud shouted.

The cheering erupted into a near roar, rippling from the elders through the young warriors and then throughout the huge camp. The entire area came alive with celebrating. Even their first buffalo hunt this year had been fruitful. Hope was alive after all! Every direction in which Buffalo Dreamer looked, she could see skins stretched for drying, meat hanging in strips for curing, while more of it hung over hot fires, fat dripping and hissing against hot coals. Bellies would be full next winter!

This was indeed a time to celebrate. In spite of uncalled-for attacks on innocent women and children, the white soldiers had known no real victories, certainly no victories that could be called honorable.

Throughout camp, warriors from various tribes began their drumming, singing, and dancing, all filled with new hope, new determination. They were strong again. They could survive and fight even though the white buffalo robe had never been recovered. Buffalo Dreamer could not help wondering where it was now, and when she would see and touch it again . . . for she would. She believed that with all her heart.

"Do you hear it?" Rising Eagle asked her, leaving the circle of elders as they broke up, each going to join his particular clan.

"Hear what?"

"Crazy Horse! He has decided to honor Curly's bravery in the battle last year with the Arapaho, and to fulfill both his son's vision and *mine*! Come!" He pulled her with him to a circle of tepees where old Crazy Horse had begun his duty of making the announcement about his son. His family had prepared a great feast for the Hunkpatila headmen, for Crazy Horse came from the Hunkpatila clan.

Buffalo Dreamer put a hand to her heart when she heard the words, for they only verified Rising Eagle's insightful gift of visions of the future. He, too, had seen a battle against many soldiers, just as she'd seen in her own dream of long ago. Now she heard the last fulfillment of Rising Eagle's vision of riding into battle with a young warrior called Crazy Horse.

My son has been against the people of unknown tongue, old Crazy Horse sang as he walked among the lodges with his announcement.

> *He has done a brave thing.*
> *For this I give him a new name, the name of his father,*
> *And of many fathers before him.*
> *I give him a great name.*
> *I call him . . . Crazy Horse!*

Buffalo Dreamer looked up at Rising Eagle. "The hope we found on Medicine Mountain is renewed, my husband," she told him.

Rising Eagle nodded. "This is truly a great moment. United we can know great victories, as will our sons. Brave Horse will know the vengeance he deserves. Seeing the last of my vision fulfilled tells me so."

Buffalo Dreamer felt a happiness she thought, after Blue Water Creek, she would never know again. Old Crazy Horse, who announced he should now be called Worm because his offspring would become someone much greater than he, continued his song.

> *I give him a great name . . .*
> *I call him Crazy Horse.*

MARCH 1860

Moon of Falling Rains

CHAPTER SEVENTEEN

"WE HAVE ANOTHER letter from Robert," Florence told Abel. She sat down at the kitchen table and eagerly opened the letter just delivered.

Abel leaned back in his chair and sipped some coffee while Florence scanned the letter. "Well?" he asked.

Florence smiled. "He is getting very good grades, at the top of his class!"

"And did you expect any less from your son?"

Florence paused to glance at him. "I suppose not." She watched him lovingly. "So much of this is thanks to you, Abel. Where would Robert be now, and where would I be, if you had not taken my hand and led me out of the terrible life I was leading?"

"It isn't the what-ifs that matter, Florence. I helped a Lakota woman, and then I fell in love with her. I haven't regretted one minute of our lives together."

"Nor have I." Florence glanced back at the letter.

"*I wonder what Rising Eagle would think of this place,*" she read aloud.

"Indeed," Abel commented.

Florence thought what a different world Robert lived in now, compared to the way he grew up among the Lakota. She slowly shook her head. "Who ever would have thought that the tiny, sickly baby I gave birth to would turn out like this?" She sighed with pleasure. "My son, a student at the University of Michigan, studying to be a doctor." She met Abel's eyes. "You have brought me so many miracles, Abel."

He studied her lovingly. "And you, my dear, have made *my* life amazingly interesting and challenging. Your son's intelligence comes from your own intelligence, you know. You learned everything so fast, and as you learned, I loved you more and more. It's been exciting being married to you, to say the least."

Florence laughed lightly. "I am not sure how to take that remark."

Abel chuckled. "Let's just say life might have been much more boring without you in it. The women of this parish find you delightful, and I am glad you don't mind their questions about Lakota life. And having you here in Springfield, you being so lovely and refined and well-spoken, only shows them that the Lakota are just as worthy and intelligent as any white man. It helps in my efforts to raise money to keep sending missionaries west to convert the Indians to Christ."

Florence's smile faded slightly. "There are some who will *never* leave the old ways, Abel."

"Like Rising Eagle?"

Still, after all these years, his name caused a sharp little pain in her heart. "Yes," she answered. "Life must be very hard for them now, with more and more whites going west, more forts being built, more soldiers. And now we are reading that they might even build a railroad all the way across the country to California. It seems impossible, and I can't help wondering what the Lakota will think of something like that. It will surely chase away buffalo." She stared blankly at the letter. "I worry, Abel. We know men go out there now to hunt the buffalo, just for their hides. The articles in the paper talk about thousands and thousands of buffalo killed." She met his eyes. "Without the buffalo, my people will die. Life must be getting very hard for them."

Abel reached across the table and took her hand. "We can

only pray for them, Florence. Things are changing. This country is growing fast, and it can't be stopped. Eventually the Lakota will *have* to learn a new way."

She shook her head. "Many lives will be lost before they will ever change. There are surely terrible times ahead."

Abel leaned back again, running a finger around the rim of his coffee cup. "I'm afraid you're probably right, but there isn't much we can do about it."

Florence looked back at her son's letter and continued reading.

"In three more years I will be a real doctor. I can hardly believe it myself. I owe so much to you, Abel, and to the parish for being so generous in raising the money for my education. Please thank them again for me at your next service, and tell them how hard I am working to achieve good grades and earn my degree.

How is William doing? Is my little brother behaving?"

She put the letter down again, her heart aching at the question. She closed her eyes. Poor William, still so unhappy.

"Florence?"

She couldn't look at Abel, knowing what he was going to say.

"Robert has to be told the truth," he said. "You know that. I've told you over and over. And William also has to know."

Florence rose, turning away. "No. William is having enough trouble with his mixed blood. He doesn't need to be told that the people he thinks are his parents aren't his parents at all. It would be too hard for him. And Robert . . ." She faced Abel again. "How can I tell him I've been lying to him all these years? He is happy thinking he has a brother. What is the harm in letting them believe they are brothers, and letting William believe I am his mother?"

"Someday it might be important for them to know, Florence."

She studied his soft brown eyes, so intense and honest. In spite of his age, Abel had remained a slender man . . . and he was such a kind man. "I hope that day never comes; but if it does, then I will have no choice but to tell them. I pray every day that will not happen."

"With William's attitude lately, it wouldn't matter if he knew his Indian blood came from Rising Eagle and not from you," Abel said with a sigh. "Either way, he hates that side of himself. He and Robert are so different. Robert is proud of his heritage. William, on the other hand, worries me. It's mostly the children at school that create the problem. Every time the newspaper runs an article about Indians attacking whites out West he gets teased. We probably never should have brought him here to Illinois."

"You missed home," Florence told him. "You deserved to come back; and being here has made it easier to send Robert to travel to Michigan for school. He's adjusted so well. Robert has never been affected by remarks from others. I wish William could handle his heritage the same way."

"Robert is twenty-seven years old, old enough to handle the situation maturely. And he lived the Lakota way the first eighteen years of his life. He understands that side of himself better than William ever will. William is only fourteen, a pretty tender age, and I am afraid he has his father's temper. He's got Rising Eagle's pride and stubbornness. He just doesn't realize where he gets it from, and he doesn't quite know how to handle that pride and all that anger inside him."

Florence sighed. "I'm sorry William has become such a problem, Abel. I talk to him and talk to him, but he seems to resent me, his own mother."

"Because he blames you for his Indian blood. He should know, Florence, that he doesn't have a drop of your blood in his veins."

"Lakota blood is Lakota blood." It still hurt to think about William coming home a bloody, dusty mess two days before, after a fistfight with two white boys who had teased him about being a "savage Indian." They had shouted war whoops and asked him if he liked to get naked and dance around campfires, and if he dreamed about white girls. William had lit into them and licked both boys. That fury, that anger, that strength and pride—it all came from Rising Eagle.

Suddenly the back door was opened. Florence stiffened as young William, tall for his age, stomped inside, slamming the door behind him. Her heart ached at the sight of him, his face still bruised, a cut on his cheek still red and puffy.

"Is it true we're going to war against the South?" he asked.

Abel rose, scooting back his chair. "I don't know, son. It certainly looks like that could happen."

"If it does, I'm going to join the army and go fight those Confederates," he declared. "I hate school, and I hate it here."

"William! You're only fourteen years old!" Florence exclaimed. "The army won't take a fourteen-year-old boy!"

"I look older than fourteen. If I join the army and fight the Confederates, the white boys will see I'm not Indian at all. I'll fight right alongside white soldiers, and maybe some day I'll even go out West and fight Indians. Then they'll know. They'll know I'm not like you at all."

"William!" Abel said sharply. "You will speak to your mother with more respect."

The boy scowled at Abel. "My mother is the reason I don't have any friends," he answered. "She's the reason I get teased."

Florence turned away, pain piercing her heart.

"You will not join the army," Abel said sternly. "And you will never again say such hurtful words to your mother."

"You can't stop me from doing whatever I want," William answered. He turned and marched out of the kitchen and up the stairs to his room, slamming that door, too.

Florence felt Abel's footsteps behind her, felt his firm grip on her shoulders. "He'll grow out of this, Florence."

She thought about William's last words. *You can't stop me from doing whatever I want.* Oh, yes, he was very much Rising Eagle's son.

MAY 1861

Moon of Sweet Grass

CHAPTER EIGHTEEN

"HEY, STUART, YOU want this thing?" Private Randy Biggart grunted a little as he threw the white buffalo robe over a hitching post in front of Stuart's Supply, a trading post near Fort Laramie. "I can't take it with me where I'm going."

Stuart Templeton, a large man whose breathing always sounded painfully labored, lumbered down the steps in front of his store. He put his hands on his hips and coughed up phlegm, then spit into the dirt before replying. "I don't know, Private. Story is, that robe is bad luck."

Young Biggart snickered. "Hell, Stuart, you chicken, too? I've had this thing for six months, and I ain't had one problem."

"Why are you unloading it on me then?"

The private shrugged his slender shoulders. "I've been assigned to head back east to fight for the North. God knows I'm ready to leave this damn place, all this sun and all this dirt."

Stuart sniffed. "Yeah? Well, I lived in Louisiana once. You think it's hot here, mix that heat with lots of humidity. You'll be wishing you were back here if you end up doing your duty in the South in the summertime. If the heat doesn't get you, the bugs will."

Private Biggart waved him off. "Heck, we'll lick the South so fast it won't matter. They don't have a chance."

Stuart fingered the white buffalo robe, then scratched at a two-day-old beard. "I wouldn't be so sure of that. They're a stubborn bunch, them southern boys. And right proud." He looked toward the fort. "I hear tell there's been some problems among the troops left here, those from the South and those from the North. Some of the southern boys have deserted."

Stuart nodded. "Between that, and the North needing the rest of us, there won't be many soldiers left out here to defend against the Indians."

"Yeah. That worries me, let me tell you. Once Red Cloud and Rising Eagle and some of them other troublemakers get wind of that, they'll have a heyday, no doubt. I'm just glad I'm down here and not up by Montana way. It's the whites moving into gold country up there that the Sioux are riled against right now. The army is going to have trouble defending the forts up there along the Bozeman, that's sure."

"I'm just glad I'm not one of them," Stuart answered. "Now, what about this robe? I've got to report at Pittsburgh soon as I leave here in two days. I can't be hauling this thing with me."

Templeton looked down at the robe again, running a hand through his oily hair. "I don't know. Rumor has it that Lieutenant Spear back at Fort Kearny was somehow spooked by the thing. And the man who first stole it died a terrible death. The major who decided to keep it after Spear got himself thrown from a horse and broke his neck. I'm not sure who had it after that or how it got over here to Laramie, but it sure seems like it doesn't stay in anybody's hands very long." He looked intently at Private Biggart. "You sure you haven't had any bad luck with it? Sure there isn't some other reason you're trying to get rid of it?"

Biggart hoped the man couldn't read through him. He'd had stomach problems ever since buying the robe off another soldier eight months earlier for a pouch of tobacco. That man claimed he'd had no bad luck with it, that he was just tired of lugging it around and couldn't figure out a good way to send it back home; but he'd seemed awfully nervous at the time.

"Heck no," Biggart answered the hefty trader. "I just thought it would be something unusual to own, figured I'd take it home with me. But with being assigned right to Pennsylvania, I can't take it along, that's all. I figured maybe you could sell it to some passer-by. I mean, how often do you come across a white buffalo robe? Maybe you could even hawk it as having special powers, something like that. Hundreds, heck probably thousands, of settlers come through here every summer. I expect you could talk some hapless, ignorant immigrant to pay you way more than it's worth, if you feed him some concocted story about it. Tell them it belonged to Red Cloud or Rising Eagle."

Stuart grinned. "Now there's an idea. In fact, instead of selling it, I could put it in a special room in back and charge people to look at it—tell them it has magical powers, and tell them how rare it is. I could put a sign out front: 'Come in and see a rare albino buffalo robe—once belonged to Rising Eagle!' I could charge two cents a look, something like that."

"Sure! There you go!"

Stuart rubbed his chin, thinking. "What will it cost me?"

Biggart had not even considered a price. But heck, Stuart Templeton ought to have plenty of money. And he might make plenty of money off this thing. "Well, I'll tell you." He paced a moment, studying the robe. "It's got a burn mark on it where some soldier dropped a cigar or something on it, so it's not perfect. But it's still something pretty rare. I'll let you have it for—" He hesitated. "How about three pouches of tobacco and the papers to roll plenty of smokes? And along with that, ten dollars."

Stuart scowled and shook his head, his double chin jiggling rather sickeningly. "Two pouches of tobacco and five dollars."

Biggart loved to smoke. "Three pouches, and two dollars."

Stuart grinned again, putting out his hand. "Sold!"

Biggart laughed, shaking the man's hand. "I'll stop by for my pay when I leave out. Hey, good luck with the robe, Stuart. I hope you make lots of money with it."

"By gosh, I think I will. And I wish you luck in the war back east, son."

"Well, like I said, I don't expect it to amount to much."

"We'll see, boy. We'll see."

Private Biggart glanced once more at the robe, then nodded to Stuart and turned to head back to the fort. *By God, I feel better already.* He'd finally unloaded that damn robe.

JANUARY 1862

Month of Deep Cold

CHAPTER NINETEEN

FLORENCE STARED VACANTLY at her husband's gravesite. It had all happened so quickly. Nothing felt real. One minute they were sitting in the parlor talking, and in the next minute Abel had slumped from his chair, dead.

Was this just some hideous nightmare? How would she go on without Abel Kingsley? He was her rock, her refuge. No man could match him in goodness and patience.

"We're so sorry, Florence. The entire congregation will miss him so."

The words came from Esther Lillibridge, wife of one of the church deacons. Florence faced her, unable to clearly distinguish the details of the black bonnet the woman wore, because of the tears in her eyes. "Thank you, Esther," she answered.

A large crowd stood around the open grave as men gently lowered Abel's coffin into the gaping hole that would swallow up her husband forever. Florence forced back an urge to scream at them to please bury him on a scaffold the Indian way, facing the sky and the sun. That way Abel could more easily get up and walk the starry road to heaven. She hated the way whites buried their dead. Her greatest consolation was the number of people who'd come to Abel's funeral. He'd been so well liked.

Putting a handkerchief to her nose and mouth with one hand,

she moved her other arm around William's shoulders. She could feel him shaking with silent tears. This would be very hard on William. He'd always been able to talk to Abel more easily than to her. Her son seemed to carry such a deep resentment toward her for giving him his Indian blood, his Indian looks; but they didn't come from her at all. And now it would be harder than ever to tell him that. How could she do so without Abel's help? How could she risk losing her son now, when she needed his company more than ever?

For today William seemed more loving. She knew it was because his heart was so broken and he felt she was all he had left. She moved her woolen, fur-lined cape around him against the cold, glad that at least there was not a stiff wind today. Thank goodness, it was actually sunny, a rarity this time of year, but the brightness of the snow that covered the ground hurt her eyes. She thought what a difficult time the gravediggers must have had, with the ground so frozen. It seemed to her like a terrible time of year to die. She wanted to open the coffin and lie down beside Abel to keep him warm. She didn't want to put him in that cold, cold ground.

She heard nothing of what the guest preacher from another church said in his closing words. All she could think about was Abel, that first time he'd walked up to her back at Fort Pierre, stretching out his hand to an alcoholic prostitute called Fall Leaf Woman. Memories came flooding in, Abel teaching her to read and write, and giving her a white woman's name; Abel's sister, Belinda, teaching her how white women dressed and wore their hair, white women's manners and conduct; Abel bringing her to Christianity; Abel nervously asking her to marry him; Abel generously agreeing to let her keep and raise William after his real mother swore she never wanted anything to do with him. He'd loved William like his own, loved him because *she* loved him. Now Abel and Belinda were both gone.

Abel had taught her so much, and he understood her like no other white person ever could or would. Only her eldest, Robert, who was himself raised Lakota, understood what it was like for a Lakota to live among whites. Only Robert knew that deep inside, so much of her still clung to the old ways. She had not even written Robert to tell him about Abel. She knew Robert still considered

Rising Eagle his real father, even though he'd actually been sired by a cruel, drunken white trapper who had threatened to "drown the little rat" because Robert's fingers and toes were deformed when he was born. She would never regret giving that baby boy to Rising Eagle to raise.

In his later years Robert had also learned to love Abel, after he came to live with them. She should have written him right away, but she didn't want to interrupt his important work. What could he have done anyway? Nothing. And she wasn't even sure where Robert would be right now. She could only pray that he was not wounded, or worse. The fighting in the War Between the States had become very ugly, according to newspapers. Lists of the dead were posted every week in town and everyone read them with dread, afraid that they would recognize the name of a loved one.

She would write Robert soon. Somehow a mail carrier would find him. She would tell him to finish his work, that there was nothing he could do for her now anyway. The women of the congregation had been bringing over food, and a deacon had told her after a meeting that she would be allowed to stay on at the parsonage if she could find a way to pay for upkeep. They were going to build a new and bigger parsonage for whoever replaced Abel. That project was already underway. She would have shared the new parsonage with Abel, but that would never be now. She supposed she would have to turn to her talents as a seamstress to support herself. She'd done it once. She could do it again.

The gravesite services ended. She and William each bent down to pick up a fistful of dirt, throwing the cold soil onto the coffin. Oh, it was so hard to keep from totally breaking down! She needed to wail and keen like a Lakota woman, but these people would think that a heathen thing to do, and it would probably embarrass William, who hated anything "Indian." Instead she stoically forced back her need to sob and raised her chin, displaying her ability to hide her feelings. White people seemed to respect such things, as though any display of emotion was somehow despicable. Abel had always allowed her to show her emotions in the privacy of their home, but even he preferred not to do so in public. How different these people were from the Lakota in that way.

Still, she'd made her choice a long time ago, and this was her life. These truly kind people would accompany her to the church now for a supper in Abel's honor. His coffin would be covered, a headstone erected. Tonight she would go home . . . and sleep alone.

JULY 1862

Moon of the Red Cherries

CHAPTER TWENTY

"THOSE ARE THE white man's supply wagons, Brave Horse, and look how *many* there are!" Rising Eagle turned to his son. "We are not so many miles from Medicine Mountain. That is a place the white man must never touch, or even go near." He studied the long supply train of wagons snaking its way northward, toward a place where white men had found even more gold. They had etched a road right through Powder River country, heading north out of the place where the big-horned sheep grazed and into land already promised to the Lakota. "I do not like seeing those wagons so close to something so sacred."

"In their last treaty, the *wasicus* promised to save this north country for us," Brave Horse commented.

Rising Eagle sneered at the sight below. "They don't know the meaning of the word 'promise.' Their word is good only until they find something they want."

He faced his son and young Crazy Horse. Though now only twenty summers, Crazy Horse had already fought Crow and Arapaho. He had proved himself daring and surprisingly adept for his age, a born leader. Brave Horse was equally respected. Rising Eagle could hardly contain his pride at the fact that his son was a Shirt Wearer, a member of the *Akicitas*, the War Society. He and Crazy Horse rode together on many excursions against enemy tribes.

"Remember this," Rising Eagle told them. "Pride is worth dying for. Honor is worth dying for. Those who have chosen to abide by the white man's treaties, those who now drink the white man's fire water and who hang around Fort Laramie waiting for handouts, they have no pride and no honor. Some of us must cling to the old ways, and we must always *teach* the old ways, so that the true Lakota way will never be lost. I trust both of you to hold this in your hearts and to hand it down to your children, and teach them to do the same for *their* children so that no matter what happens, the Lakota way will live forever. When I look at the two of you, I see the hope of our Nation."

"Those are treasured words from a man I honor beyond measure," Crazy Horse told him. "I can only hope to match your own wisdom and bravery, Grandfather."

Rising Eagle smiled rather sadly at the term Grandfather, used as a sign of respect by younger men and women for their elders. Yes, he supposed that at fifty-four summers he should be called Grandfather. His youngest son, now called Thunder because of a vision quest, was eighteen summers. Even now he was riding with yet another war party, determined to steal horses from the Crow. Thunder, too, made Rising Eagle a proud father, as did his daughter. Once they returned to the main camp along the Powder River, he and Buffalo Dreamer would host the rite of Her Alone They Sing Over, a celebration of their daughter's coming of age. She Who Sings was now thirteen summers. It was time that she ceased the ways of a child. In another three or four summers he would be giving her away in marriage, but the man who took her for a wife would have to be worthy of the hand of Rising Eagle's daughter. It would cost him many horses . . . and much more.

"I think we should ride down and burn those wagons," Brave Horse told his father, interrupting his thoughts. "This is a good time to stop the white man. There are few soldiers here to protect them because of their own war against each other far away."

"Perhaps those soldiers will never come back here," Crazy Horse commented.

Rising Eagle nodded. "I would like to think that. It is interesting that the white men have told us we must not fight enemy tribes, yet now they fight each other in their own war. I will never understand their twisted tongues." He turned to the young men. "Go and get the others who wait for us back along the creek, Brave Horse. Tell them about the wagon train below and that we will make sure it does not reach its destination."

"Yes, Father!" Brave Horse turned and rode off. Rising Eagle saw a raging fire in Crazy Horse's eyes at the thought of attacking the wagon train.

"You have said that according to your medicine, you must always ride in the lead when attacking the enemy, Crazy Horse. When Brave Horse returns with the rest of the warriors, you will ride out first. I trust your medicine."

Crazy Horse held his chin proudly. "I am honored."

Rising Eagle raised his lance. He might carry the title of Grandfather, but that did not mean he was too old to do battle. Because of the words of the Feathered One in his most potent vision on Medicine Mountain years ago, no white man's bullet could touch him. He was to die by the sword, and so he could ride into any battle where white men used their guns to fight, and he would not be harmed. In the medicine bag he wore tied to his inner thigh were some of the hairs of the white buffalo, a gift from Buffalo Dreamer that had saved him from death when the white man's spotted disease attacked him. Yes, he was well protected!

Brave Horse returned with a force of forty more young warriors, all eager to put a good scare in the white men who now invaded one of the last strongholds and some of the best hunting grounds of the Lakota. It was time to teach them a lesson!

Rising Eagle nodded to Crazy Horse, who let out a war whoop and charged down the rise toward the wagon train. Rising Eagle and Brave Horse followed, side by side.

Yes. We are still strong, and we belong here. These young warriors will keep us strong! They charged the twelve very large wagons, each pulled by several oxen. Rising Eagle and his war party had the advantage, for the wagons were caught in a place where they could not circle for protection, and they were too heavy and cumbersome for a quick escape.

Rising Eagle was not close enough yet to use his lance, and so he shoved it into loops at the side of his horse and quickly whipped out an arrow from the quiver slung on his back. Although he now owned more than one of the white man's shooting irons, he still preferred bow and arrow in battle, something that took much more skill, something that was still a part of the old ways, the way a man *should* fight.

Guiding his well-trained war pony with only his thighs and feet, he positioned the arrow into his bow, drawing back and taking aim. The movement took only a moment, and in less time than a flash of lightning, the wagon driver who was his target fell with the arrow sunk into his neck. All around them rifles were fired, yet their bullets did not hit him. He knew that they would not. His medicine was great.

Now Crazy Horse was riding daringly up and down the long train of wagons, taunting the drivers. He rode right up to one and buried his hatchet into the man's skull. Brave Horse downed another with bow and arrow. Yes, his son was quite a warrior! The man fell with an arrow in his chest, but he got to his knees, trying to raise his rifle. Brave Horse rode right up to him and touched him with his coup stick.

"*Ayeee!*" Rising Eagle shouted with pride.

The man finally fell dead.

Now the entire war party rode up and down both sides of the wagon train, using arrows, hatchets, lances, rifles. These brave young men were skilled in eluding the white man's bullets, riding too swiftly for a good aim, sometimes hanging off the sides of their horses so the enemy could not see them at all. The *wasicus* would learn a good lesson today! Whoever was waiting for these men and the supplies they were bringing would soon learn that neither would arrive. They would think twice about wanting to stay in this place that belonged to the Lakota! Their soldiers were gone now, fighting their own war someplace else. These new settlers had no protection!

He saw another driver take aim at him. He yanked his lance from its resting place and charged the man, knowing no bullet could slay him. He grinned when the rifle appeared to misfire. Of course! He let out a piercing war whoop then as he rammed his lance into the man's belly, enjoying the wide-eyed horror on his enemy's face. He jerked the lance back out, and when the man fell forward over the edge of the wagon seat, he jammed the lance into his back.

The air was filled with the sound of rifle fire, screams and cries of pain, and the yips and war whoops of the warriors. In only a matter of minutes the rifle fire stopped, for there were no men left to fire them. Rising Eagle called for Two Owls, another fine young warrior who had vowed to never sign a treaty or give up lance and arrow for the white man's plows and hoes. Two Owls was their fire carrier, the man who kept hot coals with him at all times, stored in a buffalo horn.

"I am here, Rising Eagle!" The young man rode up to him, blood streaming from a wound on his forehead, a wound the young man suffered proudly, no doubt.

"Use something in one of the wagons to make a fire," Rising Eagle ordered. "Once it is burning, we will use pieces of it to set the rest of the wagons aflame."

Two Owls grinned and nodded, and Rising Eagle rode farther away to weigh the damage his warriors had inflicted in only a matter of minutes. Dead white men lay strewn about, and now the young warriors continued circling the wagons, enjoying the melee, shooting more arrows into the already-dead bodies. He heard one victim cry out to his right, and he looked to see Brave Horse scalping one white man who still lived. Then he slit his throat. He turned to face Rising Eagle, holding up the scalp. Rising Eagle grinned and held up his own bloody lance, honoring a deed well done.

Flames erupted in one of the wagons, and quickly several warriors ripped off burning canvas and pulled out other burning articles, throwing them into the other wagons, setting them on fire also. Many of the wagons were filled with lumber to build more homes in that place where more gold had been discovered. It would never arrive.

What was it about gold that made white men risk their lives to go and get it? It had absolutely no value. A man could not eat it. A man could not feed his horses with it. He could not make anything useful with it. One buffalo was worth more than all the gold that might be in those mountains, and the white men would soon learn that. If they wanted to die for gold, then let the fools do so. He himself would die for the sacred medicine wheel, for these beloved hunting grounds and for the buffalo that meant life to his people. He would die for his wife, his children, the entire Lakota nation. He would die honorably.

After several minutes all the oxen were cut loose, the wagons engulfed in flames. Rising Eagle breathed deeply with great satisfaction as he watched them burn. When more white men came along this new road and found these wagons and all their dead drivers, perhaps they would turn back.

The sky became black with billowing smoke. Brave Horse rode closer to his father, the bloody white man's scalp tied to the side of his horse. "Yellow Eagle was shot dead," he told his father. "Chasing Antelope is wounded and needs our medicine man."

Rising Eagle nodded, feeling sad for the loss of Yellow Eagle. "Yellow Eagle died bravely. We must tell his father and mother. We will wrap his body and make a travois to take it back with us for burial." He breathed deeply. "Still, only one of our warriors killed and one wounded . . . that is good. Look at all those dead white men." He raised his chin. "We are much better fighters than they, and our men are much braver. See how weak and useless these people are without their soldiers to protect them?" He shook his head. "What fools they are."

Brave Horse nodded in agreement. "We have much to celebrate when we return to camp."

Rising Eagle watched the burning wagons. "When I see something like this, see the smoke billowing into the sky, I try to let it take with it all the painful memories, all the loved ones I have lost over the years. I remember thinking once that Fort Pierre was as far as the *wasicus* would ever come. Now they swarm over this land like ants. Their numbers seem endless. But we will continue to fight them. I could never live like those who have chosen to give up the fight, those Laramie Loafers, begging for food. We might die trying to stop the white man's coming, but we will die proudly."

Brave Horse raised a fist and let out a long, screaming war whoop as Crazy Horse rode toward them, returning the scream with his own cry of victory.

AUGUST 1862

Moon of the Drying Meat

CHAPTER TWENTY-ONE

"WILLIAM, PLEASE WAIT until your brother comes home. Talk to him. At least *write* to him first and get his opinion. You have always respected his advice." Florence sat at the kitchen table with sixteen-year-old William, who scowled darkly at her pleading not to join the Union Army.

"Robert has been gone a long time. Our worlds are very different, and he doesn't have the same feelings about being Lakota that I do. He doesn't understand me anymore, and I don't understand him. Besides, I wouldn't know where to send the letter. He could be anywhere, now that he's volunteered to earn his degree by doctoring Confederate soldiers."

William spoke the last words with a sneer, then rose, kicking back his chair. "Can you believe it? Robert helping the *Confederates?*"

"He's doing what he has to do to get his degree, William. And knowing Robert, I doubt he's actually chosen sides. He is simply out there helping wounded men. He is a healer, William. That's all."

William shook his head, turning his dark gaze toward Florence again. "A healer. You always say that like you're talking about a medicine man with a rattle. You never stop, do you, Mother?"

"What do you mean?"

"You know what I mean. You dress like a white woman, speak like one, wear your hair like one. All your women friends are white, and you married a white man. But down inside you're still Lakota. I guess if you weren't still so Indian at heart, maybe I wouldn't get so angry about it. Sometimes I wish I could scrub off the outer layer of my skin and turn it white. I even used to try to do that when I was little." He turned away. "It never worked."

Florence felt the awful pain in her heart again. *You are the son of Rising Eagle*, she wanted to tell him. *You should be so very, very proud.* He'd met Rising Eagle only once, back at Fort Laramie when he was little. It was when Rising Eagle brought Robert to see her, and then he and Robert ended up helping heal William of a terrible fever and chest cold, using herbs and prayers.

William never knew then that it was his own father who held him in his arms and prayed over him that night. She never should have waited so long to tell William the truth. Now she feared it was too late, too hopeless.

"I am so sorry you feel as you do, William, but running off to join the army won't erase anything."

"It will help me feel better about myself, maybe earn me some respect. Maybe I will even go to West Point after this stupid war is over and become an officer." He faced her again. "Do you think the congregation might be able to arrange that for me?"

Florence's hopes brightened at least a little. Maybe if he did go there he would learn to have more pride in himself. And as he matured, maybe he could handle his heritage better and not be so hateful toward her. "I'll talk to them about it. I am sure that if your father were still alive, he would do everything he could to get you into officer's training, but he's gone. Maybe Robert could—"

"I'm not waiting for Robert, Mother. I have to get out of Springfield. I've completed my schooling, and my grades were good. Maybe that, combined with the fact that I've already joined the army, will help get me into West Point. Just have someone from the congregation write a letter, or maybe the new pastor. They all like you. They've even built that new parsonage and let you stay here. In the meantime, I might prove myself in some other way in the war." He paced. "You know how unhappy I am here. I'm old enough to join the army, and that's what I'm going to do."

Florence felt a painful lump in her throat. "Will you write?"

He shrugged. "Sure."

Florence fought tears, thinking how much he resembled his father, such a tall, strong stature, so stubborn. He looked much older than sixteen, and he was quite handsome, a young Rising Eagle, but not quite as dark, and slightly more slender. "Please write often, William. I'll be so worried, and so lonely, with both my sons gone in that awful war."

His scowl softened slightly as she sat down again. "I'm sorry I blame you for everything, Mother, but I can't help how I feel." He sighed deeply. "I'll write as often as I can so you won't worry about me. Maybe—maybe I'll even learn not to be so angry all the time. I don't know. It's just that when I read some of the stories we see in the newspapers about what the Sioux are doing out West, those damned killers like Red Cloud and Rising Eagle, murdering innocent whites, taking scalps . . ." He clenched his fists. "It just makes me so ashamed to carry that blood. I don't know why it doesn't bother you more."

You are talking about your own father. "William, it doesn't bother me because I understand how the Lakota are feeling right now. So does Robert, because he lived with them. How would you feel if it were the other way around? What if there were many more Lakota than white men, and they came here and told us we had to leave this place where whites have lived for many, many years? What if they came here and said they wanted this land and we had to leave it or die? What if they took away our only means of survival? How would *you* feel about something like that?"

He waved her off. "It's not the same. It's just a matter of a superior race, a more educated people taking over."

"Superior race? How *dare* you talk that way! There are many ways in which the *Lakota* are superior to the *white* man! I have tried so hard to teach you that, William. Education has nothing to do with it. And if the white man were not trying to take everything away from them, they would not do some of the things they do. They are becoming *desperate!*"

He leaned back, rolling his eyes. "It's just the way of progress, Mother. It can't be helped. The whites are here to stay. They're more educated, have superior weapons, and there are a hell of a lot more of them than there are Indians, so what must be must be. In the meantime, I have to deal with the fact that I am half Lakota. I have to deal with the lousy remarks every time another slaughter by savages hits the newspapers. All they have to do is settle down on reservations and learn our ways and learn to live like civilized people, like you learned to do. And Robert. Why is that so hard for them? Why do they have to murder and rape and pillage and scalp? They *deserve* whatever happens to them. And if by joining the army that means I'll have to go out West someday and kill Indians, then I'll do it, without one ounce of guilt. Heck, even the Crow and the Shoshoni help scout against them now."

Florence felt sick. "Fine." She held his gaze firmly. "You have chosen your way, William, but I promise you that the day will come when you will regret such words. The day will come when you understand. I don't know how it will happen, but it will happen." She looked away. "Go then. Go join the army and get a taste of killing. You had better get used to it if you intend to do the same against your own people someday."

The room hung silent for a moment. Then William rose. "I'm sorry this hurts you, Mother, but don't call them my people. They are *your* people, not mine." He walked around and put a hand on her shoulder. "I'm leaving in the morning."

He gave her shoulder a squeeze and left the room. Florence put a hand to her mouth, smothering the sound of her sobs.

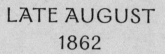

LATE AUGUST
1862

Summer Moon

CHAPTER TWENTY-TWO

THIS WAS A proud and glorious moment for Buffalo Dreamer. Her daughter had graduated to womanhood today. She was the center of attention in the *Her Alone They Sing Over* ceremony. Buffalo Dreamer danced around a central fire with other women, while their husbands and prospective lovers sat in an outer circle watching proudly.

"Her alone they sing over," Buffalo Dreamer sang about her daughter. The men joined in the singing, and drummers kept the rhythm of the songs and dancing. Once called Songbird, now renamed She Who Sings, the young girl danced with her mother, a red stripe painted down her nose and across her forehead, signifying that the Oglala medicine man, Walks With Wolves, had given her all the instructions she must hear on becoming a woman and remaining chaste. She Who Sings wore a beautifully quilled, white fringed tunic, much like the tunic Buffalo Dreamer wore when she celebrated this same rite. Her dress then had been made by her beloved grandmother many years ago, and the memory remained painfully sweet. Buffalo Dreamer had loved her *Uncheedah* deeply, and she would never forget the night before she was given in marriage to Rising Eagle, when she slept in her grandmother's arms for the last time.

How could so many years go by so quickly? Once Brave Horse

and young Thunder took wives, and once She Who Sings married, she would likely be a grandmother herself soon thereafter. How quickly she had gone from being a granddaughter to being old enough to be a grand*mother*. She dearly wished her own mother could have been here to watch She Who Sings's coming of age, but this was not a night to be mourning the dead. It was rather a night to celebrate her daughter's womanhood. She Who Sings was beautiful indeed, a daughter of whom they could be extremely proud.

Buffalo Dreamer continued the dancing and singing, feeling very proud of the grand feast she'd prepared to share with the entire clan, sweet, juicy buffalo meat from a special hunt Rising Eagle and Brave Horse conducted so that the family could properly celebrate this moment by sharing their joy and bounty with others. She felt the relief of having the ceremony over with. Preparations and just plain nervousness over being the hostess of such an important event had finally vanished into this moment of joy and dancing.

Buffalo Dreamer felt beautiful herself tonight, proud that she'd not grown fat in her advancing years. Whenever she came into the area where Rising Eagle sat, she swayed a little more provocatively, smiling enticingly at him, moving to the rhythm of the drums. She liked the admiration and desire in his handsome eyes.

Yes, he was still strong, hardly changed from their younger days. He still rode into battle, still faced his enemy with courage and daring, still brought home plenty of meat. It was because of men like Rising Eagle that the Lakota remained strong and realized many a victory. In their last raid on a white man's wagon train Rising Eagle and his warriors had come upon a supply of rifles and ammunition and had brought them back. Now this clan of Oglala was well armed, ready for more raids against the foolish, insistent white men who just did not seem to understand that the more they tried to invade and conquer Lakota land, the more of them would die.

Let them come! The Lakota were ready. With leaders like Rising Eagle and Red Cloud, and young, brave warriors like Brave Horse and Crazy Horse to step into their place in the future, there was much hope for her People.

Hope. It was what she and Rising Eagle had found on Medicine Mountain after the terrible massacre of so many of their people at Blue Water Creek. It was what she saw in the eyes of every young warrior and every young woman. It was what she heard in their songs and in the drumming. It was what she felt as she danced. Hope.

She danced in front of Rising Eagle again, and he got to his feet, still standing tall and straight, his belly still flat. He was very fetching tonight, coup feathers in his hair, wearing the bear claw necklace she'd made for him so many years ago, from the claws of the hump-backed bear he'd killed to show her father his worthiness. He still bore scars on his shoulders and back from a near-death battle with that bear before it finally died by Rising Eagle's knife. He liked telling that story, liked bragging about the scars.

She danced closer to him, studying the white stripes of peace he'd painted on his face for his daughter's ceremony. No Lakota woman could ask for a more stunning man as husband, and looking into his dark eyes, she knew she would die for him, and he for her.

She moved closer, and the drums seemed to echo her own heartbeat. Indeed, the Lakota considered the drum to be the heartbeat of their people, the heartbeat of Mother Earth. This moment, this night, was filled with magic, with joy, life, love, celebration. The singing came easily. Rising Eagle began moving with her, both of them dancing now. He kept in rhythm with her, their movements building a provocative, sensual desire they both still enjoyed for each other.

Buffalo Dreamer remained in one place, slowly turning, while Rising Eagle danced around her. His manly essence permeated her womanly senses, stirring her deeply. After all they had been through, all they had lost over the years to the enemy, to the elements, to the white man's diseases; after all the terrible mourning, there still had been moments of joy like this one, and there would be more.

Rising Eagle picked her up in his arms. Several other couples had already gone off into the darkness or to their tepees. It was expected during dances like this one. A few young couples visited under the blanket, a way of courting. Married couples did much more, and she rested her head on Rising Eagle's shoulder as he carried her out of the light of the fire and into tall grass not far from the river.

"You never change," he told her. "Because you are a holy woman, you are blessed with eternal beauty."

"And in my eyes you also have not changed," she whispered in his ear.

"Nor has my desire for my wife changed." He laid her down into the grass and ran his hands along her thighs, pushing up her tunic. She had worn nothing under it, fully expecting this to happen, wanting it to happen. They were happy tonight, and being happy and in love could only lead to the most intense demonstration of that love.

She sat up slightly and helped him untie his breechcloth, gently caressing his already-swollen shaft. "I am full of joy this night. I feel great hope, Rising Eagle, and I feel great pride in being Rising Eagle's woman."

He leaned down, tasting her mouth as he forced her back into the grass. She opened herself to him, and he filled her with fiery thrusts, moving rhythmically, sometimes pulling himself away to tease her and make her beg him to come back inside her. Finally she felt the exotic pulsating he sometimes brought out in her that made her groan his name and arch up to him in sweet abandon, wanting every inch of him, wanting to please him, aching with the pleasure of being his chosen woman, and the fact that in all these years he'd kept his promise to never take another wife, even though she could no longer give him children.

They moved in rhythm with the beating drums, in rhythm with Mother Earth. Buffalo Dreamer looked beyond him to the stars that glittered in the black sky, thinking how somewhere up there was the holy Feathered One who cared for all their ancestors.

Once Rising Eagle's life spilled into her, he relaxed against her, and they lay there quietly for several minutes before he spoke. "I was very proud of you and of She Who Sings today."

"I am glad."

He sighed and rolled onto his back in the grass. "Do you know that Brave Horse shared the blanket tonight with Red Eagle's daughter?"

"Beaver Woman?" Buffalo Dreamer sat up. "Did they stay long under the blanket?"

Rising Eagle laughed lightly. "Long enough. I have a feeling he will be playing his flute for her."

"But you said that just a few days ago he swore he could never love again after Yellow Bonnet."

"I have seen it coming, the sly, fetching looks Beaver Woman has been giving him, his stubborn refusal to acknowledge that he is touched by her beauty. He is still young and virile. He can't help but desire a woman again, and want children of his own. I think Beaver Woman can make him see he cannot mourn Yellow Bonnet forever."

Buffalo Dreamer lay back down. "I hope you're right. I would like to see him take a wife. Now, if we could by some miracle find the white robe, we would be assured that nothing but happiness lies ahead."

"I fear we will never again see the robe." Rising Eagle said, as he moved on top of her again.

Buffalo Dreamer ran a finger over his brow. "I believe we will, my husband. I have had dreams in which I am covered with the white robe. Somehow, some way, it will again belong to us."

He leaned down and licked her mouth. "Just as *I* belong to *you*." He trailed his tongue down to lick her throat, and she breathed deeply with sweet ecstasy when again he entered her. Yes, this had been a very good day. Perhaps she could not give this man more children, but their blood would live on in their grandchildren, and that was good.

PART TWO

Our land is more valuable than your money. It will last forever. It will not even perish by the flames of fire. As long as the sun shines and the waters flow, this land will be here to give life to men and animals. We cannot sell the lives of men and animals; therefore, we cannot sell this land. It was put here for us by the Great Spirit and we cannot sell it because it does not belong to us. You can count your money and burn it within the nod of a buffalo's head, but only the Great Spirit can count the grains of sand and the blades of grass of these plains. As a present to you, we will give you anything we have that you can take with you; but the land, never.

—RESPONSE BY AN UNNAMED BLACKFOOT CHIEF UPON BEING ASKED TO SIGN AWAY LAND NEAR THE NORTHERN BORDER OF MONTANA. DATE UNKNOWN.

JULY 1863

Hot Moon

CHAPTER TWENTY-THREE

JULES CARPENTER YANKED the white buffalo robe he'd purchased at Fort Laramie out of his canvas-topped wagon. He slung it over the branch of a dead cottonwood tree along the river where he'd parked the wagon.

"Damn thing," he muttered. He swore the robe was the reason his wife and daughter were so sick. They probably picked up some kind of ungodly illness from something in that robe, probably because it had once been used by dirty Indians. Could germs live that long?

What the hell did he know about germs? He only knew that all Indians had lice and were filthy. He wished he'd never bought the thing from that trader's wife, but how often did a man come across a white buffalo robe? He'd figured it would make an interesting conversation piece over the fireplace of the home he would build when he reached California.

Caroline leaned out the wagon gate then and vomited again, while their little three-year-old girl, Lilly, lay crying inside. There wasn't much he could do but sit and wait, hoping they both got better so they could rejoin another train of wagons that might come along.

Things had gone pretty well since leaving Independence, until he bought that robe. Then he'd had a wheel freeze up on his wagon. After that one of his oxen up and died, and a few days later he fell and sprained his knee. He still limped from the pain. Now it was so hot he could barely stand it, and Caroline and Lilly had taken ill. He just couldn't bring himself to force them to continue laying miserably in the constantly bouncing, jostling wagon. They needed true rest, so he'd left the wagon train and stopped here.

He hoped another wagon train would pass this way in not too many days or he and his family would have to finish out this trip by themselves. He didn't look forward to that, considering all the Indian trouble out here. The worst of it seemed to be up north in Montana, or so he'd been told, but here along the Platte River it was Cheyenne who created most problems, damn beggars!

He unhitched his oxen and tethered them near the river, then knelt on the riverbank and splashed cool water over his face. He removed his hat and dipped it into the river, then put it on his head to let the water spill over him. Its coolness helped his spirits, and he decided he'd better make camp and fill some buckets for Caroline and Lilly to sponge away the heat. Maybe it would help them feel better.

He rose and walked back to the wagon to begin unloading supplies, then heard the pounding hooves of several horses. He hurriedly climbed up the front of the wagon and grabbed his rifle from under the wagon seat. Just beyond his camp and the few trees surrounding it was wide-open land, and he could readily see the approaching riders. He watched them warily, glad to see they were white men, not Indians. Still, out here a man couldn't trust anybody.

Maybe he should have at least continued on to Independence Rock or the South Pass, where there was a chance of finding others. That would have put him in Shoshoni country, according to the wagon master who'd left him behind. Shoshoni were supposedly friendly, but you couldn't trust the Cheyenne, and they roamed all over these parts, as did buffalo hunters, men not much more trustworthy than the Indians. The group approaching him looked more like such men.

He kept his rifle ready in his right hand as the riders came closer, a motley-looking bunch of unshaven men wearing soiled buckskins, some wearing only leather vests with no shirts because of the heat. He counted five men and three extra packhorses piled with buffalo hides. He nodded as they came closer, realizing he had the greatest protection there was, especially if they meant to do harm to his wife.

"You'd best not come any closer!" he called out to them.

They reined their mounts, glancing at each other, all gruff looking.

"Just comin' in for water, mister. Don't mean no harm," one of them spoke up. "Name's Dustin Myers. These men with me are all buffalo hunters."

"I figured that. You ought to know my wife and kid in the wagon are sick. Might be cholera. They haven't drunk out of the river yet, or washed in it, so you're probably okay. Just don't come near the wagon."

The men slowly dismounted and led their horses to the river, watching Jules as they moved cautiously around him at a distance. They spoke quietly to each other. Jules stayed close to the wagon, resting against the wagon wheel, still not sure he should trust them. A rugged man himself, not afraid of much, the fact remained they were five against one.

All five men literally fell into the river to cool off, and Jules couldn't blame them. The July heat was miserable, and he couldn't help wondering if that wasn't all that was wrong with Caroline and Lilly. He felt half-sick from the heat himself.

The hunters finished their refreshment and turned to leave the river when one of them spotted the white robe Jules had draped over the tree limb. "I'll be goddamned!" the man commented. He turned to Jules. "That your robe?"

Jules shrugged. "It is, but I kind of regret getting the thing."

The hunter walked closer to the robe, as did the others. The one who'd asked Jules about it fingered the white fur, then looked the robe over more closely. All five men commented to each other about the good condition of the robe, except for a burn spot. It was obvious to Jules that they greatly admired the robe, and the man who had spoken to Jules first left the others, walking back to Jules.

He was taller and broader than the others, and meaner looking. Jules suspected he was more or less the leader of the bunch.

"My name is Clete Harris," he told Jules, tobacco juice showing at the corners of his mouth. He spit before continuing. "Where'd you get an albino robe?"

Jules removed his hat and wiped sweat from his forehead with his shirtsleeve. He hung the hat on a hook at the side of the wagon, feeling pity for his wife when he heard her moan. He was glad that Lilly had at least stopped crying. "Got it back at Fort Laramie," he answered. "Supposedly belonged to the Sioux leader, Red Cloud. Who knows? The woman who sold it to me ran a trading store there and was getting rid of everything. Said the robe was bad luck; something about it being full of Indian spirits. I guess some army man had it a while and fell off his horse and broke his neck. Then some kid private got it and claimed he didn't have bad luck, but he sold it to the trader woman's husband because he was going off to fight for the North. The woman said she was sure she saw Indian ghosts around the trading post after her husband bought the thing, and then he just dropped dead one day. She wanted to get rid of it, and I figured it would look nice over a fireplace in my home, once I get to California." He sighed. "But I've had bad luck since I got the thing. Now my wife and kid are sick. Something tells me they'll get better if I get rid of the robe."

Clete grinned. "I'll take it from you, mister. I've got no worry about bad luck. Hell, an albino robe could bring us some good money back in St. Louis. We'll be heading that way soon. What do you want for the robe?"

Jules ran a hand through his dark hair and realized how badly he needed a haircut. At least he managed to wash and shave every morning, which was a lot more than these men did. Their odor was beginning to upset his stomach. "Heck, I don't know. What's worth a lot to one man isn't worth much to another. The woman gave me the thing for a buck. I reckon' that's all I have a right to ask."

Clete nodded. "Well, now, mister, you're a right honest man." He looked Jules over in a way that told Jules that if he'd tried to drive a hard bargain, these men would simply have taken what they wanted whether he liked it or not. The man reached into a small, deep pocket sewn onto his buckskin shirt and pulled out a few coins, then counted them out to Jules. "There's your dollar. And I'm right glad my friends and I stopped here."

Jules nodded. "Good luck."

"We just *had* ourselves some good luck," Clete answered. He let out a "yee-hah!" that made Jules jump. He gripped his rifle tighter as Clete told the others he'd just purchased the robe "for a lousy buck!" Jules figured he'd probably just been cheated, but who cared? It was worth it to get rid of the robe and get rid of the hunters. The others laughed and slapped Clete on the back as he took the robe and slung it over the top of a stack of other robes on one of the packhorses. He tied it down, then mounted his horse and gave Jules a mock salute. "Hope you make it to California all right, mister, and that the misses will be okay."

Jules nodded in reply, and the five men turned their horses and rode off, still laughing and celebrating as though they'd struck gold. Jules breathed a sigh of relief that they had left with no trouble. He walked to the back of the wagon to ask his wife how she was feeling.

"Who was here?" she asked weakly.

"Some buffalo hunters. They bought the albino robe off me."

"They did? I'm glad. Something about it bothered me."

"Me, too. Anything I can do for you, honey?"

"No. Lilly is sleeping. She seems to be a little better. Her fever is gone. I'm beginning to feel a little better myself."

"Really?"

She sat up, rubbing her eyes. "Yes. Ever since I was sick a half-hour or so ago, I've begun to feel better. And as soon as I heard the men riding away, the sick feeling in my stomach began to leave me."

Jules turned to watch the dust cloud that showed the men were still riding hard toward the east. "My God," he muttered softly. The damn thing really *was* cursed.

NOVEMBER 1864

Beaver Moon

CHAPTER TWENTY-FOUR

FLORENCE PUSHED ASIDE the lace curtain at the front door. "Robert!" She flung open the door and fell into her son's embrace. "You're home and you're well and—" She leaned back a moment to look him over. "You *are* well? You haven't been wounded?"

Her son shook his head, smiling. "I suffered one very minor wound. I was never really in the Confederate army, you know. I just agreed to doctor the wounded soldiers as part of my training, and I am very glad I did, Mother. Look what I found in Tennessee!" His grin widened as he urged a very young woman to step forward. "This is my wife, Rebecca."

Florence put a hand to her mouth in surprise, gazing at a very pretty, dark-haired woman who was just barely that, more a young girl. Her son was thirty years old now, and as though to read her thoughts . . .

"Becky is nineteen, and the sweetest, most uncomplaining, most generous young lady you could ever meet."

Rebecca blushed and shook her head. "Robert exaggerates," she told Florence.

Florence took hold of both her hands. "Oh, my, I can't believe this. You're so lovely . . . and . . . oh, I have so many questions!"

"And we will answer all of them," Robert told her. He enveloped both his new wife and his mother in his arms. "I'm just glad to be home, and to have both my favorite women right here. I know it won't take long for the two of you to get to know and love each other." He kissed his mother's forehead.

"Are you home to stay?" Florence asked, wanting to cry for joy.

"Yes, I am. I am a full-fledged doctor now, graduated and all."

"Oh, Robert, this is such wonderful news! I've been so lonely and so . . ." She burst into tears. "After Abel—" She nearly collapsed against his chest, and Robert wrapped his arms around her and helped her inside. Rebecca picked up two carpetbags and came in after them, closing the door.

"I'm so sorry, Mother. By the time I received your letter he'd been gone several weeks. I'm sorry you had to suffer that alone."

"It's all right. Your letters helped. I knew it would be impossible for you to be here." Florence wiped at her eyes. "He was my whole world, Robert."

"I understand."

"He changed my life so completely all those years ago, and he taught me everything I know. I've been trying to decide what to do, where to go. The parishioners have let me stay here at the old parsonage, but I feel guilty doing so. I didn't know when you might return, or if you'd decide to do your doctoring farther east. I've just been so lost. You have no idea how good it is to see you."

"Mrs. Kingsley, I'm so sorry," Rebecca told her. "I wish we could have come home sooner."

"Let's sit down, Mother. Can Becky and I get you anything?"

"No." Florence shook her head, leaning on Robert's arm as he led her into the parlor. "Just sit beside me, both of you, and let it sink in that you're really here. A new daughter-in-law! I am so glad for both of you. Tell me how you met. I don't want to talk about Abel's death. I want to know about this marriage. How and when did all this happen?" She pulled a handkerchief from a pocket in the skirt of her dress to wipe at her tears while the three of them sat down on a sofa, Florence between her son and her new daughter-in-law.

"I'm sorry I was never able to see Abel again," Robert told her, taking a moment to swallow back his own tears. "I loved him as a father, the same as I loved Rising Eagle in my early years." He quickly wiped at his eyes. "I was blessed with two wonderful and very different men as fathers. God only knows if I'll ever see Rising Eagle again." He shook his head. "One thing we know for sure is that he's certainly still alive, considering the fact that he's actually made the newspapers in the East." He laughed lightly. "Can you imagine what he would think of that? He'd probably be very proud that he's known in the East as a notorious and feared Lakota leader."

Florence smiled through tears. "I am sure he would." She wiped at her eyes again and took another good look at Rebecca, a slender, tiny woman with dark eyes that seemed too big for her petite face. "You are so pretty, and your eyes tell me Robert was right about how sweet you are. We have so much to talk about, don't we, Rebecca? Oh, how I wish Abel had lived to see you, to know Robert is married." She took hold of the woman's hand and then Robert's, facing her son. "How did this happen?"

Robert wiped at more tears. "I met Becky while I was moving with soldiers through Tennessee. She was very sick and needed doctoring. Her father was, shall we say, not extremely happy that the man who came to help her was Indian. He wasn't going to let me touch her, but her mother threatened to shoot him if he didn't let me help."

Florence smiled through tears, shaking her head.

"I might have died of a snake bite if not for Robert," Rebecca added, her words coming in a strong southern drawl. "And since then I've seen him treat some pretty terrible wounds after an engine accident on the riverboat we took when we left Tennessee. I've even helped him a time or two. He's a wonderful doctor, Mrs. Kingsley."

"Please call me Mother." Florence studied her lovingly. "I always knew he'd make a good doctor. He grew up being taught by an Oglala medicine man, and then he wanted to learn the white man's way. And we found out he was so smart, so quick to learn. He has a gift, you know. Some of his healing is spiritual."

Rebecca's eyes filled with love. "I know. I felt it when he healed me. It's his Indian side that gives him a kind of spiritual power."

Florence squeezed her hand. "Then you understand that part of him, and you don't care that he's . . . that Robert is half Lakota?"

"Of course not. What does it matter? He's a wonderful, gentle, caring man." Rebecca's smile faded. "I'm afraid I never quite convinced my father that was all that mattered."

"Oh, dear." Florence looked at Robert again, noticing he wore a well-tailored wool suit. How handsome he was, and so much more filled out and manly looking than when he first left to go to medical school. His hair was black and shiny, but he wore it cut short now, like a white man. "Her father gave you a lot of trouble?" she asked her son.

Robert rose and walked to the fireplace. "Let's just say that right now he's probably wondering where we are." He faced her again. "We eloped."

"We had no choice," Rebecca added. "I know my mother understands, but Father never would have accepted it."

"Oh, how sad."

Rebecca rose and went to stand beside Robert. "It can't be helped. I'll miss my mother dearly, but she knew I was running away. She urged me to go. My place is with Robert now, and I've never been so happy."

Florence thought how wonderful they looked together. "How I wish William could have accepted his Indian blood with the strength and pride you have, Robert."

"You still haven't heard from him since he ran off to join the Union Army?"

"No. He promised to write often, but I knew he wouldn't. Now, once I do hear from him, I'll have to tell him that the deacons here just couldn't pull enough strings to get him into West Point. You know how hard it is to get into a place like that. It takes prestige, the right connections, recommendations." She felt more tears wanting to come at the hurt she'd suffered over William. Should she tell Robert the truth about the boy's true parentage? "William was so hopeful. Now he'll blame his inability to get into West Point on the fact that he has Indian blood. We have no way of knowing if that's true or not, but he is so bitter, Robert."

"Mother, I don't believe he really hates you," Robert soothed.

"He blames everything that goes wrong in his life on the fact that he is half Lakota," she said, shaking her head. "I ache for him to just be my sweet little boy again. And I worry so. He told me once that if he couldn't get into West Point that after the war he would definitely try to join with troops who would be sent West. He wants to go back out to where he spent his childhood, only not for fond memories. He wants to go to fight Indians." She shook her head, crying quietly for a moment. "To fight Indians," she repeated. "He is so angry inside . . . so confused. I wish you could have been here to talk to him, to reason with him."

Robert came over to sit beside her again, putting an arm around her shoulders. "Mother, he'll come around some day. And I promise to try to find him and talk with him. In fact, if we follow through on my plans, we just might find him anyway. Maybe we'll even find Rising Eagle again."

"What?" Florence blew her nose and dabbed at her eyes. "What are you talking about?"

He sighed. "Well, actually I came here to spend some time with you before Becky and I go west. I've decided I want very much to find Rising Eagle, and I want to use what I've learned to help the Lakota."

He leaned back, and Rebecca rose and walked to stand behind him, putting her hands on his shoulders. "Things are going to get gradually worse for them, Mother. You and I both know that," Robert continued. "Maybe there is something I can do to help. I don't know just what, other than be there to help doctor them. They would trust me more than a white man's doctor, and with more and more whites going west, there is going to be more disease among the Lakota, and maybe eventually starvation. They can't provide for themselves like they used to, and you know more soldiers will end up being sent west again. With all of that, and William probably ending up out there himself, I think I should head west and see if there is anything I can do." He gave Florence a squeeze. "And now that Abel is gone, and you feel you should leave here, why don't you come with us?"

Florence dabbed at her eyes again. Robert had always been so good-hearted and thoughtful. She thought about what a cruel, drunken abuser his father had been; she believed that gentle side came from his Lakota blood. She looked up at Rebecca, then looked around the parlor. "It will be so hard to leave this place where I've spent the last several years with Abel. But Illinois is Abel's home, not mine."

"That's right. Your true home is out in Nebraska and Wyoming, the Dakotas or Montana. All of it belongs . . . or I should say belonged . . . to the Lakota. That's home to you, Mother."

Florence rose and walked to a window, surprised at how her heart rushed at the thought of going back to her roots, maybe even finding some of her people again . . . maybe finding Rising Eagle and Buffalo Dreamer . . . and William. She faced Robert. "I wouldn't want to be a burden."

"Oh, I'm sure you won't be," Rebecca spoke up. "I am already—" she reddened again "—with child. It would be wonderful having you with me out there. I wouldn't know anyone else, and I'd be afraid, having my first baby and all. And Robert might be so busy that I'd be alone a lot. I would love to have you with me."

"A baby! Oh, my goodness. I get to be a grandmother!" Again the tears wanted to come. "You two have made me so happy. An hour ago I wondered if I could ever be happy again, and you show up at my doorway bringing me so much hope, so much to live for." She turned to Robert. "Where exactly will you go?"

"I figure Fort Laramie is our best bet," Robert told her. "And with the Union Pacific already nearly reaching Omaha we can take a train most of the way now. We'll stay here a couple more weeks and help you decide what to keep and what to sell. I want to thank the congregation for what they've done for me, and for you, maybe have a picnic or something." He sobered. "And, of course, I want to visit Abel's grave. He was the most wonderful, generous man I've ever known, and the way he accepted me when I decided to stay and live with you, I'll never forget that. I owe it to him to find his son and do what I can to erase the anger in William's heart and bring him closer to his mother again."

But William isn't Abel's son . . . or mine, Florence was tempted to admit. *No, not now.* The moment was too wonderful, and Robert had enough to think about for now. "I hope you can do all that, Robert. And I think it's wonderful that you want to help your people. I am so glad you have always had pride in who you are."

He smiled sadly. "Rising Eagle instilled that pride in me. It hurt so much, having to leave him all those years ago; but strangely enough I think he understood why I chose to stay with you." He sighed. "I owe him so much. He is the one who taught me I was meant to be a healer. And when I think about the miracle of my own healing on Medicine Mountain, about the power of that man's spirituality, then I understand the importance of being Lakota, and the power I also have to heal. I have never lost touch with that part of me, Mother."

Florence walked over and took hold of his hand again, looking down to study his fingers, fingers that were deformed when she gave him as a baby to Rising Eagle ... fingers that were miraculously healed one night on Medicine Mountain, through Rising Eagle's prayers. "All right, I'll go west with you," she told him. "That's where I really belong, where my heart still lies. I'll write William and tell him where I'm going. I'll just have to pray he gets the letter, and pray that if he does end up going west, we'll find him." She squeezed his hands. "And I hope you find Rising Eagle. That will be very difficult. He's considered a hostile now, among those who refuse to abide by any treaty and refuse to go live on the designated reservations. He is crafty, and he apparently rides with a leader named Red Cloud, and a reckless young warrior called Crazy Horse. He most certainly won't want to come near any white man's fort to see you."

"Then I will just have to go out and find him, won't I?"

Florence smiled through tears. "That won't be easy either. If Rising Eagle doesn't want to be found, he won't be found. And yet he could be right behind you without you knowing it. That's how clever a Lakota warrior can be."

"Do you think I don't remember that?" Robert grinned as he stood up. "I feel good about this, Mother. Something is telling me it's important that I do this. I had a dream once, a long, long time ago. The one I called brother as I was growing up, Brave Horse, was wounded and needed me. I know how important dreams are, and I see much trouble ahead. Once this terrible Civil War is over, the government will turn its attention to problems with the Sioux and other tribes. Things can only get worse then. I'm afraid for the Lakota . . . for Rising Eagle and Brave Horse and the woman I called mother for so many years, Buffalo Dreamer."

Florence nodded. "Then we will all go west and do what we can to help." She looked at Rebecca. "Are you sure you can do this?"

An obvious look of concern came into Rebecca's eyes. "It frightens me a little, but where Robert goes, I go. As long as I am with him, I'm not afraid."

"Good." Florence felt stronger, comforted. "Then it's Fort Laramie for the three of us."

DECEMBER 1864

Long Night Moon

CHAPTER TWENTY-FIVE

"A TERRIBLE THING has happened to the Shihenna!" a crier announced. He charged through the Oglala camp shouting the announcement. "Again the white man has done a terrible thing!"

Rising Eagle heard dogs barking excitedly. He recognized the voice of the crier as that of Two Owls. He rose from where he'd been sitting peacefully smoking a white man's pipe, one given to him long ago by Agent "Broken Hand" Fitzpatrick.

"What have the *wasicus* done now?" he grumbled, wrapping a wolf-skin cape around himself before ducking outside the tepee.

Buffalo Dreamer told She Who Sings to stay inside and watch a pot of buffalo meat and turnips that cooked over the central fire. Already wearing her knee-high winter moccasins, she wrapped herself in a bearskin cloak and followed Rising Eagle outside, joining other women who'd gathered to see what was going on. The Northern Shihenna were their good friends, as well as allies against the white man.

Buffalo Dreamer felt alarm at the sight before her. She counted thirteen Shihenna, three women, two children, one young warrior and seven old men making their way into camp. All but one old man walked, for they had only one horse among them. They brought no travois, no supplies, and they were huddled into blankets. One older woman fell, and several Lakota women rushed to help her. These visitors were obviously starving, and suffering from the freezing weather. None were dressed warm enough. She and several other women rushed to help the rest of the women and the children, taking them to various tepees to help them get warm and to feed them.

So, what was the terrible thing the white man had done this time? Buffalo Dreamer helped one old man and woman to her dwelling, and Rising Eagle followed, offering his wolf-skin cape to the woman. Buffalo Dreamer removed her winter moccasins and gave those to the woman also.

"They will still be warm inside," she told the woman. "I have another pair for myself."

She Who Sings spread out an extra buffalo robe for the woman. "We can give you something to eat," she told her.

Buffalo Dreamer removed her bearskin cloak and draped it over the old man's shoulders. "Both of you stay close to the fire."

The old man, skinny and withered, nodded, his white hair crusted with ice.

"This is our daughter, She Who Sings," Buffalo Dreamer explained, nodding to her daughter. "I am Buffalo Dreamer, and this is my husband, Rising Eagle," she added, nodding toward Rising Eagle as he sat down near the old man.

"We know of you," the old woman told Buffalo Dreamer. "And we are grateful for the shelter and the sharing of robes."

"What has happened?" Rising Eagle questioned the old man.

Buffalo Dreamer noticed a tear run down his cheek as he watched She Who Sings stirring the mixture of turnips and meat.

"It is hard for him to talk about it," the old woman replied. "He is called Old Beaver, and he saw his granddaughter killed by the white men who attacked us. I am Red Horse Woman, Old Beaver's cousin."

"What white men attacked you?" Rising Eagle pressed Red Horse Woman.

"We are not sure. They were not the regular Blue Coats. We were camped with Black Kettle's band at Sand Creek, waiting for supplies and for the Colorado soldiers to come and tell us where we were to go next. We had been told to wait there, and so we did.

Black Kettle is a peaceful man. He did nothing to cause trouble. He even flew the flag of the white man above his tepee and wore a medal of peace given him by the white man's great leader in that place called Washington when soldiers took him there once to visit and show him that place."

Her voice began to crack, and Buffalo Dreamer offered the woman some water. Red Horse Woman drank from a leather pouch before continuing.

"They attacked for no reason. Suddenly our tepees began exploding. Those terrible big guns were being fired at our village, and many were hurt or killed by pieces of flying metal from the explosions. None of us were ready for the attack, and in our camp were mostly women and children and old men. They rode down on us like wild men, looking like they were hungry to kill. They chased down little children and sliced open their throats or split open their heads. They ran their swords through women and old men. We are lucky to have escaped with our lives. Hundreds were killed, and I saw them cutting open women's bellies and pulling out their insides and cutting off their breasts."

The old woman suddenly burst into tears and began keening.

"They raped my granddaughter and then split her open," the old man said. "They cut off her breast and scalped her." He looked at Rising Eagle, more tears on his cheeks. "It was like nothing I have ever seen. No other enemy of ours has ever done something so terrible, not even the Pawnee. Nor have we ever done such things to our enemy. These white men, they have no honor when they fight. They kill women and little children and call it a great victory." He shook his head. "I do not understand such men." His frail body jerked in a sob.

"What the soldiers did at Blue Water Creek was bad enough," Rising Eagle fumed. "But what they did at Sand Creek sounds much worse! They are *cowards*, and they should *die* for this!"

Red Horse Woman quieted her keening, wiping at tears before she spoke again. "We ran away to the north to find our Lakota friends," she said, staring at the cook pot hanging over the fire. "Yours is the first camp we came upon. Others fled in other directions. We are not sure who survived and who did not. They burned all our belongings." She looked at Rising Eagle. "You are camped too far south. It is dangerous. You should stay in the Black Hills, or in the north country, along the Powder River."

"That's where we usually stay," Rising Eagle answered, "but we came farther south to find buffalo. Every year it becomes harder to locate a herd, thanks to the white man. And now he tries to come into the north country to find more gold, right through the mountains of the big-horned sheep. We have attacked his supply trains often and will keep doing so if he keeps coming."

Old Beaver shook his head. "After what I have seen, it is obvious they have no honor. Their words cannot be believed or trusted."

"That's why I have never put my mark on any of their treaties," Rising Eagle answered. "Their promises are never kept, and so I make no promises in return." He turned to Buffalo Dreamer, and again she saw in his eyes that look of terrible vengeance. "I will send runners out to the other clans, the Brule, the Santee, Minneconjou, Hunkpapa, and Teton, even to the Arapaho, who until now have been our enemy." He turned back to Old Beaver. "We will offer other tribes the war-pipe, asking them all to join us and the Shihenna in our fight against the white man. It is only by banding together that we can conquer them. They are great in numbers, but so are we. Always before we have all gone our own way, splitting up for hunts, never needing to always stay together. We could even fight enemy tribes as separate clans. This new enemy is different. We must be strong, and great in numbers."

"Do you think others will accept the war-pipe?" Buffalo Dreamer asked.

Rising Eagle reached for another cape to pull around himself. "They will when they learn what has happened to our Shihenna friends. This calls for counsel with all the chiefs, Red Cloud, Two Face, Blackfoot, and Shihenna leaders also. I will tell them I think we should start by protecting the Powder River area. Now is the time to take advantage of the fact that most of the white man's soldiers are gone off to their own war. We will show the white settlers how foolish they are to come here. They must pay for what they have done to our Shihenna friends at Sand Creek!"

Old Beaver slowly nodded, tears still on his cheeks. "It would make my heart happy to see all our people, the Shihenna and the Lakota, come together to do great battle against the white man. It must be done, to protect our children and their children, and the chaste young women like your daughter. If we do not keep the white man at bay, he will come and steal your daughters and do terrible things to them. He will take all the game and steal and burn all the things we need to survive."

"We won't let that happen," Rising Eagle promised. He rose, turning again to Buffalo Dreamer. "Feed them and keep them warm. I will speak with some of the others who came here, and then hold council. I will appoint runners to send to the other tribes."

He ducked outside, and Buffalo Dreamer thought how quickly the white man could change a peaceful, happy moment into one of fear, confusion, and horror. This terrible thing done to the Shihenna would not be forgotten, ever. Surely one day even the white man would know disgrace from what they had done.

JANUARY 1865

Snow Moon

CHAPTER TWENTY-SIX

BUFFALO DREAMER'S HEART pounded with anticipation. In the distance lay the town the white man called Julesburg, where the special coaches that carried white settlers into this country stopped to change horses. A large settlement had grown there, stocked with valuable supplies. Since the white man was gradually stealing their hunting grounds, killing their buffalo, and not keeping their promises of providing needed food and goods for survival, the Lakota would take what they needed from the white man's own supplies.

They were not so far from the place where just two moons ago so many Shihenna women and children had been brutally and needlessly butchered, their bodies desecrated. Now it was time to retaliate for the horror. Now it was time to show the white man what happens when promises are broken and when peaceful tribes are attacked for no reason. This peaceful rest stop for white travelers would be attacked in return. At the same time the Lakota would grab badly-needed supplies, food and blankets, cooking pots, winter coats, matches for fires, guns and ammunition.

She and several other women were here to collect the bounty once the warriors secured the area. This attack would be only the first of many attacks on white settlements from the Platte River northward to the Powder River, where She Who Sings waited with the rest of the women and children in a large camp of Lakota and Shihenna, as well as warriors who'd stayed there to protect them.

This was an exciting moment! Buffalo Dreamer would not just stay behind with the other women. She would ride beside Rising Eagle! The Lakota believed her presence brought them good luck.

She looked at Rising Eagle, who sat proudly on his painted war pony. Because of the freezing temperatures, he wore a heavy, beaver-skin vest over his deerhide shirt. The front of his leggings were protected by a layer of bearskin flaps tied to them to keep his knees and thighs from becoming wet and cold, and he wore knee-high, bearskin moccasins. His head and ears were protected by a hat made of more beaver skins, and coup feathers were tied to the base of his hair below his hat.

The fur outerwear made him look even bigger than he already was, and his face was painted red, for blood and war, with black circles around his eyes to protect them from the sun's glare, and to signify death to the white man.

She, too, wore a good deal of fur outer garments, a hooded cape of wolf skin covering most of her body except for the holes through which she could put her arms when necessary. She wore sleeves of more fur over her arms, and in her right hand she gripped a hatchet.

"I am ready, Rising Eagle," she told her husband, imagining the white men doing to her beautiful, innocent daughter what they had done to Old Beaver's granddaughter. If this was what it took to keep something like that from happening, then she would gladly join in any war campaign to that end.

Rising Eagle met her gaze, and she thought how frightened she would be of him if she was seeing him for the first time. Indeed, he presented an intimidating picture of virile manhood and fearless warrior.

"It is time to avenge the Shihenna," he told her, his dark eyes glittering with a desire to kill. He looked to his left and to his right at a line of warriors one thousand strong. Just as he'd wanted, many more Lakota and many Shihenna had joined together for this important campaign. By their horrendous act against the Shihenna, the white man had created much trouble for himself. Brave

Horse rode to Rising Eagle's left, and Oglala chiefs Two Face and Blackfoot had also joined them. So had many Shihenna, including Chiefs Dull Knife and Two Moon. Red Cloud and Crazy Horse would follow for yet a second attack on this place, then join them for more warfare farther north.

Rising Eagle nodded to Brave Horse. "I will let you lead the attack, so that you can take home a story of bravery and victory to Beaver Woman's father. Then they will know you are worthy of their daughter."

Brave Horse grinned, and it warmed Buffalo Dreamer's heart to know her son loved again and would marry Beaver Woman once this campaign was over. For many weeks he had played special songs for her on his flute, and finally she'd set a bowl of food outside her tepee for him, showing him that she accepted his pledge of love. Now he had only to bring home three white scalps, five white man's blankets, and two white man's rifles in payment to her father before he could take Beaver Woman for a wife.

Brave Horse raised his lance, and Buffalo Dreamer thought how he seemed a replica of Rising Eagle at thirty summers. Her son charged ahead, and the rest of the thousand warriors followed, descending on the Julesburg station in full force, snow and dirt flying from under the feet of their horses. Approximately four inches of snow helped in their surprise attack, since it cushioned the sound of their thundering war ponies.

In only minutes they were circling the settlement. Arrows sang through the air. Warriors dodged bullets from guns fired by desperate, unprepared settlers and station attendants, who were soon overwhelmed by sheer numbers.

The air resounded with gunfire, screams, the smell of smoke and war cries. Flaming arrows made their way into coaches and tents, homes and covered wagons, and soon many establishments were aflame. Buffalo Dreamer rode down on a fleeing white man and landed her hatchet between his shoulders, then realized another white man nearby had his rifle aimed right at her. In a flash a fur-clad warrior charged between her and the man with the rifle, letting out a blood-curdling war cry. It was Rising Eagle, and before the man could fire, Rising Eagle rammed a lance into the man's neck. Before his victim could slump to the ground Rising Eagle grasped hold of his hair, then yanked out the lance. Ramming it into loops at the side of his horse, and still clinging to a fistful of the man's hair, he whipped out his knife and sliced off a piece of the man's scalp before letting him fall.

He whirled his horse to face Buffalo Dreamer and handed her the scalp. "This belongs to you." Fire glowed in his dark eyes as Buffalo Dreamer took the scalp and tied it to the side of her horse. Then she saw Brave Horse, who had dismounted and was in hand-to-hand combat with another white man. The young warrior rammed his hunting knife into the chest of his enemy, then cut off a piece of his scalp, holding up the bloody prize and letting out a victory war whoop.

Now Shihenna and Lakota warriors were everywhere, burning, killing, looting. Women and children cringed behind barriers and were not harmed. Buffalo Dreamer rode up to a group of cowering women and shouted to them in the Lakota tongue.

"Go home! You do not belong here! Hear me, women. Take your children back to the land of the rising sun where they will be safe. This is not a good place for you!" She grabbed up three blankets from a wooden table nearby and rode off.

Now it seemed everything was on fire. Remaining white men began giving up the fight, throwing out their rifles and cringing behind wagons and barrels or running inside buildings left unburned. The warriors began screaming shouts of victory, and women brought in horses and travois to gather supplies. In minutes a good stash of supplies was taken, and they headed north to seek out more settlements and wagon trains to plunder.

Yes! The white man would learn a hard lesson over the next few weeks. He would be sorry for what he'd done to the Shihenna at Sand Creek!

APRIL 1865

Moon of the Birth of Calves

CHAPTER TWENTY-SEVEN

FLORENCE WATCHED THE new troops arrive, never sure if or when William might end up among them. Fort Laramie had changed and grown since she and Abel had lived here years ago. Back then it was a converted trading post called Fort William, and there were not nearly so many soldiers here, and with rumors that the Civil War was nearly over, the South all but defeated, more and more soldiers were being sent here . . . to fight a new war against a new enemy, one much more formidable even than the Confederate Army.

She had not realized how much she'd changed over the years of being married to Abel until she came back here and saw the Indians who lived near the fort, those who'd already given up and settled for the white man's promises of handouts. Laramie Loafers, some of the soldiers called them, as, so she'd been told, did the hostile Indians who still refused to settle for a life of sitting around begging for supplies.

She could hardly believe the sight, a hundred or more tepees sprawled in the area of the fort, many Indian men just sitting around drinking whiskey. It brought pain to her heart to see her people this way, even worse pain to remember she once lived by the bottle herself.

She, Rebecca, and Robert had been here only two weeks.

She'd taken work as a seamstress for the soldiers, and Robert served as a doctor at the fort, tending both Indian and soldier. He tried to help some of the Lakota stop drinking, tried to teach some of the younger ones how to speak and read English; but most of them resented his efforts. They saw no need for such learning, and most would not let Robert doctor them, not trusting the white man's means of healing, even though Robert was more Indian than white.

Florence thought how her people were caught in an odd middle road now, clinging to old ways, yet unable to survive that way; needing to learn a new way, but refusing to do so because of their distrust of the white man. Some were being lured into acting as scouts against the hostiles, helping the soldiers hunt down their own people. It sickened her to realize the white man had discovered his best weapon against the Lakota—divide and conquer. She had no doubt that such tactics would inevitably be the downfall of a proud people.

Now the government was already building forts along the Bozeman Trail, which led to the gold fields of Montana. Such an invasion of prime Lakota hunting grounds was specifically forbidden in the Treaty of 1851. She could not blame the hostiles for being so angry over all the broken promises. Even she felt great anger over it. A man's word should be good, and not changed just for convenience.

She waited for the new contingent of troops to arrive. She'd spotted them approaching from the east, fresh soldiers to reinforce the troops already here, some of whom would be sent farther north to help with the building of the forts to protect the Bozeman travelers along the Powder River. She suspected those soldiers would find life quite precarious. Already Red Cloud, Rising Eagle, and others were waging a campaign against all whites, and stories of death and destruction seemed to come in every day.

As the soldiers came closer, she smoothed her gingham dress, not sure what she would even say to William if he did show up here.

"More soldiers?"

Florence turned to Rebecca, who walked up beside her. "Yes."

She moved an arm around Rebecca's waist. "It's awfully hot today. You shouldn't be out here in your condition. Why don't you go inside the cabin and rest, Becky?"

The young woman sighed, resting her hand on her ever-growing belly. "It's even hotter in there."

Florence nodded. "I guess it is. It isn't usually this hot out here in May. It won't last." She gave the girl a light hug. "Actually, you would be more comfortable in one of those tepees, I assure you. See how they are rolled up at the bottom? Tepees are quite comfortable in hot weather. When you roll up the bottom, it lets air circulate, but the buffalo-hide skins are a great sun barrier and actually create a pleasant area inside. Perhaps I should construct a tepee for us instead of staying in the cabin." She laughed lightly. "At least I *think* I can remember how to construct one."

"You really used to live like that?"

Florence sighed with nostalgia. "The first twenty years of my life." She watched the new recruits parade past, then drew in her breath and put a hand to her chest. "Go and get Robert!"

One of the soldiers, who looked very Indian, halted his horse and put up his hand, signalling those behind him to stop. He was apparently some kind of officer. He stared down at Florence, and their gazes held. Florence could not help the tears that came to her eyes, and she put her hands to her face.

"Is it William?" Rebecca asked.

"Yes," Florence whispered. "It's William."

Nineteen. He was only nineteen, but he was filled out and experienced and looked twenty-five. Not only that, but William wore the stripes of a sergeant. How could a nineteen-year-old already be a sergeant?

"I knew you would be here," William spoke up. He glanced at Rebecca. "You must be Robert's wife."

"Yes," she answered with a smile. "How did you know?"

He moved his gaze back to Florence, who watched him with joy and relief to see he was all right. He had not contacted her the whole time he'd been gone after joining the army. "I got Mother's letter, and I stopped in Springfield after being reassigned. I had two weeks before I had to head west. I spoke with several of the church members, and of course I wanted to visit my father's grave once more."

So, at least he had gone home. At least he'd cared that much. Florence wondered if he would have visited *her* grave if she were the one who'd died? Surely he would hate her even more if she told him the man he mourned was not his real father at all.

"Where are you staying?" William asked.

Florence pointed to a log cabin outside fort grounds. "I have a room inside the fort," she told William. "I pay my way by mending uniforms. Robert and Rebecca live in the cabin. Robert came out here to doctor the soldiers and the Lakota who live around the fort."

William glanced out at the numerous tepees with a sneer on his lips. "The Laramie Loafers?" He looked back at his mother. "You mean you aren't living out there in one of those tepees with them? I thought you were so proud to be Lakota, Mother." He shook his head. "Maybe now that you've seen how lazy and drunken they have become, you're not so proud anymore. Maybe now you understand why I hate being identified with people like that."

William turned his horse and yelled out an order for the infantrymen behind him to follow him into the fort. "I have to report," he said, riding forward. "I'll be back."

Several of those who marched behind William turned to look at Florence as they passed. She supposed she was quite a curiosity for them, a Lakota woman among the "heathen Indians," dressed as she was, and speaking good English.

"Nothing has changed," she told Rebecca, her heart heavy. "I had hoped being away might help."

Rebecca touched her arm. "Robert had some hard times working with the Confederates," she told her mother-in-law. "Some wouldn't let him doctor them because he was an Indian. They sometimes teased him, saying no Indian was going to take a knife to them, saying he would use it to do more than fix their wounds. I have no doubt William has also had some bad experiences and suffered a great deal of teasing because of his Indian blood. Robert never let it bother him, but I can see William does. I am so sorry."

Florence smiled sadly. "Go find Robert, and meet me at the cabin. We'll wait there for William."

Rebecca kissed her cheek and left her, and with a heavy heart Florence walked to the cabin to wait.

CHAPTER TWENTY-EIGHT

IT WAS NEARLY an hour before William arrived at the cabin, still in uniform, which sickened Florence. Surely to Lakota men like Rising Eagle the uniform represented a hated enemy. Robert, who had let his hair grow straight and long again, greeted his brother at the door. They shook hands, and then Robert embraced a rather reticent William.

"I'm glad to see you made it through the war all right," he told him.

"You sure?" William answered. "I thought you were a Confederate." The words were spoken with a hint of a teasing smile, which relieved Florence.

"I was a *doctor*. That's all," Robert answered. "I would have helped any man, gray uniform or blue. Frankly, I thought the war was ridiculous, a tragedy, a terrible waste of young lives. I'm glad you weren't one of them."

William stepped inside, removing his hat and greeting Rebecca with a nod. He turned back to Robert. "You have a real pretty wife, Robert. Where did you find her?"

Robert grinned. "In Tennessee. She was very sick. I treated her and then carried her off. She is my white captive."

Rebecca reddened and grinned, and William laughed lightly. "I can't stay long," he said then. "I have orders to take a company out on patrol tomorrow, and I'm damn tired. Word is we might be moving out soon up into the Powder River area." He glanced at Florence. "To search for hostiles."

Florence felt her chest tighten with dread.

"I think our mother deserves a hug from her long-lost son," Robert told William. He gave his brother a stern look of demand. Always the "big brother," Robert had a way of handling William that no one else had.

William nodded with a sigh and turned to Florence, who stepped back.

"I will not be embraced out of duty," she told him. "If you have no feelings for me, then why embrace me?"

The room hung silent for a moment, the tension thick. William closed his eyes for a few seconds. "You are my mother," he said then, meeting Florence's gaze. "Of course I have feelings for you. I am fighting a battle on the inside, Mother, and seeing you only reminds me what that battle is all about, but it can't change the fact that I love my mother."

Florence felt like crying. "Well, I appreciate those words, son." Her eyes teared. "I have missed you so much. Why couldn't you have at least written to tell us you were all right?"

He stepped closer and embraced her, and Florence wrapped her arms around his middle.

"I'm sorry I didn't write," he told her. "I just couldn't."

Florence kissed his cheek, then stepped back, looking him over. "You look quite handsome in uniform, I must say. And please tell us how it is you are a sergeant at nineteen years old?"

William shrugged. "That's the war for you. A lot of younger men became officers, sometimes just because there wasn't anyone else around to take command. For a while I served under another man really young for the job, a colonel named George Custer. He was pretty cocky, I'll say. Ten to one he'll be out here fighting In—" he hesitated. "Indians—real soon," he finished. He sobered, a hint of anger coming into his eyes. "Only reason he ended up with such a high rank is because he's a West Pointer."

Florence felt the sting of the words.

William turned to Robert. "I'll never be able to get any higher than sergeant, but I've learned to settle for that."

"The army suits you then?" Robert asked.

William nodded. "Yes. For a while I thought I might just go ahead and get out after fighting those southern boys, but I still . . . there are still things I want to accomplish."

"Like killing Indians?" Florence asked, holding her chin proudly.

He met her eyes, remaining silent at first. "Maybe," he finally spoke up.

"And maybe all you're doing is fighting yourself," Robert suggested. "Maybe you think this is going to free you of all that pent-up anger, William, but it won't. If you fight the Lakota, you'll destroy your soul. They are your people."

William rolled his eyes. "Let's not get into that again. I will wrestle with this whole thing my way. Right now I like the idea of showing the rest of those boys out there that I am one of them. I came out here to fight Indians just like they did, and I'll do my job to the best of my ability. The Lakota can settle peacefully, or answer to our howitzers. It's their choice."

"You will end up tearing yourself in two," Florence told him. "And tearing *me* in two."

He shook his head. "You're a strong woman, strong and stubborn. And you're sure of your place, Mother. But I'm not sure of mine, and I won't be sure until I go out there and face the enemy."

You could end up fighting, even killing, your own father and brothers, she wanted to shout.

"I have to go," William said then, looking agitated. "Like I said, I have duties to fulfill and I have to report back. I don't know how much I'll be able to visit with any of you. I could be leaving here any day. I just wish you would all go back to Illinois. Get the heck away from the mess out here. It's only going to get worse now that more soldiers are being sent here. The hostilities have to end, whether anybody likes it or not. People are dying on both sides, and white settlement can't be stopped. The Lakota will just have to learn that. They can learn it the easy way, or the hard way. It's their choice."

He put on his hat, looking at his mother pleadingly. "Please leave, Mother. This is not a good time for you to be here. Please go home."

"I *am* home, William. This land *is* my home. And I tell you now, my son, that yes, I am sure there are hard times ahead for the Lakota, but there are also hard times ahead for you. I *need* to be here, as much for you as for my People. And if my being here somehow embarrasses you, I can't help that."

William closed his eyes and shook his head. He turned to Robert. "You have a lovely wife. Congratulations. I might not even be around for the birth of your child, but I look forward to my new niece or nephew. The only thing I don't understand is . . ." He glanced at Rebecca. "Pardon me, ma'am. It's nothing against you as a person." He looked back at Robert. "I just don't understand why you married a white woman and brought her out here to doctor the Lakota. Which are you, Robert? Are you Lakota? Or are you white?"

"It isn't a matter of choosing, William. I'm simply Robert Kingsley, and I am also Spirit Walker. I've combined both those worlds in my practice of medicine, and I'm proud to carry the blood of both nations. You should also be proud. And there are better ways of helping the Lakota than going out and shooting them down. It's those of us who have mixed blood who can help meld both cultures together."

William looked away. "Why should I help a people who have brought me only shame?"

"The shame is in your own mind. If you had known them as I did, as I knew the medicine man Moon Painter, and my adopted father, Rising Eagle, you would feel differently."

William sighed. "I can hardly believe you have fond memories of a man who makes war on innocent settlers and savagely murders them."

Robert shook his head. "There is so much you don't understand, William, and you never knew Rising Eagle."

William turned to his mother. "I'm sorry but I really do have to leave. I have duties."

Florence nodded. "I understand. By all means, go and perform your duties, William. Your father taught you to be a responsible man. Just remember that you are also responsible for your own personal actions and decisions . . . and their consequences. Just remember that your brother and I are here whenever you need us. God go with you, William."

He studied her a moment longer, then turned and walked out. Florence went to the door to watch him, the son of a great Lakota leader, wearing the blue coat of that man's most hated enemy.

MAY 1865

Moon When the Ponies Shed

CHAPTER TWENTY-NINE

RISING EAGLE SAT in council with all the most esteemed Lakota leaders, he and the others members of *naca ominicia*, joined by leaders of the *tokalas*, the Police Society; the *akicitas*, those of the Warrior Society; the *wakincuzas*, or Pipe Owners; and the Shirt Wearers, of which Brave Horse was one. He could think of no greater joy than what he felt now, having his own son sitting beside him among the *wicasa itacans*, the supreme counselors.

Over two thousand Lakota had gathered here several days north of Fort Laramie, joined by close to a thousand Shihenna, whose own leaders also sat in this council. Rising Eagle's efforts at bringing the various tribes together had been successful. The white man was learning a good lesson, and he was paying for the awful thing he'd done to the Shihenna at Sand Creek.

The pipe of peace was passed among the circle of leaders, each man offering it in the four directions before discussing their next plan of attack.

"Scouts tell us that many soldiers have gathered now at Laramie," Red Cloud spoke up.

"It is a bad sign," an Oglala chief, Two Face, told them.

"I think they are afraid," Crazy Horse offered. "I think that after our celebrations here, and after praying at the Sun Dance and

cleansing ourselves in the sweat lodges, we should go after those soldiers along the Platte. They should know we are not afraid of them."

"I agree with my friend, *Tashunka Witko*," Brave Horse said.
"Many of us are ready to go against the Blue Coats. Crazy Horse
and I have no fear of them."

"We must be careful not to concentrate too closely on one
place," Rising Eagle warned. "If they are sending out more soldiers,
perhaps it means their war with each other has ended. Perhaps they
will send many more into the north to build more forts along the
Powder River. Do not forget that the white man is determined to
go into the land north of the mountains of the big-horned sheep,
where he has found more gold. Some of us must go there to protect
our last best hunting grounds. Many of the whites there are also
killing buffalo, just for their hides. Without the buffalo, we die. We
must protect those hunting grounds."

For a moment there was only silence, as the leaders, both
elders and young warriors, pondered his warning.

"I agree," Red Cloud finally spoke up. "I am for protecting the
Powder River."

They all nodded, again taking a moment to think about what
should be done about the seemingly unstoppable invasion of a new
enemy.

"I say this," said Blackfoot, another Oglala leader. "In our camp
is a white woman and her child, Shihenna captives. We can use
them to show the *wasicus* we will settle for peace along the Platte
River. We will take the woman and child to them as a gesture of
this peace. Then perhaps they will stay away from the Powder
River and leave us alone. They will abide by the Treaty of Horse
Creek in which they promised that land would be ours forever. If
they do not, then we will continue attacking all white settlements
and forts and wagon trains along that road in the north. Crazy
Horse, you should not attack again in the Platte River area until we
return the captives. Maybe then they will not even send more soldiers. They will see we truly want peace, that all we have been
doing is protecting what is ours."

Several of them nodded.

"It could be dangerous," Rising Eagle warned. "Who will take the woman to Laramie?"

Blackfoot rubbed his chin. "It's my idea. I'll take her."

"I'll go with you," Two Face spoke up. "You and I have been good friends for many years. We will go together, representing the Oglala, and show them no harm has come to the woman. They should understand this, after what they did to the Shihenna at Sand Creek. They did terrible things to Shihenna women and children, yet we bring to them a white woman captive of the Shihenna who has not been harmed. I think it is a good gesture. If we can have peace along the Platte River, then we will be able to better protect the north country."

Many nodded their heads in agreement.

"What do you think, Crazy Horse?" Rising Eagle asked.

Crazy Horse looked at Brave Horse, who sat to his left. "I think Brave Horse and I would rather have some fun with the Blue Coats and make them afraid."

Several of them chuckled.

"Spoken like a reckless young warrior," Red Cloud said with a grin. "But a brave one. When I see the eagerness in our younger men, I feel confident about the future of our people."

Again they all nodded, and Rising Eagle felt within this circle of men a wealth of wisdom and courage, honor and power. Then one of them, who until this moment had said nothing, spoke up. He was Hunkpapa, a warrior called *Tatanka Yotanka*, Sitting Bull.

"We all must remember one thing," he told them. "One of the greatest among us, Rising Eagle, was told by the Feathered One that bad times are ahead, that we must remain very strong. And his wife, the holy woman called Buffalo Dreamer, once dreamed that many soldiers, perhaps two hundred or more, would be surrounded by thousands of Lakota and Shihenna and turned into a pool of blood. We know that Rising Eagle's visions are true, and that the dreams of the woman who has seen and spoken with the white buffalo are also true. This means peace with the Blue Coats will not come so easily. We must keep this in mind in all our dealings with them, and also remember that the white man speaks with a split tongue."

The circle of men sobered, again returning to a contemplative mood.

"Sitting Bull's words hold much meaning," Red Cloud told them.

Many nodded.

"That does not mean we cannot keep trying for peace." Two Face stood up. "Let us try. Perhaps it will give us time to hunt and store up plenty of meat over the hot season. The winters have been hard on us because the hunts have not been good. And when we have to spend time fighting the Blue Coats, it leaves us less time for the hunt. Let Blackfoot and I take the white woman and her child to Laramie first and see if it will help."

Rising Eagle also rose. "It is true much trouble surely lies ahead, but in Buffalo Dreamer's vision we defeated many Blue Coats, and we were strong and many. We should take hope in that. Yet there are many among us who are very wise in wanting to show the white man that all we want is peace, and to be able to live freely on land promised to us. Each of us is free to do what he chooses, to fight or to hope for peace, to remain free to live and hunt where we choose, or to join the Laramie Loafers and go off to the places the white man calls reservations. I choose to remain free. And I believe that the Powder River area is one we should watch closely. I say we should let Blackfoot and Two Face take the white woman to Laramie and see what the white men say about it."

Several nodded again.

"Then it is decided," Red Cloud spoke up.

"Some of us will go with Blackfoot," Crazy Horse said. "I for one will go."

"As will I," Brave Horse added.

"I, too, will go," Rising Eagle told them. "I will ride at my son's side, and I will take as many more with me as choose to go, but we will not go down to that place. If we mix too closely with the soldiers, it could only bring even more trouble. We will gather a distance from the fort and taunt them and make them afraid. Then they will think even harder about listening to us and accepting our offer of peace in the Laramie area. It is many days' ride from here.

We will leave after the Sun Dance. I wish to pray and to first cleanse myself in the sweat lodge."

"Some of us will head north," Red Cloud told them. "We will camp along the Tongue River and hunt."

All agreed, and the councilmen parted. Rising Eagle headed back to the tepee, where Buffalo Dreamer waited. He went inside to find her mending his war shield. She looked up at him anxiously. "What did you decide?"

He moved to sit down on a bed of buffalo robes. "After the Sun Dance we will take the white woman captive of the Shihenna to Fort Laramie, as a token of our desire for peace. We need to settle things here along the Platte so that we can concentrate on the hunt and on protecting our hunting grounds in the north. Perhaps if we can realize some peace here, they will not pay so much attention to the Powder River and will not send soldiers there."

Buffalo Dreamer set the war shield aside. "Do you truly believe that?"

Their eyes held in mutual understanding. "We have to try, Buffalo Dreamer."

She sighed. "I do not like the thought of you going there. Something tells me it will not bring peace at all."

"We will see." Rising Eagle came around to where she sat, leaning close. "Where is She Who Sings?"

"Our daughter is at the menstrual lodge. We are alone."

He grinned, pushing her back and resting his arms on either side of her. "Good. I wish to make love to my woman before I begin fasting for the Sun Dance."

Buffalo Dreamer grinned. "This is a sudden change of mood, but I don't mind."

He licked at her mouth. "When I begin to worry over what lies ahead, it makes me want to make love to you, to enjoy these peaceful times, which are becoming rare." He nuzzled her neck, savoring such moments more than he ever had before, never sure how long they would last in this world that had become so uncertain for his people.

JUNE 1865

Moon of Making Fat

CHAPTER THIRTY

"IT'S HIM, ROBERT!" Florence, Robert, and Rebecca watched from an outlook post of the log fort, where they could see the Lakota leader in the distance, riding back and forth on his painted Appaloosa, taunting the soldiers.

"He's frightening," Rebecca said in a near whisper, as though being in the warrior's presence brought on an almost worshipful attitude. "What is he saying?"

Florence and Robert listened for a moment, then both grinned, Florence laughing lightly.

"Do you see me?" Robert said, interpreting for Rebecca. "I am Rising Eagle. You should be afraid. Do you see me? I do not kill women and children. I am not a coward like you white men with blue coats. Do you see me? I am Rising Eagle. You should be afraid."

"He has not changed since when I knew him in his younger days," Florence said.

"I have to see him," Robert said.

Rebecca put a hand on her husband's arm. "He might not realize it's you, Robert."

"Don't worry. No honorable warrior will kill one man riding out to him unarmed. He will wait to see what it is I want. I can't pass up this opportunity. I might not get another chance."

"Talk to William," Florence said. "See if there is any way he can go out there with you."

"He won't want to do that."

"Your medicine and Rising Eagle's prayers saved his life when he was a small boy."

"William doesn't care about that now. Besides, Rising Eagle won't be too happy discovering that the young boy he saved now wears the blue coat of the white man's army. And the army wouldn't like him going out there."

Florence watched Rising Eagle again. "I suppose you're right." Her heart felt painfully heavy. "Those other young warriors with him, Brave Horse is probably among them. You could see the one you once called brother. And maybe you can reason with them, Robert. Tell them how strong the army is, and that they will get stronger. Tell them about the howitzers. Tell Rising Eagle many Lakota lives would be saved if he will bring them here and go to the reservations the white man's government is creating for them in the Black Hills. They can live at peace there. Maybe he will listen to you. He trusts you."

"Wait." Robert studied the small group of Lakota sitting on the rise a safe distance from the fort. Three of them rode forward then. "Look. Doesn't that look like a woman riding in front of one of those men?"

Both women watched as the two men came even closer.

"It *is* a woman!" Rebecca said. "And it looks like she's holding a baby. What are they doing?"

They heard orders being shouted below. Soldiers positioned themselves, leveling their rifles.

"They are coming in peace!" Florence turned and climbed down the ladder, not waiting for Robert and Rebecca. Robert would have to help his wife down the ladder, since Rebecca was seven months' large with child. Florence lifted the hem of her gingham dress, dodging around horse dung being shoveled by a private and hurrying over to the fort commander. She did not care for Lieutenant Malcolm Griggs, since he was only in temporary command and knew next to nothing about dealing with the Lakota.

She mounted the steps to the command post. "Lieutenant

Griggs, the Indians out there are presenting some kind of peace offering. Please don't order any shooting."

The young lieutenant turned to scowl at her. "My interpreter says the one shouting at us is Rising Eagle, a hostile. And he is calling my soldiers cowards."

· "That is the warrior way. Taunting the enemy is almost more important than actually fighting him. There are three more men approaching the fort with a white woman and a small child. I assure you, this is some kind of peace offering."

He looked her over rather scathingly. "Mrs. Kingsley, might I remind you that you are simply a civilian here. I respect the fact that your son is a soldier here, and your other son has helped doctor some of my men. But I am not of a mind to take orders from a woman, a Lakota woman at that. And I don't feel much for peace when Lakota hostiles come here with a white woman prisoner. God only knows what she has been through."

Florence thought how sad it was that white men could murder and rape Cheyènne women; yet now the fact that the Lakota were bringing in just one captive white woman as a sign of peace angered and excited the lieutenant.

"Please, you must listen to what the men coming in peacefully have to say," she told Griggs. "I am only asking that you don't fire on any of them, Lieutenant. Rising Eagle is holding back, as are the others out there. That is a sure sign that he means no harm at this time. He only wants you to see how strong and ready they are, but he means no attack. This could be a chance to avoid further lost lives. My son, Robert, is going out to talk to Rising Eagle. He will try to reason with him and convince him to surrender himself and his people and go to the Black Hills and live peacefully."

Griggs, a clean-cut young man who seemed to resent having to serve here in the West at all, shouted an order to open the gates of the fort. "Don't worry, Mrs. Kingsley, I won't start anything if they don't. But if they think they can bring back an abused white woman without suffering some kind of punishment for what they have probably done to her, they can think again."

"That woman is probably Mrs. Eubanks, the woman captured by Cheyenne, not Lakota. She's one woman. And she isn't even a

Lakota captive. If nothing else, don't punish the Lakota for something the Cheyenne have done."

He looked at her again, obvious irritation in his eyes. "The Lakota and Cheyenne have joined forces, which makes one just as guilty as the other."

"Lieutenant! This is a sign of *peace*! Don't do something to change their minds!"

"And don't purport to order an officer of the United States Army!" he barked angrily. "Go away, Mrs. Kingsley! Go sew on some buttons and leave army business to me! As far as I am concerned you are only one step above the enemy!"

Florence stiffened, thinking what a fool he was. How she would enjoy seeing this man try to stand up alone to a warrior like Rising Eagle. She turned away, just as the gates opened to allow the entrance of two elder Lakota men, one of them wearing a war bonnet. A Cheyenne leader rode with them, and Florence wondered if Griggs and the others even knew the difference between Cheyenne and Lakota. A beleaguered-looking white woman, wearing an Indian tunic, her face sunburned and her hair a mass of tangles, sat in front of one of the Lakota men, carrying a baby in her arms. She screamed for help before her captors even reached the entrance. She jumped down, baby and all, and ran to one of the soldiers standing guard, then began carrying on hysterically.

"Let me go to her," Florence offered. "I can interpret the proceedings for you."

"I have my own interpreters," the lieutenant answered. "Either go back to work or go to your quarters."

"I am not one of your soldiers to be ordered around!" Florence told him.

Griggs faced her, smoldering anger in his eyes. "No, you aren't. But your son *is*. Do you get my meaning, Mrs. Kingsley? I can make life here hard for him, or rather easy. It's up to you."

Florence wanted to hit him. Her Lakota pride set in, and she could see how easy it would be to want to make war against such men. She walked away, approaching Rebecca and moving an arm around the young woman's waist. She could tell Rebecca was frightened by what was happening.

"I'm afraid for him," Rebecca said, referring to Robert, who had mounted a horse and rode out of the fort to go to Rising Eagle. At the same time soldiers surrounded the three Indian men who had brought in the white woman.

CHAPTER THIRTY-ONE

RISING EAGLE WARILY watched the man approaching on horseback. He trusted nothing these white men did, but as the man drew closer, he could see he was not white. Although he wore the pants and shirt and woolen outer jacket of a white man, his skin was dark. He wore no hat, and his long, black hair was tied in a tail over his right shoulder.

Rising Eagle ceased galloping his war pony to and fro, ceased his shouted taunts. This was a time to be watchful. Two Face and Blackfoot had taken the white woman prisoner to the soldiers at Fort Laramie, accompanied by a Cheyenne chief, Four Antelope. Now someone dressed as a white man rode out to greet Rising Eagle. The man stopped several yards away and called out to him.

"Rising Eagle! My heart is happy to see you!" He spoke in the Oglala tongue. "You are the one I once called *ate*."

Father? There was only one Lakota man other than his own children who would say that. Could it be? Cautiously he rode closer, studying the younger man, who was quite handsome. Now he knew who it was, for in spite of his dark skin and hair, the man had blue eyes. "Spirit Walker?"

The man smiled and nodded. "I hoped to see you again, Father, but I never thought I would find you so soon!"

Rising Eagle felt a surge of joy, in spite of the gravity of the moment. He looked over his adopted son, this man who was once a deformed baby, given to him by Fall Leaf Woman to raise. "You dress like a white man."

Spirit Walker rode closer, reaching out to grip Rising Eagle's wrist. "I am called Robert Kingsley now; but I am still Lakota at heart. I have been to the white man's school of higher learning. I am a doctor now, Father; but even though I often use white man's medicine, I sometimes sing a medicine prayer over my patients. I still believe in the power of *Wakan-Tanka*, who to me is the same as the white man's God, Jehovah."

Rising Eagle grasped Robert's wrist in return. "Then you are not here to come back to your true people?"

"I am here to beg you to go home, Father, to *Paha-Sapa*. Go home and remain there. It will save many lives. The white man's government will provide for you, and if you go there, I will go, too. I will teach the Lakota children, doctor them, make sure that promised supplies reach you. You can meet my wife. She will give birth to our first child soon. We can all be together again. Even my mother would go. She would like nothing more than to be with the Lakota again, to go home to the Black Hills."

"Your mother? She is here?"

Robert nodded. "Her husband, the preacher, Abel Kingsley, died. She is alone now except for me."

"You married a Lakota woman?"

Robert finally let go of his wrist. "I married a white woman, but she has a good heart, Father, just like Yellow Bonnet has a good heart, even though her skin is fair and her eyes blue."

Rising Eagle stiffened. "Yellow Bonnet was killed at Blue Water Creek."

Robert's eyes closed, and Rising Eagle knew that he took great sadness in the news. "Who else?" he asked. "Is Buffalo Dreamer still alive?"

Rising Eagle nodded. "Her father was killed there. And my sister, Many Robes Woman. Runs With The Deer. Old Moon Painter. Many others. Most of our relatives are gone now."

Robert sighed, rubbing his eyes. "I'm sorry. Moon Painter taught me so much about healing, and I thought of him as Grandfather."

"I cannot go to the reservation," Rising Eagle told his adopted son. "I will never trust the white men or their leaders. Do you know what white men did to the Shihenna at Sand Creek?" He could see the agony in Spirit Walker's eyes.

"I know."

"It must be avenged."

"If you try that the killing will just go on and on, Rising Eagle. And it will end badly for the Lakota. I can't impress on you enough how many whites there are in the land of the rising sun, nor how determined and greedy they can be. They want this land and they will do anything they can to get it. They have more men and better weapons."

"But they have no honor."

"Some of them do."

"Not when it comes to how they treat my people and other Nations. Some have decided to go the way of the white man, like the Pawnee, some of whom now scout against us. But they will find out in the end that they will get no great favors for it. In the end they, too, will discover they mean nothing to the white man. I feel it in the wind."

Robert sighed, looking past him. "Is Brave Horse with you?"

Rising Eagle raised his hand and shouted his son's name. Brave Horse rode forward. "Do you recognize this man?" Rising Eagle asked him.

"I heard him call you *ate!*" Brave Horse answered, riding closer to grasp Robert's wrist. "He is the one I once called brother! We have good memories, Spirit Walker!"

Robert smiled with obvious tears in his eyes. "Yes, we do. I have missed you, Brave Horse. And look at you! So tall and strong! You look just like your father. Tell me about my youngest brother and sister."

"Thunder is twenty-one summers now and a brave warrior who rides with Red Cloud. She Who Sings is sixteen. I myself will marry when we return to our camp. Her name is Beaver Woman, the daughter of Red Eagle."

"I am glad for you." Robert's smile quickly faded. "But I implore you, Brave Horse, to convince Rising Eagle and Buffalo

Dreamer to go home to the Black Hills and abide by the orders of the white man's government. I know the meaning of the vision you had all those years ago at your first vision quest, and I can tell you that your vision only means more whites coming into Lakota lands."

Brave Horse frowned in wonder. His horse whinnied and pranced restlessly, as though sensing his alarm. He softly commanded the sturdy Appaloosa to settle. "What do you mean?" he asked Robert.

"Your vision told of an iron horse with a fire in its belly, carrying white faces across the prairie. In the East white men often travel by railroad. A large black iron steam engine fueled by burning wood pulls cars on wheels that sit on iron rails. It's called a train, and the cars it pulls can carry up to a hundred or more people at one time. The white man's government plans to build train tracks all the way from the East through Lakota and Cheyenne hunting grounds and beyond the western mountains, all the way to the other side of the country. They have already started building this railroad, and now that their war with each other is nearly over, this building will go much faster. They will also use the trains to bring out more supplies, things with which to build more forts, even cities. The railroad is what you saw in your vision, Brave Horse. You can see down there that the government is already enlarging the fort, constructing many new buildings. This place will become quite a large settlement before long. Some soldiers have their wives here, and children. They plan to build a supply store, and some white civilians have settled around the fort."

He turned to Rising Eagle again. "Don't you see, Father? There are simply too many white men for the Lakota to keep fighting them. I have seen it with my own eyes. I would not lie to you. More will come, and more and more and more. Their numbers will never stop, but the Lakota numbers will fall like stones down a mountain, because the white man will take away the buffalo, their only means of survival."

"This is what you came out here to tell us?" Rising Eagle asked, irritated by the warnings. "That we should just give up what has been ours since *Wakan-Tanka* created us? That we should live like women, hoeing the ground? That we should become beggars, like the Laramie Loafers who sit around drinking the white man's fire water and waiting for his handouts, waiting for the white man to keep his promises? If fighting for the right to hunt where we please, fighting to protect the buffalo, fighting to protect our women and children and to save our own honor means having to die, then we would *rather* die!"

"And so would I, and Crazy Horse!" Brave Horse added. "He is my best friend, and he waits over there with the rest of the warriors we brought with us. Remember his name, my brother, for you will hear it often among the soldiers, as you will hear *my* name and our *father's* name. Soldiers will speak these names with much fear!"

Brave Horse turned his horse and rode back to the six other waiting men, letting out a war whoop as he did so. Robert turned his gaze to Rising Eagle.

"I did not come out here to create bad feelings. I am only trying to reason with you, Rising Eagle, because I care, and because I have seen the things I have told you about. I have lived in the white man's world and I know what he is capable of doing."

Rising Eagle slowly nodded. "And I know what the Lakota are capable of doing. If the white man continues to force our hand, he, too, will discover the power of the Lakota warrior. But do not fret, my long-lost son. We are still considering peace. We are still hoping beyond hope that the white man will stop lying to us. We are thinking of once more talking peace. This is why we have brought the white woman here, as a gesture of peace to the white man. We spoke about this in a great gathering of *tokalas*, *akicitas*, *wakincuzas*, and *naca ominicia*. We wish to quit fighting here along the flat river and go to the land in the mountains of the big-horned sheep, which was promised to us in the great treaty signing at Horse Creek. We already know we cannot stop the thousands of whites who come through here along the great medicine trail to the land of the setting sun, but there are still not so many in the Powder River hunting grounds. It is there we wish to continue the fight, for that land was promised to us, and now the white man comes there searching for his gold." He nodded toward the fort. "I will think about what you have said, after I see if the soldiers accept our peace offering."

Robert turned his horse to face the fort, watching soldiers escort the two Lakota chiefs and the Cheyenne chief into the fort, along with the still-hysterical white woman. "Then I will wait with you, but I have to tell you, Father, that the soldiers down there won't understand the gesture. Most of them understand nothing about the Lakota way. Mother and I try to explain such things to them, but they don't listen." He sighed deeply. "And I have to tell you, Father, that my young brother, William, the little boy you helped me pray over when we came here all those years ago for the Horse Creek Treaty . . . he has grown to hate his Lakota blood. He wears a blue coat."

Rising Eagle felt a sword pierce his heart. "Fall Leaf Woman's son is a *soldier*?"

"Yes," Robert said sadly. "He had some bad experiences growing up in the white man's world. He never lived among you as I did, never learned the pride of being Lakota. His actions have broken my mother's heart."

Rising Eagle sat silently for several seconds, watching the fort, waiting to see if Two Face, Blackfoot, and Four Antelope would come out to signal they could come into the fort for peace talks. "Once, on Medicine Mountain, the Feathered One told me there would be bad times for us, and that our people would become divided," he told Robert. "When I think of those like William, and those Laramie Loafers down there, living on the white man's handouts, some of them even scouting against us, I know what the Great Being meant. But He never told me to stop fighting for what is right, what is ours. I expect it to be hard, because the Feathered One already warned me of this." He looked at Robert. "I know that you understand why we cannot give up completely. It would mean we are no longer men. We have lived one way since before even our ancestors can remember." He studied Robert. "I can see you are happy. I'm glad. I missed you greatly after you chose to live with your mother."

"And I missed you, but I believe I was destined to live among the whites, to be a link between them and the Lakota."

"Perhaps. Each man has to do with his life what he thinks is best."

They both watched the events below, quietly enjoying each other's company for the short time they would have together. Suddenly there arose a commotion along the top of the log wall of the fort. It looked as though some soldiers were struggling with someone. "What are they doing?" Rising Eagle asked with alarm.

Robert studied the movement. "I don't know."

Brave Horse rode down closer then, other young warriors with him, including Crazy Horse, who rode up beside Robert, holding out his hand. Robert took hold of his wrist.

"I am *Tashunka Witko*," Crazy Horse told him. "Remember my name. The soldiers will speak it often."

Rising Eagle could tell Robert was impressed by Crazy Horse, who always wore the painted lightning bolt on the side of his face and the painted white hail spots on his chest. Robert nodded to him, then turned to Rising Eagle.

"You had a vision of one day riding into battle with a warrior named Crazy Horse."

Rising Eagle nodded proudly. "My medicine is good."

Robert looked down at his hands, opening and closing them. "How well I know."

Rising Eagle glanced at the man's fingers, remembering that strange night on Medicine Mountain, when his prayers miraculously healed Robert's fingers and toes.

"Look there!" he heard Brave Horse shout. "What are they doing to Two Face and Blackfoot?"

Rising Eagle watched in confusion as the two Lakota chiefs' bodies were lowered over the side of the fort wall.

"My God!" Robert exclaimed. "What the hell—"

"What is that around their necks!" Crazy Horse demanded.

"And hanging from their feet!" Rising Eagle added.

"Stay here!" Robert ordered. "There are too few of you. If you make a move to help, the soldiers will kill *all* of you! I will go and see what's happening."

Rising Eagle watched as Robert charged back to the fort, riding up to the chiefs' bodies, which dangled from the fort wall. Now

Four Antelope's body was also dropped over the wall. All three chiefs' bodies twisted and contorted in a struggle for life, but in moments they hung limp.

Rising Eagle watched Robert ride over to a group of soldiers and began shouting something to them. Then some of the Lakota who lived around the fort seemed to take alarm. Some of the women began screaming and running, gathering up children, and climbing onto horses, as did many of the men. They rode out toward Rising Eagle, apparently frightened.

"You must go!" one of the men shouted to Rising Eagle. "The soldiers, they hanged those Lakota and Cheyenne chiefs! They put iron chains around their necks, and tied heavy iron balls to their feet so that they would choke to death!"

Brave Horse looked at Rising Eagle in horror. "When a man dies by choking, his spirit cannot reach the place of our ancestors!"

Rising Eagle kept his eyes on Robert, seeing him riding back toward them now. "Wait for your brother," he told Brave Horse.

"Why have they done this?" Brave Horse demanded as soon as Robert was within hearing distance. "They hanged Two Face and Blackfoot! You know that is the worst way for a Lakota man to die! We came here in *peace*!"

Robert looked just as angry as they when he rode close to Rising Eagle, panting with anger and excitement. "Those in command at the fort didn't understand your gesture of peace, which is what I feared." He looked back at the fort, swearing under his breath, then met Rising Eagle's gaze again. "I'm sorry, Father. There is so much the white man just does not understand about the Lakota way."

"We are afraid they will kill us, too!" said one of those Rising Eagle deemed a Laramie Loafer. "We wish to go back with our people where we belong! Some of us, we can still fight and hunt. We are tired of begging from those white men!"

"I think we should fight them right now!" Crazy Horse exclaimed through gritted teeth. "The war along the flat river is *not* over after all!" Screaming a chilling war cry, he rode off toward the fort before anyone could stop him. Brave Horse and the other younger warriors with him followed.

"No! Wait!" Robert shouted to them. He turned to Rising

Eagle with a pleading look in his eyes. "You must *stop* them, Rising Eagle! They'll be shot down!"

No more had he spoken the words than shots rang out, and Brave Horse fell from his horse.

"Sweet Jesus!" Robert groaned.

"My son!" Rising Eagle started forward, but Robert grabbed his arm.

"Wait, Father! There will be a better time. There are at least two hundred soldiers down there, all thirsty for Lakota blood. You have to go back to wherever you're camped and hold council first! There are too few of you. You *know* that!"

"Brave Horse! I cannot lose another son!"

Crazy Horse bravely dismounted amid the gunfire and helped Brave Horse climb back onto his war pony. Then both young men and the rest of the younger warriors rode back to where Rising Eagle waited with Robert out of firing range. Robert hurriedly dismounted and helped Brave Horse climb down from his pony. At the fort soldiers raised rifles and let out their own war cries, as though they'd just experienced some kind of great victory. Now even more of the Laramie Loafers were packing belongings and preparing to run away.

Brave Horse groaned and went to his knees, holding a hand to his lower left side, where blood spilled through his fingers. Robert knelt beside him, studying the wound. "You all have to get *out* of here for now!" he told Rising Eagle, looking up at him. "Leave Brave Horse with me. I can help him!"

"Our own medicine man can help him!"

"Damn it, Rising Eagle! I've treated a hundred such wounds in the white man's war! Bullet wounds are much different from arrows and knives! Let me help him! You know you can trust me! I am Spirit Walker."

"They will make him a prisoner! Or they might hang him, too!"

"I won't let that happen! I *promise*! I had a vision once, years ago, in which I saw myself helping a wounded Brave Horse. This is my vision. Nothing can happen to him! Just go! Go, and leave him with me. I promise I will see that he finds his way back to you when he is well!"

"Spirit Walker is a *white* man now!" Crazy Horse shouted. "You cannot believe anything he says!"

Rising Eagle shot the young warrior a scolding look. "He grew up as a son to me! His heart is still *Lakota*! And he is right. This is not the time to attack. We came here in peace. You should not have gone down there, Crazy Horse. There will be a better time." He turned his horse in a circle, glaring with bitter hatred toward the bodies still hanging off the fort wall. "Another cowardly act that will not be forgotten!" He turned to Robert. "This is our last expression of peace. The Blue Coats will suffer for this." He saw tears in Robert's eyes, and he remembered the young man had always had a soft heart. "Let nothing happen to my son."

"I will always honor you as my father, and Brave Horse as my brother," Robert answered. "No harm will come to him. I will help him and see that he gets back to you. Go now. Hurry, before the soldiers decide to come out here and shoot the rest of you down."

Rising Eagle held his gaze a moment longer, then rode closer to Robert and Brave Horse. He reached down and touched the top of Brave Horse's head. "May the Great Spirit be with you, my son. You can trust Spirit Walker. And you can be sure this cowardly act will not go unanswered."

Brave Horse cast him a look of devastation. "My medicine . . . was not strong. I am ashamed."

Rising Eagle shook his head. "If Spirit Walker had a vision of helping you, then there is a reason for this. It has nothing to do with the power of your medicine, my son. Let Spirit Walker help you. His medicine is also strong."

Panting and grimacing with pain, Brave Horse nodded. "Go, Father. The others must know about this."

Rising Eagle turned again to Robert. "I may never see you again, Spirit Walker. May the wind always be at your back. Perhaps those like you can learn a new way, but some of us never will. To live the way the white man wants us to live is like being walking dead men. We would have no purpose."

"Damn it, Rising Eagle, I'm so damned sorry." Agony in his eyes, Robert looked toward the fort again. "It looks like they're assembling." He looked at Rising Eagle again. "Go! Quickly."

His heart heavy at leaving Brave Horse, Rising Eagle turned and rode off, the other warriors following. He could only pray Spirit Walker was right in saying no further harm would come to Brave Horse. How sad that this meeting with his long-lost adopted son had to end this way . . . another example of the cowardliness and stupidity of the white man.

CHAPTER THIRTY-TWO

REBECCA HELPED ROBERT wrap clean gauze around Brave Horse's middle, while the still-painted young man lay semi-conscious from drinking laudanum for pain. Getting him to drink the medicine had been a difficult argument for Robert, since Brave Horse trusted no medicine used by white men. Besides that, a Lakota warrior took great honor in the pain he suffered from fighting the enemy. He could not be considered brave if he did something to take that pain away. Only when Robert convinced him that drinking the laudanum was the same as blowing on a whistle during the pain of the Sun Dance did Brave Horse finally agree to swallow the medicine so that Robert could treat his wound.

"I've never seen a truly wild Indian this close," Rebecca commented.

Robert chuckled. "I do believe you have seen *me* up close, and Brave Horse is no different from me." He enjoyed the color that came into her cheeks.

"You know what I mean." She sighed as Robert tied off the gauze. "Do you think the commander will leave him alone? I mean, he won't try to put him in prison or something, will he?"

"I would help him escape if that happened."

Rebecca folded her arms in front of her. "That frightens me. I worry that you will end up being arrested yourself, Robert. Maybe we should go back to your old home in Illinois until these Indian wars are over."

Robert covered Brave Horse, who lay on his and Rebecca's rope-spring bed. He turned to Rebecca, moving his arms around her. "I can't leave now, Becky. You know that. There are too many people out here that I care about. They might need me, just like Brave Horse needed me. William might end up needing me also." He kissed her forehead. "I can understand how you must feel, afraid for yourself and for the baby. As long as we're here at Laramie you needn't worry. It's the soldiers who go out on patrol for wood-cutting expeditions and the like who are in danger."

She rested her head against his chest. "I wouldn't leave you no matter what the danger. If you don't want to leave, then I'm not leaving either. I just worry about your involvement in all of this, and what it does to you on the inside to see these things happening to the Lakota."

Before he could reply there came a knock at the door. He gave Rebecca a light hug, then left her to open the door to his mother and William. He cast William a look of chastisement. "Did you come to hang another peaceful Indian?" he asked his stepbrother.

William raised his chin, a gesture that reminded Robert of Rising Eagle. Over the past few weeks, now that William was more man than boy, he'd noticed a peculiar resemblance between William and Rising Eagle. A white man would simply say that was because all Indian men looked alike, but they did not, and William's resemblance to Rising Eagle was uncanny.

"I came because our mother claims to have something very important to tell us," William answered curtly. "I'm off-duty, but I don't have much time, so let's get this over with. And, by the way, I did not participate in that hanging, although after what the Lakota did to that poor woman, it didn't bother me much."

Robert stepped aside to let Florence and William in. "Knowing the Lakota, I have no doubt the woman exaggerated," he told William. "And don't forget that Mrs. Eubanks was the prisoner of the Cheyenne, not the Lakota. They are the ones who raped her, as she put it. I am not even going to attempt the Indian explanation of that word. Actually, it doesn't exist in the Lakota tongue, and when an Indian man claims the enemy's woman, it has a whole different meaning than when a white man rapes for his own selfish, insidious pleasure. And I suppose it was all right for the men at Sand Creek to not only rape the innocent women there, but also to cut open their bellies and rip out babies and reproductive organs, as well as run swords through little children. Do you agree?"

William rolled his eyes, then glanced at Brave Horse, who lay lightly moaning on the bed in the corner of the one-room cabin. "You know you're just inviting trouble for yourself, treating that hostile, don't you?"

Robert shrugged. "Maybe." He turned to his mother, leaning down to kiss her cheek. "Let's sit down, and you can tell us why you've brought your reluctant son here," he told her. He pulled out a chair made from hand-hewn logs, and Florence thanked him and sat down at the table, also homemade from planks nailed to logs. William, Robert, and Rebecca took the other three chairs, and Rebecca asked if anyone wanted coffee from the pot she'd kept heated over hot coals in the stone fireplace.

"No. Just sit, Rebecca," Florence told her.

Robert realized his mother seemed extremely agitated. "Are you all right?" he asked her.

"No."

The woman looked as though someone had just died.

"What is going on, Mother?"

Florence blinked back tears as she looked over at Brave Horse. "He looks so much like his father," she said rather absently. Then she turned to William. "As do you, William."

All three of the others frowned.

"What the heck are you talking about?" William asked with a frown.

"Look at him, William," Florence said quietly. "Look at Brave Horse. Don't you see the resemblance?"

Still scowling, William took another look at Brave Horse. "He's Lakota. Of course we resemble each other."

"That's white-man talk," Florence said.

William sighed. "So what? That's how I think and feel."

Robert began to get a very eerie feeling. "Mother, you're talking in puzzles. What is it you asked us here for?"

Florence closed her eyes and put a hand to her head. "I asked you here to tell you I've . . . lied to both of you . . . for years."

"Lied about what?" William asked.

Florence swallowed as though afraid of something. "That handsome young warrior lying on that bed . . ." She opened her eyes and faced William. "He's your brother, William. Your *blood* brother. Not just Lakota blood, but . . . Rising Eagle's blood."

Robert felt a rush of cold sweep through him, and Rebecca drew in her breath. William just sat staring at the woman he'd called mother all his life. His jaw flexed as the blood seemed to literally drain from his face. "What the hell are you talking about?"

Florence blinked back tears. "At the risk of losing your love, my son, you have a right to know the truth. Twenty years ago a white woman was brought to this very place, much like Mrs. Eubanks was brought here today. She'd been a captive of Rising Eagle, who agreed to turn her over to Agent Thomas Fitzpatrick in exchange for rifles. He kept the woman's stepdaughter."

"Yellow Bonnet!" Robert spoke up. "You met her mother after Rising Eagle gave her back?"

Florence nodded. "She . . . was carrying a child . . . Rising Eagle's child."

After a moment of silence, while the reality of what she was implying began to set in, Robert put his head in his hands. "Oh, my God. When I came to you all those years later, you led me to believe William belonged to you and Abel."

"This is crazy!" William said, intense anger in his dark eyes. "It's *crazy*! You're making this up!"

"I am finally telling you the *truth*, William!" Florence said, raising her voice. "The woman didn't want her baby because it was fathered by a Lakota man. She wanted to go back home and pretend none of it ever happened. Her husband had been killed by Rising Eagle, and she felt if people knew the truth of what happened to her, no white man would even look at her! She stayed here until she gave birth and then she left. She abandoned you, her own precious son, and I took you in and I loved you like my very own! I couldn't have any more children after I had Robert, and I dearly wanted another baby. I had given Robert to Rising Eagle to raise because I was an alcoholic and couldn't take care of him. But by the time you came along, I was healed and married to Abel, and all those years I missed my firstborn son. I *ached* for him! Then when you were born I had a baby to hold and love again, and I *do* love you, just as much as I love Robert, who *is* of my own blood! But he isn't *your* blood brother, William. That young warrior lying on that bed *is*! Brave Horse is your half-brother, and Rising Eagle is your real father."

William kicked back his chair and rose, fists clenched. "Why didn't you tell me a long time ago? And why didn't you just give me to the *Lakota* to raise?"

"Because I wanted a baby to hold again," Florence answered, tears starting to trickle down her cheeks. "I had given my son to Rising Eagle, and now I had a chance to raise one of *his* sons. I made Thomas Fitzpatrick promise never to tell Rising Eagle, because I was afraid he would come and try to take you from me. Sons mean *everything* to a Lakota man."

William turned away. "This isn't true. It *can't* be true!"

"If you hadn't joined the army and come out here to fight Indians, I might never have had to tell you," Florence answered. "But now that you might go out there and end up fighting your own father, and your own brothers, you have to know. Rising Eagle has three living children, Brave Horse, and another son and a daughter. They are your brothers and sister, William. You can deny it all you want, but it's the *truth*!"

He turned to face her again. "How *dare* you! How dare you do this to me! For God's sake, I'm signed up for five more years! What the hell do I tell my men whenever we find ourselves caught in a battle with the Lakota? 'Don't shoot! You might kill my father and brothers?' " He walked to the door and put his fists against it, bending his head. "Jesus!"

The room hung silent for a moment.

"Dear Lord," Rebecca said then in a near whisper.

Robert sighed and rose. "What about Brave Horse? Should we tell him when he comes around?"

Florence shook her head. "I don't know. I will leave that up to you, Robert. You knew him best. You grew up with him."

Robert studied the agony in her eyes. "I can't say this doesn't upset me, Mother. After all, I've thought of William as my blood brother all these years."

"I hope you can forgive me, Robert." She looked at William. "And I hope you can also forgive me, my son."

"Don't call me son," William groaned, hanging his head as he still faced the door.

Florence covered her face and wept. Robert walked over and placed his hands on her shoulders. "We'll work this out. It will just take some getting used to. And you were right to tell William."

"The hell she was!" William said, finally turning. "Except for one good reason." He walked closer. "Now I know why I never felt close to you, Mother. You weren't my mother at all! And now I know why I hate the Lakota! I hate them because my *real* mother hated them for what they did to her! She hated *me* and she hated the man who planted my seed in her. I *also* hated him, for creating a son who has had to live in two worlds and has never belonged to either one of them! I've had to choose, and I chose the white man's world. That's where I am *staying*! And don't expect me to care whether or not I might end up setting my rifle sight on Rising Eagle or Brave Horse or any of the rest of them! They mean *nothing* to me! Do you understand? *Nothing!* And don't you dare mention this to any of those men out there. I never want them to know! I've had a hard enough time making myself credible and respected in this army! The last thing I need is for my men or my commanding officers to know that one of the most wanted Lakota hostiles is my *father!*" He walked to the door. "Damn you," he said coldly. "*Damn* you!"

He walked out, slamming the door so hard that it jolted Brave Horse awake for a moment.

"Ate," he murmured, moaning for his father.

JUNE 1865

Moon When the Green Grass Is Up

CHAPTER THIRTY-THREE

"THIS IS OUTRAGEOUS!" Robert fumed. "Moving all the friendly Lakota to Fort Kearny will only unite them more firmly with the hostiles and make things worse, not better!"

The order had come only two days after the incident of the hanging and Brave Horse's injury. All friendly Lakota, meaning mainly the Laramie Loafers and any other Lakota who wished to come in peacefully and settle for handouts from the government, must move away from Fort Laramie, east to Fort Kearny.

"Kearny is in the heart of Pawnee country! The next thing you know they'll be wanting to move them into Oklahoma Territory. They could never survive in country like that. The government is ordering peaceful Lakota out of land already promised to them!"

"The order includes us," Florence told her son as she read the diction. She looked up at Robert from where she sat at the kitchen table. "We are to go also, just because we have Lakota blood. Even the Bordeauxs have to go. James Bordeaux has had a trading post here for years. He is no threat at all. But his wife is Sioux, and so they all must go."

Robert glanced at Brave Horse, who now lay on blankets on the floor, having voiced his dislike of the soft bed he'd first been laid in. Robert could see confusion in his adoptive brother's dark eyes over his own obviously agitated state.

"Colonel Moonlight is an idiot and an ass!" he grumbled, sitting down to the table.

"Yet he is the commander here," Florence reminded him. "And his orders have come from—" She looked at the printed orders again. "A Major General Grenville Dodge, the new commander of the Department of the Missouri. He is most likely a man who knows nothing about how to deal with the Lakota."

"And word is Moonlight once was just a Kansas volunteer," Robert added, "schooled by none other than Colonel John Chivington, the same sonofabitch who led the attack on peaceful Cheyenne at Sand Creek. Such are the kind of men who are in charge of Lakota affairs! The hostiles are already furious over the fact that the bodies of Two Face, Blackfoot, and Four Antelope were dragged to that scaffold west of here and left there to rot, an obvious attempt to further disgrace the Lakota. No man should be allowed to hang in the open, covered with flies and maggots and picked at by buzzards! The Lakota wouldn't do that to their worst enemy!" He rubbed at his eyes. "How in hell can I explain this to Brave Horse, or convince him that he and Rising Eagle and the others are better off turning themselves in and settling for peace? This is just another example of the stupidity of the United States government! They will end up wanting yet another treaty, changing the promise that the Lakota could stay in the area between here and the Powder River forever. When they hear about this order, they'll panic. This will only unite all of them against the whites."

Rebecca turned from where she'd been kneading bread dough. She rubbed at her stomach. "This is not a good time for me to have to pull up and travel somewhere."

Robert glanced at her sadly. "Let alone the danger the move could present from the hostiles." He closed his eyes and shook his head. "I'm sorry, Rebecca. I didn't expect this. I figured you'd be here when you had the baby, where there are plenty of supplies and decent facilities; not walking across the plains."

"Robert, the army can't order us to do anything," Florence told him.

"They can if the order comes directly from the government.

They want Laramie populated with soldiers only. A lot of people have settled around here, mostly Lakota and half-bloods. Laramie is considered government property now. If they tell us to get out, we have to get out." He rose again, pacing. "The fools think that by getting rid of all of us, their troubles will be over." He glanced at Brave Horse. "They will learn that their troubles have only begun, I'm afraid; and if I wasn't devoted to my doctoring and my lovely white wife, I'd be half tempted to go join up with Rising Eagle."

Rebecca returned to kneading the bread, using more force and energy than normal because of her frustration. "What about William? He is also a half-blood."

Robert glanced at his mother again, and she looked at her lap, twisting at a ruffle on the skirt of her dress. "What happens to William happens. There is nothing we can do for him. He won't *let* us do anything for him."

"He's a good soldier. No one can deny that," Robert said. "He'll likely be allowed to continue with his service, as long as he keeps his hair cut short and obeys orders. This will only make his job harder, that's for sure."

"Which will make him even more unhappy," Florence said quietly.

Robert sighed, turning back to Brave Horse, who now was sitting up, looking around the room with a look of a prisoner in his eyes. When the young brave finally returned Robert's gaze, he spoke.

"I want to go now."

"You're too weak," Robert answered in the Lakota tongue. "And right now is not a good time, Brave Horse." He walked over to sit down in front of his brother. "I need to explain something to you, and you have to listen if you want to live to return to Rising Eagle. You have to trust me, Brave Horse."

Brave Horse frowned. "What has happened? You are angry about something. Do the soldiers want to hang *me*, too?"

Robert shook his head. "Not if you stay here quietly with us and do what I tell you. But if you make one move that leads the commander of this fort to think you are going to hurt someone, he won't hesitate to kill you, Brave Horse; or worse, put you in the fort prison. He has imprisoned other Lakota, one of whom I have been treating for an infected leg from where it's been rubbed raw from the iron cuff and ball he has to wear. Prisoners are put in chains, Brave Horse. I don't want to see that happen to you. Colonel Moonlight hates the Lakota. What I am angry about right now is that he has sent out an order given him by a new Indian agent appointed by the white man's government. All Lakota in this area, peaceful or hostile, are supposed to move away from here. They are to go east, to Fort Kearny. The order includes the half-bloods, like myself and my mother."

Brave Horse stiffened. "I will not go where it is even hotter, where there are no mountains, no trees! That is *Pawnee* country! No Lakota should have to go there! The white man promised this land and the land along the Powder River would be ours forever!"

"I know what he promised."

"I have to go!" Brave Horse tried to rise, but Robert grasped his arms.

"No, Brave Horse! Trust me on this! You have to stay right here for now. Your best chance of escaping is after we start moving east. Once we're on the move there will be fewer soldiers. They will send a company to guard us. Some of the friendly ones have already fled, so it won't be long before Rising Eagle will know about this order. You and I both know he's probably out there somewhere right now watching out for you, waiting for you to return. He knows you will be with us when we make the move. My gut tells me this will not be a peaceful movement at all. The Lakota, especially ones like Rising Eagle, and Red Cloud will never settle for this."

"There will be *war!*" Brave Horse sneered. "The white man cannot start ordering us to move to little pieces of useless land, where the buffalo are already gone and the game and wood are scarce. We will not leave the north country! I must go to my father! And to Beaver Woman! She is to be my wife!"

"You will get to them, Brave Horse. I promise you. But you will never make it if you don't listen to me and trust me. Besides that, you have to be stronger, more ready for an escape. If you move around too much right now you could pass out from weakness after losing so much blood just three days ago."

Brave Horse studied him intently. "What will *you* do? Are you going to the land of the Pawnee?"

"Not if I can help it. I am a university graduate with a medical degree, and my wife is white. I think I can convince the commander to let me stay, especially since Rebecca is carrying. It's possible Florence can also stay, since she's a seamstress and earns her own way here. Besides that, they think—" Robert hesitated. Should he tell Brave Horse? "They think William is her son, and he's a sergeant here, a good soldier, from what I can tell. Even if William gets shipped off someplace else, they might be lenient with Florence and let her stay here because she's his mother."

Brave Horse shook his head. "The white man has strange values. We should not have to lower ourselves to him and beg for the things we want. It is like begging them to keep their promises. No Lakota man would think of breaking a promise."

Robert sighed in agreement. "I have learned how to deal with them, but this order is completely unfair."

"When are we to go?"

"In about ten days."

"That is too long! I will not stay in this place that long!"

"You have to, Brave Horse. Be patient."

Brave Horse scowled, tossing his hair behind his shoulders. "Where are my weapons?"

"We will smuggle them out with us when we leave. When you need them, you will have them. I promise."

Still scowling, Brave Horse lay back down, staring at the ceiling. "I do not like this place. How can you live inside four walls, in a place where the Great Spirit cannot find you; where you cannot look at the stars when you sleep?"

Robert grinned. "I often sit outside at night for a while before I go to bed. My wife understands."

Brave Horse moved his gaze to Rebecca, then to Florence. "I think that your wife should stay behind during this march."

Robert was glad Rebecca could not understand the words, since their conversation was in the Lakota tongue. Rebecca would be very upset at the mention of staying behind, but that was exactly what he himself thought should be done. The trip was too dangerous for her, not just because of possible trouble, but because of the baby. That would be a good way to get the commander to also allow Florence to stay. Rebecca would need her if she went into labor. "I agree," he told Brave Horse, "but I'll go myself, mainly to make sure that if you get the chance, you can escape."

Brave Horse touched his arm. "I will make sure you are protected," he told him. "And if possible, I will see that William is not hurt, even though he wears a soldier's uniform. He is still Lakota, the son of Fall Leaf Woman."

Robert glanced at Florence, reading the anxious look in her eyes.

"Don't tell him," she said quietly. "It would break Rising Eagle's heart to know a son of his wears a blue coat. If William won't acknowledge the relationship, there is no sense telling Brave Horse or Rising Eagle."

Robert rose, facing her. "The day will come when they will have to know, Mother. Instinct tells me that. And some day William has to face the truth, and face Rising Eagle. He should not let the man go to his grave without making things right."

"That's William's choice to make, not ours. I thought I was doing the right thing by not telling him a long time ago. I just . . . I suppose I never thought it would come to this." She looked at Brave Horse. "How are you feeling, Brave Horse?" she asked in the Lakota tongue, putting on a smile.

"I have pain," he said, putting a hand to his side. "But I wish to leave this place."

"You can trust Robert. If he says you are not ready, you should listen to him. And he is right about waiting until you are away from here to try to go back to your camp."

Brave Horse looked up at Robert. "What happened to the bodies of Two Face and Blackfoot? And to the Cheyenne leader, Four Antelope? Were they taken out where my people can pick them up and give them a proper burial?"

Robert felt sick inside. He sat down in a chair and faced Brave Horse. "I wish I could say they were," he answered. "But they were taken out to a scaffold west of the fort and left hanging there to rot. It is our commander's way of trying to frighten the Lakota into obeying what they are told to do."

An icy look came into Brave Horse's dark, angry eyes. "They will pay for such an insult!"

Robert nodded. "I have no doubt they will, Brave Horse. Bad times are ahead."

"That's because white men stole my mother's sacred white buffalo robe."

"What?" Robert well remembered the importance of the white buffalo robe, not just to Buffalo Dreamer, but to all the Lakota.

"Many years ago. Father and Mother were camped alone, and white men snuck down after dark and stole it from where it hung outside their tepee to air out. It broke my mother's heart. She cut her hair and let blood, and she and Rising Eagle went to Medicine Mountain to pray for its return, and for strength and wisdom to survive without its protection. The robe has never been found. Rising Eagle believes *Wakan-Tanka* is just teaching us a lesson in how to be strong even without the sacred white."

"This is sad news," Robert said, shaking his head. "I can just imagine how hard that was on Buffalo Dreamer." He gave Brave Horse a reassuring look. "Maybe someday the robe will be found and returned to its rightful owner."

"*Aye.* I always include the return of the white robe in my prayers." A sad look came over Brave Horse's face. "Do you still have the pipe Rising Eagle gave you long ago, my brother?"

"Of course I do. Do you wish to smoke the pipe with me?"

"Yes," Brave Horse answered, grimacing as he sat up again. "It will give me strength. Then you can sing and pray over me the old way."

Robert nodded, smiling. "I will be glad to sing over you, Brave Horse."

"No matter what happens, we will always be brothers."

Robert felt a lump in his throat. "We will always be brothers." How he wished William could feel the same way.

JULY 1865

Moon When the Chokecherries Ripen

CHAPTER THIRTY-FOUR

BRAVE HORSE NEARLY choked on the dust from the long line of wagons ahead of him. The procession of soldiers and Indians began with the leader of the 135-man escort, Captain William Fouts, a balding, gruff soldier with nothing but contempt for the people he led to Fort Kearny. The man was often drunk from white man's fire water, his face red and puffy, his personality hateful.

Ten army wagons filled with tents and supplies came first, followed by a wagon carrying Fouts's wife and two daughters, as well as Mrs. Eubanks and her baby. Another army wagon carried one of the Lakota prisoners, his leg festered from abrasions caused by the iron cuff he was forced to wear. Three more prisoners, in chains, rode on horses, looking miserable. Fur traders with Indian wives and half-breed children followed in their own wagons, accompanied by their livestock. Then came the Lakota, mostly Oglalas and Brules, pulling travois piled high with their belongings and accompanied by their own horses and several dogs.

He was glad Robert had managed to convince Rebecca and Florence to stay behind at Laramie, relieved that the despicable, hated Colonel Moonlight had agreed to allow Robert's request because of Rebecca's condition. Rebecca had begged to go, hating to have Robert out of her sight, but finally she gave in to his demand that she stay behind. He promised to return as soon as possible, and Brave Horse made a promise to himself to protect him if necessary.

The behavior of the soldiers made Brave Horse burn inside with fury, all the more reason for Florence and Rebecca not to see this. Now he knew for certain he could never live on a reservation under the hand of such slovenly, ruthless, and dishonorable people. Sometimes soldiers would throw an Indian baby into the river to see if it would swim. And sometimes they took young Lakota girls into their tents. The Lakota were helpless to do anything to stop it . . . but soon . . . soon . . . the soldiers would pay!

Robert had heard talk among the Laramie Loafers. The Lakota were planning an escape, and there were as many as fifteen hundred hostiles out in the hills waiting to help them! Brave Horse had no doubt that Rising Eagle and Crazy Horse were among them. He could hardly wait to see his father and his good friend again. Thunder would probably also be with them. He'd missed his brother. Once he rejoined his clan, these soldiers would soon regret their inhumane treatment of his People!

The first two days of the forced march seemed to drag mercilessly slow. Some of the younger Indians raced horses after making camp in the evening, needing to make the time pass; but just last night Fouts had ordered no more racing, worrying it might lead to escape attempts. He had declared that anyone caught racing would be tied to a wagon wheel and given fifteen lashes with a whip.

Dusk fell, and the long train of soldiers and Indians halted along Horse Creek to make camp. Brave Horse dismounted the war pony Robert had kept for him after he was wounded, and he and Robert unloaded their horses and rolled out blankets. They turned their horses out to graze and sat down to rest, both taking some jerked beef from their supplies to nourish themselves. Brave Horse, his side still aching, drank some water from a canteen.

"I will need my knife and my handgun," he told Robert in the Lakota tongue. "Tomorrow morning you would be wise to look to the soldiers and go where they go for cover."

Robert nodded. "That's when they will make their break?"

"Yes."

Robert reached into a supply sack and took out Brave Horse's handgun, which Brave Horse had stolen from a dead white man at Julesburg. He cautiously handed it over.

"I hope you know, Brave Horse, that when the shooting starts, I will have to fire against the Lakota. I have to do so to protect my mother and my wife. If the soldiers think I had anything to do with the escape, they could arrest me, even hang me."

"I understand, my brother."

"I won't really try to hit anything, but I have to make it look good. Where will these Lakota get weapons?"

Brave Horse grinned arrogantly. "They are clever. The soldiers think they have taken all our weapons, but my people know how to hide things well. The soldiers will be surprised." He sobered. "My heart is sad that it has to be this way, Spirit Walker. After tomorrow, I may never see you again. I wish it were not so."

Robert nodded. "So do I." He took a deep breath. "And there is something I think you should know. My mother disagrees, but I feel I am right in telling you."

"What is that?"

A dog ran between them, barking and throwing dirt, and a young Indian girl ran after it. All around them the camp was a bustle of wagons and horses, and soldiers shouting orders.

"William," Robert said, moving closer to be heard. "He is not really my blood brother. Florence is not his mother."

Brave Horse frowned. "Why do you tell me this?"

"It's important that you know. Florence adopted William to raise as her own son. His real mother was a white woman, the woman Rising Eagle captured years ago and then gave to Broken Hand Fitzpatrick in trade for rifles."

Brave Horse thought a moment, then felt the reality hit him so hard that he gasped. "We share the same *father?*"

Robert nodded. "William is your half-brother, Brave Horse. Florence never told Rising Eagle because she was afraid he would try to steal the boy away. Now she doesn't want Rising Eagle to know that a son of his own blood wears an army uniform and hates his Lakota blood. However, I think he *should* know. Someday it might be important. I leave it up to you if and when Rising Eagle is told."

Brave Horse wiped sweat from his dusty face, feeling stunned. Rising Eagle had another son he knew nothing about, and that son wore a blue coat! "Does William know?"

"Yes, but he hasn't known for long. Either way, he claims it doesn't matter to him, that he is a soldier out here to fight Indians, and that he feels no connection to his Lakota blood. He's had plenty of opportunity to come and talk to you, but he won't do it. I'm sorry, Brave Horse."

Brave Horse felt the pain of realizing how cleverly and decidedly the white men were beginning to divide his people. "There are others of our own blood who have begun to betray us. And William was raised in the white world. He knows nothing of the Lakota. You understand, because you were raised with us."

"I felt you had to know. Years ago I had a vision that one day I would help you when you were wounded. That day came, and I believed there had to be a reason for it. Now I believe that reason is to have the chance to tell you the truth about William."

Brave Horse nodded. "Perhaps." He turned to watch soldiers making camp on the east side of Horse Creek, away from the dust and commotion of the traders and Indians. "It is here that we came to sign a treaty many years ago, a treaty promising land to us that now the white man says is no longer ours. Now I find I have a blood brother who will fight against us." He felt a pain in his heart. "Everything has changed. Everything is wrong. The white man brings so much confusion. Nothing he does makes sense." He sighed, shaking his head. "We cannot believe anything they tell us. And now they are beginning to divide us." He looked back at Robert. "But this march, this betrayal of the Horse Creek treaty *will* unite us. We will never forget the sight of the bodies of honorable chiefs left to hang and rot in the sun, food for crows. And even if my own brother has to die for that, then I cannot stop it."

"I understand." Robert put a cork back into the mouth of his canteen. "Will you tell Rising Eagle?"

Brave Horse frowned. "I don't know. I'll think about it."

Robert nodded. "You'd better get some rest. You'll need it for tomorrow."

Brave Horse smiled, looking upward. "The skies are clear. I

think tomorrow will be a good day to die, if that is what must be; but I do not think many Lakota will die. Perhaps it will be soldiers who die."

Robert felt tears sting his eyes. "Tell Rising Eagle that I will always miss him and pray for him."

Brave Horse gave his adopted brother a warm smile, and Robert could see that he, too, had tears in his eyes. "He knows. And you and I will always be brothers."

Silently the Lakota took weapons from under blankets and made ready their horses, while the soldier escort and their wagons got underway at sunrise. The traders and half-bloods followed, but the Indian camp did not move.

"Go now," Brave Horse told Robert. "Take your horse and hurry to join the soldiers. Tell them you think there will be trouble and you want to help them."

Robert grasped his wrist. "God go with you, Brave Horse."

Brave Horse felt the pain of parting once again, as they had to part so many years ago when Spirit Walker chose to stay with his mother after finding her at Fort Laramie.

"I wish it could be different," Robert told him.

"As do I. Go now."

Robert turned away and mounted up, heading out at a slow trot at first, not wanting to present too much alarm. Brave Horse mounted his own horse, his heart racing with a thirst for battle and freedom. Soon he would be with Rising Eagle and the rest of the Oglalas who still chose freedom over the filth and boredom of reservation life.

Now Fouts was circling the Indian camp with a few of his men, shouting and cursing at them for not breaking camp and following the half-bloods. It was time to get under way, but the Lakota were making no move to leave. Then Brave Horse let out a blood-curdling war cry, followed by several yips, a signal to the rest of the camp.

Instantly warriors mounted their ponies and women grabbed children and bundles of supplies and ran for the river. All knew it was possible some would drown in the swift, cold current, but it was worth the risk. Brave Horse rode close to the screaming, angry Captain Fouts and pulled out his handgun, shooting the man through the heart.

Fouts fell from his horse, and Brave Horse and other warriors chased down his escort and shot them down. Now bullets were flying everywhere. The surprised soldiers farther ahead began shooting back, and the half-bloods and traders were caught between. Some tried to quickly circle their wagons, as did the drivers of the army wagons, causing some of the wagons to careen sideways and fall over.

The entire camp became a bedlam of flying bullets and arrows, screaming women and cursing, confused soldiers. Women and children as well as warriors who were herding spare horses forded the river. Brave Horse shouted to some of the other warriors to help him free the Lakota prisoners. He charged in their direction, shooting down the soldier who guarded them and ripping keys from his body that could unlock the chains on the prisoners.

He felt the whiz of bullets everywhere, but he managed to free the three prisoners who were still able to walk or ride. The prisoner with the festered leg was in an army wagon, and it was impossible to get to him without being killed. Reluctantly he had to leave him.

Because they had planned this, the Lakota were more organized than the soldiers, and they managed to steal some of the army horses as they made their way to the north side of the North Platte, where more Lakota, some of the hostiles, appeared from over a rise to help them.

"Father!" Brave Horse muttered, spotting Rising Eagle. He charged up the hill. "I knew you would come!" he yelled before he reached the man.

"My son! You are alive!"

"Spirit Walker sang over me. I have much to tell you, Father."

Crazy Horse rode up to them then, shouting a cry of joy at seeing that his good friend was alive. Both young men screamed war whoops and rode down with Rising Eagle and others who'd come to fight. They rode into the river to help women and children struggling out of the cold water. Rising Eagle handed Brave Horse a rifle, and both men took aim, downing more soldiers.

"Where is Thunder?" Brave Horse shouted amid the gunfire.

"He stayed at the village with those who will protect the rest of our women and children," Rising Eagle answered.

"Spirit Walker is down there, Father!" Brave Horse warned. "Do not shoot at anyone who does not wear a uniform!" Should he tell his father he even had to be careful of shooting at the men *in* uniform, that he might shoot his own son? There was no time to explain. Brave Horse's heart fell when from where he sat he could see soldiers dragging the sick prisoner he'd had to leave behind from the army wagon. Then they shot him. A soldier who appeared to be full of arrows managed to walk up and lean close to the prisoner, shooting him once more in the head. It looked as though another soldier was scalping him.

After another hour of shooting and keeping most of the soldiers pinned down, the Lakota finally escaped. Rising Eagle, Crazy Horse, and others who'd come to help had brought extra horses for those who had none. Women and children mounted up, and the several hundred Lakota who were being marched to Fort Kearny in hated Pawnee country made their way north, toward the Powder River and the beloved hunting grounds that were supposed to be theirs forever.

Brave Horse could only pray that Spirit Walker . . . and William . . . had not been harmed. He might never know, for he doubted he would ever see either one of them, or Fall Leaf Woman, again.

JULY 1867

Time of Ripeness

CHAPTER THIRTY-FIVE

BUFFALO DREAMER WORE her finest tunic to the powwow, invited as an honored holy woman to sit behind her husband at the important meeting. Excitement prevailed among the elders present. This summer's Sun Dance would resound with power and victory, as more young men shed blood to *Wakan-Tanka* and joined the mighty force of united Lakota and Shihenna who had enjoyed significant victories the past summer. On into winter they continued a relentless harrassment of soldiers at the three major forts along the white man's road that led to northern gold mines, as well as attacking all travelers, until nearly all movement through their northern hunting grounds came to a halt.

Just last winter the Lakota, led by Red Cloud, Rising Eagle, and Crazy Horse, had ambushed a troop of over eighty soldiers several miles outside of Fort Phil Kearny. Every last man was killed, and many weapons were stolen. It was a great victory, especially for Red Cloud, who led most of the raids; and for Crazy Horse, who initiated a very successful plan of luring soldiers into areas where they were then trapped by a larger force of Lakota. His trick worked well and continued to be successful. Red Cloud's strategy of constant attacks on any soldiers who left the confines of the northern forts seemed to be working beyond their expectations. Lakota and Shihenna warriors made it almost impossible for soldiers to go out on important wood-cutting expeditions, which meant freezing winters with little or no heat for warmth or for cooking. Soldiers and settlers who traveled the Bozeman did so at great risk.

Now, here in the valley of the Little Big Horn River, were gathered the most important leaders of the Oglala, Brule, Hunkpapa, Minneconjou, and Sans Arcs, as well as northern Cheyenne and Arapaho. *Mahapiya-luta*, Red Cloud, again reminded them that it was only by remaining united this way that they could continue striking out at the new soldier forts along the Bozeman. He suggested they concentrate on Fort Phil Kearny, near the only good source of wood. "White men have built a mill there, where they cut hundreds of trees for lumber and for wood to burn. Many of those trees are still fresh and alive. I hear them cry with pain when they are cut down."

"The easier place to attack would be the place called Fort Smith," the Shihenna leader, Dull Knife, protested. "It is far to the north and has fewer men. It is less protected."

The rest of the leaders present began discussing the matter, and Buffalo Dreamer took pride in the fact that Brave Horse was among them. She thought how no greater example of the bravery and power of the Lakota could be found than right here at this powwow.

"These are the best hunting grounds left to us," Red Cloud spoke. "We must be vigilant in protecting them. If we continue creating enough trouble for the soldiers, they will leave. I think it is best to continue attacking the forces that are sent out to cut wood for Fort Phil Kearny."

"We are strong now, many in numbers since we are more united," Rising Eagle answered. "Perhaps we can attack more than one fort at a time. If the esteemed leader of the Shihenna, Dull Knife, wishes to attack the fort farther north, it might be possible to do both."

Many of them nodded. Then Crazy Horse rose to speak. "Let me and those who wish to ride with me attack the wood cutters at Fort Phil Kearny. We can gather at least a thousand warriors for this. Dull Knife could take another six or seven hundred of his braves farther north. If we strike more than one fort at once, it might wear down the soldier resistance more quickly. We can starve or freeze them out! They will give up and go home!"

Brave Horse raised his fist and shouted three yips of agreement. Others joined in, and soon all were shouting war whoops of support.

Rising Eagle rose then, putting up his hand for quiet. The yips and shouts diminished as they waited for him to speak. "Our scouts have told us that the one called General Connor once gave his men an order that all male Lakota and Shihenna and other tribes over the age of twelve summers should be attacked and killed. Now I give an order, that all *white* men, especially those who wear the blue coats, should be killed!"

The shouting and yipping rang in full force again.

"It will be easier for us," Crazy Horse yelled. "They keep themselves confined to the areas of the forts and go out in groups to cut their wood. But we know how to scatter when they come after us. They cannot catch us! They cannot even find us!"

Buffalo Dreamer smiled, feeling compelled to join in more shouts of war, as the circle of elders and warriors broke up. Drummers began pounding their rhythmic tempo, breaking into songs of war and victory. As was necessary in order to gain even more strength and courage for more planned attacks, warriors began dancing around a huge central fire, built by the women. All drew strength from their songs and prayers to *Wakan-Tanka* for protection and success.

Hundreds more gathered around the dancers, joining in song, so that by dusk the air resounded with singing mixed with war whoops and yips of eagerness to attack and kill.

Buffalo Dreamer watched the celebration with pride. *Yes, we are strong! United!* Wherever the white buffalo was now, it could only bring bad luck to the white men who had it in their possession. That was why so many were dying at the hands of the Lakota!

Life was good. Brave Horse had married Beaver Woman not long after he escaped the soldiers at Horse Creek, and now, at last, she was a grandmother! Beaver Woman had given birth to a little girl the previous summer. Small Flower was beautiful and healthy.

It was time to take out the deer hide she kept rolled up in her personal parfleche and paint more scenes on it, adding to the circle of life she recorded there, scenes that depicted important events in her life, the birth of family members, important victories for Brave Horse, Thunder, and Rising Eagle.

Thunder rode with his brother and Crazy Horse now. Both her sons were proud, accomplished warriors. She Who Sings was being courted by a prominent young Shihenna man called Black Hawk. Perhaps by next summer she would have yet another grandchild. Now, if only she could recover the white buffalo robe, life could be almost perfect.

Men and women alike danced around the bright fire, from which embers flew upward into the black sky. In the early hours Beaver Woman joined Buffalo Dreamer in the circle of women who also danced around the fire, but then she left to tend to Small Flower. The dancing continued into the night, until some fell down exhausted, men and women alike. A few couples snuck away to make love, and Buffalo Dreamer wondered why Brave Horse did not go to Beaver Woman's tepee. Instead, panting and sweating from so much activity, he came to his mother to tell her he must speak with her and Rising Eagle.

"I already told Father earlier I wished to speak with him and you alone after the dancing."

Puzzled, Buffalo Dreamer waited with Brave Horse for Rising Eagle to finish his war dance, not wanting to interrupt any prayers he sang. Buffalo Dreamer never failed to be impressed and moved by the energy and virility of her husband, in spite of his age of sixty-one summers. He was still just as capable in battle as the younger warriors, many of whom followed him faithfully. When he finally joined them, his nearly-naked torso boasted hard muscle and a still-flat stomach. He wore a beaded armband Buffalo Dreamer had made for him, his hair twisted at the side into a quilled hair ornament.

"Come to our dwelling," Buffalo Dreamer told her son.

The three of them walked the nearly half-mile to Buffalo Dreamer's tepee, moving through circle after circle of other tepees, for the gathering of Lakota here was one of the largest yet. Buffalo Dreamer ducked inside, taking her place to the left of the central fire, as was custom. Brave Horse and Rising Eagle moved to the right and sat down, crossing their legs.

The fire had dwindled to simmering coals, and Buffalo Dreamer added wood to it to help shed light inside the tepee. In moments the wood sputtered and crackled into flames that cast a soft yellow glow on all three of them. Rising Eagle lit his prayer pipe and shared it with his son before speaking.

"What is it you wish to tell us, Brave Horse?" he asked.

Brave Horse glanced first at his mother, then back to Rising Eagle. "It is something that I have known since the escape at Horse Creek, something that Robert told me. It is about Fall Leaf Woman's son, William."

Rising Eagle frowned. "I must tell you that I have had strange feelings of connection to William ever since I first saw him as a small boy, when Spirit Walker and I prayed over him because he was sick with fever. When I held him, I felt a force move through me that I could not explain."

Brave Horse sighed. "I know the reason for the force, Father. I have wrestled with whether or not I should tell you, for your heart was heavy over the fact that the Lakota had become divided. But now we are united, and so you should know that there is still one division that could be very important, one that you should both include in your prayers."

Buffalo Dreamer felt a hint of alarm. "What is it, my son?"

Brave Horse turned to his father, meeting his dark eyes squarely. "William is *your* son, Rising Eagle, by the white woman you captured many years ago, Yellow Bonnet's mother."

Buffalo Dreamer drew in her breath, and she watched Rising Eagle stiffen. He remained silent, his jaw flexing in the mixture of emotions Buffalo Dreamer knew he must be suffering.

"My son!" he finally said in a near whisper.

"The white woman hated the baby. She did not want it, and so, lonely for another child of her own, and missing Spirit Walker, Fall Leaf Woman took the baby and raised him as her own. She was afraid to tell you, for fear you would try to take him away. She had already given Spirit Walker to you to raise, and she . . . loved you. And so she was proud to raise the son of Rising Eagle as her own."

Rising Eagle closed his eyes and breathed deeply. "Now I understand the force I felt when I held him in my arms." He moved his gaze to the small fire. "A son of my own blood . . . wearing a soldier's uniform." He closed his eyes. "Every time I put my rifle sight on a soldier, he could be my own son. I might have already killed him without knowing it."

"The last I knew, he was at Fort Laramie, so it's not likely he has been among those we have killed here in the north," Brave Horse told him.

"You saw him, then, at Laramie?"

"Yes, Father."

"And does William know I am his father?"

"Yes, but he doesn't care. He claims he is not Lakota, that he will never think of himself as Lakota. He is a soldier in the white man's army, and if that means risking killing you, then he will risk it. He hates his Lakota blood. When I lay wounded in Robert's dwelling, he never came to talk with me, his own blood brother. I saw him a few times, but he never spoke to me. It makes me sad, as I know it will also sadden you. That is why I was not sure I should tell you; but I could not keep it from you any longer. William, and the half-bloods who live like whites and serve the white soldiers with supplies and trade goods, they are the ones most responsible for the division among the Lakota. I fear one day Lakota will end up killing Lakota. It is the white man's plan, the surest way of defeating us. Already such division has worked against us by keeping us from being as strong as we could be, but I take hope and strength in how the rest of the Lakota have come together with the Shihenna."

Rising Eagle slowly nodded. "The worst division is father against son, son against father."

"We must pray for his soul, Father. A man cannot live forever divided against himself. Although he works and lives among the whites, Spirit Walker has remained Lakota at heart; but William's heart has no love for that part of himself. I believe that someday the choices he has made will come to haunt him. If he dies before acknowledging his Lakota blood, he will go to a bad place and never be able to be with his true ancestors. I only care because I do not wish such a thing for my brother. I fear our biggest fight will not be with the white man, but with each other, a fight to keep the Lakota one people, united forever."

Rising Eagle closed his eyes. "I thank you for telling me this. Go to your wife now, Brave Horse. Leave me alone with Buffalo Dreamer."

Brave Horse sighed. "Yes, Father." He rose, taking a moment to touch his father's shoulder before he left. Buffalo Dreamer waited quietly for Rising Eagle to speak then, and finally, after staring at the fire for several minutes, he met her eyes.

"I have another son, and he wears a blue coat. This is something that was never shown to me in my visions. When the Feathered One told me there would be bad times for us, and division among our people, I never thought that would include a son of my own blood."

Buffalo Dreamer thought a moment before answering. "Perhaps there is another way to see this, my husband. The half-bloods will force the white man to acknowledge his own blood has been mixed with the very people he tries to kill. Through the half-bloods we can bring the Lakota way into the white man's world, whether he likes it or not. Perhaps in this way we *can* remain strong after all."

He closed his eyes. "I must pray about this. I am a leader of my people, a respected elder. It shames me to have a son fighting on the side of the enemy."

"No, Rising Eagle. Feel no shame. When you planted your seed in that woman in order to disgrace her and her husband and all our white enemies, you invaded the white world in a way they cannot stop, and in a way all half-bloods have invaded their world. You created a human being, one with the strength of Lakota blood. I believe that one day William will understand that part of himself. He cannot deny it forever. And now, because of William, a part of the great Rising Eagle will lie among the enemy, so that even if they kill you, you will live on, not just through Brave Horse and Thunder and our daughter and their children; but also through William and any children he might father. A part of Rising Eagle will forever belong to both worlds."

He slowly nodded. "Yes." He met her gaze. "One day I will see and touch William again. I believe this in my heart. And when I do, he will know his true self."

She studied him lovingly. "May it be so, Rising Eagle. I will pray for it." She felt tears come to her eyes at the thought of how vividly and painfully the white man had changed the world they once knew, a world of beauty and peace and the Lakota way, a world in which she and so many other of her people were not even aware of the existence of the *wasicus*.

AUGUST 1867

Moon of Dry Dust Blowing

CHAPTER THIRTY-SIX

"I DON'T SEE any Indians," Private Gibson reported to Sergeant William Kingsley.

William adjusted his hat, gazing out at the Sullivant Hills to the east. "That doesn't mean they aren't around, the sneaky bastards," he answered. "Where is Commander Powell?"

Gibson nodded toward Little Piney Creek, about four hundred yards from camp. "Taking a bath in the creek."

"I wouldn't mind doing that myself," another private, Nolan Deming, spoke up. "Good way to cool off."

"Good way to get an arrow in the ass, if you ask me," William answered.

They all chuckled, but William felt the same nervousness as the others. Their camp was made up of nothing more than an oblong circle of wagon boxes, which would be used for cover in case of Indian attack. Construction, and fuel for cooking and heating at Fort Phil Kearny, five miles away, required lots of wood. The only source of a good supply was here at upper and lower Little Piney Creeks, where soldiers and civilian woodcutters came in constant shifts to cut and haul wood to the fort's saw mill. Constant Indian attacks plagued them, and a camp had been set up here in a spot where both branches of the creek could be guarded.

William had been assigned to Company C of the Twenty-seventh Infantry, soldiers who guarded these far-reaching outposts, set up mainly to protect the Bozeman Trail; but the Sioux and Cheyenne were making such guard duty extremely treacherous. The soldiers were always on edge; but at least now they had new rifles, Springfield-Allin .50 caliber breech-loaders, guns that could be loaded and fired much faster than their old weapons. That gave all of them some comfort. If the Sioux attacked, they would be surprised by how fast a few soldiers could fire on them before they could get close.

Still . . . one could not forget the slaughter of Captain Fetterman and eighty men last December. He hated to say it, but Fetterman almost deserved what he got after declaring he could defeat the entire Sioux Nation with eighty men. He'd learned the hard way. Crazy Horse was getting damned clever with his ability to lure soldiers into a trap. Poor Fetterman had ended up shooting himself in the head before the Indians got hold of him.

Not only was there danger from an all-out attack, but sometimes a man simply went down from a single arrow or a gunshot from a sniper. Trying to find the culprit was like finding a needle in a haystack. Nobody knew this country like the Sioux.

"I don't know any sneakier people than the Lakota," he said aloud, still watching the hills.

"Aren't you talking about your own kind?" The question came from another private, John Garrett.

William scowled at him. "Watch your mouth, Private, or I'll send you out there as a prime target, just to see if there *are* Indians out there somewhere."

Garrett grinned. "Yes, sir."

"We know you're one of us, Sergeant Kingsley," Private Gibson added.

William rolled himself a cigarette. "Yeah, well I sure as hell am not one of *them*." He looked around some more, then took a moment to light the cigarette. "I don't like this. It's too quiet."

"Hell, you can hear the woodcutters chopping away, sir," Gibson reminded him.

William shook his head. "It isn't that. I just have an eerie feeling." He held the cigarette in his mouth as he lifted his chin and ran a finger around the inside of his shirt collar. God, he hated this heavy, sultry weather. It was 7 A.M. By this afternoon the steamy August day would be almost unbearable.

He couldn't help wondering how his mother was getting along back at Fort Laramie. Most of the half-bloods had been allowed to return after the Indian escape at Horse Creek. Rebecca had delivered a baby boy two years ago. Named Abel, after his grandpa, William figured the boy must really be growing by now. He'd only been able to see the child those first few months before being shipped up here to duty at the northern forts.

He turned to study the rest of the twenty-six men who lounged around the wagon-box corral, most of them sitting against wagon wheels, two men playing cards, all of them confident in their protection, their rifles, and in the fact that the fort was only five miles away. But five miles was damn far if you needed help in a hurry.

Duty here was nerve-wracking, to say the least. Indian attacks were constant, adding to his hatred for that part of his blood. In the distance he could hear the voices and shouts of the woodcutters, the rhythmic ring of axes, and the cracking sound of a tree coming down. Things were peaceful enough, for the moment. He wondered why in hell the government hadn't built Fort Phil Kearny right here instead of five miles away. There was no figuring some government decisions, except that the fort did have to be closer to the Bozeman Trail. Still, they could have figured something better than this. This was too damn dangerous.

He threw down his cigarette and stepped it out, then walked to a water bucket, dipping a ladle into it and drinking from it, then splashing some of the water over his face. That was when he heard the words that made his stomach turn.

"My God!" Gibson exclaimed. "There are thousands of them!"

William turned toward the Sullivant Hills to see Sioux and Cheyenne swarming down the hills.

"It's like they just rose right up out of the ground," Private Deming said with a tone of awe in his voice.

"Jesus, we're done for now," Private Garrett commented.

Suddenly they heard gunfire from the direction of the wood-cutting expedition at the Lower Piney, and already men were running from there, headed for the wagon-box corral. Captain Powell made a mad dash for the corral from the creek where he'd finished bathing.

"Take your positions!" William told the privates, shouting the same to other men. It seemed that almost instantly the air resounded with yipping and war whoops, gunfire from the wood-cutting area, and the whinnying of frightened horses. The attacking warriors, painted hideously in white, green, and yellow, broke into sections, one group charging toward the army's mule herd and chasing it off. Several began dashing daringly back and forth on painted ponies in front of the soldiers, chanting war and death songs, while the entire force of several hundred, maybe even a thousand, began surrounding the wagon boxes.

"We'll never live through this," Gibson almost whined.

"Just keep those rifles ready and start firing as soon as you see the whites of their eyes," William ordered.

"If they get inside the wagon boxes, I'll shoot *myself* before I let those bastards get hold of me," Deming said. He quickly began untying his boot, ripping out the laces. William knew the plan. The men had talked about it often. Tie their laces together, with a loop at each end. You could stick your toe in one end, and the other end was hooked to the trigger of your rifle. A man could stand up, position the rifle under his chin, and pull the trigger with the shoelace. They preferred blowing their heads off to being captured by the Sioux.

"Forget the damn shoestrings and start shooting!" he ordered.

The warriors chanted and raced back and forth, brandishing spears and rifles, then began their attack on the wagon-box corral. Some men leaped inside the wagon boxes for protection, others took positions inside the ring of wagons, standing to shoot over the tops of them or kneeling behind wagon wheels or barrels.

The onslaught was horrendous. Before long the dust stirred up by the Indians, combined with rifle smoke, made it difficult to even see the warriors. There were only thirty-two soldiers, and it was impossible to guess how many Indians. William and the others loaded and fired their Springfields as fast as their hands could maneuver, which wasn't always easy because of simple nervousness.

In spite of the rapid fire from the Springfields, the warriors remained daringly close, some dropping over the sides of their horses and firing arrows into the corral from under the horses' necks. Others got close enough to throw spears, while more fired so many times at the wagons that they began splintering up the top boards.

It irked William that he couldn't help a hint of respect for the fighting abilities of the Lakota. They were as organized as any regular army, and sometimes seemed more capable. One man with binoculars shouted that there appeared to be chiefs farther back on the hill giving orders to couriers who dashed back and forth from them to the warriors doing the fighting.

"No doubt Crazy Horse and Brave Horse are part of the ones trying to get our scalps!" Gibson shouted. "And I'll bet Rising Eagle and Red Cloud are up there telling them what to do!"

William fired just as fast as the others. Why did he feel this distant pride at the abilities of the very people trying to kill him? Why did it bother him that he could be shooting at his own brother, maybe even his father? He'd always figured that if this moment came, he would gladly kill them, just to get rid of them so he could stop thinking about them.

Suddenly the Indians retreated. William heard a few whispered curses.

"They're surprised by these new rifles and the rapid fire," William reassured his men. "But be prepared. No doubt they're regrouping."

A tethered pony not far away was so full of arrows it had to be shot, a shot that seemed too loud in the sudden eerie silence. Minutes later warriors on foot made a second attack, and William was grateful that they were well supplied with ammunition. The rifle fire started all over again, as arrows whizzed through the air and landed in all directions, and bullets pinged and crashed into wagons and barrels. The soldiers fired until gun barrels became red hot. Flaming arrows sang through the air and landed inside the corral, igniting horse manure and one wagon. The stench of burning manure, sweat, and gun smoke made William's lip curl.

Finally the Indians retreated again, and during the lull some warriors daringly charged forward to retrieve their dead and wounded.

"I've never seen such horsemanship," one man commented.

The air hung silent again, but not for long. There came an odd humming sound from a gully only about one hundred yards away. Some men stood up to see what it was.

"Get down!" William ordered.

Before long they could see hundreds of nearly naked warriors coming on foot from the gully, chanting their death songs. In spite of more desperate firing from the soldiers, the warriors kept coming, even though some bullets went right through a warrior in front and landed into the warrior behind him, so that bodies began piling up.

William had never seen anything like this, not even in the Civil War. There was a kind of desperate determination about these Sioux. They were deliberately risking their lives to make a point—get out of our hunting grounds or risk being constantly attacked, no matter how many of us have to die.

Damn! Why did he feel this unexpected pride at being half Lakota? It made him angry, and he fired as fast and as accurately as possible. His gun barrel turned red, and he had to set the rifle aside and grab up another, wondering how many rifles would end up ruined today from warping.

"Look there!" Gibson shouted. "Some of the chiefs are riding down closer! I'll bet one of them is Red Cloud. Rising Eagle might be there, too!"

"Shoot them!" someone else yelled. "Get rid of Red Cloud and Rising Eagle, and we'll destroy their spirit!"

"I hope to hell we've killed Crazy Horse," another shouted. "I wish I knew what he looked like."

William took careful aim, studying two older Indians who had ridden closer. They wore splendid war bonnets. Could one of them really be Rising Eagle? Suddenly the shouts and gunfire that had rung in his ears for the past couple of hours became dim. All he could see were the two men he'd set his sight on, moving the sight from one man to the other.

Why in God's name couldn't he pull the trigger? What was

stopping him? This was ridiculous. He had a good chance to kill two obvious leaders of this onslaught, and he couldn't bring himself to do it. Was he looking down his sight at his own father?

For a brief moment it seemed everything stood still. The splendid-looking chief he aimed at just sat there staring right back at him, as though he knew something about him. In spite of gunfire everywhere, the man did not seem afraid. No bullets hit him. William blinked at sweat that suddenly dripped into his eyes, making them burn. He ducked his head to wipe perspiration from his eyes and forehead onto the sleeve of his uniform, and when he looked back up the two chiefs were gone!

"What the hell—"

They had disappeared like ghosts. Now, finally, the rest of the warriors began a retreat, unable to continue their attack against the horrendous, unending gunfire from the Springfields. Minutes later those who had retreated to the hills began splitting up, and William heard the boom of a howitzer.

Men began to cheer. Help had come from the fort! The Indians began to scatter, and William wilted down against a wagon wheel, his face black from gunpowder.

"This wagon is shot all to hell!" someone said.

"Take care of the wounded!" someone else shouted.

A few began to shout their own war whoops of victory.

"One more attack and we'd have been goners!" someone else exclaimed. "I've never seen anything like that. They just kept comin' and comin'!"

William sat there quietly, weary, sweaty, confused. Was that his own father he'd faced? Why couldn't he pull the trigger? It would have been so easy. "You're a damn fool, William Kingsley," he muttered, wondering what his name would be if he'd grown up among the Lakota.

AUGUST 1868

Harvest Moon

CHAPTER THIRTY-SEVEN

BUFFALO DREAMER JOINED Rising Eagle and Brave Horse as they rode down on Fort Reno, the last of the three forts along the Bozeman Trail to be abandoned by U.S. soldiers. The government had ordered the soldiers to leave the forts and promised the Powder River area as permanent Lakota hunting grounds, "unceded Indian Territory!"

Red Cloud had won his war for the northern hunting grounds, sticking to his word that he would not talk peace until the forts were abandoned. The Lakota gladly burned them to the ground, first Fort C. F. Smith, then Forts Phil Kearny and now Fort Reno. They allowed the inhabitants of the forts to first leave peacefully, then celebrated by burning each hated fortress.

Buffalo Dreamer, always proud to hold the honor of riding with Lakota warriors, set a torch to hay inside Fort Reno, joining in victorious war whoops as the entire fort was gradually consumed. They rode up a hill to join thousands of others who watched, singing and drumming as smoke billowed into the sky.

It felt good to ride free, to know that they could hunt all over this land without fear of soldier attacks. The soldiers could no longer cut sacred live trees and dirty the waters. They could no longer hunt precious game badly needed by the Lakota. This whole, big land, as well as the sacred Black Hills, belonged to the Lakota, forever!

By nightfall, after torching the last fort, the celebrations continued within a huge camp of thousands of Lakota, mostly Oglala. Buffalo Dreamer rode beside Rising Eagle through camp, as part of a procession led by Red Cloud. How good it felt to see happy faces everywhere! Dogs dashed about, barking and wagging their tails as though even they understood the importance of this moment. They rode past Beaver Woman, and her father, Red Eagle. She Who Sings was with them, holding two-year-old Small Flower in her arms. The Shihenna warrior who hoped to marry She Who Sings rode now with the others, an accomplished warrior whom Rising Eagle at last considered worthy enough for his daughter's hand. Brave Horse also rode in the parade of conquering warriors, his brother, Thunder, at his side, both wildly celebrating with Crazy Horse. Wolf's Foot, Little Bear, Two Owls, Bear Dancing, Black Horse, and Old Beaver, all relatives of Rising Eagle, participated in all the battles that led to this moment.

Rising Eagle held his war lance high, and Buffalo Dreamer rode beside him, weaving through circles of tepees, enjoying cheers of praise.

Red Cloud wore his sacred war bonnet, reveling in his day of glory, a well-deserved moment for him.

The noise that filled the air almost hurt Buffalo Dreamer's ears: cries of victory, horses whinnying, circles of women singing, drummers pounding rhythmically, the drumming accompanied by the equally rhythmic jingling of tiny bells worn around the ankles of dancers.

Buffalo Dreamer gave out a light scream when Rising Eagle suddenly grabbed her from her horse as though taking a captive. She sat sideways in front of him then, resting her head on his shoulder. "It has been many years since I knew such happiness," she told him.

"As it has for me," he answered. He headed away from the resounding celebrating, urging his sturdy mount up another rise and over its crest, down the other side to a stand of trees where they could be alone. He halted the horse, lifting Buffalo Dreamer down and dismounting. He took his riding blanket from his horse's back and spread it on the ground over soft grass. "Sit," he told Buffalo Dreamer.

Smiling, she obeyed, watching him take a flute carved from wood from the parfleche tied to his horse. To her surprise, he sat down next to her, his dark eyes dancing as he put the flute to his full lips and played a song for her. It sounded familiar. He stopped then, grinning.

"Do you remember that song?"

Buffalo Dreamer frowned in thought as he played it again. Then she brightened. "Rising Eagle! You remembered that after all these years?"

He looked her over lovingly. "When I first came for you, a young maiden so frightened of the man who was to be her husband, I watched you dance around the sacred stone wheel on top of Medicine Mountain, and there you became my wife, though unwillingly. I took you home to the Oglala. Because of the circumstances of our union, I was not able to court you properly."

Buffalo Dreamer felt like crying at the memories. "Then you were badly wounded trying to protect me from Crow attackers. I thought you would die. I knew then how much I loved you and wanted you to live."

Rising Eagle reached out and ran a hand down the side of her dark, flowing hair. "It was your presence at my side that made me want to live, your words of love. And it was then I realized that every young maiden deserves to be courted, deserves to be allowed to fall in love with the man who woos her. And so I began playing my flute for you, pretending you were not yet my wife at all."

Buffalo Dreamer laughed. "You played for so many days and nights that I was beginning to wonder if you would ever stop and come back inside the tepee and be my husband."

"But finally I did. And later we went to Medicine Mountain to pray for fertility, and there Brave Horse was conceived."

"And it was on Medicine Mountain that we later took Spirit Walker to pray over him, where the Feathered One spoke to you and healed Spirit Walker's crippled fingers."

He set the flute aside. "We will go there again, Buffalo Dreamer, to the sacred medicine wheel. There we will be close to heaven."

Buffalo Dreamer nodded, her smile fading slightly. "How long do you think we can enjoy this victory, my husband?"

He shook his head. "I don't know. Shihenna who join us from the south have told us about the iron horse, just like what Brave Horse saw in his first vision, a huge black horse with fire in its belly, charging across the plains and prairie, pulling coaches behind it filled with white people. Brave Horse's vision has been realized, and even as we celebrate getting rid of the soldiers here, more whites come into this land in the south, riding the railroad. They keep coming, and so I have no idea how long we can enjoy this victory. The others think we have won forever, that this is the end of our troubles, but because of the warnings of the Feathered One, I know more bad times will come." He pulled her against him. "For now we will revel in this happiness, and we will share our bodies, for I love you just as much as when we were young. My desire for you never lessens."

"Nor mine for you," she whispered against his neck. He laid her back, and Buffalo Dreamer ran her hands over his arms. "This has been a good day." She reached up and touched his graying hair. "We will celebrate the peace we have for now."

He licked her lips. "We will go on one more hunt, then go home to *Paha-Sapa*. Now we can roam from the Black Hills in the east to here along the Powder River in the west, even into the mountains of the big-horned sheep and the Big Horn River. There is much left to us." He shifted to unlace his leggings and untie his breechcloth.

"I look forward to the peace and rest of the Black Hills, Rising Eagle. Perhaps there our daughter will marry Black Hawk and give us more grandchildren, as will Beaver Woman and Brave Horse." She drew in her breath when he leaned close and moved his hand along her thigh, pushing up her tunic.

"And Thunder will take Daisy for a wife," he said, "and they, too, will have children. Our blood will live on in our grandchildren."

He pushed the hem of her tunic to her waist, and Buffalo Dreamer opened herself to him. He entered her gently, moving to the rhythm of the distant drumming.

Peace! There would be peace and freedom now, at least for a while . . . a year? Three years? Forever was a pleasant thought.

PART THREE

Our Nation is melting away like the snow on the sides of the hills where the sun is warm, while your people are like the blades of grass in spring when summer is coming . . .

—RED CLOUD

MAY 1869

Season of the Wildflowers

CHAPTER THIRTY-EIGHT

THOMAS KELP OPENED one side of the large, wooden wagon he called "Kelp's Traveling Dry Goods Store." He draped his white buffalo robe over the front of the dropped door so it would be prominently displayed, glad he'd made it here to Promontory City, Utah, in time to witness the joining of the Union Pacific and Central Pacific Railroads. The "city" was really nothing more than a hodgepodge of tents, but the crowd here perfectly fit the kind of customers Kelp was after, at least seven or eight hundred people, most of them rich and in a happy, celebrating mood.

The occasion was filled with all the usual tomfoolery of such historical moments, speeches by railroad magnates Thomas Durant and Grenville Dodge, more hand shaking than Kelp had ever witnessed, bands playing, and a gathering of wealthy men who didn't know a damn thing about the West or the Indians. Such men were easily fooled into spending a lot of money on worthless items. Many had their wives with them, and the presence of women in such remote, uncivilized places as western Utah meant women who needed pills and spirits for headaches and other womanly ailments.

Whatever they needed, he had it. He had traveled these parts for years, distributing his goods to people who otherwise had to travel long distances for simple items like buttons and laudanum, creams, bolts of cloth, cough syrups, pots and pans, blankets and such. He could usually ask outrageous prices for his goods, because to some people it was worth saving a long trip. He always enjoyed having something "unusual" to hawk along with common goods, and the white buffalo robe was certainly that. He intended to ask a lot of money for it, so he'd saved it for just this occasion, knowing full well there would be plenty of people here with top hats, silk vests, gold watches, and plenty of money in their pockets.

"Thomas Kelp here, folks, ready to supply you with all your needs!" he announced, standing inside the wagon just behind the buffalo robe. Behind him were shelves and drawers filled with common necessities.

This was the official joining of the great railroad across the continent. The smell of smoke from the flash powder used by countless photographers still hung in the air. The crowd of witnesses to the historic event broke into smaller groups that lingered and strolled about, looking giddy and excited. One couple in particular caught Kelp's eye. The man's suit and his wife's dress gave them away as wealthy, and he took note that the woman kept glancing his way. Something interested her, and from what he could tell, it was the white buffalo robe. When she finally pointed at it and said something to her husband, he knew his bait had worked.

"Come and see the white buffalo robe that once belonged to Red Cloud, the infamous Sioux leader who chased all the soldiers out of Montana!" he announced. "That's right, folks, this is a genuine albino buffalo robe, powerful medicine to the Sioux! A brave buffalo hunter stole this robe off Red Cloud himself! That's the story, folks! The robe is said to possess powerful Indian spirits."

A woman urged her husband closer.

"Come on up and touch the magic white buffalo robe, and your prayers will be answered! Feel the power of the great Red Cloud! This robe might even have been touched by the infamous Rising Eagle, or perhaps by Crazy Horse! For the right price, you might even be able to own this unusual and rare white buffalo robe!"

Now the woman looked excited.

"I have other goods here, folks," Kelp continued, as others drew near. "I have medicine for whatever ails you. I have perfumes and creams for the ladies! I have tobacco and chain watches for the men! I have blankets, stockings, boots, and hats! You'd be surprised how much I can get in this wagon, folks! It's extra large and full of just about anything you might need! That's why it takes four oxen to pull it. Just tell me what you're looking for, and I probably have it!"

The couple stood close now. The woman touched the white buffalo robe almost reverently. She seemed quite enamored with it. "Can I help you, sir?" Kelp asked the man, who sported a mustache and a silk top hat.

The man grinned. "Well, it seems my wife has taken quite an interest in this white buffalo robe. Doesn't interest me, mind you, but Louella is always enamored with anything rare. Costs me an arm and a leg at times."

Kelp joined him in laughter, thinking how glad he was to hear that. "Well, sir, you don't get much more rare than an albino buffalo robe."

Louella smiled, looking up at him. "Did it really belong to Red Cloud?"

Kelp frowned. "Well, ma'am, that's what I was told by the last man who owned it. Now, mind you, they say the robe is haunted. I got it from a merchant in Denver whose store burned down. Low and behold, the robe was one of the things they saved."

The woman sobered, still running her hand over the robe. "Yes. What else do you know about it?"

Kelp rubbed his chin. "The man in Denver said he got it when he bought supplies in St. Louis. He bought it from a trader there whose wife went mad. The trader blamed it on the robe and was anxious to sell it. He got it from some buffalo hunters who brought it to St. Louis to sell. They told him some white man sold it to them because he believed it made his wife sick, and he in turn got it from some trader way out at Fort Laramie in Wyoming. I don't know anything about its history before that, except that the trader at Laramie claimed it had belonged to Red Cloud. You can bet this beautiful robe once belonged to somebody very special. The Sioux consider a white buffalo very sacred. I can tell you, ma'am, that if you want to own something very rare, this would be the most cherished item in your home. I'll bet you have a very beautiful home back east, don't you?"

"Yes, we have a lovely mansion that overlooks the Atlantic," her husband answered for her. He extended his hand. "My name is Harry Bentley, and I own a considerable share of the Union Pacific."

Yes, I'll bet you do. "Glad to meet you, Mr. Bentley. And if you'd like to buy this robe for the missus, I'm ready to give you a good bargain."

"Well, I don't know. If the robe is going to bring us some kind of bad luck—"

"Oh, I wouldn't worry about that, sir. Some people just happen to have bad luck and want to blame it on something. I think most of the things that happened were pure coincidence, but then again, what a wonderful conversation piece the robe would be for you when you hold parties and dinners at your home, especially for people back east who have never been out in this land, never seen an Indian or seen anything like a buffalo robe, let alone a white one. Why, I think this robe is perfect for people like you. And surely you are too educated, sir, to worry about superstition and such."

Bentley laughed. "Yes, I most certainly am." He looked at his wife. "What do you think, dear? Would you like to have it?"

Louella Bentley put a hand to her chest and breathed deeply. "Oh, Harry, I'd love it! What a perfectly charming, intriguing item to have around when we hold our annual Thanksgiving ball this fall!"

Bentley shook his head, looking up at Kelp. "All right, how much is this robe going to cost me?"

Kelp frowned, as though giving the matter deep consideration. "Hmmm. Well, Mr. Bentley, I paid ten dollars for this robe," he lied. Why tell the man that the merchant in Denver had practically begged him to take the robe just to get rid of it? "I'll let you have it for twelve. I do have to make a little something, mind you."

"Twelve dollars!" Bentley pushed back his top hat.

"Oh, Harry, twelve dollars is nothing for such a thing," his wife said. "Please don't dicker about the price. We simply must have this robe."

Mrs. Bentley looked several years younger than Mr. Bentley. Kelp readily perceived that the pretty young thing was accustomed to getting her way. "You really can't go wrong paying that price, sir," he put in. "The robe is well worth it, I assure you. You'll find out when you get it home and learn how many people will try to buy it from you just to have it."

Bentley sighed as he studied the robe a moment longer, running his hand over it himself. "I suppose." He studied it a moment longer, then reached into his pocket. "I only have five on me. I'll have to get the rest from our private car on the train." He handed out the coins. "Hang on to the robe and I'll be back with the rest."

"Certainly, sir, and I greatly appreciate it. You won't regret this, I assure you!"

"Yes, well, I had better not."

"Oh, thank you, Harry!" his wife said, turning to give the man a quick hug.

Bentley smiled, patting her back. "You stay here and admire your latest rarity while I go get the rest of the money." The man left, and Louella turned again to admire the robe.

"This is so exciting," she told Kelp. "I can't wait to get it home."

"Well, ma'am, I am glad for you," Kelp answered. "I am always happy when my *customers* are happy." Actually, he was glad to get rid of the damn robe. All the stories he'd heard about it spooked him. He'd bought the thing because of the possibility of making money on it, and he most certainly had, considering he only paid one dollar for it. But the stories he'd heard about it had worried him all the way north from Denver. So far his only problem had been a terrible ache in his left foot and a slightly upset stomach ever since bringing the robe on board. The pain had not left him for the entire trip into Utah. He'd find out soon enough if it was the robe, as soon as he handed it over to the Bentleys. One thing was sure, he deserved getting twelve dollars for taking the risk of carrying it this far. He would be glad to be rid of the thing.

He began hawking his other wares to the rest of the crowd that mingled nearby. Louella Bentley pressed her cheek against the robe as though it were the most wonderful thing she'd ever seen, and Kelp hoped that once she owned the robe, she wouldn't experience any bad luck until he was well out of sight.

JUNE 1869

Moon of Ripe Cherries

CHAPTER THIRTY-NINE

BRAVE HORSE WATCHED his brother, Thunder, laugh with the joy and power of still being free, in spite of all the white man's attempts at shoving them onto reservations. Thunder was twenty-five summers now, and Brave Horse himself was thirty-five, both prime warriors walking in the footsteps of their honored father, Rising Eagle.

"These are good times, with all the soldiers gone from the Powder!" Thunder told Brave Horse, forced to shout in order to be heard above all the yips and howls and war cries coming from the hundreds of younger warriors who were celebrating yet another great occasion. Crazy Horse had just been declared war chief of the Oglala! Runners had already come to tell them that the same designation had been given to Sitting Bull of the Hunkpapa. Both leaders brought new life to all the Lakota, who still enjoyed their victory over the United States Army in forcing them out of the Powder River area and burning their forts.

Brave Horse had something more personal to celebrate. Beaver Woman had given birth to a son, Little Bear, just one month earlier. Last summer his sister, now twenty, married Black Hawk and now was with child. Thunder had yet to take a wife, more concerned about proving himself a warrior to be feared and respected. Just last month he had suffered his second Sun Dance sacrifice.

Thunder, more slender than he, was proving very strong, and very brave, as any son of Rising Eagle should be.

Amid all the shouting and dancing and drumming, Brave Horse could not quite bring himself to celebrate as loudly and with as much enthusiasm as the others. His thoughts turned to William. Where was his half-brother now? Was he alive, or dead? To think of him reminded Brave Horse that there still remained a dangerous division among the Lakota—between those who remained hostiles here in the Powder River area, and those who had chosen to sign the Treaty of 1868 and to live on reservations.

Among the reservation Indians was Red Cloud himself. Now that he'd known a great victory, the man who'd led them now seemed satisfied with bowing out of leadership. The white man's government had named an agency after him, which had puffed Red Cloud up with too much pride. It had left him feeling praised and honored by the white man, and so after first refusing to go to the reservation and continuing to hunt along the Powder River, he had finally retired to the Pine Ridge Reservation, where he'd begun trading with whites and accepting government handouts.

Brave Horse wondered if Red Cloud's memory had been fogged by age. He, of all Lakota, should realize that the white man should never be trusted to keep a promise. No white man truly cared about an Indian.

He frowned, turning away from the others.

"What's wrong, Brave Horse?" Thunder asked, turning to walk with him.

Brave Horse walked farther away, where it was more quiet. "I don't really know," he finally answered, facing Thunder in the moonlight. "I have this feeling—"

Thunder waited, his youthful eagerness making him impatient. "About what?"

Brave Horse walked farther away, and Thunder followed, sitting down beside him in the soft grass along the Powder River. "Everything," Brave Horse answered. "My face smiles, but my heart tells me to be wary." He sighed. "I want you to be wary also, Thunder."

"Wary of what? These are good times for us! I'm ready to ride with Crazy Horse against the Crow, since our enemy now licks the hand of the white soldiers. The Crow even scout for the soldiers against *us*! They will soon learn to regret it. Already we have raided Crow camps, taking many scalps and stealing Crow horses and supplies. You and Crazy Horse now are members of the *Kangi Yuha*, the Crow-Owners, our most highly-honored warrior society. One day I also hope to belong to the Crow-Owners. We have never been stronger, Brave Horse. We have chased away the soldiers, and all this land has been promised to us forever."

Brave Horse remained quiet for a moment before finally speaking again. "Just as other land was promised to us forever, until the white man decided to risk everything to have it. So far he has managed to steal everything he's come after, no matter how hard we fight. He has backed off for now, but for how long? His government still says we are hostiles and should go to the reservations. If we try to trade for guns and powder anywhere outside the Powder River area, soldiers still shoot at us. We are not on a reservation, yet we are confined to this area for survival. We have always needed to travel far and wide for the hunt. We are free, yet we are not free at all. One day the wild game here, too, will thin out. Then what do we do for food?"

"We will just keep growing stronger here, strong enough to regain some of our other hunting grounds some day."

Brave Horse pulled at some of the grass. "If we were all still truly united, I would think that might be possible. But the Crow and the Shoshoni are friends with the soldiers now. And Red Cloud has taken many Lakota to the reservations, dividing us. Even the Northern and Southern Shihenna are divided, not because of differences, but because the white man's railroad and settlements are between them now, and the Shihenna cannot move north and south without being attacked. The Southern Shihenna are also on reservations now. The white man has found many ways to divide us, Thunder, making us weaker." He shook his head. "I have always dreaded the day I would see my vision of long ago come true, the black, iron beast bringing more and more whites west. Now we know my vision was of the white man's railroad. It is a bad omen."

"But the Northern Shihenna are still our friends. They fight with us."

"Still, they are divided. And so are the Lakota. And the fact remains we cannot leave the Powder River. We have won it back, yet we are prisoners here. If we go to our beloved Black Hills we will be fired upon unless we give up and go to the reservations. I am afraid we will never regain enough power in numbers to take back the rest of our land."

"What are you saying, Brave Horse? That we should give up? Remember our mother's vision of thousands of Lakota and Shihenna surrounding hundreds of soldiers and killing all of them. We have yet to kill that many soldiers at one time. That is all ahead of us. Great victories still await us!"

Brave Horse nodded. "This is true. And I am not saying we should give up, Thunder. I am saying we must be careful. We still must always save up as much food and skins as possible for each winter. We still cannot trust any of the white man's promises, and we must do all we can to keep the Lakota from becoming even more divided, to keep those with us now from giving up and going to the reservations. Our father has told us many times the words of the Feathered One, that very bad times lie ahead, but that we will one day prevail over the white man. The Feathered Being never told Rising Eagle when that would be, whether it would be in our time, or in a future time. We must be strong and never lose faith, no matter what happens."

"But if we do see the day when thousands of us kill many soldiers, surely that is when we will see our strength return."

"Father is not so sure. It could be the beginning of bad things for us. The one person who can help hold us together is Crazy Horse, but for all his power and honor, I am worried."

"Crazy Horse is your best friend! You know our enemies fear him, and that bullets from their guns cannot harm him."

"This is true, but Crazy Horse has told me in secret that his heart aches for a woman I will not name. She is married to another.

If he should try to steal this man's wife, it will cause a lot of hard feelings and possibly more division. Crazy Horse is popular and honored, and some have grown jealous of him. We cannot forget that in Crazy Horse's vision some of our people were holding him back. That could mean a lot of things. I have warned my friend that it is best he ignores his desires, that his prominence as a leader means he must always put the People first. Our own mother and father each loved someone else before they married, but they ignored their own desires for what their visions told them to do. They were complete strangers, yet they wed each other because it was their destiny. They understand the importance of adhering to what our visions tell us must be. Crazy Horse must always remember this and walk carefully."

Thunder nodded. "I agree with you, brother."

Brave Horse rose. "I just want you to remember these things, Thunder. You are young and eager, but be cautious, and always be true to your own dreams and what you know is right for the People. Crazy Horse is a great leader, but one day, if he makes a wrong choice, he could create an even greater division among us. Be wise, Thunder."

"I will."

Brave Horse touched his brother's shoulder reassuringly. "Let's go back and enjoy the celebrating. We will pray to *Wakan-Tanka* that those of us still fighting for what is ours can remain united."

Both young men returned to join the dancers. Of all those who shouted their war cries, Crazy Horse was the loudest, holding high his Crow-Owners Society lance, its shaft painted red and wrapped in otter fur, eagle and owl feathers tied at one end, the stuffed skin of a crow bound just below the spear-head. He led the dancing, and the others followed faithfully, feeling strong and victorious. Thunder joined in, but Brave Horse held back. He was not jealous of Crazy Horse, his good friend of many years. He was just worried.

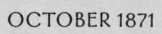

OCTOBER 1871

Moon When the Water Begins to Freeze

CHAPTER FORTY

ROBERT APPROACHED RED Cloud with feelings of awe and honor, in spite of the man's infamous reputation as the Oglala chief who chased the soldiers out of the Powder River. He was surprised to hear the aging warrior had agreed to settle at the agency named after him here in South Dakota. He supposed Red Cloud thought that because they had burned the forts and chased out the soldiers, the Powder River area was now safe from white settlement, but already travel along the Bozeman was again picking up. Robert had no doubt that within a few years the area would see a good deal of white settlement, in spite of the fact that those northern hunting grounds had been promised to the Lakota in the latest treaty.

Such blatant and deliberate refusal to abide by a treaty infuriated him as much as any Oglala, but he understood and knew they all must accept the fact that white migration westward would simply not end, especially if there was gold to be found, let alone the many other resources this country offered, as well as free land and rich prairie earth for farming.

How sad that the Lakota fought so hard and gave up so much for what could only be fruitless campaigns. Still, Red Cloud had fought a good fight. He had probably decided that he would end his leadership campaign with a victory and not take a chance on ending it some other way.

He nodded to the astute and still strong and handsome warrior chief as he came close. Red Cloud wore a full war bonnet, a fancy beaded shirt, earrings, and a bear-claw necklace, obviously wishing to make a good impression on the adopted son of Rising Eagle. He motioned for Robert to sit down beside him on the grassy hill that overlooked a large camp of reservation Oglala.

"I am Robert Kingsley," Robert said in the Oglala tongue, as a formal introduction. "I was called Spirit Walker when I lived with Rising Eagle and the Oglala. I am honored to meet you, Red Cloud, and I thank you for agreeing to speak with me."

Red Cloud sat straight and proud. "It is also my honor to meet the adopted son of Rising Eagle, and the brother of Brave Horse." He lifted a prayer pipe that he'd placed across his folded knees. He offered it in the four directions, then smoked it and offered it to Robert, who did the same, handing it back with a smile.

"I am glad you have chosen to convince some of your people to settle here," Robert told the Lakota leader.

Red Cloud sighed. "I am content to know that I have saved our sacred hunting grounds." He looked Robert over admiringly. "You have come to ask about your Lakota family?"

"Yes. My mother and I are both concerned. Is Rising Eagle well? And Buffalo Dreamer?"

Red Cloud nodded. "They are both well, as is Brave Horse, and their son Thunder, and their daughter, She Who Sings. Brave Horse has taken a wife, Beaver Woman. They have a daughter called Small Flower, and a son called Little Beaver. He should be about two summers now."

Robert smiled. "I'm glad. Thunder and She Who Sings?"

Red Cloud smiled. "The last I knew, Thunder was courting a Shihenna maiden called Daisy. She Who Sings is now the wife of a Cheyenne warrior called Black Hawk. I do not know if they have children."

"Buffalo Dreamer must be very proud of her two grandchildren."

"As well she should be."

Robert's smile faded. "Is there any chance any of them will come here to the reservation?"

Red Cloud thought a moment. "I think not. In my own heart I suppose I am myself still a hostile, but I have won my war, and I have decided to trust the white man's promises. I have grown weary of fighting. But Crazy Horse, Brave Horse, and the other younger men among the hostiles still do not trust the Blue Coats and the Great Father in the East. Nor do they wish to live in one place. I am satisfied with the food and blankets and tobacco I receive." He set his pipe aside. "If I were younger, perhaps I would remain a hostile. I think one day the others will also weary of the fighting and will come here to live in our sacred Black Hills. This is our true home."

Robert nodded. "I wish they would come here so I can always know they are safe." He paused before continuing. "I have something else to ask you, Red Cloud. You know that I am schooled in white man's medicine. I have learned many valuable things that could help the Lakota, and I am hoping you will agree to allow me to doctor the reservation Lakota. Actually, what I need is for you to convince them to *let* me doctor them. I fully support Lakota medicine and I will gladly work with your medicine men. I can also help with white man's medicine, but most of your people don't trust it."

Red Cloud waved his arm, indicating the hundreds of tepees below. "It is not easy to change the minds and hearts of a people who have lived one way since they were formed. It was not easy convincing many of them to come here. Even though they are here, there is much about the white man they will never trust. It will be many generations before that happens, but I will speak with some of them. If they trust you, it will only be because you are Rising Eagle's adopted son."

"I understand, and I appreciate anything you can do." Robert rose. "Thank you for speaking with me, Red Cloud. I'm glad you chose to come here. I hope that one day Rising Eagle and his family will do the same."

Red Cloud smiled sadly. "You know that with the Lakota, safety does not come first. What is *right* comes first. What belongs to them comes first. We are all willing to die for those things."

Robert felt as though someone were squeezing his heart. "I know that all too well, and it is what I fear the most for my Lakota family." He put out his hand, and the two men grasped wrists. Robert left, feeling sad at realizing he might never see Rising Eagle and the others again. At least he could tell Florence that they were all well . . . for now.

And they'd heard from William. He was presently back at Fort Laramie, having reupped his army service. Robert could not imagine why. The pay was lousy and living conditions certainly not terribly comfortable. He'd hoped his brother would finally end his army career, but William had signed up for another three years, according to his most recent letter. The only reason Robert could figure was that the Indian wars were still far from over, and William still seemed to think he could prove he was not Indian by staying in the army. Robert wished he would settle down into a normal life, take a wife, and have some children. Maybe then he could know some real happiness.

He sighed, glancing back at Red Cloud, who still sat alone on the hill. It sickened him to know the man would one day learn his long battle to save the Powder River hunting grounds was all for nothing, except perhaps a page in history.

FEBRUARY 1872

High Water Moon

CHAPTER FORTY-ONE

BRAVE HORSE WAITED on a ridge, watching Crazy Horse ride back toward him after going to find the body of his friend, High Back Bone. High Back Bone had been killed four days before by Shoshoni when he and Crazy Horse and others raided a Shoshoni camp along the Yellowstone River. The rest of the Oglala involved in the raid had already returned to the main camp, chased off by the Shoshoni.

Brave Horse could see the weariness and dejection in Crazy Horse's countenance, even in the slow walk of his horse. Buzzards circled in the distance, a sign that High Back Bone's body had probably already been picked clean.

Brave Horse could not help but feel angry at the approaching Crazy Horse, for Crazy Horse was the root of the current bad luck among the Oglala. They had seen more than one battle lost against the Shoshoni, a new division among the clans, and more whites moving into the Powder River area against their promises to stay out. Just as he had predicted to Thunder, Crazy Horse's lust for another man's wife had caused great turmoil among the People.

It was over now. His good friend had eloped with Black Buffalo Woman, wife of No Water. In retaliation, No Water had sought them out, and had shot Crazy Horse in the upper jaw at close range. People from Crazy Horse's clan in turn had shot a mule left behind by No Water after he'd fled. They'd demanded that No Water be sent to them for punishment, but No Water's clan, led by Bad Heart Bull, had refused to turn him over. Only some fast talking and reasoning by some of Crazy Horse's uncles had helped resolve the situation to some degree. They'd sent Black Buffalo Woman back to Bad Heart Bull's camp to be returned to No Water. No Water in turn had sent three ponies to Crazy Horse's father, and the matter was supposedly closed.

There was one reason why it would never really be closed, as far as Brave Horse was concerned. Not long ago Black Buffalo Woman gave birth to a girl with light, curly hair. No one else among the Oglala had hair like that, except Crazy Horse, who had been a long time recovering from a shattered upper jaw. He still carried a deep scar on his upper lip, which forever marked him as a once-honored warrior who had put his own wishes before the important unity of the People. He'd been stripped of his ceremonial shirt, and since then, the eager pride and unity of the Lakota as a whole seemed to melt away, and the situation with white intrusion grew worse. Crazy Horse's younger brother, Little Hawk had been shot by white miners farther to the south. Crazy Horse had ridden down there alone to find his body and raise it on a scaffold.

Now this—another raid against the Shoshoni ending in disaster. Crazy Horse looked at him sadly when he drew closer. "You blame me," he said bluntly.

Brave Horse sighed. "I cannot fully blame you, my friend. When I was much younger, my heart ached for the white girl my father had captured and raised. Do you remember her?"

Crazy Horse nodded. "Yellow Bonnet."

"I wanted her, but my father considered her a sister. I was not sure if my father would accept the fact that I wanted to marry her. I had already made up my mind that if he did not allow it, I would run off with her. That would have shamed both of us, perhaps caused me to be banished from the clan; but I was ready to do it anyway. I understand how it is to want someone so badly you can hardly stand it, so badly that you will risk even honor to have her."

Crazy Horse put a hand to the scar on his lip. "I have caused more division among our People. I never wanted to do that. And now I am no longer a Shirt Wearer. My brother is dead. My good friend, High Back Bone is dead. I have a new wife, and Black Shawl is good to me, but she is not Black Buffalo Woman. I have a daughter among Bad Heart Bull's clan, and I cannot see her. Now they have all gone to live at Red Cloud's agency."

He sighed, turning his painted horse around to move beside Brave Horse, staring out into the valley where High Back Bone's bones lay bare. "What are you thinking, my friend?"

Brave Horse looked around at the beauty of the land around the Yellowstone River. "I am thinking that one day we will have no choice but to go to reservation life. It hurts to think of it."

Crazy Horse nodded. "Yes. And I am thinking that my vision of my own people holding me back means that one day my own people will kill me."

Brave Horse frowned, facing him. "You truly believe this?"

Crazy Horse breathed deeply. "I have had dreams about it. My friend, if there is any one cause for losing our fight against the white man, it will be the division among our own people. Now I have contributed to that division. I will never stop being sorry for that. If I die at their hands, I will deserve it." He cast Brave Horse a sly glance then, actually grinning. "But let me tell you something else. I will go down fighting. I have nothing to lose now, Brave Horse. Black Shawl carries my child, but if we are destined to live on a reservation, it matters little to me how many sons and daughters I can claim. They will not be able to live as free men and women. Nothing will be the same; and so, my friend, I will now fight as I have never fought before. I have thought about this for a long time. I plan to rekindle the spirit of the Oglala and of all the Lakota. All those who still feel we should fight will find new faith, new determination. This is my vow: to remain in the north and do what I can to bring the Hunkpapa, Minneconjou, Sans Arcs, and Oglala all together again. There are still many thousands of us left in the Powder River, if we also bring the northern Shihenna into our group. They will join in renewed fighting, because they, too, still have the desire left deep in their hearts to give the white man plenty of trouble. What do you say, Brave Horse? Do you want to be known in the history of the white man for hanging your head and walking away to the reservations? Or do you want to be known as one of the great leaders of a Nation of people who fought valiantly to keep what is rightfully theirs?"

Brave Horse smiled then himself. "You know the way I would have it."

Crazy Horse straightened, puffing out his chest slightly. "I am also thinking that if we can give them a good fight in the Powder River and along the Little Big Horn, our people will be left with the spirit it will take to never turn over the Black Hills—ever. Not for any amount of money. No treaty giving away our precious homeland should ever be signed."

Brave Horse nodded. "I agree!"

"Then we will fight! It matters not what happens to me now, and so I will show the Blue Coats how reckless and brave a Lakota warrior can be! I will fight as I have never fought before! Are you with me?"

There was the magic again. Crazy Horse had a way about him that made a man want to accept whatever challenge Crazy Horse put to him. "I am with you, my friend."

Crazy Horse raised his fist and let out a chilling war cry that brought back memories of his wildest days of fighting. Brave Horse laughed and screamed his own war cry. Both men turned their horses and rode off at a hard gallop, heading north, toward the Powder and the Little Big Horn Rivers.

SEPTEMBER 1873

Moon When the Deer Paw the Earth

CHAPTER FORTY-TWO

WILLIAM PEEKED AT his poker hand. Three queens. Two tens. With only four other players, a man would rarely lose with such a hand, although he wasn't so sure the prize was worth much. Supposedly white buffalo robes brought decent money in places like St. Louis, but the one he was gambling for now looked pretty old. The underside had yellowed, and someone had dropped a cigar or pipe ashes or something into the shaggiest area, burning some of the hair and leaving a dark spot.

He wasn't even sure why he wanted the thing . . . more curiosity than anything else, he supposed. The owner, Sergeant Jerry Cook, was out of money and offered the robe instead, teasingly warning that whoever owned it just might end up with all kinds of bad luck.

"It's never affected me that way," Cook added, "but the thing has been through several owners, so I'm told. Every one of them ended up getting rid of it because they think it's full of some kind of evil Lakota spirits and brings them a trail of woes."

"Where did you get the thing?" another player, Private John Bailey, asked.

"Got it off a miner when I was stationed at Fort C. F. Smith. He said he got it from a rancher he stayed with on his way north. The rancher claimed *he* got it from some wealthy-looking man in

Cheyenne. The man apparently bought the robe back during the celebrations at Promontory City in Utah. The rancher said the guy stepped out of his car when the train stopped in Cheyenne and offered the robe to the highest bidder, right then and there. He claimed his wife got real sick after he bought the robe off some peddler. He wanted to get rid of it, sold it for two dollars to the rancher. I guess nobody else wanted it because they thought it was bad luck. I don't believe in such things, mind you." Cook dealt the draw cards as he talked.

William waved him off. "I'm good," he said. He shifted in the wooden, straight-back chair, thinking how he didn't even need to light a smoke for the relaxing benefits. There was enough smoke hanging in the air of the barracks tonight that all a man had to do was breathe. In their time off, the men had to think of things to do for recreation, and lately they'd had plenty of leisure time during the lull between riding with George Custer to protect Northern Pacific Railroad engineers, and waiting for their next assignment. Now that the Northern Pacific was bankrupt, he supposed Crazy Horse and Rising Eagle and the rest of the hostiles in the Powder and Yellowstone River areas were having quite a celebration. Not only had they won back the Bozeman and burned all the army forts there, but they then gave soldiers so much trouble over the building of a railroad through that same country that they chased out the railroaders *and* "Long Hair" Custer.

Most of the Oglala and other Lakota still refused to go settle on the new reservations in the Black Hills. They kept up an endless and frustrating battle to keep their hunting grounds in southern Montana and northern Wyoming.

Stubborn sons of bitches, I'll hand them that. "What about the rancher and the miner?" he asked Cook aloud. "Did *they* have bad luck with the robe?"

Cook shrugged. "They never said."

"Seems like it's gone through an awful lot of hands. Maybe that bad luck story is true," William suggested.

"Nah!" Cook waved him off. "It hasn't affected me any, and if it saves me money tonight, that's *good* luck," he laughed.

"Hell, Sergeant," Bailey spoke up, "I wouldn't exactly say you ain't been affected with bad luck by that robe. Didn't you take an arrow in the thigh last year helping General Custer defend the Northern Pacific?"

Cook frowned. "It just went through the flesh at the back of my thigh and pinned my leg to my saddle. I pulled it right back out and went on fighting."

They all laughed lightly. "Quite the brave man," William teased.

Cook stuck a cigar in his mouth, chewing on the end of it as he studied the cards he'd drawn. "Yeah, well, where are *your* war wounds, Sergeant Kingsley? I think you're charmed on account of your Lakota blood. Those hostile bastards won't shoot at you."

William quelled the temptation to let anger take over, always hating references to his Indian looks. He knew Cook was just teasing, but he'd taken such teasing for too many years. "I wouldn't say getting your hat shot off is a sign no one is shooting at you," he answered. "I felt the wind of that bullet so strong it whistled. A half-inch lower and I wouldn't be sitting here."

"Oh, yeah," Private Bailey answered. "I remember that. That's the day Crazy Horse's bunch snuck across the Yellowstone and attacked Custer's surveying party. Shot ole' Long Hair's horse right out from under him."

They all laughed again, having actually enjoyed seeing the arrogant general's horse go out from under him. Custer was a damn good soldier in many ways, but some thought him too reckless. Everybody knew the young general had been in trouble with his superior officers several times in his career, even earning himself a demotion once. Still, the man was a charmer, and sometimes almost too brave. Some thought it was more foolishness than bravery. Either way, he always managed to pick himself up and get right back into the action, earning back the rank he'd originally earned too early in his career, during the Civil War.

The bidding went around again. William threw in money to match the highest bet, then doubled it.

"Hell, I'm not even sure my robe is worth it," Cook laughed.

"It's worth it," Bailey said, squinting as smoke drifted into his eyes from the cigarette he held at the corner of his mouth. "How many white buffalo have you ever seen? They're damn rare. I'm taking that robe home and use it when I brag to my grandkids about the Indian wars." He frowned then when he looked at his extra cards. "Maybe."

William wasn't quite sure why he wanted the robe himself. Why own something that supposedly brought a man bad luck? Then again, it was probably a bunch of hogwash anyway. Maybe he would give the thing to Robert, or better yet, to Florence. He still thought of Robert as a real brother, and Florence as his mother. They lived at Red Cloud's reservation now, in the Black Hills. They wrote often since he'd been reassigned here to Fort Abraham Lincoln, east of the reservation, but he seldom got around to writing back.

Robert still doctored both Indians and soldiers, and Florence worked as a seamstress, a damn good one, he had to admit. He remembered how good she was at things like that as he was growing up.

Even though he knew now that he and William were not blood brothers, Robert still seemed to think he had some kind of responsibility toward him, and William didn't understand why . . . except that he was supposedly Rising Eagle's son, and Robert still had a strong affection and respect for that renegade. So what if Rising Eagle was his father? William didn't know the man and probably never would. For all he knew that bullet that knocked his hat off came from Rising Eagle's rifle, or maybe even Brave Horse's. They didn't care about him, and he didn't care about them.

"Show your cards," Sergeant Cook said, laying down a flush of diamonds.

"Shit," Bailey grumbled, throwing in his cards. One other man threw his cards away also, leaving William and one other man.

William squinted to see the man's cards by the dim lamplight. He glanced at the robe again, which was tacked to the barracks wall over Cook's cot. Between all the smoke and the pale lighting, it looked even rattier than he'd thought. Hell, maybe Florence *would* like to have the thing.

He laid down his hand.

"Holy shit," Cook commented. "That was *dealt* to you?"

"Sure was," William answered with a grin.

The last man threw in his cards. "Beats me."

Bailey picked up the cards to redeal, and Cook rose and walked over to where the robe hung. "It's all yours," he told William.

"For what the dingy old thing is worth," William answered. "Something tells me I've just been cheated."

They all laughed as Cook yanked out the tacks that held the robe, then took it down and brought it over to William. "Here you are, Chief." He draped it around William's shoulders, and suddenly the comments and laughter of those around him seemed to fade into the background. William felt an odd warmth surge through him with such force that almost instantly he began to sweat, and he swore he could hear distant drumming.

CHAPTER FORTY-THREE

RISING EAGLE STARTED awake, bathed in sweat.

Ate.

He looked around the tepee, dimly lit by dying embers of the central fire. Who had called him? He and Buffalo Dreamer were alone. He rose and stepped outside, looking up at a black sky glittering with thousands and thousands of stars, then sucked in his breath when he saw a white streak shoot through the heavens.

What was this all about? To see a star streak through the night sky could only be a sign from the Feathered One. Something had awakened him, something out of the ordinary. Someone had called "Father," but it had not been a child's voice. It was a man's.

He gazed around the quiet camp, circles of tepees inside which men, women, and children slept. No one was around to call out to him. The scouts and guards were far off around the camp's perimeter.

"Do you feel it?"

Rising Eagle turned to see Buffalo Dreamer standing at the tepee entrance. "Something woke you, too?" he asked.

Buffalo Dreamer walked closer, and he thought how young she still looked in the soft starlight. "I dreamed about the white buffalo," she told him. "It came to me and wrapped its robe around me. I felt warm and happy. The white buffalo licked my face, and I woke up to find a wetness on my cheek. Then I noticed you were not lying beside me. Did you also have a dream?"

Rising Eagle frowned in confusion. "I am not sure. I suddenly woke up covered in perspiration. Someone called out to me, saying 'Father,' but it was the voice of a grown man. I came outside, but there was no one around."

"Do you think it was Brave Horse?"

Rising Eagle again looked up at the heavens, slowly shaking his head. "No. You know that Brave Horse sleeps soundly nearby." He continued scanning the heavens. "When I came out here, I saw a star fall through the sky, leaving a white streak. It was a sign from the Feathered One, which means whatever woke me was very important, as is the dream you had."

Buffalo Dreamer also looked up. "It is the white buffalo robe. Someone close to us has touched it. I feel sure of it."

Rising Eagle thought for a few quiet moments. "Still, why did I hear someone call 'Father,' as though calling to me alone?"

Buffalo Dreamer shook her head. "Perhaps it was William."

He wiped at perspiration on his forehead with the back of his hand, still sweating even though he stood in the cool night air. "The son who wears a blue coat. The son who wants nothing to do with his Lakota blood."

"He cannot always fight the true Human Being within himself. His father is Rising Eagle, a man of great spiritual powers. There will always be a connection between you two." She moved an arm around him. "Something must have happened to make him feel close to you."

Rising Eagle shook his head. "He does not even know me. He would gladly kill me in battle. And for all I know, I have already killed *him*, my own son."

"No! If you ever raise a hand against each other, you will both know it."

"I hope you are right." He put his arm around her shoulders. "And you believe that someone close to us touched the white robe?"

She sighed, settling against him. "I can think of no other reason for the dream. Since the night it was stolen I have prayed that somehow it would again come into my possession before I die. I want it placed on my burial platform, so that I can take it with me to the great beyond."

He kissed her hair. "If you have prayed for it, as have I, then it will be so."

"I hope you are right."

A wolf howled in the distant hills, and Rising Eagle continued to watch the sky. "It burdens me to have a son I don't know, and who denies me," he told Buffalo Dreamer. "I will take my prayer pipe and go away from camp to pray that someday I will know him, that someday he will no longer deny me and will seek me."

"I'll get your pipe and a blanket," Buffalo Dreamer said, leaving him to retrieve what he needed.

Rising Eagle looked up to see yet another shooting star. "What is this feeling?" he murmured.

Ate! This time the word was whispered in the wind.

JULY 1875

Moon of the Horse

CHAPTER FORTY-FOUR

THE SUN DANCE lodge resounded with drumming and singing, mixed with whistle-blowing, as the participants danced around the central sacred pole, leaning away from it so that the skewers in their breasts would cause more bleeding and pain. The more they suffered, the more likely their prayers would be answered.

Buffalo Dreamer closed her eyes and sang her own prayer song, her arms bleeding where she had cut away some of the flesh in her own sacrifice for answered prayer. These were desperate times, when it was important to stay together to fight for what was most sacred of all to the Lakota, *Paha-Sapa*.

"Great Spirit, hear my prayer. Save my people," she sang, raising her arms and letting the blood flow. "Great Spirit, you see my blood. Know that my prayers are sincere."

The Lakota's most dreaded worry had come true. White men had begun invading the Black Hills in search of gold, led by none other than *Pahuska*, the long-haired soldier the whites called Custer. As always, whenever white men heard the word gold, they became like crazy men and scrambled to find it.

Many Lakota who'd agreed to settle on Red Cloud's reservation had left there the past summer and fled northwest to join Rising Eagle, Crazy Horse, and the rest of the Oglala. Sitting Bull and his Hunkpapa had also joined them, as well as Spotted Eagle and his Sans Arcs, and the Minneconjou under Touch the Clouds. The Lakota who'd fled the reservation had given up their allegiance to Red Cloud, who seemed more and more content now to settle into the sedentary life of a reservation Indian.

Rising Eagle, Crazy Horse, Sitting Bull, and others here would never let that happen to them. They were much too proud. Death would be better than allowing the white man to invade the last beloved stronghold of the Lakota.

They were strong and united again. Although Crazy Horse did not hold his once-prominent position as a most respected leader, the current situation helped others forget their differences. Once again many looked to the wily warrior for help in fighting this new threat.

The Shihenna had joined them in great force. All were angry. The white man's persistent invasions had gone far enough. Not only were they again swarming into the Powder River area, but now they had contaminated the heart of Lakota land. This could not be tolerated! It was time to again unite, time for blood sacrifices, purification rites, constant prayer.

Buffalo hunters were killing off game by the thousands with their big guns, yet they took only the hides. Once Buffalo Dreamer saw white men collecting the bones left behind, after the carcasses were picked clean by vultures. The bone collectors traveled with large open wagons piled high with skulls and other large bones. Where they took them and what they did with them she didn't know, but never had she seen such hideous waste, nor such disregard for an animal so precious and sacred.

Pahuska! Long Hair was becoming a sore in their side. The Shihenna hated him for raids he'd led against them seasons earlier. At least Crazy Horse, Sitting Bull, Rising Eagle, Brave Horse, and other prominent leaders managed to chase the arrogant Blue Coat out of the northern country, where the white man had tried to build another railroad, another effort at moving into Sioux lands. The Lakota had stopped the invasion, but now, again, Long Hair was staging yet another invasion. The white man's government had again declared Rising Eagle and all the great leaders here, as well as the thousands who followed them, hostiles, insisting they return to Red Cloud's reservation.

Never would they live that way, even though the campaign to bring them in was heating up. Rising Eagle and Brave Horse sang prayer chants with others, while the sacrificial dancers gradually began to fall away in a faint, the skewers tearing their skin as they fell. Thunder was among them. Buffalo Dreamer knew Rising Eagle was proud to sing for his youngest son. He, too, held up his arms as he sang, letting blood flow from the cuts he'd given himself.

Sixty-five summers in age, he was, yet look how he danced, how much strength and energy he still possessed! Although a highly honored elder now, he still often rode into battle with the younger men.

She herself was fifty-six summers. Her hands and face were wrinkling, and many gray streaks showed in her hair. Still, Rising Eagle always seemed to see her as young and beautiful. They still shared bodies in exquisite lovemaking, sharing a special closeness felt only by a man and woman destined by *Wakan-Tanka* to be together.

"Death to Long Hair!" Rising Eagle sang. "Death to all white men!"

Thunder blew on the whistle Rising Eagle had carved for him to use in this, his second Sun Dance. Just as Brave Horse kept his whistle as a special treasure from his father, so would Thunder.

She continued praying until Thunder finally collapsed when the skewers tore away from his breasts. Only then did Rising Eagle cease his singing. He knelt beside Thunder, who lay on his back, bleeding and sweating. The young man said something to Rising Eagle, who nodded, then rose and held up his hands.

"Death to Long Hair!" Rising Eagle shouted at the top of his lungs.

"Death to Long Hair!" many shouted in reply, adding war cries to the chant.

"Death to Long Hair," Buffalo Dreamer said wishfully.

NOVEMBER 1875

Frost Moon

CHAPTER FORTY-FIVE

FLORENCE OPENED THE door to greet an army courier, who nodded. "Ma'am, I'm Private Wilson from Fort Abraham Lincoln. I
have a rather large package for you. It's from your son, William."

"Oh?" She looked past him to see two pack horses loaded with
various bundles. She knew a good deal of it was just mail. What on
earth was William sending her? He hardly ever wrote a letter, let
alone sent a package. "I have no idea what it could be, but please
bring it in."

He tipped his hat. "It's a little heavy. I figured I'd wait and
make sure you were home first."

"Fine." Florence smiled at him, and the private turned to walk
back to the horses. Beyond the small log cabin Robert had built for
her, she had a view of the sprawling Red Cloud Reservation, where
she'd moved with Robert three years ago, helping her son tend to
the medical needs of those Lakota who'd chosen to stay here, as
well as doing seamstress work for the many government employees
and white traders who lived here. Her cabin was next door to
Robert and Rebecca's, which she truly enjoyed, since she often
helped watch her grandchildren, Robert's ten-year-old son, Abel, a
six-year-old son called Stan, and a three-year-old daughter, Lynn.
They brought Florence great joy, a warm, close family she once
could only dream of having.

How she wished William would fall in love. Maybe then he would mellow some and learn to accept himself. The trouble was, not all white women would accept him, and he in turn would not want a Lakota woman for a wife. Her heart ached for the young man's bitter confusion about his identity.

Surprised at the size of what the courier carried to her now, she stepped back and let him come inside and lay it on the floor. Whatever it was, it was rolled up and wrapped in an army blanket, tied with rawhide straps.

"My goodness!" she exclaimed. "What on earth—"

"Not sure, ma'am. All I know is when I stopped at Fort Abe he brought this to me and said to bring it to Florence Kingsley at the Red Cloud Reservation; said to tell you you'd understand once you saw it, and to do with it whatever you think is best."

Florence shook her head. "Well, thank you. Can I pay you?"

"No, ma'am, no problem. Just doing my job." He tipped his hat again and left, and Florence, still frowning with confusion, knelt down to untie the leather straps. She unrolled the blanket, gasping when she saw what it hid . . . a white buffalo robe!

"Dear God in Heaven!"

Immediately she rose and ran outside to Robert's cabin, grateful to find him there after she pounded on the door. "Come quickly!" she said as soon as he opened the door.

"Why? What's wrong, Mother?"

"Just come!" Florence heard him tell Rebecca to stay with the children until he came back. She felt him hurrying behind her.

"Mother, what's wrong? Are you all right?"

"I'm fine. I'm fine. Come and see what William sent me." She rushed inside, realizing only then that in spite of the cold, she had not even grabbed her woolen cape before running over to get Robert, and she'd left her door wide open. Robert closed it behind him once they were inside, and they both stamped snow from their feet.

"Look." Florence told him, kneeling next to the white buffalo robe. "What do you think of this?"

She watched Robert's eyes widen. "Dear God," he muttered. He knelt beside the robe, spreading it out fully and running his hands over it. "Dear God," he repeated. He fingered an area that looked as though someone had dropped ashes on it and singed the fur. "I don't believe this."

Quickly he folded the robe over to take a look at the reverse side, where there was no fur. Florence watched him run his hands over the soft skin, leaning closer, as though looking for something.

"Could it be the one that once belonged to Buffalo Dreamer?" she asked.

Robert folded the other end back, studying a circular-shaped discoloring on the hide. "I don't believe it. No two skins could possibly be marked the same, and I've never heard of another white buffalo robe in existence among the Lakota. I remember this marking." He met her gaze. "It's Buffalo Dreamer's robe."

Florence covered her mouth, her eyes tearing. "How on earth would William have come to own it? He had a courier bring it here and told him I would know what to do with it."

Robert lifted the robe a little more, only then noticing a letter that had been sandwiched between the robe and the blanket it was wrapped in. He grabbed it up and opened it, reading aloud to his mother.

"Mother, I won this robe three years ago from another soldier in a card game. The thing gives me the creeps, as I feel a feverlike warmth rush through me every time I touch it, and I've been having frequent headaches. I meant to send it a long time ago, but I got caught up in various campaigns and just never got around to it. I have a feeling if I get rid of the robe, I'll feel better. Figured you might have use for it. A white robe must mean something special to your people. . . ."

Robert stopped and looked at her. *"Your* people, not his." He shook his head. "He still fights it."

She closed her eyes and nodded. "How well I know." She put a hand to her heart then. "And we both know why the robe had such an affect on William. It's a connection between him and Rising Eagle." She looked at Robert. "I don't suppose that would matter to him."

Robert sighed. "I don't know, but I intend to write him and let him know. I'd better do it right away before he gets shipped off to some other fort and I lose track of him again."

"Finish the letter, Robert."

He studied the letter to find his place.

"I gave the damn robe to someone else, but he said he felt sick all the time, and he'd heard stories about it, said everyone who owned it had some kind of bad luck. I don't like such crazy talk, and I don't like being connected to something some people think has some kind of strange powers, especially when it apparently has something to do with the Lakota. I don't mean to turn that bad luck on you, but maybe if it's owned by a full-blood Lakota that person will have good luck instead of bad.

"I am still here at Fort Abraham Lincoln but might be leaving soon for expeditions into the Powder River area. An Indian inspector called Mr. Watkins has recommended that troops go after the hostiles and round them up and 'whip them into subjection,' to repeat his words. I don't know what will come of it, but I suppose I'll find myself ducking arrows again in the near future. Figured it was time to update you on my whereabouts and what I'll be doing. I might get to ride with General Custer himself. I am very excited about that.

"If you don't want the robe, maybe some of the Sioux there at the agency will want it.   *William."*

Robert leaned against the wall and closed his eyes. "Good God, he's going out with that idiot general. Custer is a good soldier in some ways, but he's terrible at following orders. I can't believe the army let him back in and gave him back his rank after kicking him out a few years ago." He leaned over and fingered the robe again, shaking his head. "I can't believe this. I can't believe Buffalo Dreamer's sacred white robe has ended up in our laps." He looked at Florence. "What do you think we should do with it?"

Florence touched it herself again. "I'm not sure. It shouldn't go to just anyone. It belongs to Buffalo Dreamer. Surely she would die to get it back." She met her son's gaze. "I don't want anyone to know about this yet, Robert. Let's wait and see what happens with this new campaign. Maybe we will find some way to see that it gets back to Buffalo Dreamer and Rising Eagle."

Robert nodded. "I agree." He sighed. "Maybe I should pack it up and go to Fort Abraham Lincoln, offer to ride with whatever troops William rides with. If the army is successful at rounding up the hostiles, maybe by some miracle I'll find Rising Eagle and Buffalo Dreamer. It will give them great hope and comfort to get the robe back."

Florence's eyes teared over at her son's dedication to his people. "I agree. Thank you so much, Robert, but please be very careful. I couldn't bear to lose you, and you have three little ones depending on you."

"I'm just glad you moved here. You'll be great comfort to Rebecca and the babies. Don't worry about me. I'll be all right."

Florence fingered the robe again. "I will pray for you, son, and for William. And I will pray for Rising Eagle and Buffalo Dreamer, that this robe will again fall into their possession. It would warm my heart to know we were able to do that much for them." Suddenly she jerked her hand away.

"What is it?" Robert asked.

She rubbed her hand. "I felt a sudden, strange numbness, and I could swear I heard drums and singing."

Robert closed his eyes, touching the robe himself and breathing deeply. He slowly nodded. "I hear it, too!" He looked at his mother. "Finding this robe is surely some kind of omen, Mother. I just wish I knew what it means."

MARCH 1876

Windy Moon

CHAPTER FORTY-SIX

"SHIHENNA! MANY SHIHENNA! Prepare your lodges for them!"

Buffalo Dreamer and Rising Eagle ducked outside their tepee and were quickly joined by Brave Horse, Crazy Horse, and others. The men mounted their ponies and rode to the southern edge of the huge encampment of Lakota at the northern end of the Rosebud River. Mud splattered as the horses galloped over the partially thawed ground.

Buffalo Dreamer watched the riders greet Wolf's Foot, the crier who'd announced the arrival of many Shihenna. She shivered against the cold, damp air. A good deal of snow remained on the surrounding mountains, as well as on the grounds of the camp, in places where over the winter it had drifted deep. She rubbed the backs of her arms while she waited, curious at the arrival of so many Shihenna. As she watched them approach, she realized they had suffered some kind of tragedy. Most of them walked, some of the old ones bent over and shivering under thin blankets, much like the refugees who had come to them after the Sand Creek massacre. Some struggled with no blankets at all. Most of them carried what few possessions they had in their arms, as they dragged only two travois with them. Little children ran along behind their mothers. Several men and women appeared to be wounded by the way they stumbled as they walked.

"Blue Coats," Buffalo Dreamer muttered under her breath. No one needed to explain to her what had happened to their Shihenna friends. Obviously they had suffered yet another unwarranted attack. She and Rising Eagle had followed Crazy Horse here to the northern reaches of their hunting grounds to join up with Sitting Bull, after messengers had come to them three moons before to tell them they must go to Red Cloud's reservation by the end of the Moon of Strong Cold, or face soldier attack.

The request was cruel and ridiculous. The Moon of Strong Cold fit its name. It was the coldest month of the year. To expect thousands of Lakota to go that far in such weather was like writing them a death sentence. The snow was too deep and the horses too weak, let alone the kind of temperatures under which they would have had to travel. All the white man's government needed to do was wait until spring, and many of the Lakota who'd fled the reservation would return on their own. The rest were willing to at least speak again to the white leaders . . . all except Crazy Horse, Rising Eagle, and Sitting Bull, who still vowed never to live the reservation life.

Now she saw Brave Horse riding in her direction. She waited for her son, seeing the anger in his eyes when he reached her.

"Soldiers attacked their camp!" he said, dismounting even before his horse came to a halt.

"Long Hair?" she asked.

"Not this time. They are not sure who the leader was, but they attacked Old Bear's peaceful camp, where He Dog had gone to stay. They burned all the lodges and possessions and ran off many horses, leaving them to suffer in the cold with no food or supplies." His hands went into fists. "I *curse* them! They could see there were many women and children among them. It was not a camp of warriors."

"Tell your father to bring some of them to our tepee," Buffalo Dreamer told him. "I will build up the fire and begin preparing something to eat. We are low on our own supply of meat and blankets, but we can still share."

"I will help also," Beaver Woman spoke up. "Bring some of them to our tepee, also, Brave Horse."

Brave Horse nodded, and Buffalo Dreamer could see the pain in his eyes. He turned and leaped onto his horse and rode off.

"This is inexcusable," Beaver Woman told Buffalo Dreamer.

"It doesn't surprise me," Buffalo Dreamer answered. "Over and over again they attack peaceful camps. It's all so unnecessary. Why can't our people wait and go back after the summer hunt? We were promised this land for hunting. Why do we suddenly have to leave?" She scowled as she watched some of the battered Shihenna come closer. "The Blue Coats have no conscience, and no honor. They speak of peace, yet they do these things that only make us more angry, more determined never to go to the reservation."

Beaver Woman touched her arm. "We should prepare the fires." She left Buffalo Dreamer to return to her tepee, and Buffalo Dreamer ducked inside her own dwelling, hurriedly putting more wood on the fire and enjoying its warmth herself. Then she sat back on her heels, staring at the flames for a moment, remembering her youth, when they never had the kind of worries they had now. Back then life was a joy. They had complete freedom to live and hunt wherever they wanted, from the Black Hills all the way west to the mountains of the Big Horn sheep, north to the land of the red-coat soldiers, and south to Pawnee country along the wide, flat river there. The buffalo were so plentiful there that herds moved like rivers of dark waters across the plains and prairies. There were no Blue Coats, not even a white man of any sort in this land; and no noisy, smoking iron horses. Game was plentiful, streams were bright and clean. All was peace and beauty.

White men had spoiled all of it.

She heard Rising Eagle's horse outside, and she looked up when he came in. She understood his rage, saw it in his blazing, dark eyes.

"We had a treaty," he said, sitting down on a robe near the fire. "All of this land was supposed to be ours forever, yet now they come and tell us we can no longer be here! And worse, they attack peaceful camps just because we refuse to go to the reservation in the dead of winter!" He looked away for a moment, his jaw flexing in anger. "I was considering hunting here in summer and going to the reservation for winters." He met her gaze again. "But now I want only to *fight*! Crazy Horse and Sitting Bull feel the same. We will hold a council meeting with the Shihenna leaders and decide what to do next. The soldiers will *pay* for their stupidity."

Buffalo Dreamer quietly nodded, again looking down to watch the flickering flames of the central fire. "I have not yet realized my dream of long ago, of many Shihenna and Lakota surrounding hundreds of soldiers and killing all of them." She met his gaze again. "I believe I am closer than ever to realizing that dream."

Rising Eagle sighed, his look suddenly turning to one of affection. "Perhaps you should go to Red Cloud's reservation after all, and take Beaver Woman and the grandchildren with you. You would be safer there. I fear this is going to be a long summer of fighting."

She shook her head. "Never. I will never leave your side, my husband. If you are wounded, I should be with you; and if you die, I, too, must die."

Their gazes held for several quiet seconds, and then he nodded. They reached across the fire, clasping hands, letting the heat penetrate their skin, as though to seal their pact.

MAY 1876

Moon When the Ponies Shed

CHAPTER FORTY-SEVEN

ROBERT RODE UP beside William, slowing his horse again to the gait of the rest of the 925 men heading west from Fort Abraham Lincoln, all under Brigadier-General Alfred Terry. Behind Terry's lead rode General George Custer and his Seventh Cavalry. William's troops rode under Major Reno, who reported to Custer, which irked Robert. Custer was cocky and confident, and knowing the Lakota warriors like Crazy Horse, Robert almost wanted to laugh at Custer's confidence.

"Why did you insist on coming along on this campaign?" William asked him, staring straight ahead as he spoke. "You and the other civilians along are crazy. This is going to be a long, hard march."

"You know why I volunteered to come. I have a sick feeling my services as a doctor are going to be needed."

William snickered and shook his head. "For the Lakota?"

"Don't be so cocky. You're as bad as Custer."

William coughed from the rolling dust stirred up by hundreds of horses. "I'm being practical. Between Crook coming from the south, Gibbon from the west, and us with nearly a thousand men heading from the east to meet the others, the Sioux are going to be surrounded by close to three thousand soldiers."

"And what if there are five or six thousand Lakota? Maybe more than that?"

William turned to look at him for a moment. "What the hell makes you think there are that many out there?"

Robert shrugged. "Look how many left the reservation last summer. Do your arithmetic, brother. There could even be up to *ten* thousand Lakota out around the Powder and the Little Big Horn. As far as I'm concerned they've done a lousy job of planning this campaign. Why don't they just relax and let the Lakota come back to the reservation? If they wouldn't push them so much, they might do just that. They're running out of their source of livelihood, namely the buffalo. Eventually they will *have* to come in whether they like it or not. All this isn't necessary. It's a dangerous risk of a lot of lives."

"And you are a doomsayer," William replied. "Besides, this is a refreshing change to the boredom at Fort Abe. I though we'd never get another assignment."

"And you know Custer's reputation for riding his men hard. Our rear ends are likely to be red meat by the time this march is ended."

"Getting soft?"

"Getting old. I guess the two go together."

William laughed lightly, and the sound warmed Robert's heart. At least William was a little easier to talk to than he'd been a few years ago. He decided to risk the question that might bring on his anger.

"Tell me something, brother," he said, determined to use the word brother even though they were not blood related. Maybe if he used the term enough, William would loosen up and they could regain some of the closeness they'd known when William was younger. "Why do you think that white buffalo robe you sent to Mother gave you headaches? Do you really believe it was the robe?"

William sobered, looking straight ahead again. After several seconds he replied. "I haven't had a headache since I shipped it off."

"Why did you keep it so long?"

"I don't know," William answered, frowning. "It was a great topic of conversation, I guess."

"You didn't feel some sort of . . . connection to it?"

"Don't be ridiculous."

"Well, you said it gave you headaches. Why in heck do you think that was?"

"Just forget about it, all right?"

Robert shook his head. "I'm afraid I can't. I happen to know something about that robe."

William glanced his way. "And you're determined to tell me."

"I am." Robert gave him a soft smile. "When I was a young boy, my adopted brother, Brave Horse, and I often slept on that robe. My adopted mother, Buffalo Dreamer, always claimed it saved our lives once when smallpox swept through our camp and killed our little brother and sister."

Commanders ahead of them shouted orders to halt where they were and take a noon break. William raised his hand and shouted the same orders to his men, telling them to dismount and give their horses a rest. He looked at Robert then, a mixture of surprise and near dread in his eyes. "What are you saying?"

"You know what I'm saying. That robe once belonged to Buffalo Dreamer, and it is very sacred. It's been touched by Rising Eagle, who has great spiritual powers. That's why you got a strange feeling every time you touched it. And you got headaches because you've been denying your real heritage most of your life. Rising Eagle was trying to get to you through that robe."

William maneuvered his horse around Robert's and rode up closer, facing him. "You know, Robert, you're a good brother, but I'm getting really tired of you hounding me about Rising Eagle."

"I just don't want you to keep denying the true man inside, William."

"Oh? And who is that?"

"That's for you to find out. All I know is, I'd bet my life that every time you touched that robe, Rising Eagle felt something, maybe even Buffalo Dreamer. They are out there somewhere, and I have no doubt their greatest desire is to have the robe returned to them. I came along on this mission to see if I can find them and return it. No matter what happens, that's what I'm going to do, or die trying."

William closed his eyes and looked away. "My God," he said quietly. He faced Robert again. "And here I thought you came along for *my* sake."

"Oh, I did. You're as much a part of this as they are. Your real father is out there somewhere, William, and this just might be your only chance to see him again. Don't you remember anything about him from when you were little and he and Buffalo Dreamer came to see Florence and found out you were sick? Don't you remember when Rising Eagle held you in his arms and prayed over you, not even knowing then who you were? Remember how easily you warmed to him? You were totally fascinated by the man. Don't you remember any of that?"

William removed his hat and ran a gloved hand over his hair. "Only vaguely. I can't picture his face." He put the hat back on. "You had no right doing this, Robert. I need to concentrate on army duties. I don't need you harping on me about a man I don't know or want to know, a man who's probably waiting out there to kill all of us if he gets the chance."

"That's quite possible. That's part of the reason I came along— to stop that from happening if I can—and to help you or Rising Eagle, or both of you, if the chance arises. You will never be a happy man, brother, if you don't acknowledge your true father, before you, or he, dies."

William looked around, obviously uncomfortable. "Keep your voice down. I've never told anyone, and considering the point of this mission, it wouldn't bode well for me if these men knew whose son I am, and it would be even worse for my commander to know. Keep it to yourself."

"Like you've been doing for years?"

"I mean it, Robert!"

Robert slowly nodded. "Don't worry. I won't tell your terrible secret."

William rolled his eyes. "You have the robe with you?"

"On my pack horse."

"Well *keep* it there out of sight."

"I intend to, unless I find Rising Eagle and Buffalo Dreamer. Maybe you don't care if you ever see them again, but I certainly do. It's been years since I saw my adoptive parents and brother. Considering the sad future they face, and the fact they'll most likely end up fighting two or three thousand soldiers for reasons that aren't even their fault, I want to find them before it's too late."

"This *is* their fault! All they had to do was come in to the reservation and this all could have been avoided."

"In the dead of winter, with few supplies, weak horses, and below-freezing temperatures? The government couldn't wait until summer?"

"I can't help the decisions of the president or my own commanders."

"Of course you can't. But then you didn't have to keep re-upping your service either, did you? What's the *real* reason for that, William? You hoping to face your own father one-on-one?"

"Shut up!"

Robert felt sorry for him. "Yes, sir." He backed up his horse. "Just remember I'm around if you need to talk to me, William. And you watch yourself. I have a real bad feeling about this campaign." He turned his horse and rode off to join the party of civilians who'd come along for the adventure. "A real bad feeling," he repeated to himself.

JUNE 1876

Moon of Making Fat

CHAPTER FORTY-EIGHT

"LOOK AT THEM!" Rising Eagle exclaimed. He stood with Buffalo Dreamer on a rise overlooking the huge camp sprawled along the Little Big Horn, circles of tepees for as far as the eye could see. "How many strong do you think we are?"

Buffalo Dreamer breathed deeply, feeling her husband's great joy at the sight. "Eight thousand? Ten thousand? It's hard to say."

"I think ten. Never have the Lakota been so united. Hunkpapas, Oglalas, Minneconjous, Brules, Blackfeet, Two Kettles, Sans Arcs, as well as most of the Northern Shihenna, and most of those who had settled on Red Cloud's reservation are also here." He looked down at her, then he smiled. "The scouts tell us many soldiers are coming, but with so many of us here, they would be crazy men to attack us now, especially after our defeat of General Crook on the Rosebud!"

Buffalo Dreamer felt elated at the memory. Only a few days before a large contingent of soldiers coming from the south under the white man's General Crook were discovered by Lakota scouts. What excitement they'd enjoyed that day, and for the next several days, as warriors led by Crazy Horse attacked Crook and his men, driving them back over and over. The soldiers' forces included many Crow scouts, which made the battle even more exciting, for not only could the Lakota and Shihenna fight the Blue Coats, but also their long-time enemy, the Crow, who had gone the way of the white man and now fought with him against the Lakota.

Many women had watched the fighting, and in one instance Crazy Horse rode into the midst of a group of Crow scouts who were whipping Jack Red Cloud, son of the Oglala Chief Red Cloud. Crazy Horse scattered the Crow scouts and grabbed Jack, carrying him back to safety, shouting "Today is a good day to fight! Today is a good day to die!" It was their most exciting battle yet with the Blue Coats, and it whetted their appetite for more confrontations. Crazy Horse indeed had a way of inspiring others.

"The white man's soldiers are discovering we are a formidable enemy," Rising Eagle told her. "And when I rode beside our sons into battle on the Rosebud, my heart has never known such happiness. Whatever happens, our names, and the names of Crazy Horse and Sitting Bull and others will long be remembered by the white man."

They watched warriors riding back and forth in camp, shouting war whoops. Women trilled in reply. In the distance several young boys raced horses. The entire camp was alive with excitement. Victory tasted wonderful!

"The day of my dream is near," Buffalo Dreamer told Rising Eagle. "I can feel it."

Rising Eagle nodded. "We will make a fire here, you and I. We will pray together." He looked down at her, his smile fading. "These will be our glory days; but we know they could also be our last days, for this is only the beginning of the coming of more and more soldiers. The scouts tell us that Long Hair is coming here from the east, and more soldiers are coming from the west. They intend to surround us, but they have no idea how many of us are here. They will be very surprised, but even if we defeat the new ones who come, they will send more again. With little to eat and nowhere to go except back to the reservation, we cannot hold out forever."

Buffalo Dreamer took hold of his hands. "But we will give them a good fight," she told him. "And I will be at your side through all of it."

Their quiet moment was suddenly interrupted by shouts from

below. "More soldiers!" The cry was faint because of their distance, but they could understand the words. "Warriors! Come south! Soldiers have killed women and children on the River of Greasy Grass! More soldiers! Hurry!"

"I have to join them!" Rising Eagle pulled away and ran down the hill. Buffalo Dreamer followed, her heart pounding with both excitement and dread. Never before had so many soldiers and so many Lakota come together in conflict!

JUNE 25, 1876

CHAPTER FORTY-NINE

"THE SOUTHERN END! The southern end!" Brave Horse shouted to Rising Eagle as he and several hundred more warriors charged past him.

"My hatchet and war shield!" Rising Eagle ordered Buffalo Dreamer. "And my rifle!" He leaped onto the back of his swiftest horse, which was tethered near their tepee. The day was very hot, and he wore only his breechcloth, an apron, and moccasins. Several coup feathers were tied into his hair, which was braided into two queues over each shoulder. There was no time to apply his war paint, no time for a council meeting or prayer. This was every man for himself.

Buffalo Dreamer handed him his war shield and hatchet. He slipped the war shield over his left arm and grasped the hatchet in that hand, then took the rifle into his right hand. Their eyes held for just a moment as more and more warriors charged past them, sod spewing in every direction. Women were running with their children and papooses, heading for a ravine.

"*Wakan-Tanka* be with you, my husband," Buffalo Dreamer told him.

"And with you." Rising Eagle charged away, using only his feet and thighs to guide his very dependable war pony. Now even more warriors joined him, the air alive with their shrill war cries. In spite of his sixty-six years, Rising Eagle suddenly felt like a young man, alive with the chance to again show the Blue Coats what a formidable enemy the Lakota could be. He thought how ridiculous it was that the soldiers had come after them, when all they had to do was wait out the summer. After the summer hunt and the Sun Dance celebrations, many of the Lakota here would go back to the reservation willingly. It was as though the Blue Coats *wanted* a fight . . . and so they would get it!

As he neared the south end of the River of Greasy Grass he noticed several dead women and children sprawled about, which gave him more determination to take part in battling the Blue Coats who had committed this surprise attack.

He charged into the melee of soldiers in combat with Lakota and Shihenna. He raised his repeating rifle, stolen from a dead soldier in the battle on the Rosebud just a few days ago. Using only one hand, he fired at two different soldiers, slaying both of them. The noise was incredible, screaming warriors, screaming soldiers, horses whinnying, the air filled with gun smoke, bodies of Indians and soldiers alike sprawled everywhere. More and more Lakota and Shihenna joined them, until they overwhelmed the soldiers.

Rising Eagle tried to see if Long Hair was among them, but he did not spot the soldier called Custer. Now the Blue Coats began to retreat, as well they should! He felt a bullet whiz past his head, then tossed his own empty rifle aside and rode down a soldier fleeing on foot, landing his hatchet between the man's shoulder blades. The soldier fell into the river, turning the water red where he landed.

It was then Rising Eagle felt it, the deep pain of a bayonet in his left side. He whirled his horse, hatchet raised, but suddenly he stopped with his arm in mid-air. Strangely, the soldier he faced did the same thing, looking ready to stab him again but holding back.

Suddenly everything seemed to become quiet, as Rising Eagle stared into the eyes of what looked like a Lakota man. He wore a blue coat. The man, whose Lakota features had obviously been softened by white blood, sat his horse right beside Rising Eagle. He could easily stab or shoot him now, but the soldier hesitated.

Rising Eagle felt an odd force move through him, as though perhaps he'd been struck by lightning. The man he faced was no Crow scout. As the rest of the soldiers began their retreat, Rising Eagle lowered his hatchet. "You are William," he said, speaking in his own tongue, but saying William's name in the only way he knew it, the English way.

The soldier's raised bayonet was covered with Rising Eagle's blood. The younger man's eyes first showed hatred, then an awareness of whom he faced.

"Rising Eagle?" William asked, using the Lakota term for his name.

Yes, he knew! Rising Eagle looked down to see blood running out of the wound at his side. Already it trickled down his thigh. Many years ago, on top of Medicine Mountain, the Feathered One had predicted he would die by the sword while riding to war with Crazy Horse. He glanced at the retreating soldiers to see Crazy Horse charging back and forth in front of the lead ranks of soldiers.

So, his time had come. He had never dreamed it would be his own son who would kill him. He looked back at William, who now had tears streaming down his cheeks. The young man threw his rifle down and turned, fording his horse into the river to join the rest of the soldiers. The river ran swiftly today. Several soldiers and their horses had been swept away. Rising Eagle could see their drowned bodies being dashed about, but William made it across.

Lakota and Shihenna swarmed around Rising Eagle, cheering loudly, some still shooting at the soldiers. A few even turned and bared their bottoms at the retreating Blue Coats, taunting them with defeat. Rising Eagle stared at the one soldier who'd suddenly changed his whole world. William reached the other side and rode toward a gully where soldiers had taken refuge. He turned his horse and looked back once, then disappeared into the gully.

"Pahuska!" A Shihenna man shouted the name. "Follow me! Long Hair and many more soldiers! Today is a good day to die!"

Rising Eagle looked down at his side again. Yes, today was a good day to die, and as long as there was life in him, he would continue to make the soldiers regret coming for him. He joined Brave Horse and others who now followed Crazy Horse, charging northward to fight Long Hair. Rising Eagle hoped he could cling to life long enough to fight one more battle.

CHAPTER FIFTY

BUFFALO DREAMER HELPED She Who Sings, Daisy, and Beaver Woman herd the children to safety, wondering what the future held for her four grandchildren now, a granddaughter and grandson by Brave Horse and Beaver Woman, a grandson by She Who Sings and Black Hawk, and a granddaughter by Thunder and Daisy.

She led Small Flower, now nine summers, by the hand. Beaver Woman carried five-year-old Little Beaver as she ran alongside Buffalo Dreamer. She Who Sings clung to the hand of her own five-year-old son, Red Pony, and Thunder's wife, Daisy, carried their infant son, Running Elk, in a papoose on her back.

The women and children scurried to a ravine, where Buffalo Dreamer left them. "I must see what is happening!" she told her daughter and daughters-in-law.

"Be careful, Mother!" She Who Sings told her.

Buffalo Dreamer grasped the black mane of her favorite horse, a red mare called Sunset, who had followed her as she ran. She leaped onto the horse's bare back and kicked its sides with her heals, noticing that on a distant rise the warriors were now headed north. More warriors charged past her, shouting *"Pahuska! Pahuska!"*

Long Hair! The man who had dared to bring white miners into the Black Hills was here!

"Death to Long Hair!" some men were shouting.

"Little Bear!" Buffalo Dreamer screamed out, addressing one of Rising Eagle's nephews. "Where is Rising Eagle!"

"They chased off the soldiers at the south end of camp!" he answered. "Now we go after Long Hair!" He charged away, and Buffalo Dreamer followed, as did several hundred other women, bound to see the battle that would take place to the north. It was exciting to watch their men at war, and all wanted to be close in case of injury or death.

Buffalo Dreamer could not help wondering if at last she would see the battle about which she had dreamed. She could already hear constant gunfire and the screams of men. By the time she and the others reached a high hill overlooking the battlefield, she knew this was the moment. Never had she beheld such a sight.

Already the soldiers were moving from scattered locations toward one area where they could circle and fight. Some had pulled their horses down to use as barriers. Some of the horses kept kicking and moving, but others were obviously dead. She tried to determine how many soldiers there were, as thousands of Lakota and Shihenna warriors began circling them . . . just like in her dream. As far as she could determine, there were at least two hundred Blue Coats, probably more.

Dust rolled high into the air, which was filled so loudly with gunfire and shouting that it almost hurt her ears. She wondered why soldiers from the south did not come to help these men, but she realized they might not even hear the noise. In this part of the land the rolling hills had a way of muffling noises.

She searched frantically for Rising Eagle amid the melee below, then thought she spotted him landing his hatchet into one soldier. Was that blood on his leg? He'd been wounded! She put a hand to her chest, searching then for Brave Horse. She spotted him riding near Crazy Horse, but quickly she lost all of them again in the dust.

Gradually the gunfire lessened. She squinted to see if Long Hair indeed was among the soldiers being slaughtered below, and finally she spotted his blond curls, nearly at the center of the fighting. His hat was gone, and it appeared he'd cut his hair a little shorter. He looked wounded, but he was still fighting. One thing that could be said about the daring, arrogant Long Hair Custer was that he seemed to be a brave man, or perhaps he was just stupid and careless. It was hard to determine which description fit him.

She joined the other women there in cheering on their men as soldier after soldier fell. The dust thickened again, and after a while the gunfire stopped almost completely. Now she could hear only war whoops. As the dust cleared, she could see the warriors stripping the bodies of dead soldiers, taking their blue coats, their weapons, some of the horses that were still alive. She felt a sick feeling of dread, for Sitting Bull had warned all of them the day before that through a vision he'd been told they must not take anything from the soldiers or defile them in any way the next time they fought them. Sitting Bull's dreams were highly honored, yet now the warriors were doing the very thing he'd told them not to do. Victory tasted too good to them to think about anyone's warnings.

Some of the women ran down to the scene to steal even more items: knives, guns, supplies, blankets, boots. Now Buffalo Dreamer could see Long Hair, his body full of arrows, sprawled across his horse. For almost as far as she could see over the valley before her lay the bodies of dead soldiers and dead horses. Slowly she rode Sunset closer, but she refused to dismount and touch the bodies or steal anything from them. She searched frantically for her sons and Rising Eagle, and finally the three of them approached, Thunder and Brave Horse on either side of their father, who was obviously gravely wounded.

"My husband!" she called out.

He rode close to her, holding his right hand over a wound in his left side. "A bayonet wound," he told her.

She gasped, a lump rising in her throat. Both knew he would die by the sword. She'd seen her dream of many Lakota and Shihenna circling and killing many Blue Coats come true, and now the Feathered One's prediction of how Rising Eagle would die also seemed to be taking place.

"Father!" Brave Horse spoke up, reaching out to touch his arm. "We will take you to the medicine man, Bear Dreaming."

"No," Rising Eagle objected, his gaze still on Buffalo Dreamer. "Your mother and I will go to Medicine Mountain."

"You will never make it that far!" Thunder told him. "You are too weak. And there are more soldiers out there! They will shoot you down!"

"They will not harm us." Rising Eagle looked at Thunder, then turned to Brave Horse. "Both of you know the only place I should die is at the top of Medicine Mountain."

"Then we will go with you!" Brave Horse told him.

Rising Eagle shook his head. "Your place is with your wives and children, and with your sister. Both of you know that in spite of our victory here today, more soldiers will come, and they will be even more determined. The Lakota cannot hold out forever. One day we will be forced to live on the reservation. Those who want freedom must go north to the Queen Mother's country, where Sitting Bull will go now. Go with him. Save yourselves."

"It's not worth it if we lose our freedom!"

Rising Eagle closed his eyes, obviously weakening. "Listen to me." He breathed deeply. "What is most important is preserving the Nation, saving the children. And you yourselves must live to teach them the Lakota way and make sure they never forget. They in turn must teach *their* children, and then the next generation, so that the Lakota way and the Lakota spirit is never lost. This is a great victory that will . . . long be remembered." He took another deep breath. "And the final victory will be . . . never giving up *Paha-Sapa*, not for any price. One day . . . the land will be ours again . . . when the Feathered One returns with all our ancestors to reclaim it. Watch for . . . the messenger of *Wakan-Tanka* . . . and for the birth of a white buffalo. It will be . . . a sign."

Buffalo Dreamer brushed at tears over the look of despair in the eyes of her sons. "You must do as your father tells you," she said. "He will go to his death happy in the knowledge that his family will live. When the day comes that you return to the reservation, ask for your adopted brother, Robert. If he is there, he'll help you. He knows the white man's way. He'll make sure you are not harmed."

"We love you, Father," Thunder said through tears.

Rising Eagle nodded. "As I love you. That is why I ask these things of you. You must . . . obey what I tell you."

Brave Horse looked away. "I thought this would be the happiest day of my life."

"It is, son," Buffalo Dreamer told him, reaching over to touch his hand. "You have taken part in a battle that will forever be remembered, both by our own people and by the white man. And your father can go to his death after realizing a great victory. It's the only way for a great Lakota leader to die. I will help him get to Medicine Mountain, and you should be glad that he will die there, where he has known great visions and has spoken to the Feathered One Himself. The old ones like your father have known their glory. Now it is your turn. Never despair, Brave Horse . . ." She turned to her youngest son. "Thunder. This is a happy day. Go and find your families. Have you seen Black Hawk? Is he all right?"

Brave Horse sniffed. "He already went to get our sister and their children."

"A wise decision. Go now, both of you, so I can take your father to Medicine Mountain. It is not so far south of us."

Thunder wiped at his nose and eyes. He handed over an army blanket he'd stolen. "Take this. You might need it."

Brave Horse handed his own repeating rifle to Buffalo Dreamer. "Here. You might need it to protect Father until you reach Medicine Mountain." He handed her a box of cartridges, and a parfleche he'd already had tied to his horse before the soldiers came. "There is some dried meat in my parfleche."

Buffalo Dreamer took it, shoving the cartridges into the parfleche and draping the supply bag over her horse's neck. She held the rifle in her left hand, then took hold of the rope bridle of Rising Eagle's horse. She looked from Brave Horse to Thunder. "Tell She Who Sings where I have gone, and that I love her and will be with her and the grandchildren forever in spirit . . . and with both of you, my precious sons." Tears trickled down her cheeks.

"You are not coming back?" Thunder asked her.

Buffalo Dreamer met Rising Eagle's gaze. "Where your father dies, I die," she answered. "I will not go on without him."

Both sons wept as Buffalo Dreamer started off, leading Rising Eagle's horse. "Go," she told them. "Go to your families. Head for the land of the Queen Mother before more soldiers come."

"Good-bye, *Ate,*" Brave Horse told his father softly.

Buffalo Dreamer remembered the time when he was just a baby, and he called out for his father, *"Ate!"* just before running naked out of their tepee to tease his father with a race. That was when he was stolen by Pawnee warriors. She'd taken part in the Lakota and Shihenna raid on the Pawnee camp where Brave Horse had been taken. That was the first time she'd ever actually ridden into battle at her husband's side. So many memories! So many years!

Feeling as though someone was ripping out her heart, she turned away and headed south, toward Medicine Mountain. Her vision had been realized, as had the prediction of the Feathered One about Rising Eagle's death.

JUNE 27, 1876

CHAPTER FIFTY-ONE

"MY GOD!" ROBERT muttered, drinking in the scene before him. Buzzards circled, and the buzzing of flies over the mostly-naked, dead bodies was so loud it rang in his ears. One needed not ride closer to know most of the men below had been scalped and otherwise mutilated. Many lay with upwards of a hundred arrows in them.

"Custer is down there somewhere," William said, his voice stony. "His brother, Tom, too. I feel sorry for Custer's wife."

Robert sighed. "It's obvious my services aren't needed down there." He turned to William. "Thank God Terry and Gibbon relieved us back there. I never thought I'd end up shooting at my own people myself, but I have to say, I was damn scared." He'd hung back with other civilians while Major Reno and his men fought the Lakota and Cheyenne at the south end of the Little Big Horn. Indians there kept them pinned down for nearly two days, and Robert stayed busy dressing wounds. None of Reno's men had any idea what had happened to Custer and his men here at the north end of the river. Nearly five miles of rolling hills separated them. Custer wasn't even supposed to be here, but what had really taken place here was something for the army to settle. "This is certainly one battle for the history books."

William slowly nodded, covering his face with his arm to help ward off the stench in the air. He looked at Robert. "Thanks for coming down and helping us fight back there."

Robert studied his half-brother's face, black with gun smoke and dust, streaked by perspiration. He knew he must look the same. "Quite a fight, wasn't it?" He smiled sadly, and William did the same.

"Yeah." He sighed. "Want to know something *really* funny?"

"What's that?"

"My latest stint in the army ended five days ago."

Robert frowned. *"What?"*

William nodded. "I didn't even have to come along on this campaign, but I volunteered to use up my last days with the army to come along. I figured I'd sign up again, but I'm not so sure I will." He dropped his arm to wipe at the dirt on his face, curling his nose at the smell. "I'm tired of it all, Robert. And . . . something happened back there I didn't tell you about."

Several soldiers ordered to do so moved down to the battlefield to begin trying to identify bodies. Robert noticed one of them leaned over to vomit. "What's happened?" he asked William, looking back at his brother.

William wiped at his eyes, turning his horse then and riding at a gentle walk away from the horrible sight below. Robert followed. "What is it, William?" He realized then that his brother was crying. William took a few deep breaths before continuing.

"I saw him."

"Who?"

William swallowed. "My real father."

Robert felt his heart beat faster. "Rising Eagle?"

William nodded. "I didn't know it was him . . . until after."

"After what?"

William faced him, his eyes bloodshot, new, lighter streaks on his face from fresh tears. "After I stabbed him with my bayonet."

Robert felt as though the blood was draining from his body. "You *stabbed* him? How do you know it was Rising Eagle?"

"I just knew, the minute he turned. Our eyes held, and he had his hatchet raised, but he stopped mid-air and just looked at me. Then he spoke my name. He knew . . . and then *I* knew. I remembered seeing him once before . . . at a distance during the Wagon Box fight. I had my rifle sight on him . . . but I couldn't pull the trigger . . . wondering if it was Rising Eagle." He swallowed again. "Still . . . I never really thought . . . if something like that did happen, that it would bother me." He removed his hat and ran a hand through his hair. "My God, I've killed my own father. I'm not a religious man . . . but the way I was brought up . . . by a preacher and all. I can't help wondering how God will punish me for this."

Robert wanted to weep himself. Was Rising Eagle dead? He'd wanted desperately to get the white buffalo robe to him and Buffalo Dreamer. He had to at least find Buffalo Dreamer. He shook his head, swallowing back his own tears. "God won't punish you, William. You didn't know." He looked over the vast rolling hills to the north, where more dead bodies lay, the bodies of Lakota and Cheyenne. "My God, man, you were in a fight for your life. No one would expect you to stop and ask who is who in a battle like that." The only thing that warmed his heart was to discover this really bothered William. Seeing Rising Eagle had touched something in him. "Maybe you'd feel better if we found Buffalo Dreamer and took the white robe to her."

William smiled sadly. "Hell, she'd probably shoot me. If she didn't, Rising Eagle's sons certainly would. The mood they all must be in right now, there's no sense trying to find them."

"Yes, there is. You need to find them, William. You need to meet your brothers and sister. You need to meet Buffalo Dreamer. She can tell you lots of stories about your father."

William sighed. "I don't know. I just . . . I see that mess there behind us, and all the dead Indians we've seen on the way here, and I wonder what it's all for. I thought I hated them, but the way they fought . . . a part of me understands why. Why didn't the government just wait a while longer, let them get used to the idea of the reservation, see how many might have come back after the hunting season?" He shook his head. "I'm so torn, Robert. I never thought I'd feel this way. I was fine till I looked him in the eyes and realized that was probably the one and only time I would ever see him. And I'm the one who sank my bayonet into his side. How am I going to live with that?"

Robert closed his eyes. "Damn." He breathed deeply, thinking for a few quiet minutes while around them soldiers shouted orders. Some of them were cursing the Lakota, one man was crying loudly. "I have an idea," Robert said.

William took a thin cigar from a pocket inside his uniform jacket and lit it. "What?" He puffed the cigar while he waited for an answer.

"You are officially a regular civilian now, right?"

William took the cigar from his mouth and stared at it. "Yeah, I guess so."

"That means you can ride away from here. There isn't anything the army can do about it."

"So?"

"Look around us, brother. We won't exactly be a welcome sight to these men. Fact is, the mood these soldiers are in, one of them might go mad and shoot us just because we have Lakota blood. This isn't exactly the safest place for us right now."

Robert smoked quietly for a moment. "And?"

"And there are several women and children and a few men south of here who've been captured and will be taken to the reservation. We could ride down there and talk to them, see if any of them knows what happened to Rising Eagle and Buffalo Dreamer. Rising Eagle is a damn tough man. He just might not be dead yet. If he isn't, I want to go to him and see if I can do anything for him. I can hardly stand the thought of him dying before I can see him again. I'm going to see what I can find out, and you might as well come with me."

William smiled sadly. "In a blue uniform? Are you crazy?"

Robert shrugged. "I have some extra clothes in my supplies. Take off the uniform."

William looked down at pants, took off his hat, and looked at it. "I've been wearing an army uniform for a lot of years."

"And you've never found happiness. Why not try life as a civilian for a while? It's time to settle down, William, find yourself a good woman. And it's time to go back and make amends with my mother, face the reality that you *are* half Lakota. And you need to pray, brother, for forgiveness. Most of all you need to give yourself the chance to talk to Rising Eagle, if he's still alive. You'll never be a happy man if you don't own up to your heritage, William. You have to get rid of all that hate inside of you. You can't live divided against yourself forever."

William kept the cigar in his mouth as he slowly removed his army jacket, then tossed it and his hat aside. "Maybe you're right. I'm not saying for sure yet, but you've been a loyal, if irritating, brother, I'll say that." He looked at Robert, his eyes still swollen and red. "Hand me a shirt."

JUNE 28, 1876

Moon When the Green Grass Is Up

CHAPTER FIFTY-TWO

BUFFALO DREAMER KEPT to the cover of trees as much as possible, amazed at how infested with white settlements this land of mountains and rivers and millions of buffalo had become. Every few miles she also spotted more soldiers. They swarmed the hills and valleys like ants. She had no doubt soldiers would rain down on the Lakota now like a heavy storm, and her heart ached for her children. She could only pray they would make it to the safety of the Queen Mother's land in the north. If anyone could get them there, Sitting Bull could. She had no idea what Crazy Horse would do now, but she felt confident that if Brave Horse's good friend wanted to do something reckless and foolish, Brave Horse would stick to his promise to head north.

"I saw him," Rising Eagle told her. He rode bent over, still holding his side. His color was turning to a sickly gray, and Buffalo Dreamer knew it was taking all the courage he'd ever mustered just to hang on to life until they reached Medicine Mountain.

"What are you talking about, my husband?"

He did not answer at first, and she realized it took what little strength he had just to speak. As they'd hurried away from the battlefield on the Little Big Horn, she'd stopped to steal three neck scarves from three dead soldiers, then tied the ends together to make them long enough to wrap around Rising Eagle's wound.

Although the yellow scarves were heavily bloodstained, it looked as though the blood had dried. The outer bleeding had stopped, but she knew Rising Eagle could still be bleeding on the inside. His whole left side and back were purple. She'd seen wounds like this before and a person seldom survived them, no matter how much the medicine man prayed over the victim. Still, Rising Eagle had himself survived extremely grave wounds in his lifetime . . . but when he was much younger and stronger.

"Rising Eagle?" she spoke up again.

He lifted his head slightly. "What?"

"You said that you saw him?"

He closed his eyes. "My son . . . William."

Buffalo Dreamer's eyes widened in surprise. "William! With Custer's men? Is your son dead?"

"I don't know. He was not . . . with Custer. I saw him . . . at the south end . . . where we first rode. He did not know . . . who I was . . . until after he stabbed me . . . with his bayonet."

Buffalo Dreamer halted her horse and turned it to face Rising Eagle, who clung to his horse's mane in a desperate effort not to fall off. "*William* did this?"

"It was meant to be. I believe . . . it was the only way . . . to awaken his Lakota heart."

Buffalo Dreamer let out a sigh of shock and disappointment. "It should not have taken the death of my husband, his own father!"

"Do not blame him. He will be . . . Lakota now. I feel it . . . in my heart."

"You are sure it was him?"

He sat up a little straighter, grimacing. "I made ready to kill him . . . after his bayonet plunged into my side, but I could not . . . do it. I saw his face . . . and then I spoke his name. I knew by his eyes just as he knew."

"Then he must live with the terrible guilt." Buffalo Dreamer turned Sunset and moved forward again, leading Rising Eagle's horse by its rope bridle. What was this world coming to? If the Crow and Shoshone and Pawnee could have come to peace with the Lakota and Shihenna, the Arapaho, perhaps some of the southern tribes she'd heard of, Apache and Comanche . . . what if all of them could have joined together against the white man? How different might things have been? But for centuries warring among the tribes had been the way and the white man knew that. He'd used that to divide and conquer, then finished off his plan by killing nearly all the buffalo, so that there was no way to survive but to go to their hideous reservations and beg for food and blankets. Maybe those who went to the Queen Mother's land would fare better.

Who was to say what would happen next? She and her husband would not be here to watch it. They would be with the Feathered One, and all their loved ones who had gone before. They were old and weary now. It was time for the younger ones to take their place, to keep the Lakota spirit alive.

She moved out of the trees into a flatter, more open area, anxious to make better time and get Rising Eagle to the sacred peak of Medicine Mountain. Thankfully, one side of the mountain offered a gradual ascent, in such a way that in years past, when her people went to the sacred circle of stones at the top, they'd carved a pathway up the side of the mountain.

Even the Lakota did not know how the stone medicine wheel came to be. Perhaps the *Wakan-Tanka* Himself had caused it to be there. No one even knew who'd first discovered it, a layout of stones shaped exactly the way the poles of the sacred Sun Dance Lodge would be shaped. All considered the place highly sacred, and it held special meaning to her and Rising Eagle. Now they would go there to die. It was fitting.

They came over a rise, and it was only then that she saw a camp of white men ahead, three of them, hunters, most likely. Quickly she lifted the rifle that lay across her lap, glad that Brave Horse had given her one of the newer army repeating rifles.

"Hey!" she heard one of the men shout. They all rose, and Buffalo Dreamer was not about to wait to see what they would do. She raised her rifle, took aim, and fired. One man went down.

"Son of a bitch!" one of them yelled. He dived to the ground, and the other reached for his rifle, which was propped against a stump.

Buffalo Dreamer retracted the lever, spitting out a spent cartridge, then fired again. Before the man could even raise his rifle, he, too, went down.

"*Wakan-Tanka* is with us today!" Buffalo Dreamer told her husband.

The third man got up and started running for his horse. Buffalo Dreamer left Rising Eagle for a moment and charged her horse down the hill to get a better shot. As the man climbed onto his horse she fired again, opening a hole in his back.

Again she retracted the rifle lever and spilled the third spent cartridge. She held her chin proudly, allowing a soft breeze to blow her hair away from her face and feeling quite proud of herself. She turned and rode back to Rising Eagle, smiling. To her surprise, he had his head up, watching her. He, too, was smiling.

"My . . . warrior woman," he said teasingly.

She laid the rifle across her lap again and took hold of his horse. "Nothing will keep us from reaching Medicine Mountain. Nothing."

JUNE 30, 1876

CHAPTER FIFTY-THREE

"WE CAN CATCH them! I know we can! I know exactly where they're headed." Robert urged his horse down a steep escarpment. "And I know the shortcuts." He looked back to see William right behind. One good thing William had learned in the army was how to handle a horse well, but then he was also half Lakota. Was there a Lakota man alive who couldn't handle a horse from the time he was three or four years old?

He grinned at his own memories of learning to ride. Rising Eagle had taught him. He couldn't let the man die without seeing him once more!

"You're going to kill these horses," William shouted from behind.

"They'll be all right if we keep switching with the spares."

They made it to the bottom of the gravelly hill with no mishaps. The Oglala men they had questioned gladly gave them four of their best horses, trusting William to return them to the reservation. The men he'd talked to had been at the Custer slaughter, but then headed for the reservation. They had seen and spoken with Brave Horse, so they knew where Rising Eagle had headed.

Robert was not surprised it was to Medicine Mountain. If Rising Eagle was dying, there was no place else he would want to be but at the top of that place of magic, where the Feathered One could easily find his soul.

He prayed that Brave Horse and the rest of the family would make it to Canada. That was where he intended to go next, to make sure they were all right. Rising Eagle and Buffalo Dreamer would want him to do that. And somehow amends had to be made between them and William. He hoped poor Rebecca would understand later. She'd been so good about the things he felt he needed to do for his family, but he dearly missed his wife and son, and Florence, who would be devastated to learn Rising Eagle had died. He just hoped he could reach his Lakota father while the man was still alive.

William caught up to him then. He wore civilian pants and boots now, a white cotton shirt open at the neck because of the July heat. "What about Rebecca?" he asked, nearly shouting the words as they kept the horses at a rapid gait. "She'll be worried."

"I told one of the army scouts to be sure to let her know where I've gone once they get their prisoners to the reservation. And I know Florence will be glad to know we've gone after Rising Eagle and Buffalo Dreamer. She'll make Rebecca understand."

"Do you think Florence will forgive me for what I've done?"

"She's a good, Christian woman. She'll forgive you. I have already forgiven you."

"Well, I'm not so sure Brave Horse and my other siblings will."

"Let's take one thing at a time. There is a lot of healing to be done on all counts," Robert told him. He rode shirtless today, liking the feel of the sun on his skin, remembering when he often rode this way in his younger days living with the Lakota. He slowed his horse. "Let's rest them a little."

William followed suit, and his lathered horse snorted and shook its mane. "What do you really think will come of all this, Robert?"

Robert shook his head. "The whites are bound to make Custer into a martyr, and portray the Lakota as nothing but untamed murderers. There is so much they don't know about the Lakota culture, the things that drove them to what happened back there on the

Little Big Horn. But it won't matter, not for a long time. Our people will be called savages, and life is going to be hell for them, both for the ones on the reservation and for those who've fled north. There are hardly any more buffalo in Canada than here anymore, and Canada has its own Indian tribes to deal with. Eventually Sitting Bull and the others will have to come back south and settle on the reservation."

They both remained quiet for the next several minutes of travel, and Robert knew how William must be suffering inside. He hoped he was doing the right thing, taking him to Rising Eagle. He couldn't help but think he was. The only thing that would help William get over what had happened was to reconcile with Rising Eagle.

"You sure you know where you're going?" William asked him then.

"I'm sure. And like I said, between Rising Eagle's wound and the fact that they will have to be careful to stay out of sight, they'll be moving slowly. With us riding hard and taking some shortcuts, dangerous as they are, we can get there practically the same time as they, I'm guessing."

"I hope you're right. But I have to tell you, your shortcuts are about to give me a heart attack. I'm beginning to wonder if *we* will make it there alive. This is damn rugged country."

"You can handle it. You've been in the army out here for a long time now, brother. You're trained for this."

"Lord knows I should be." William sniffed. "What the heck is that smell?"

Robert frowned, slowing his horse and sniffing the air. "Damn! Smells like dead bodies."

"I think you're right. God knows I've smelled that odor too many times in my army career."

Pain ripped through Robert's heart. The smell came from the direction anyone would have to ride to get to Medicine Mountain. Had Rising Eagle already died? Still, if he had, Buffalo Dreamer would have nothing to wrap him in. And if she could have built a scaffold, she had no way of raising him up. Maybe she'd had to just leave him, but even then she would have at least covered him with stones. He turned to William. "We'd better check it out."

He saw equal concern on William's face, which warmed his heart a little. William was actually learning to care. They headed in the direction of the smell, curling their noses as it became worse. Buzzards circled in the distance. The horses began to balk and whinny as they drew closer, wary of the smell, but both men managed to urge them closer to what looked like three bodies and a dead campfire.

Finally the horses would go no farther. Both men tied their horses and the two spare mounts. They took their rifles from their boots and headed toward the sight. Robert put his arm over his nose and mouth, and William did the same as they came even closer to see three bloated bodies. From what they could tell, they were white, although they wore buckskins. Their camp looked undisturbed, and two horses grazed not far away, still wearing bridles. A small wagon full of buffalo robes sat nearby.

"Buffalo hunters," Robert commented, relieved they were not the bodies of Rising Eagle and Buffalo Dreamer.

"Who do you think shot them?" William questioned.

Robert shrugged. "Indians, most likely."

"Buffalo Dreamer?" William asked.

"Who knows? I only know she would kill anyone who tried to get in her way of getting to Medicine Mountain."

Repugnant as it was, Robert leaned a little closer to the bodies, trying to determine how long they had been dead. "My guess is no more than twenty-four hours. Doesn't take this kind of heat long to have these effects on a dead body, and if it was longer than twenty-four hours, they would look even worse than this, and they would be picked practically clean by the buzzards or torn apart by wolves."

William made a face and turned away. "Maybe we're only a day away from Rising Eagle and Buffalo Dreamer."

Robert studied a pathway of crushed grass, leading away from the campsite exactly in the direction Buffalo Dreamer would have to go to reach the mountain. He nodded. "Maybe."

William left to get the horses. "We'd better get moving then. There is still some daylight left."

Robert watched him a moment, then hurried to join him. "You giving me orders, Sergeant?"

William grinned as he untied his horse and a spare, then mounted up. "It's going to take me a while to get used to *not* giving orders."

Robert's horse reared slightly after he untied it, still skittish from the smell of dead bodies. "Whoa, boy!" Robert climbed up as the gelding turned into a circle. He calmed the animal and untied his pack horse, taking hold of the lead rope. "Well, you're right about covering more ground before dark. Let's get going."

A shadow passed over them, causing both of them to look up then to see an eagle gliding above them, lower than either of them had ever seen an eagle fly in the vicinity of humans. It called out, as though beckoning them, heading south, then circling back and crying out again in the unique squall of an eagle. Again it headed south.

"I'll be damned," William commented.

"It's a sign," Robert told him.

William frowned. "You going to get into that Lakota spiritual stuff again?"

"I don't need to. You can see it for yourself. Don't forget your father's name."

William glanced up as the magnificent bird circled back yet again. He shook his head as he moved his gaze to Robert again. "Lead the way," he said, looking a little irritated.

Robert subdued an urge to smile. He knew Rising Eagle's spirit was calling to them, but it wouldn't do much good to try to convince William of that. Let him learn for himself about the spiritual powers of men like his own father.

JULY 2, 1876

Moon of the Horse

CHAPTER FIFTY-FOUR

BUFFALO DREAMER COULD hardly stand watching her husband's agony. Never had she seen him more brave, able to bear more pain, not even when he suffered the horrors of smallpox. At last they had made it here to the one place he could die in peace, and she was grateful that the July warmth had even made it up here, on top of the world, at the flat top of Medicine Mountain. Between two of the stone spokes of the Medicine Wheel she'd brushed smaller stones away and spread out her only blanket so that her husband could lie down. They had arrived late morning, and now the warmth of the late afternoon helped comfort Rising Eagle as she sat next to him, singing her prayer song.

> Wakan-Tanka, *hear me.*
> *Spirit of the white buffalo, hear me.*
> *Take away my husband's pain.*
> *Take it to the heavens and blow it away.*
> Wakan-Tanka, *hear me.*
> *Take his spirit with you.*
> *Leave the pain behind.*
> *Spirit of the white buffalo, hear me.*
> *Take away my husband's pain.*

Tears wet her cheeks as she sang, knowing that the answer to her prayer would mean she'd lost Rising Eagle in death.

Rising Eagle's breathing was labored, his groaning constant. She stopped singing for a moment and leaned closer. "Let it go, my husband. Let your spirit go," she wept.

"Not . . . yet," he whispered. "Something . . . tells me . . . not yet."

Her stomach ached at the agony of watching this once virile, handsome, proud warrior lying in such horrible pain. How she wished she could help him. How she wished she had the white buffalo robe to cover him with. She looked up to the heavens to pray again, and then she saw it, a very large eagle sitting on a nearby rock, completely silent. Could it be a vision of the Feathered One? A sign of some kind?

"*Ate!*" someone cried then.

Buffalo Dreamer put a hand to her heart, looking around. Had the eagle cried the word "father?"

She felt Rising Eagle's hand tighten around her own when someone called the name again. "*Ate!*" Father!

"He . . . has come," Rising Eagle said softly.

"Brave Horse?" Buffalo Dreamer asked him.

"No. The son . . . who would deny me. I feel him near me. My soul told me . . . I could not die yet. There is one last thing . . . I must do."

"*Ate!*" came the call again, this time closer.

"Lie still, my husband," Buffalo Dreamer told him. "I will go and see." She rose, walking from the center of the stone Medicine Wheel to the edge of the circular structure, watching as two men with four horses appeared over the crest of the trail leading to this sacred place.

"Buffalo Dreamer!" One of them rode closer while the other held back. When the first man reached her, she realized it was Robert, Fall Leaf Woman's son, the very man who as a baby had been healed of his deformities here at this very place because of Rising Eagle's powerful spirituality. That same spirituality had told her husband to hang on to life just a little longer . . . for this.

"Spirit Walker!" she called out, still using Robert's Lakota name. He dismounted and walked up to embrace her.

"I have come from the Little Big Horn," he told her. "I heard that Rising Eagle was wounded. I couldn't let him die without seeing him once more, Buffalo Dreamer, and not without giving you something I know you've prayed for." He led her to his pack horse, untying a large bundle that looked like blankets. He unwrapped them, then lifted and held up the white buffalo robe stolen from her so many years ago.

Buffalo Dreamer nearly fainted from surprise. "The robe!" she gasped. She covered her mouth. "How did you get it?"

"I'm not sure how many men have owned it, but it ended up in the hands of William, Rising Eagle's son by the white woman. He sent it to me and my mother. I knew the moment I saw it that it was yours." He draped it around her, and she fell to her knees.

"My prayers are answered!" she wept. "The robe is mine again!"

Robert knelt near her, putting a hand on her shoulder. "You have William to thank for the robe, Buffalo Dreamer. I have no doubt that Rising Eagle told you it was William who stabbed him, but William didn't realize until it was too late. It changed his life, Buffalo Dreamer, and I feel certain bringing him here was the right thing. There was a reason for him finding the robe, and for what happened at the Little Big Horn. He is here, Buffalo Dreamer. He wants to see Rising Eagle."

Grasping the robe tightly around her, her eyes so full of tears she could not see well, Buffalo Dreamer stood up, Robert helping her because of the weight of the robe on her weakened body. "Tell him to come closer," she said.

Robert called to William, who dismounted and approached them hesitantly.

"Speak to me, son of Rising Eagle," Buffalo Dreamer told him.

William cleared his throat before replying. "I . . . something . . . made me come here," he told her, using what he knew of the Lakota tongue. Buffalo Dreamer realized Florence and Robert must have taught him, when he was young. "I ask your . . .

forgiveness," he said. "I thought I could fight and conquer that part of me that is Lakota . . . but I can't. I wish to see my father . . . if he still lives."

Buffalo Dreamer held the robe together with one hand while she reached out between the folds to touch William's chest. "Rising Eagle would want me to forgive you. You only did as the Great Spirit wished you to do, William. Rising Eagle was told long ago that he would fight in a great battle against the Blue Coats, riding beside an honored warrior called Crazy Horse. All of that came to be. He was also told by the Feathered One that he would die by the sword. You have only fulfilled that prophecy. He is dying from wounds suffered in a great battle. It is the only way a man like Rising Eagle can die, and he is not afraid."

She turned to Robert. "My husband has been suffering terribly, clinging to life because he kept saying there was something he must do."

She turned to William again. "Now I know what he was waiting for." She turned. "Come with me, both of you. Speak with your father once more, William; and Robert, you called Rising Eagle father for the first eighteen summers of your life."

"I will always think of him as my real father. And how can I ever thank him enough for the prayers that healed my hands?"

"Rising Eagle was only a connection between you and the Feathered One." Buffalo Dreamer hurried through the circle of stones to kneel beside Rising Eagle. "My husband! Your son, William, found the white buffalo robe! He has brought it back to us!"

Rising Eagle's eyes opened as she lay down beside him, throwing the robe over both of them.

"We are safe now. We can finally be at peace. We have the robe! We have the robe! All will be well!" Buffalo Dreamer rested her head on his shoulder as William knelt down on the other side of Rising Eagle, tears in his eyes.

"Please forgive me . . . *Ate*," he said, speaking in the Lakota tongue.

Rising Eagle managed to raise his left hand, and William took hold of it hesitantly. "You did . . . what the Great Spirit . . . directed you to do," Rising Eagle told him, so softly that William had to lean closer to hear him. "You had . . . no choice."

William swallowed. "I am sorry I never had the chance to know you."

"You will know me . . . in spirit."

Robert knelt at Rising Eagle's head, leaning down and kissing his forehead. "*Ate,* I have missed you. I wish our last meeting would not be like this."

"Stay," Rising Eagle whispered. "Both of you. And when I am gone, help my sons . . . and my daughter . . . my grandchildren."

"You know I will," Robert told him.

"I will try," William told him. "I have a lot to learn."

Rising Eagle's eyes closed.

"He is so tired," Buffalo Dreamer told them. "Just stay beside him for a while. He should not talk any more." She drew the white buffalo robe closer around herself and her husband and closed her eyes. "I can't believe it," she said, still stunned she again possessed the white robe. Surely this meant something good lay ahead for the Lakota.

CHAPTER FIFTY-FIVE

WEARY FROM THE hard ride, William left Rising Eagle and Buffalo Dreamer to get a blanket from his gear. Robert walked with him, both men thinking their own quiet thoughts. Robert retrieved a medicine rattle from his supplies, and to William's surprise, he carried it over to where Rising Eagle and Buffalo Dreamer lay and began chanting over them, shaking the rattle and singing for *Wakan-Tanka* to take Rising Eagle soon and spare him his pain.

William spread his blanket out near Rising Eagle and lay down, feeling uneasy being here at such a sacred place, yet finding it strangely calming to realize he was Rising Eagle's son and had a right to be here after all, in spite of it being his own bayonet that had gravely wounded the man. After all, Rising Eagle himself had told him it was meant to be. He'd actually fulfilled a vision without even realizing it.

He closed his eyes, listening to Robert's chanting. It was calming, and it brought back glimpses of another time, when an Indian man held him in his arms and sang over him. Now he remembered. It was Rising Eagle. A lump rose in his throat, and he realized that more than ever he wanted to know more about that part of him that was Lakota. As he drifted to sleep, he thought how it would please Florence to know that.

* * *

A sudden, deafening clap of thunder woke William. He gasped and sat straight up, then leaped to his feet and backed away as he watched wide-eyed at a bright shaft of light that shone down on the very spot where Rising Eagle and Buffalo Dreamer lay. For a moment he could swear he saw the ghostlike images of Rising Eagle and Buffalo Dreamer floating upward, but as quickly as he thought he saw them, they disappeared. He ducked when a bolt of lightning ripped through the black sky and popped against a large boulder, which appeared to actually move.

Suddenly all was silent, and to his astonishment, there was not a cloud in the sky. The moon was just a sliver, and other than that the sky was a mass of stars! Where in God's name had the lightning and thunder come from?

He looked around, trying to adjust to the darkness. "Robert?"

"I'm here."

William shook his head and waited for his eyes to adjust, then saw Robert sitting near Rising Eagle and Buffalo Dreamer, where he'd been when William fell asleep. "What the hell just happened?"

"They're gone. The Feathered One has taken them."

"What? What do you mean, them? Is Buffalo Dreamer all right?"

There came a moment of silence. "She's dead. Now only the shells of their bodies remain."

William frowned, stepping closer. "But there wasn't anything wrong with Buffalo Dreamer."

Robert leaned down, and now William could see he was covering Buffalo Dreamer's and Rising Eagle's faces with the white buffalo robe. "She was a holy woman," he said quietly, "destined to always be at her husband's side. She's gone with him to the Great Beyond, where all is peaceful and buffalo are plentiful."

"But . . . how—"

"Never underestimate the powers of the Lakota, William. Or the power of love."

William felt a terrible sadness engulf him. "Should we . . . bury them?"

Robert rose and walked near him. "No. They're already buried. What better burial platform could a proud Lakota warrior and his holy woman want than to lie together at the top of Medicine Mountain? All is as it should be. We'll leave them here."

"What about the robe?"

"It's where it belongs, thanks to you." Robert put a hand on his shoulder. "Let's go down."

"But it's dark!"

"I know the way. And once your eyes adjust, you'll be able to see good enough. I don't want to be here in the morning."

William leaned down and picked up his blanket. "If you say so." Tears stung his eyes. "I hate to leave them here alone like this." He could feel Robert's smile.

"They aren't alone. They're very happy, William, I assure you. You'll see them again someday. Don't worry."

His emotions running wild with curiosity and a feeling of deep loss, William followed Robert down the long, winding pathway to a more level area partway down.

"We can camp here," Robert told him. "We'll go the rest of the way in the morning."

William started to unload his blanket again when he heard it . . . drumming and singing. He was sure it came from the top of the mountain. "Robert! Do you hear that?"

Robert spread out a blanket of his own. "I hear it."

"But there's nobody up there!"

"Go to sleep, William."

"But—"

"Don't ask, brother. Just believe."

William left his horses to graze and spread out his blanket, staring at the top of the mountain, from where not only was he sure he heard the drumming and singing, but he thought he saw a faint light. "My God," he whispered. Astounded, he sat down, suddenly remembering the date. How ironic that in just two days from now the United States would celebrate its first one hundred years of independence, yet the Lakota, who were here first, would probably never again know true freedom.

And yet again, some will always be free. Where did that thought come from? Why did he get the eerie feeling that if he went back up the mountain in the morning, Rising Eagle's and Buffalo Dreamer's bodies would not be there? He decided it would be best to never know.

EPILOGUE

AFTER THE CUSTER battle of June, 1876, and through the first three months of 1877, Crazy Horse continued his determined fight to resist life on a reservation. He finally relented when the Lakota became more scattered, many dying from hunger and exposure. Differing opinions about what to do and loyalties to various other leaders led to further arguments and division among the Lakota.

Once Crazy Horse finally surrendered, the attention he received from curious soldiers and citizens created more jealousy among his people, and continued misunderstandings, as well as problems with white interpreters deliberately changing some of Crazy Horse's words to make him sound threatening to the Indian agents and white leaders, only made things worse for Crazy Horse. Other agency Indians began to blame him for all their troubles.

Crazy Horse again fled the agency, then returned on an invitation to come in and be taken to Washington to meet with leaders of the white man's government. However, General Crook, afraid for his life because of rumors, instead ordered Crazy Horse to be confined. Accompanied by men from his own Oglala tribe, Crazy Horse saw the tiny barred windows of the guardhouse where they were leading him, and he realized his own people were taking him to imprisonment. He balked, pulling a knife and turning, slashing one of the Oglala men, Little Big Man, across the forearm. Little Big

Man grasped Crazy Horse's arms, shouting "Don't do this! Don't!"
Most likely he was just trying to stop Crazy Horse from doing something that could get him killed, but it was too late. A Private
William Gentles bayoneted Crazy Horse in the back twice, once
through the kidneys. Crazy Horse died the next morning. Thus,
Crazy Horse's vision of his own people holding him back was
fulfilled.

There are conflicting stories about what really happened that
day, and the true intentions of the Oglala who accompanied Crazy
Horse to the reservation, and about whether his stabbing was
intentional or an accident. Whatever the truth is, the Lakota came
to realize he was one of their greatest and bravest leaders. Today a
monument to Crazy Horse is under construction near Mount Rush-
more in South Dakota.

The Medicine Wheel remains atop Medicine Mountain in
northern Wyoming and is open to the public, but the stones form-
ing the Medicine Wheel are surrounded by a chain-link fence to
prevent theft of the sacred stones by visitors. It is rumored that
those who do manage to steal any of the stones live to regret it.
One such woman was plagued with so much bad luck that she
drove all the way back from Pennsylvania to return stones she had
taken from the sacred site. Once she did, her bad luck ended.

One curiosity about the Medicine Wheel is that on a nearby
mountaintop is a stone arrow that points to it. Why is it there?
Who would be able to see it and what it points to, except from
above? I leave the answer to the imaginations of my readers.

One last note: The Sioux have never sold the Black Hills.
Paha-Sapa remains sacred to them, and belongs to them, to this
very day.

FROM THE AUTHOR

I HOPE YOU have enjoyed my *Mystic Dreamers* series. If you would like to read the personal story of Robert and Rebecca and how they met, you can buy it from *Mightywords.com*. Just download the story and you have a tiny missing piece from *Mystic Warriors*. It's called "The Touch of Love," and is a moving love story, only about seventy-five pages long.

If you haven't read them yet, Book #1, *Mystic Dreamers*, and Book #2, *Mystic Visions*, are both available in hardback and in paperback through your local bookstore, through Amazon.com, or directly from Forge Books. For information about other books I have written, send a self-addressed, stamped envelope to me at P.O. Box 1044, Coloma, Michigan 49038. I will send you an updated newsletter. You can also check my Web site at *www.parrett.net/~bittner*. Thanks for your support!